Set the Moment

THE MOMENTS SERIES

ZIYE' TAYLOR

ISBN: 979-8991796019

Publisher: Ziye' Taylor, 2025

Book Cover by Claudia Bonet

Partial Editing by English Proper Editing Services

First Edition October 2025

Contents

Content Warnings   1

Playlist   2

Ency-Clit-Pedia   3

Authors Note   4

Prologue   6

Sienna's 21 Before 21   11

1. Jace   12

2. Jace   18

3. Sienna   24

4. Jace   34

5. Sienna   39

6. Sienna   44

7. Jace   52

8. Sienna   56

9. Sienna   64

10. Jace   72

11. Sienna   79

12. Sienna   86

13. Jace   94

14. Sienna 101

15. Jace 105

16. Sienna 109

17. Jace 117

18. Sienna 123

19. Sienna 134

20. Jace 142

21. Sienna 148

22. Jace 154

23. Sienna 159

24. Sienna 165

25. Jace 171

26. Sienna 182

27. Jace 190

28. Sienna 197

29. Sienna 205

30. Sienna 207

31. Jace 215

32. Jace 216

33. Jace 227

34. Sienna 236

35. Jace 241

36. Jace 245

37. Sienna 248

38. Sienna 251

39. Jace 256

40. Jace   259

41. Sienna   263

42. Sienna   266

43. Jace   271

44. Sienna   275

45. Sienna   277

46. Jace   281

47. Sienna   285

48. Jace   289

49. Sienna   294

50. Jace   299

51. Sienna   302

52. Jace   307

53. Jace   318

54. Sienna   324

Epilogue   326

Acknowledgements   334

About the author   336

Content Warnings

Though Set the Moment is more of a romantic comedy, it does tackle some strong themes....

Triggering topics may include: parental neglect, mentions of alcohol use, on page death, anaphylactic shock, feelings of abandonment, pregnancy mention, vulgar language, strained parental relationships, explicit consensual intercourse descriptions, and on page violence.

These scenes are graphic and may be triggering. Please only continue if you can handle it.

Remember that you are loved and seen.

Playlist

Eyes Off You –PRETTYMUCH

six thirty–Ariana Granda

One Life–Justin Bieber

Into You–Ariana Grande

No More Hiding–SZA

safety net–Ariana Grande (ft. Ty Dolla $ign)

Garden (Say It Like Dat)–SZA

Pretty Little Fears–6LACK (ft. J. Cole)

History–One Direction

nasty–Ariana Grande

Better–Khalid

Dance For You–Beyoncé

pov–Ariana Grande

Secret–Ann Marie (ft. Yk Osiris)

Miss possessive–Tate McRae

I'm Pretty–KATSEYE

Tonight I Might–KATSEYE

Heartbreaker–Justin Bieber

Sweet Dreams– Beyoncé

WORLD WE CREATED–GIVĒON

0X1=LOVESONG (I Know I Love You)–TOMORROW X TOGTHER

Purple lace bra–Tate McRae

Ency–Clit–Pedia

For all my clit-thinkers who'd love to get their smutty fantasies on or avoid it like the plague, spice can be found in the following chapters:

Twenty-Four

Twenty-Five

Thirty-Two

Thirty-Seven

Authors Note

Set the Moment has many flashback scenes along the course of the book and to make this book accessible to everyone, these scenes will have page breaks like the one below.

Happy reading!

Dear perfectionist, this one's for you.
Welcome home, angel.

Prologue

BLOOD POOLS IN MY mouth as I chew on the inside of my cheek, my heart racing.

"No seriously, Keegan! Sienna has such a stick up her ass..." I hear my classmate, Natasha, laugh.

I don't mean to flinch at her words. My nanny raised me better than to let foolish haters affect me.

But I do.

I cringe as Keegan laughs. The sound is wheezy and loud, like a toy rooster as she cackles away at my expense.

"It's because her family is famous, Tash...She wouldn't be in this program without Mommy and Daddy."

Hello pot, meet kettle.

It's always *Daddy's money* this, *Mommy's money* that when people talk about me, as if I had gotten into one of the most competitive dance programs on my parents' merit alone.

I rest my head back on the wall behind me, covering me from their view as they continue to spew their nonsense.

Today's the last day of classes at NYU before the summer break begins, and it's also my last day *ever* in this cesspit. From the moment I stepped foot on campus two years ago, my life has been a living hell.

I've had random people follow me from cafés to my condo, a study date with a weirdo from my econ class who wanted me to take his *feet* pics, and not to mention all the times where my things would come up "missing" in the studio with the girls in my class being a pain in the ass.

I mean seriously, who puts a nail in someone's pointe shoe?

Heaving a sigh, I prepare to enter the cold room when another voice stops me in my tracks. My skin boils with anger as the person giggles with the two dancers.

"Oh c'mon, girls, you two both know her parents don't love her enough to pay for schooling. That's why little Miss Perfect's always overachieving. I bet all she needs is a good fucking to get her out of that bitchy attitude she has."

My heart sinks as none other than Valencia McAllister, my idol, current mentor, and professor for Dance Technique, speaks.

Never meet your idols, they say.

I smooth a stray, brown coil from my face, take a deep breath, and straighten my spine. I refuse to give these assholes the satisfaction of my tears.

"Oh, you're so right! Anthony told me that she was a frigid bitch who wouldn't put out when they had a date a while back." Keegan cackles.

My breathing shakes as I try my hardest not to cry. They've been nothing but cruel to me since I stepped foot on campus. I could storm in there and give them a piece of my mind, tell them all off.

But I don't.

It would bring shame to my family if I ever did something worth headlines. That's my cousin Zola's job. She's the star in that department.

Deep breath in...

Hold for ten seconds.

Exhale.

The breathing technique from yesterday's hot yoga class is no use. Everything feels like it's caving in on me.

The walls are closer, I'm as tall as the ceiling, and my legs are wobbly.

"Oh! Hey, Sienna!" A familiar voice calls out to me like a life raft, but I don't take it even though I need to. Instead, I sink further into the depths of my mind as the girls in the room gasp, now fully aware of my presence.

Ignoring the voice, I get out of there as fast as I can. I don't think about the fact that we have evaluations today or that I'm running around Washington Square like a chicken with its head cut off in a lavender leotard.

My breathing doesn't calm itself until I make it to my shell of a condo that I've lived in for less than two years. The place is cold, lacking in anything that screams Sienna Jones. The only distinctive quality in the apartment is the six-tiered pink cage that houses my pet ferret, Oscar.

Sighing, I drop my dance bag on the ground as I make my way inside, locking the door behind me and putting a door stopper up that my uncle Clef bought me.

He's a serious security nut, and me moving away from my parents' home in California to New York by myself only upped his anxiety.

"Oscar, we've gotta get out of here…I can't do it anymore. What do you think?" I ask the white ferret, pausing momentarily for him to speak.

Is this what my life has come to? Communicating with a Mustelid?

Maybe those girls were right. I haven't seen my mom or dad since they started touring in the UK last year. I have zero friends, the social life of a guinea pig, and I'm a twenty-year-old virgin who likes to read spicy books more than have human interactions. The only exceptions to that last one being my family and my cousin Cleo's two friends, Jace and Georgia.

As a kid, I would spend summers in their hometown, Summerfield, Maryland. They would go to my dance recitals in Maryland, we'd play games, and if we were lucky, we got to go on small trips together. In the winter, I'd spend the first week of winter break there, too. My uncle would try to teach us how to ice skate—Cleo and Jace were naturals, but Georgia, my cousin Ryan, and I were horrible.

I miss Summerfield. I miss the person that I was before life dealt me its shittiest hand at age ten.

Stepping into my bathroom, I discard my clothes, leave on my bra and underwear, and connect my phone to my waterproof speaker, preparing myself for the next hour I'll spend in here.

I need to wash away all the trauma I've dealt with this past decade, starting with an everything shower.

Getting my body scrubs and Nair hair removal ready, I apply the remover to my pits and legs ,then wait. Soft R&B plays in the background as I look in the mirror and take myself in.

My hair is dull and lifeless from throwing it into a bun for dance, and my skin has lost its glow.

I need to reset everything, starting with my look.

Chewing on my bottom lip, I type the number of my favorite travel stylist in the city and call her, asking for the Reset Special, which includes a wash, blow dry, color, trim, and silk press. I haven't straightened my hair in months, and I usually don't in the summer or spring. But considering the circumstances, I think it'll be okay.

My stylist, Ranae, responds quickly, saying that she'll be at my place within two hours.

Quickly turning on my favorite songs by the band Twisted Vipers, I hop in the shower. The water is hot against my skin as I wash off the Nair, exfoliate my entire body, and perform a one-woman show in forty-five minutes.

By the time I'm done showering, steam fills both the bathroom and my bedroom. I'm quicker than the speed of sound as I moisturize my body, dancing naked in the mirror.

There's something freeing about allowing myself to just *be* when I'm alone.

After letting Oscar out, I make my way into the living room. After my appointment, I'll have the entire day to do whatever I want, and I know just where to start.

I'm getting the hell out of New York, but where can I go? I refuse to go home—California may be known as the Golden state, but my life was dim. The only company around were staff and my endless flow of nannies.

Pass.

I could always go to Georgia and live with my grandparents. Papa would love to have one of his grandbabies back home to play music for, but he'd also make me eat black eyed peas every day.

Pass.

My phone dings, pulling me from my thoughts. I pick it up and raise a brow.

Cleo

> Can't do it anymore, Si Si

> I'm going home.

What the hell? Home? Last time Cleo and I talked, she seemed to be having the time of her life…Is she moving back to Summerfield? If she is, maybe I could move there too. I mean, some of my best memories were there.

He's there.

Could I?

My phone dings again.

Cleo

> I love you, but I'm transferring to SFU. I know things have been tougher for you here, too. You should think about it.

> Talked to Dad and he'd love to see you again. Gloria, too.

I smile at that. Cleo's stepmom, Gloria, makes mean empanadas and handles everything like a boss. Maybe moving wouldn't be such a bad thing. It could be a fresh start, a new me? I need a plan.

"Listly, you better not fail me now," I say aloud as I make a list, opening the app on my computer.

Lists are what keeps me from losing my marbles on a daily basis. I have morning routine lists, life goals lists, and even bathroom checklists.

If it can be a list, I probably have it.

Every good list needs a name. I type all of the things that I've always wanted to try, but was too scared in the past to do it when the name hits me.

If I'm going to do this, I'm giving it my all. What better way than to get it all done by my birthday?

"Sienna's 21 before 21," I say as I type the words at the top of the page.

By New Year's Eve, I'll be a new me.

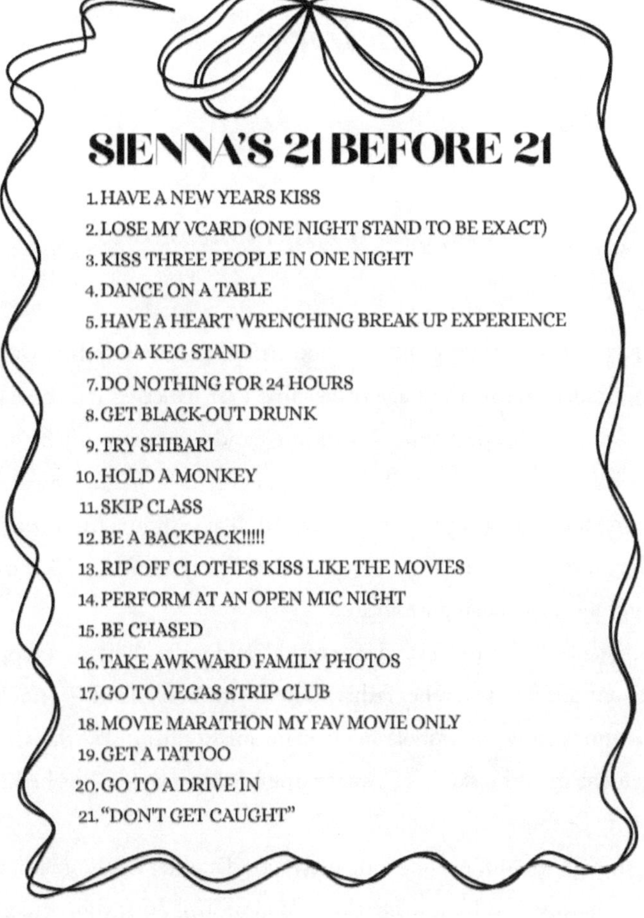

SIENNA'S 21 BEFORE 21

1. HAVE A NEW YEARS KISS
2. LOSE MY VCARD (ONE NIGHT STAND TO BE EXACT)
3. KISS THREE PEOPLE IN ONE NIGHT
4. DANCE ON A TABLE
5. HAVE A HEART WRENCHING BREAK UP EXPERIENCE
6. DO A KEG STAND
7. DO NOTHING FOR 24 HOURS
8. GET BLACK-OUT DRUNK
9. TRY SHIBARI
10. HOLD A MONKEY
11. SKIP CLASS
12. BE A BACKPACK!!!!!
13. RIP OFF CLOTHES KISS LIKE THE MOVIES
14. PERFORM AT AN OPEN MIC NIGHT
15. BE CHASED
16. TAKE AWKWARD FAMILY PHOTOS
17. GO TO VEGAS STRIP CLUB
18. MOVIE MARATHON MY FAV MOVIE ONLY
19. GET A TATTOO
20. GO TO A DRIVE IN
21. "DON'T GET CAUGHT"

one

Jace

— three and a half months later

"YOU BETTER WORK IT, girl!" My shout is loud as my non-biological niece, Delilah, prances across the stage of her first ever dance recital. Like a proud mom, I hold my phone sideways with one hand and pump my fist in the air with the other to a sound mix of classical and pop instrumental music.

"You're doing great, Deli!" my best friend, Blake, shouts from beside me in the same exact pose as me and the rest of the hockey team. I snicker quietly at how stupidly embarrassing we all are.

Tonight's Delilah's first ever dance recital, and we're all here to support our number one girl. However, her father, Derek—my best friend—is not here yet. I find it funny how the asshole made it his mission to instill the art of time management into the skulls of twenty-one hockey players, but he himself is nowhere to be found.

The thought of him not showing up for his daughter does something to my protective nature, but I know Derek. He'd never bail on anyone, especially his kid. None of us would. In the three years since we've met, Delilah has become the niece to all players on the Summerfield University Men's Hockey team.

"Dude, oh my gosh…I don't know how my mom did all that cheering for me at my Peewee games. My throat is dry." Blake frowns, taking his seat. I follow behind him, chuckling as he blows out a deep, exasperated breath.

The idiot looks crazy dressed in his "funcle fit" consisting of a #1 Uncle tee shirt, cargo shorts, black fanny pack, and Birkenstocks, topped off with a red flannel thrown over his shoulders.

"You look ridiculous," I say chuckling as Blake smiles, running a hand through his hair. "I know you do but, what do I? Wait…" He furrows his thick brown brows.

"Fucking idiot."

A hand on my shoulder pauses me from laughing at Blake. Charlie Tyson, one of my teammates, pops his head in the space between Blake and I's heads.

"How does it feel to officially be moms like Momma bear?" he asks in reference to Derek, gesturing to our semi-matching outfits.

"Puh-lese…I pull this look off better than—"

"Did I miss it?" A deep, hurried voice cuts my sentence short.

Derek Perez looks like a man who has seen better days. His usually tamed hair is a mess of damp curls around his head, the usual day-old stubble on his face has been replaced with a light beard, and he's *wet*.

"Why are you wet…" I grimace as he takes the empty aisle seat beside me, saved for him.

"The hell happened to you?" Blake's bright blue eyes furrow as he looks the giant up and down.

"And why the fuck are you late?" My tone bites as my blood rushes through my veins hotter. There should be absolutely zero reason he missed Deli on stage.

"Long story—did I miss it?" he repeats his question again, his voice hurried.

My heart sinks from the sound of desperation and sadness in my friend's voice. Derek is the "Mom" of our friend group, he's our glue. So to see him out of character has my cold dead heart feeling a certain way.

"By five minutes, man. She did amazing…take a look." My voice is softer than usual as I hand him my cell phone with the dance pulled up, watching over his shoulder as Delilah dances across the stage.

My stomach drops as I watch the video back. I was so focused on making sure to capture the moment, I didn't see it.

The look.

But it's there, clear as day.

While the rest of the girls do a turn, Delilah pauses on the stage and looks around the crowd before frowning. Her little four-year-old body is quick to recover and almost instantly falls back into line with her fellow dancers.

My shoulders fall as does Derek's. He looks around frantically as if searching the dark theater can give him the answers to all his problems.

"I've got to find my baby, she probably thinks I abandoned her..." he mumbles, but I can hear him loud and clear as he jumps up from his spot next to me, rushing out of the theater.

He was so quick, I hadn't even processed what he'd said until he was gone.

Replaying the part again, I frown as images of a past I want to forget flashes before my eyes.

Her skin is cold. She shivers beneath my touch as my small, lanky arms pull her into my body. I wrap her up in my side and kiss the top of her forehead as she shakes.

"They didn't show, was it me? I did everything per-perfectly." She hiccups, diamond-like tears falling down her mahogany face.

"You were an angel out there," I say, my eight-year-old self trying my hardest to comfort her just as my mom comforted Jackson, Asa, and I.

"I was an angel...sure, but I wasn't theirs. Why won't my parents just choose me for once?"

"Sometimes we put faith in others and don't expect them to hurt us...but they do. No one knows why, but it's never your fault that other people can't see how bright you are."

My chest caves as she turns to look up at me, her hazel eyes are bloodshot as our eyes lock, and she holds up her pinky.

"Promise?"

"Promise."

"I'm gonna go check on him." Blake coughs, snatching me back to the present as he drops his half-empty container of popcorn in my lap.

I inhale deeply, pushing the memory of *her* out of my mind. I haven't *willingly* thought about her in a year, and I refuse to start back now.

Fuck, who am I kidding? I've thought about her every day since our last encounter.

Now I can't *not* think about her. Hell, this is that incident all over again, only this time, I'm witnessing it as it happens.

What could've possibly made Derek late for this? He's usually the only person out of the team who's punctual to a T.

I take a handful of the popcorn, shoving the salty snack into my mouth.

Deep breaths, Jace.

Derek didn't bail. He's here.

Deli won't be disappointed like her.

Two more groups of dancers perform without a hitch before Blake and Derek return to their seats, flustered like two kids who'd just gotten told off. I'm about to get up to replenish my stash of popcorn and fruit snacks, when my friends slide into the seats next to me. The blue-eyed bastard of the two smiles from ear to ear while the other looks...murderous.

Interesting.

"Dude, Momma bear just got his balls *busted* by a dance teacher." Blake snickers, leaning in close to tell me.

I raise a brow over his head at Derek, who's on his phone, watching the video of Delilah I'd sent into our group chat.

"A dance teacher?" I question, eyeing the two of them.

"Yep! She was hot as hell, pink hair and everything."

Charlie leans forwards between Blake and I's seats and chuckles. "Dere-bear got his balls busted? No way."

"Way! And she was *hot*!"

I ignore Blake as he proceeds to inform the rest of our team about what had happened in the hall between Derek and Delilah's dance teacher.

I'm about to tell him not to send a text to the group chat about it when all of the lights in the theater go out.

My knee bounces as my mind recounts my favorite dancer—the Alice who'd once escaped my Wonderland. I silently reminisce about the summers and mild winters the two of us shared as children when a spotlight shines over a figure on the stage.

The woman is hunched into a ball, her body contorted to look small as she breathes heavily.

I'm immediately brought back down to Earth and all air evaporates from my lungs as light pink hair shines brightly under the stage lights. I don't notice the rest of the audience's gasps as the woman rises from her spot before dramatically falling to the ground as a piano key thuds loudly in the background.

My heart rackets as my eyes lock on the woman in front of me.

Smooth mahogany skin, light pink hair, and eyes the color of the Earth shine bright under the lights of the stage.

Sienna Jones is right in front of me.

My chest tightens as she rises from the ashes of my heart, her movements slow and magnetic as an instrumental song begins to play.

Sienna wears a black leotard with a flowy, sheer, black skirt that's languid with her body as she lets the music encompass her.

I watch in astonishment as she tells a story of feeling alone and confused in a world that was not made for her. I sit up in my seat, goosebumps kissing my flesh as I lean in to get a better look at her as she dances her heart out. My cheeks warm as she does a leap that seems to be impossible and my brain catalogs every. Single. Moment.

Sienna is captivating as she dances.

She's a lone star in a room full of darkness, shining brighter than anything else. Her eyes catch mine for a short second, and it's all my body needs to have a knee-jerk reaction.

I've been in awe of Sienna since I first watched her dance in her uncle's backyard at eight-years-old, but to see her growth as a dancer does something to me. I want to run up there and tell her how proud I am of her. Yet, another part of me wants to pick her up and run away, whisk her off to a forgotten place where she's the only star in the universe and I'm her moon.

Sienna bows, pleased with herself as the audience jumps and claps for her. She knows she's in control, and she loves it—I can see it. I can also see something else. Something much more sinister.

Is that anger, angel?

I can see it in the way her jaw clenches slightly and how her eye twitches faintly.

Sienna's livid, and I'm going to know exactly why.

I've lost my angel once before—I fell from the sky and landed in Wonderland without her. I see my shot to get her back, and if I don't take it now, I won't get the chance to do it again.

I have to have her, even if it's the last thing that I do.

TWO

Jace

I DON'T WASTE ANY time as I run out of the theater when Sienna exits the stage. Christmas came early in the form of a pink haired ballerina. It's been years since I've seen Sienna, let alone watched her dance. A normal, much more sane man would stop and think about the fact that he hasn't seen his childhood crush and best friend's cousin in nearly two years.

Except I never said that I was normal.

I have a one track mind right now, and it's set on having her. Sienna Jones isn't someone you can own or take as a possession—I'd never think to do that to her, but stealing her time with the hopes of being in her presence is something I would absolutely do.

Have I ever mentioned that pink is my favorite color? I thought it'd been green, but pink is much more enticing.

Light pink and black flashes by, and my eyes are drawn to her immediately.

We could be a million light years apart, but I'd spot her anywhere. Sienna Jones, the woman that you are.

My body aches to be near her, to talk to her. I let the invisible string tethering my soul to hers yank me forward to my missing piece, only for the string to wrap itself around my neck. My soul is yanked back into my body, forcing me to feel a choking sensation as someone approaches my little angel.

A man.

Tall and broad with deep, dark brown skin and even deeper low cut waves approaches Sienna, his smile brighter than the sun as he looks down at *my* girl.

My head tilts as the two of them laugh at something Boy Wonder says.

What the fuck is this?

Who the fuck is this?

Is he your boyfriend, angel?

Why are you here after years of radio silence?

I see red and collide with another person. A woman around my mother's age blushes as I hold her up, apologizing for not paying attention.

I've got to get this girl out of my head.

I can hear Sienna's laugh from here, and it pisses me the fuck off that it isn't me she's laughing with.

Fuck, I have to do something.

Screw her *boyfriend*. I'm Jace fucking Heart.

"Woah there, honey, what's the matter?" the woman asks, pulling my focus back to her. Her voice is soft with a southern twang and her tone reminds me of my Nonna—sweet and inviting. The lady's body language says otherwise—she looks strict and extremely put together.

I look around the emptying atrium, my jaw twitching.

Where the fuck did Sienna go that fast?

"Looking for something?" the lady asks.

"More like someone...I need dance lessons at this studio. Who can I talk to about scheduling and payment?" I cringe at my tone, but that's to be expected when the one woman who's been plaguing my mind for years shows up out of nowhere at a recital for my best friend's kid.

"You're in luck, sweet pea. I'm Calista Dupri, owner of the Madam Dupri Dance Academy. Was there a specific thing you wanted to learn or—"

"Whatever Sienna Jones teaches." I waste zero time. My breathing is harsh as I look down at the woman.

Her lips purse, clearly annoyed by my interruption.

"I'm sorry, young man, but Sienna is one of our most booked coaches. You can probably get on the waitlist for another teach—"

"I'll pay whatever, but it can only be her. I just need her...to teach me." I cringe internally by the pleading in my voice. I can hear my dad's reprimand now.

"Heart men do not beg. Only bitches beg."

I grimace at the reminder of his words, but Calista Dupri doesn't see any of this, though. Instead, she's observing me, replaying my words in her head.

I know immediately what she's about to say isn't going to be something I like, so when I see the squint in her eyes, clearly sensing my bullshit, I butt in.

"I'll give you a hundred grand for her to teach me privately until New Year's Eve—only her—and she gets all the money after."

Calista reels back as if I'd shot her and scoffs, "Excuse me?! How dare you try to bribe—"

"So? How much are her lessons?"

If my friend Georgia could see me right now still pining after the same girl years later, she'd laugh in my face. Georgia is the only person in my trio of friends who knew about my crush—considering Cleo, my other friend, is Sienna's cousin.

"I beg your—"

"Hundred grand, four months of classes with her only. Take the money or—"

Calista's eyes replicate saucers as she gasps and shouts, "You're out of your mind!" before storming away.

I sigh, pinching the bridge of my nose.

Guess I have to take matters into my own hands.

So much for that master plan to get Sienna alone.

"Honey, why would you buy a dance studio in the middle of *Maryland?* I thought you were a painter..." My mother's voice is light and questioning as I answer her fourth call of the day.

Sighing, I roll my eyes as I take a seat in front of my easel, pulling a smock over my bare chest.

"Did anyone ever question Shakespeare when he wrote all those plays?" I ask absentmindedly, positioning myself in front of my canvas. My body buzzes with energy and my fingers twitch to touch a brush.

After the recital and disappointing chit-chat with Calista Dupri, I've acquired a dance studio, a headache, and an itch to paint.

The headache and studio were a given considering the small two-story building cost me around three hundred thousand dollars and resulted in a nice, long chat with Dad. It was no surprise for Mom to call me every day, though.

What did surprise me was the itch to paint something. I haven't sat and worked on a piece in months.

"Umm...yes? What did we send you off to that school for if you're not learning—"

"Did you call me to lecture me or to talk to your favorite spawn, Mom?" My voice is teasing as I make light brushstrokes against the canvas, using lavender and light brown oil paints.

"Fine...I did have a reason for my call, sweetheart."

My eye twitches as my mother eases the term of endearment into her sentence. *Honey* was her usual nickname for all of us boys, but when Anna Heart truly wanted to get her way, she'd used *sweetheart*.

Just as I open my mouth to question her, she beats me to the chase.

"Before you get mad, I just want you to hear me out."

Gritting my teeth, I set down my paint brush and brace myself for whatever verbal torture my mother will throw out. Anna Heart may love her boys with her entire being to the point she'd become overbearing, but she also knows just the right way to get under our skin.

"I had a talk with Grace, and we just think you and Georgia should try—"

Oh for the love of God.

"Mom." I feel cold as I look out of the one lone window in my bedroom. The street light is on in front of our house, and although it's pitch black outside, I know that somewhere out there in the underworld Hades is giggling happily at my expense.

"What?! You've known the girl your entire life and you're not getting any younger. I'd at least like to see my last boy get married." The calm I'd felt earlier at the recital while Sienna danced is nowhere to be found as my mother's words hit me like a bullet train.

I'm only nineteen, but to her I'd might as well be forty-five. My parents had my brother, Jackson, when they were my age, and then got married soon after. Luckily for them, they'd been in love with one another well before Jackson came along. My brother followed in their footsteps, marrying my sister-in-law, Corinne, at twenty-one, six years ago. Asa, my second older brother, decided to rebel when he was fifteen. He's repeatedly stood on the notion that he is against marriage and would not be getting married if his life depended on it.

He's twenty-four now, single and mysterious as fuck living in New York, leaving me to bear the brunt end of our parents ideas of love, life, and family.

"Mom, you wanting me to marry Georgia is like telling me to marry Jackson's fugly ass. Gross and fucking crazy considering she's my best friend. And you aren't dying, so stop."

I should feel bad for my tone, but I can't. Hearing that you should marry one of your best friends every day for almost a decade is fucking annoying.

Georgia, Cleo, and even Ryan have been the only constant people in my life besides my family. I wouldn't touch any of them with a ten foot pole.

Georgia, with her blonde hair and green eyes is the feminine equivalent of me. She acts like me, talks like me, looks like me—and I'm pretty sure she's a demon. The thought of even *hugging* her, let alone kissing her in front of a church, gives me the heebeegeebees.

Unlike Georgia, my best friend, Cleo, is the exact opposite of me. I admit that as a kid I had a teensy crush on her and we did kiss once, but that ship sailed before it ever reached its dock because Hurricane Sienna came through wielding all the power.

I haven't been attracted to either Georgia or Cleo, because not only have I watched them grow up, know all of their secrets, but I've also seen them down twelve hot dogs between the two of them.

Only one girl remains on my mind, and I have a plan in motion to get her.

"Language…" My mom's soft voice reminds me that we're still on the phone.

"I'm sorry, Mom, but it's been over ten years of you scheming and I don't have any feelings for Georgia nor Cleo," I say, officially giving up on my painting for the night.

"Fine, I'll stop for now, Jace. You know that if you ever need help I'm just a call away right, honey?"

Chuckling as I take a seat on the foot of my bed, I nod.

"Yes, ma'am."

"Good, because I have a feeling this school year is going to have a lot more drama than last year…" My mother sighs, and with that, she hangs up.

THree

Sienna

"I'D LOVE TO TAKE you out sometime..."

My brain replays the words of the pretty stranger from last night. After my performance yesterday, my body buzzed with anger and adrenaline. I've been an instructor for the Mini age division at the MDDA since I moved to Summerfield in mid-May.

In the time that I've been an instructor, I've met every single parent—except for one. The father of Delilah Perez, my golden student. Delilah, unlike the other girls in her group, is eager to dance and the most patient. She wants to learn new things and is always front and center for warm ups. It hadn't even crossed my mind that I'd never met her dad because an older lady had been dropping her off, whom I'd assumed was her mother until Friday night.

Her "mother" asked me to babysit her for a few hours, and I'd agreed only to find out later that the sweet older woman was in fact Delilah's *grandma,* and Derek Perez, one of the goalies for the men's hockey team at SFU, was her dad.

It upset me that another young dancer's parents weren't as active in her dance life as they should've been, so when I saw Delilah on stage last night, searching the crowd for him only to be met with disappointment, I was livid.

Derek showed up a few minutes after her performance, wet, and with a pitiful look on his face. I hate to say it but, I cursed him out.

Me!

You're probably thinking, Si Si, you'd never...Oh, but I did!

I eviscerated him with my words then danced on his tombstone...and his friend.

The friend who was with him was collateral damage—he'd shown up right after the verbal lashing and got the ending of it.

After I did one of the most irresponsible things of my life with a smile on my face, I danced away all of that anger I felt towards Derek.

As I danced, I couldn't shake the feeling of being watched. Growing up, the feeling was familiar. Welcoming, even. I'd thought I was crazy at first considering I was dancing on a stage in front of about two hundred people and being watched was kind of the point, but then I saw *him*.

Or at least I think it was him.

Jace Heart.

The theater was dark, but even in a crowded room with very little light, I think I'd know the feeling of those light green eyes anywhere. My skin buzzes as my mind replays all the moments where those eyes tracked me.

"Was Jace there?" I mumble, chewing on my nail with furrowed brows. Tugging my knees to my chest, I stare at the TV aimlessly as my mind goes through last night.

"Was Jace where?" a bubbly and inquisitive voice asks, bursting my thought bubble as Georgia's intrigued face pops into my line of view.

"Bitch, oh my gosh..." I cringe back, my heart racing as she cackles, sitting back in her seat on the couch next to me.

"That was...too good," She laughs harder, the laugh bordering a wheeze as her blonde hair shakes with her body.

I roll my eyes and throw an unfolded towel at her from my stack. We'd been originally watching TV and doing laundry today to prepare for the first of the semester tomorrow, but folding laundry quickly turned into watching the first two episodes of a new reality show called, *Love in Cancun*.

"No seriously. Was Jace where?" Georgia questions as she straightens up, pausing her folding as her green eyes search my face.

My nose scrunches as I tilt my head, unsure of myself.

Was that really him? Or my imagination?

Sighing, I throw my head back. A nap would answer all of my questions—my dreams never steered me wrong. Except for that one time I dreamt my toenails fell off and thought that I'd die in my sleep.

"Nothing...I just need a nap, it's been a long day." I sigh, massaging my scalp. "Jace doesn't even go to this school, right?" I ask, my tone hopeful just as my cousin Cleo stumbles out of her bedroom and heads straight to the kitchen.

It's only been four days since she and Georgia moved into our apartment, and I wouldn't be surprised if she'd started a donut collection in our cabinet. The girl's a snacker.

"Right...he *definitely* doesn't go here." Had I been paying full attention, I'd catch the inflection in Georgia's words and the way her eyes shift quickly between the TV and I, but I'm not.

Instead, my mind wanders back to the familiar blond man and all the ways I've ruined our friendship.

"Did you eat all the powdered donuts, Si Si? I can't find any!" Cleo shouts, her voice muffled by the inside of the cabinets.

"Girl, that was all you last night," Georgia calls back, nudging my shoulder with a cheeky grin as she discreetly pulls a bag of powdered donuts out from under our coffee table, shushing me.

Masking my laugh, I force my thoughts away from the idea of the Herculean man from my past and focus my attention on the show in front of me. It's no use when images of blond hair, tanned skin, and large, rough hands wrapped around my waist flash through my mind.

No one in their right mind likes Mondays, and I'm no different. My body feels jetlagged as I make my way across the quad towards the Bloom School of the Arts building.

A sane person would've dropped their 8:00 a.m. Ballet 3303 class and hit snooze without a second thought. But for me, dropping a class means failure.

I refuse to be a failure.

The hairs on the back of my neck rise at the thought of imperfection. I have bigger fish to fry and failing isn't one of them.

Speaking of fish...I haven't checked anything off of my list in days. Rummaging through my bag, I pull out the small, crisp, pristine list of tasks I have to complete before my 21st birthday on December 31st.

Yes, I'm a New Years Eve kid. No, it's not as fun as you think. I have had little to no experience in life. Sure, I've drank a few times with my cousin and her friends, but I've never gotten drunk. I've never dated anyone for fear of what my parents would think. Oh, and my first kiss was...something.

I gulp as I think back to that day two years ago just as my body is jerked forward and I brace for impact with the concrete.

Only for it to never come.

"Shit, I'm so sor—Sienna?" A deep voice calls my name, and I freeze.

It's the guy from last night. Anthony? Ashton? I can't remember what his name was for the life of me. He smiles down at me, steadying me as he looks me over. His deep brown skin glows in the sunlight and his height almost shields me from the sun. Today, he's wearing a green sweater and jeans, typical for the early autumn weather here in Maryland. I'll admit, the man is handsome.

I tilt my head, trying to come up with his name.

"Aric." He chuckles, and I laugh awkwardly.

"Right, sorry. Things were hectic last night. Are you going to the Bloom building?"

Aric's smile brightens, a row of blinding, straight, white teeth flash me as he speaks. "Yes, actually. I have a painting course at eight."

"Painting?" My voice is distant to my ears as my mind sends thoughts to my brain—a clear image of a blond boy holding a paintbrush with a cheeky smile as he paints a picture of me.

We'd been ten-years-old and bored out of our minds that summer because a storm knocked the power out in Maryland. It'd also been the first ever summer I spent more than a week in Summerfield.

The prickling feeling I'd felt earlier rises, and instead of my eyes remaining on the deep brown ones in front of me, they flicker to the left.

Our eyes connect instantly like two magnets.

My breath catches, and I feel like I'm falling back down the rabbit hole of us. Images of him and I throughout our life in the summer and the winter of my 18th birthday flash like photos.

Cool jade eyes pull me in and refuse to let me go. No matter if I'm in a crowded room, on a busy street, or on stage, my eyes will always find his.

It's been two years since I've seen him. Should I wave? Do I say hi? Does he even remember me? I mean I look different...my hair's *pink*, for crying out loud. Did I mess up by changing myself?

I haven't even gotten to the tattoo part of my list—

He's with a girl. My head tilts as he and I keep our eyes locked on one another, unwavering, as she jumps into his arms and they lock around her instantly.

Jace has a girlfriend?

Does he call her angel, too?

"So...have you thought about my question from earlier?"

Like a bucket of ice cold water has been dumped over my head, my eyes snap back to Arin or Ashton's—I'm horrible with names—brown eyes.

Inhaling sharply, I think over his question.

I came to this school to get a fresh start, and if that means going on a date with a random hot guy, then so be it.

"Yeah, pick me up this Sunday?"

"Sunday at eight?"

Why do I feel like this could be the start of something very, very bad?

No Si Si, that's just you overthinking...tell the cute guy yes and move on with your day.

"It's a date." My heart bangs against my chest as the words tumble from my lips.

Is this normal or a sign of a bad omen?

I'll be fine...I hope.

Aric—right, that's his name—walks me to class and reminds me that he'll pick me up for our date on Sunday. I don't know if it's because it's my first date here or because I'm uncertain about whether or not he and I should be going on it, but my heart stutters.

Pushing away that feeling, my body soothes itself as I enter the studio where Ballet 3303 will be held. The room is bright and lively with chatter as people stand around. Smells of sterile disinfectant and old wood calm my nerves as I enter the expansive dance studio that I'll be spending the next few weeks of my life in.

The studio is probably the largest I've ever been in on a college campus.

Floor to ceiling windows line the expansive western wall with huge mirrors along the front. There are barres strategically placed along the middle of the room and a podium in the corner where the professor will conduct class.

I sigh, my shoulders relaxing as I drop my bag down, taking a seat beside a girl with auburn hair. She looks up at me, giving me a small smile.

It's a familiar smile, but I can't quite place it.

"Your hair is beautiful! I've always wanted to dye mine!" She giggles and I cringe back as she sticks her grimy hands up in an attempt to touch my hair.

What the hell?

Why do strangers think that because I have "pretty" and unique hair, that gives them a free pass to pet me like an animal at the zoo?

The red-head must catch on quickly because her eyes widen almost immediately and her jaw drops.

"Oh! I'm so sorry...I just thought—"

"That you could touch me even though we've never met before because my hair is unusual?" I ask, a small smile breaking my hard exterior as the girl chuckles awkwardly.

"Sorry about that...I promise to keep my hands to myself from now on. I'm Daisy, by the way." Daisy's cheeks brighten a light shade of pink, highlighting her freckles as she holds out her manicured hand for me to shake.

Grabbing it, I nod. "Sienna. Nice to meet you."

"Likewise. What brings you to Summerfield? You have that fish out of water vibe."

My brows raise and my cheeks burn as a larger smile breaks out across my face. This could be the fresh start I was searching for—a new friend!

"Is it obvious?" I ask, chuckling softly as Daisy nods, her red hair swooshing as she ties it into a bun. "My old school sucked, so I moved here for a fresh start." I shrug, looking away to our professor at the front of the room.

She's an older Black woman with deep brown skin and bright red lips. She reminds me of my aunt Melody with her short and petite physique.

"Ah, same! I just moved, too. There's someone here that I missed so I'm hoping that he and I can reconnect..." Her light cheeks redden even more as she curls into herself slightly.

My brows raise as I take in her words. What a coincidence—there's someone here for me, too, at this school...only he's dating someone else.

Daisy and I spend the rest of our first class of the semester focused on our professor—who goes by Coach K—sharing little chats here and there. Coach K tells us about all things to be prepared for over the course of this semester, including our final exam. Since Ballet 3303 is a hands-on dance course, we will all work on partnered projects and add a creative spin to our favorite dance pieces for the Winter Showcase.

The Winter Showcase, as Daisy and another student, Reagan, explained it, is a four-hour long event at the end of the fall semester where every arts major will showcase their work over the semester. Students with dance concentrations will perform their project and be graded on technique, routine, costume, and overall presentation.

The dance is worth forty percent of our final grade.

Daisy and I agree to partner up, so we exchange numbers at the end of class.

My body feels light and my brain is cleared of all fog as I make my way to my car parked near the quad.

The first day of classes went by without any casualties, and everyone has been nice so far.

I'm buzzing with excitement for tonight's lesson with my Minis. My girls are like little rays of sunshine, and since I'm already in a good mood, I'm going to get them a small treat.

The Sweet Tooth, an Alice in Wonderland inspired bakery, is just five minutes from the studio. My body practically hums with energy as I step into the sweet-smelling shop. The building smells of fresh baked chocolate chip cookies and is warm, like a hug.

"Hey, lovely, what can I get for you? Lavender Love?" Saree, the main baker greets me as I step inside, and my body warms.

I should feel embarrassed that Saree knows my order is lavender macarons off the top of her head, but nothing can beat the thrill of happiness that I'm feeling right now.

I made a friend and she's not bitchy!

That shouldn't be something to celebrate, but if you've met the people that I have in life...you'd feel the exact same way as me.

"Actually no, I'm getting treats for the girls! Can I get a dozen red velvet cupcakes and three Lavender Loves?"

A grin breaks across my face as Saree nods and gets the cupcakes. Nothing can break this good mood I'm in. Today's going to be an amazing day, I can just feel it.

Wait, no ...that's just my phone buzzing.

It takes me a minute to fish my phone from my purse with it being lodged between my e-reader and notebook. Giving myself a pat on the back when I find the lavender phone, my smile falters as my boss's name flashes across the screen with a new message.

Madam Dupri

> Sienna, report to my office after you clock in. We have business to discuss.

Business? My shoulders deflate as I reread the message.

What could she possibly have to say to me? Dupri never wants to talk to anyone...especially on Mondays.

Shrugging it off, I thank and pay Saree before heading to the studio. It's probably nothing...Dupri sends encrypting texts all the time. She probably just wants to ask how to connect her phone to the Bluetooth again or something.

Or not.

My hope turns to mush as I enter the studio. Vicky, our receptionist, who's usually as bright as the sun when I enter, greets me with a tight lipped smile and points me towards Durpi's office just off the side of the entrance. My heart rate speeds up as the world closes in on me.

I tug the sleeve of the compression top I'm wearing and sigh. Maybe this is a meeting about my performance and she wants to promote me?

Yeah, let's go with that.

"Take a seat, Sienna." Dupri's cold voice crushes all of my happy spirits as I enter her office, quietly sitting in the uncomfortable, brown leather chair in front of her desk.

"Is everything ok—"

"Are you in some sort of trouble, Sienna?"

I'm at a loss for words, my eyes wide as Dupri cuts me off, leaning into my space. Her eyes are like greedy little cameras trying to grasp any information they can as she observes me.

"Excuse me?"

"You have a new student. One who paid a lot for *you* specifically to teach them. I don't know what you've gotten yourself into, but do whatever this student asks of you." Her voice is deep and serious as her hard gaze remains laser focused on me.

The box of cupcakes in my hands feels like stones as my stomach drops.

New student?

"But what about my girls? This is their first practice after the recital and—" My voice is unrecognizable to my ears as I speak, the beat of my heart drums loudly in my ears.

"Don't worry about the Minis for now. They're being taken care of. Your student is in Studio F, so don't keep them waiting."

Her voice is cold as she dismisses me. My feet feel like lead as I drag them to Studio F on the other side of the building—far, far away from my girls and all the other classes.

The air on this side of the building is crisp, with only four unused studios. This studio is one of the older ones waiting to be remodeled to fit the rest of the academy's modernized look.

Sucking in a deep breath, I brace myself for who's on the other side of the door. Dupri made it seem like the devil himself was waiting for me.

My body thrums with anxious energy and my tongue is thick with heaviness as I turn the knob to the room.

Taking a step inside, my senses are flooded from all over. It's dark in here, save for the small orange, ambient lightning of a vintage stage light in the corner. I sneeze quietly as dust flies into my nostrils.

Dropping my bag and placing the cupcakes down beside it, I'm about to start stretching when I realize I'm not alone.

In the center of the room sits a lone figure, with over-ear headphones on, hunched over. The person is obviously male, with large back muscles hidden under a white compression shirt.

My back stiffens as I look the figure over. My heart knows who sits before me, but my eyes refuse to recognize them.

Run! It's a trap! the distant voice in my brain shouts, but my feet are stuck in their place and I'm paralyzed as the figure looks up in the mirror.

His dirty blond hair shakes with the action and my heart free falls to the pits of hell as green eyes meet my hazel ones.

"Jace?" My voice is breathless and unrecognizable, like a foreign entity has taken over my body as he smirks, still watching me through the mirror.

"Hello, angel."

Four

Jace

I WOULD'VE LAUGHED DUE to the look on Sienna's face when our eyes connected in the mirror, had this moment been funny. The deer caught in the headlights look works for her.

As if realizing her frozen state, she inhales sharply. Her shoulders relax as her eyes soften around the edges.

"What're you doing here?" Her angelic voice warms my skin as her attention flickers back and forth between my face and the sketchbook on my lap.

Had I been over the stunt she and that asshole in the tacky green sweater pulled earlier, I would respond to her with something along the lines of *"waiting for you, babe,"* or *"sitting here like an idiot because I bought a dance studio for you even though I haven't seen you in 615 days."*

But I don't...Instead, I say, "Is this not a dance studio?" My tone is clipped as my hard gaze locks yet again with hers, daring her.

The fire beneath her hazel eyes blaze alight, her jaw sets as they squint down at me.

I've never talked to Sienna like this. Cleo and Georgia, yes, but never her. She's always been the angel of my dreams, the Alice that I yearned for in Wonderland. But I know that's not the truth.

She's been a stranger to me since the day she walked out of my life two years ago.

I watch as she ducks back into herself, placing the mask I'd always pulled away as a kid back on. Sienna had been smiling when she first entered the studio until she saw me.

I take my time analyzing her differences in the mirror. In almost two years since laying my eyes on her in person, Sienna has only made one change to herself.

Her hair, once a long wild mane of Cherry Cola curls, is now a slicked back bun of pink delight.

I tilt my head at the freshly dyed hair.

Pink isn't even her favorite color, lavender is.

"Yes. It's a studio, but you're no Alvin Ailey. Why are you here, Jace?" She folds her arms over her chest, and my eyes immediately flicker to the way they push up in her shirt before flickering back to her face.

Sienna has the face of an angel, the face of someone you'd be grateful was the last person you'd see before the darkness of death takes over you. The cold, dead thing in my chest beats fast as she pops her hip out, giving me the stern look of an annoyed authority figure.

I smirk at her. I can see it in her eyes, the hidden amusement, the questions.

Trust me, angel. I have millions of questions for you, too.

"What does it look like, angel? You're a teacher, I need teaching. So teach me."

As if I had stunned her, Sienna's eyes widen and she reels back before rolling them.

My smirk grows into a full blown smile as she scoffs at my rude tone. Some things never change with her.

As kids, whenever I'd gotten annoyed with either Cleo or Georgia—which was basically all the time since my closest friends were two annoying girls who wanted to practice their makeup on me all the time—Sienna would always stand up for them, or roll those honey-like eyes at me.

I've thought about this moment for years. The day that I'd see Sienna Jones again after she'd left me on a rooftop in Manhattan on her 18th birthday, dazed and confused with the feel of her plump, pink lips still lingering on mine.

I bet she's still wearing the same lip gloss, too.

That expensive raspberry flavored one that almost every girl in the world wears because it's *'lip oil'* not gloss...or whatever the fuck that means.

I just know it felt good against mine.

That night that she'd left, I'd been trapped with the knowledge that there was a possibility I'd never see her again. She was living in New York and so was Cleo. Georgia, Ryan, and I stayed here in Maryland, and the Jones girls seemed like they were living their life in the Big Apple.

Cleo had met some guy, Marcelo, who I've played against a few times, and Sienna was doing spectacular at NYU.

The kiss was something you could only dream of. At the top of a skyscraper in the heart of the city, fireworks for the New Year went off and her lips met mine in a dance I hadn't known was already engraved into my mind and soul.

It was slow and needy like a kiss before war. Your last chance at goodbye.

Until Georgia found us on the rooftop.

The blonde she-devil equivalent to Hades found us in the most secluded corner of the world, on our little island in the midst of the New Year celebration.

She'd yelled, "Happy New—" until she realized what she'd been seeing.

And that was how I found myself alone on a rooftop, crowded with people who knew and loved me. Sienna ran away from the scene faster than a burglar and ignored my every attempt to reach out to her since.

Hell, *Georgia* even tried to get her to talk to me once.

But now, two years later, in an old unused dance studio alone without any barriers between us, we watch each other like hostile strangers.

"Seriously, Eros. I have a student I'm meeting. My boss is on my ass about this kid...so please just do me this one favor and leave." Her voice softens as does her brows as she takes her bottom lip between her teeth.

Her boss?

Does she not know that I'm the boss now?

"I'm the student," I say, my voice deadpanned as I tilt my head at her.

I see it in her eyes, the annoyance. It bubbles over like hot water on a stove. Sienna huffs, her chest rising and falling rapidly as she turns on her heels, snatching up her bag to leave, but I'm already ahead of her.

This was *not* how this *reuniting* was supposed to go. She was supposed to walk in and see me sitting here, and we would've christened the goddamned room. Instead, my angel's running away from me...again.

"Stop, Sienna." My voice is stern as I bark my words at her, mentally hating myself for being so cold towards her, but it gets the job done as Sienna stops in her tracks.

She looks bewildered as she eyes me.

"I booked you," I say with a shrug as her eyes widen.

"You...what?"

"For the next," I look down at my watch, smirking, "116 days, you're mine, angel."

Her eye twitches as the truth of my words assault her brain. "You did *what*?"

I sigh, blowing out an air of annoyance as I lean back on my hands.

"Cleared your schedule."

Sienna's brown skin reddens like a tomato as the twitching of her eyes increases.

"You self-centered, spoiled brat. How dare you come into my space and mess it up to suit your needs? I teach *four-year-olds*, for crying out loud! Do you know how hard it is for a kid to adjust to something like that? They probably think that I abandoned them because I'm not there to teach them right now since your cocky ass decided to come in here acting like you run things and taking up my time. Time is precious, and you're wasting mine right now!" She curses, pacing around the room with her bag held angrily like a vice in her fist.

My eyes widen as I take in everything she's said.

Maybe she *was* the hot dance teacher Derek and Blake said ripped them a new one after all.

I don't think I've ever heard Sienna swear in our decade of knowing one another, but as her words sink in, I realize not only have I fucked this up—I probably ruined something great before it could've ever started.

She drops her bag beside mine. I watch as a slip of paper falls from it onto the floor, but she doesn't notice it. Instead, she's gearing up to rip me a new asshole.

"You know what you are, Jace Heart?" she asks, her voice calm as her eyes narrow on me.

No...I actually do not want to know—

"You're an entitled rich boy who needs to be knocked down a notch. Find yourself a new dance teacher."

Woah...*What?!*

I didn't spend nearly three hundred thousand dollars on this studio for her to *quit*...Somehow my mind hasn't connected with my mouth, because instead of being reasonable and explaining my peace to her, I say, "You're rich, too!" like an idiot.

Sienna rolls her eyes, throwing her head up to the sky as if asking God for mercy as she snatches up her bag yet again and leaves the studio, slamming the door behind her.

Well...that went great.

With a deep sigh, I clean up the studio, grabbing the box she'd left in the room and the small white paper that fell out of her bag.

Though that wasn't how I expected our first meeting to go, it could've been worse. She's kinda cute when she's mad anyways. Like an angry chipmunk.

My hand itches to read the note that'd fallen, and as soon as I'm safely in my SUV, I do.

"Sienna's 21 before 21?"

My eyes skim over the list, growing wider and wider as they do until they land on one thing in particular.

Have a New Year's kiss.

If anyone in this world is kissing Sienna Jones on *that* day, it'll be me. And I know just how I'll make it happen.

Five

Sienna

Maybe I overreacted, but ugh! The nerve of him. Nothing screams toxic masculine energy than a man inserting himself in your space and trying to dominate everything you've worked on. Not only did he completely disregard the fact that I have ten little ones depending on me as their teacher, he ignored my set schedule that I had curated with my boss.

After leaving work abruptly, I received a nice long text message from Calista, alerting me of my new schedule, what's required of me, and new locations to meet my *student* at. Not only did Jace trample on my plans, he had to have bribed someone because I'm virtually off of work every day except for Wednesday and Fridays.

Two days that I had planned to work on the Winter Showcase with Daisy earlier today.

Heaving a loud sigh, I feel like I'm going to explode as I enter The Sweet Tooth for the second time today. My skin thrums with frustrated energy, and I try and fail to contain myself as I stalk towards the front counter.

"Back so soon?" Saree's honeyed voice is like music to my ears as she pops up from behind the counter, smiling like a mad-man.

She must sense my anger because the smile drops immediately as her brows furrow, taking me in. My clothes are slightly tousled and my hair is fuzzy from yanking on a hoodie in the car. My shoulders are bunched up, and I'm pretty sure that I'm wound so tight that the slightest touch would cause me to combust.

"Talk or eat?" she asks, looking down at the register, tapping away.

"Eat. Definitely eat." I frown, reaching for my purse when she holds a hand out to me, effectively stopping me in my tracks.

"I got this, baby girl. Go sit down and take a breather." Saree's smile is warm as she gestures towards the lavender, pink, and sage green bean bags chairs in the "quiet nook" of the bakery. The quiet nook is essentially a small area where customers have a small array of books and comfortable seating to read and eat their baked goods.

With a groan, I plop down on the sage green one and grimace, cursing it mentally for its color.

Why does my favorite chair have to be the same color as his eyes?

My frown softens when Saree brings me a small tray of Lavender Love Macarons and chocolate chip cookies with a small peach ginger tea.

My muscles unwind as I take a tentative sip of the warm tea, blowing to cool it down.

Instinctively, my hand moves without thought towards my phone, successfully pulling up the one app that kept me in touch with my friends over the past two years.

Muscle memory is a hell of a thing.

Without fail, I find myself on Jace's art page, my fingers caressing the screen as I scroll through the millions of paintings, sketches, and sculptures he's made in the time we've been apart.

I scroll until I find it, the painting of the unfinished girl.

It's a brown skinned model in a perfect arabesque. Her body is light as a feather as she reaches out with a sophisticated hand, reminding me of someone on a mission. She's graceful and poised, her shoulders relaxed with the confidence of knowing her work and executing it perfectly. But that's not what sends me for a loop—it's her face.

He'd captured the woman, up until her neck. The painting was posted a year ago and he'd titled it *Unfinished: The Girl Who Loved.*

Further down, there were more paintings of landscapes and people, but that ballerina always stuck out to me.

As I scroll to the bottom, I stop as my eyes land on a painting that hadn't been there last week.

It's me.

As a young girl, probably around twelve or thirteen, smiling as I look off to the distance. My messy array of curls are carefully painted to show the one time I'd allowed myself to not care about my appearance as a kid.

Jace had told me he wanted to paint me, and I agreed after my parents missed yet another one of my recitals in Summerfield. I did summer classes here to spend time with Cleo and her friends before going back to California for school. When I'd realized my parents hadn't shown up, I couldn't leave my room at uncle Clef's for days.

It wasn't until the scrawny, blond kid from next door with hair like Hercules and a smile that could kill stumbled into my room, grinning like the Cheshire cat, that I realized life wasn't that bad.

Jace spent that entire day trying to brighten my spirits by giving me snacks I wasn't allowed to eat at home, watching TV with me, and just being there for me.

It wasn't until he'd suggested painting me that I smiled.

He did everything to make me laugh that day...and now he's grown up to be an annoying douchebag.

Earlier today, he and that girl were all over one another, and now he has the nerve to go to my place of work and demand changes in my schedule to suit him?

What a narcissistic pig.

I'm about to let out my fourth sigh when the wind chimes of the room go off.

My head whips to the door, an unnatural feeling boils in my gut as I look at it.

Did he follow me here? Is going to apologize?

Instead, Aric stares back at me. My shoulders drop at the sight of him and the feeling in my stomach dies as he makes his way over.

"Hey! I didn't know you liked this place," he says, smiling brightly at me.

The sight unsettles me after receiving an even brighter one from a man that I loathe just twenty minutes ago.

I curl my lips in, biting them slightly before plastering on a smile.

"Of course! Who doesn't love a bakery?" I ask, but my voice sounds scratchy and unnatural.

"Right...so I was thinking about our date—"

Date? When did I...*Shit.*

I forgot I even agreed to that, and it was only this morning that I had. How can I get out of—

"So, yeah... are you allergic to anything? I have a few restaurants in mind—"

"Only strawberries."

Hello, three foot hole, allow me to dig an additional three feet because what the fuck was that? I was supposed to say, "*Oh, I'm sorry...I have to walk my pet fish, Melinda,*" or something along those lines.

Instead, I'm stuck going on a date with a man.

A man.

Eugh.

Could you see my shoulders quiver?

I don't know if it's just me or the fact that I'm awkward as hell, but the idea of going on a date with a random man gives me the creeps.

There, I said it.

I'm creeped out.

No I'm not...that's a lie if I ever told one. I *did* want to go on the date. Aric's cute enough, after all, but then *Jace freaking Heart* sat his perfectly golden ass down in my studio and now my brain is fucked up.

Fuck men. They're useless, anyways.

I don't know how or when, but I make it back home to the apartment to find the girls already in their rooms, probably getting ready for their classes tomorrow.

Dragging myself through my night routine is as easy as squeezing unripe lemons. My mind is sore from dealing with Jace and starting a new semester, and my body is sore from everything else.

By the time I'm securely in my bed, swishing my feet under the covers to warm myself and get fully comfortable, my mind wanders back to my list.

I haven't checked it at all today.

"A girls got needs...I *need* to get this list done." I huff a sigh, walking my sock clad feet against the hardwood floors of my bedroom over to the tote bag hanging on my desk chair.

Rolling my eyes at myself, I dig my hand into the bag. Wait a minute...

Pat. Pat. Pat.

It's got to be here somewhere...I never leave the house without it.

Snatching my bag off of my desk chair, I tilt it up, exposing all the bag's contents to the ground as my eyes frantically search for the missing paper.

Birth control...*Check.*

Five sticks of gum...*Check.*

Four different lip oils...*Quadruple motherfucking check.*

Where is it?!

My heart drops as my world comes crashing down on me.

No.

No.

NO.

No.

No...

My list is gone.

SIX

Sienna

"Good job, girls! I'm so proud of you all..." I trail off, my voice unrecognizable to my own ears.

My mind is on a continuous loop of the past few days and where my list could've gone in that time. Even though the blond equivalent to Hades announced that he was taking over and becoming my student, I still had other students to take care of first, which is why I'm teaching the Minis today.

The world doesn't revolve around Jace Heart, and neither do I.

Taking a sip from my water bottle, my eyes remain locked on the ten girls before me, all participating in an end of practice stretch. When I got to the academy today, Dupri told me to head to my original studio, Studio C, and I found all of my original students sitting around chatting with one another.

It felt good to see and be around my girls, even if it's only been about a week since the recital.

I miss teaching them and their little pouts when they don't understand a piece of choreography.

As the girls pack up with their moms, I begin to do the same.

My body is exhausted and my limbs feel like they're on the verge of snapping. This morning, I had another early morning Ballet course as well as a three hour lecture on the history of modern art.

History isn't my strong suit, so sitting in that lecture on a hard wooden chair for most of my school day took a toll on my body.

Rolling my shoulders out and stretching my neck, I let out a relieved sigh.

Todays over...luckily, there wasn't any crap with parents or—

"Daddy!" a familiar voice squeals. My body shutters as the sound of little feet pattering against the ground echoes in the emptying room.

Delilah's father is a tall, handsome man, and the most annoying parent that I've met thus far—and that's saying a lot considering I've only met him *as her father* once...when I cursed him out at the recital.

Before *Hades* came and took over my job, I taught at the studio for two and a half months. In that time, I'd only met Derek twice: once when I babysat Delilah and thought he was her brother...and on the night of the recital when he missed her performance, showing up late.

Besides those two instances, I've only ever met Delilah's abuela, Lidia, a short, older Latina woman who loves hugs. Lidia has picked up and dropped off Delilah from every single practice. So when I realized that it was *him* who neglected his child, I saw red.

A fiery inferno burned inside me and like a phoenix, the old "sweet" Sienna died. It was the first time I'd ever cursed at someone, and boy did it feel good. Since then, from what the other instructors have told me, Lidia has remained the sole person to show up for Delilah's practices.

My mind thrums with unbridled rage as our eyes lock. Any human who is negligent towards their kid isn't a parent in my eyes.

As I walk past the two I stop, expecting Derek to ask about his daughter's progress like the rest of the parents, but he doesn't.

He *scowls* at me, deep, brown eyes burning bright with rage. I'm a rather tall woman, but the man is a giant. And from what I heard from other young instructors, he plays hockey, too.

Figures. I bet he and Jace are friends. Two men who act like Neanderthals. One who scowls and refuses to speak, and the other who bangs on his chest and speaks *too much*.

Could Jace be friends with a person who isn't present in their child's life?

He wouldn't be, right?

My mind is infiltrated with thoughts of the blond, pulling me into the past almost instantly. The memory of us ten years ago flashes before my eyes, sucking me in.

Jace's small, lanky arms are cold as they pull me into his side. His childish body is smaller than mine, but he still manages to hold me as if he were huge like his brothers, Asa and Jackson.

"I'm sorry your mommy and daddy didn't come again, angel," he pouts, his sage eyes dim as he looks down at me. Jace's cheeks are rosy as he blows a frustrated breath, the scent of grape soda on his tongue.

My heart falls at the reminder of my parents.

Could he tell that I'm upset?

I thought that I hid it well...

"I saw you crying in the room..." he says, his voice soft as he tries to tug my small body deeper into him, like a Doe trying to protect their Joey.

"I—"

"It's okay, angel. I won't tell anyone, it can be our little secret. Pinky promise!" The young ten-year-old boy's voice is bright as he holds out his pinky to me, promising to keep my secret.

"Promise?" The softness of my voice is almost inaudible to my ears, but Jace hears me perfectly.

"Always, I won't ever abandon you. I'll go to all of your shows and be the loudest in the room!" he exclaims energetically, his pinky looping with mine as he smiles at me. The sun shines beneath Jace's irises and he reminds me of that one Greek guy that my aunt Melody likes to talk about so much.

Heracue...

Herca?

Hercules!

He's like Hercules. He's strong, nice, and looks out for me. Jace Heart is like my very own Hercules!

I giggle at the thought of him being my hero.

"You can't go to all of my shows, silly! I live in California..." I frown, but Jace laughs off my words.

"My dad has a plane! I'll just ask him and we'll go together, we can even get...cookies... together," he says, whispering the word "cookies".

I giggle at his silliness, and just like that, my once somber mood is replaced with something light and airy like the sun.

He's my sunshine.

Heaving a deep sigh, I turn on my heels and leave.

Not today, Satan. You may have taken me out of my character a few days ago, but I refuse to give this ogre the satisfaction of a reaction from me.

Nope.

Not happening.

By the time I make it back home to the apartment, I'm annoyed, hungry, and still thinking about my list. I had it before I went to class a few days ago...

The pinging of my phone pulls me out of my thoughts as my phone vibrates against my butt pocket. Looking down, I furrow my brows as I read the text from Aric.

Aric

We still on for Sunday?

My heart drops at the thought of dealing with *more* men this week. I need a break from their species. I don't think it's good to have to socialize with multiple men in less than a week. It messes with the brain.

I feel dumber just from a few hours *thinking* about Jace, let alone being around him.

I knew that I'd started losing brain cells when my first thought after being asked on a date was, "Would Jace care if I went?" rather than, "What kind of perfume should I wear?"

I'm losing my mysterious girl vibe here!

"Girl, you're letting the good air out the house! You're either in or you're out," Georgia jokingly scolds me, standing in front of me with her blonde locks in rollers, wearing a baby blue bath robe and a green face mask.

"Who's grandma are you?" I ask, cracking a smile as she rolls her eyes.

"Obviously someone has to be an authority figure around these parts...Cleo's been acting suspicious, and I haven't seen you in three days!" she groans dramatically, dragging herself to the kitchen. In an instant, she's back in front of me, holding a strawberry cupcake.

My smile widens as she struggles to eat the cupcake because of the mask, and I take a step back when she gets a little closer with the cupcake.

Georgia's the oldest of the three of us, with her being twenty-one while Cleo and I are both twenty. Georgia graduated with us because she was held back in kindergarten due to her dyslexia, which from what I heard, is how she, Jace, and Cleo became friends the next year.

Since I spent my summers and some winter breaks in Summerfield, I met Georgia. She became an instant big sister to me, always looking after me and trying to get me out of my shell.

"Missed me?" I tease, grinning from ear to ear as she hands me a paper towel with four fresh baked chocolate chip cookies on it.

My favorites.

We're a household of snackers. If you ever come over, expect to find donuts, cookies, and cupcakes at any time of the day.

"You already know I have! I haven't seen you or your Type-A cousin in *years,* and now you two are here and we haven't had a single girls night..." the blonde groans and pouts while kicking her legs out like one of my toddler dancers.

"A guy asked me out," I cringe, frowning slightly. Aric's not a bad guy, but what if he isn't the *right* guy? I get uncomfortable just from the thought of going out with him...what's to say he's not a weird serial killer?

Or.

A guy with a foot fetish.

My body shivers uncontrollably from the thought. Feet creep me out so much, and then there's people that willingly put *other* people's feet in their mouth.

Bleh.

Can you hear me throwing up in my mouth?

Georgia's arm shoots out across my chest like a mom who's just slammed on the breaks, and my neck snaps to the side from the force.

"Did you just say someone asked you out?!" she exclaims, hopping off the couch, her jaw agape.

My cheeks warm from her laser focused green eyes.

"Someone did what?! Oh my gosh, Si Si, we have to help you get ready!" Cleo's melodic voice is as loud as all outdoors as the pink clad woman rushes out of her bedroom into our shared living room.

"It's not a big deal..." I shrug, looking away from them to the TV, but the blonde-brunette duo has other plans. The girls close in, standing in front of me like Thing 1 and Thing 2 with their hands on their hips and creepy smiles on their faces.

I sink into my seat on the couch as Thing 2—Cleo—jumps on me.

"Of course it's a big deal, you *never* go out!" she exclaims, settling herself beside me as Georgia purses her lips.

I roll my eyes, smiling, "I'm sorry, ma'am. Is that the pot calling the kettle black?!"

"You go to one party, have a man eat you out, and now suddenly you're the party expert?" Gerogia adds.

"I've had boyfriends, G. When was the last time you've seen this stickler *talk* to a man?" Cleo asks, her tone clearly light and playful as she turns on the TV.

Georgia and I's eyes lock momentarily, communicating with one another.

She knows the last man I talked to. Hell, she walked in on us devouring one another's mouths.

Her eyes tell me *I won't say anything if you don't.*

And I won't. Not now, not ever. That kiss was like something out of a fairytale, but like all stories, they must come to an end. And our page turned on that night.

"Oh, shut up! Si Si's just a little inexperienced is all...I bet she'll find the person of her dreams while she's here. That guy could be her soulmate." Georgia shrugs and my nose scrunches.

Aric is not my soulmate...*that* I know for sure. Jace, too, for that matter.

I think my soulmate might just be an artsy girl who paints little portraits of me when I sleep and feeds me green grapes because she knows I hate the red ones. We'd make dinners together, she'd go to my shows, and we'd ride off into the sunset on her bike because, of course, I'd date a biker girl.

Can you tell that I read too many books?

"What was his name again?" Georgia asks, pulling my attention back to the topic.

"Aric Rogers, I think...he's an art major."

At this, Georgia's brow raises. "Rogers? He's...a guy. Just be careful, he was sweet in our Textiles class, but he does tend to date a lot."

"So I should go on the date?" I ask, chewing the inside of my cheek.

"You're still contemplating it?! Girl, go get your man!" Cleo laughs loudly, but I can tell there's something off with her. She isn't her usual, careful self right now. Matter of fact, she's been a little off since she came back from New York.

My smile is small as I look at my cousin.

Just what happened to her while she was gone? And why does the idea of saying yes to this date freak me out?

"Cheers to the motherfucking weekend!" Georgia shouts as she lifts her cocktail glass in the air, her sour apple margarita sloshing in the cup.

"Bitch, it's Thursday!" Denver, one of Cleo's new friends, jokes as Georgia giggles, throwing back her drink.

The laugh that leaves my mouth rips from the bottom of my stomach as Georgia completely misses her mouth, the drink going down her shirt while Denver's does the same.

When Cleo first introduced the beautiful stranger, my first thought was, *fuck, why is her friend a literal goddess?* Followed by my second thought of, *is she going to fit into our little group?*

We can be a bit *intense* considering we're all practically family, so it could be intimidating to others.

My thoughts of unease were put to rest immediately when Denver began to joke about wanting a margarita as soon as she stepped over our threshold.

Her outspoken thoughts soon turned into a friendly competition on who could whip up the best cocktail, with all of us making our own signature drink for the entire group.

With Cleo making her signature cosmopolitan, Denver whipping up a raspberry margarita, Georgia dazzling us with her sour apple margarita, and me fixing up my go to Caribbean storm...it's safe to say we're shitfaced.

"Wait, wait, wait! We need more shots!" I hear Denver cry out as she chases Georgia into the kitchen from their spot on the balcony as Cleo starts singing one of our favorite princess theme songs.

Life is good. Liquor thrums through my veins and I'm surrounded by good energy. This was the whole purpose of my list. I made it to let go and relax, but something won't let me. I don't know if it's because I can't find the list or because images of sage green eyes and a daring smile clouds my thoughts.

seven

Jace

LEAVE IT TO MY girl to have "pet a monkey" on her bucket list. I chuckle inwardly as I reread the twenty-one items on her bucket list, making my own edits in the notes app of my phone.

Some of these things have got to go. I mean *who* is she kissing that isn't me? And a one night stand is completely out of the question.

If I had the privilege of having Sienna Jones in my bed, one night *would not* be enough. I'd need all of eternity to make up for lost time, and the rest of infinity to make more memories with her. I could never be done with her, so let's just scratch that one off, too.

A smirk finds itself across my lips as I eye number fifteen.

Be chased...

What kind of crazy things go on in that brain of yours, angel?

Just as I'm about to highlight the bullet, a body knocks into mine on the bench, pulling me back to my current surroundings.

The Men's Hockey locker room.

Scrambling with my phone and the list, I shove both into my duffel just as Charlie settles in next to me.

Having the list is a nonissue. I'd never judge Sienna for being inexperienced or for wanting to branch out, but *the guys* don't know her. I won't subject anyone to the torture of having an entire hockey team knowing their business.

The only reason that they know my business is because I don't care enough to hide it.

Society likes to think that women are the only gender group that likes to gossip, but boy are they wrong. Men *gossip*. Hell, they may even gossip more than women.

Name one man who hasn't been secretly eavesdropping on a conversation and somehow knew something that they weren't supposed to know.

I'll wait...

Exactly.

"Sooooo..." The blond giant wiggles his brows at me, shimmying his shoulder into mine.

"So?" I furrow my brows at him, placing a protective hand on the duffle.

I'd honestly hate to have to fuck up one of my closest friends because he snooped through Sienna's private list.

Yes, I know I sound hypocritical.

Shut up.

"Are you coming to the football game tomorrow? The guys and I have a bet going for it, you could throw in a twenty on your guy." Charlie shrugs, running a hand through his sweaty hair.

My *guy* is Ryan Jones, Cleo's stepbrother and Sienna's cousin. He and I are just as close as I am to Cleo. My ears perk up as I weigh my options. If I go to this game, there's a 95% chance that Sienna would go to it, too.

When we were kids and Ryan would have scrimmages during the summer, she'd make it a point for us all to go to the game. I know it was because her parents never went to her recitals, but I'm pretty sure she's carried that tradition into adulthood, whenever she could make it.

I could spend the entire night with my girl, and she'd be forced to be around me since her morals would never let her leave in the middle of a family member's event.

She's too kind to do that.

"I'm in." I shrug, playing the role of the nonchalant guy, but deep down my blood is thrumming with energy and eagerness.

By the time the guys and I get home from practice, we're like dead men looking for a coffin.

Braxton and Alec struggle as they walk up the stairs side-by-side, attempting to go up at the same time to their rooms. I watch in silent confusion as the pair fight like a couple of confused sloths for dominance, with Alec being the smaller of the two.

Just as Brax is close to making a break, pushing his way through, Alec beats him to it. The two run up the stairs, shouting after one another, leaving me confused on where the hell they got their energy from.

I am spent.

I'm not saying any names, but some idiot freshman thought it'd be a good idea to piss Coach off by being twenty minutes late to practice tonight. You'd think he'd be the only one to be disciplined, but *no*. Clef Jones doesn't operate that way.

If one fuck head is late, we're *all* late—which resulted in twenty minutes of extended practice doing bag skates. The goalies were included on this punishment since both Derek and Ricardo Ruiz, one of our backup goalies, were late as well.

What's up with people lacking punctuality these days?

The couch dips as Blake plops down on it with a bowl of popcorn in his lap. I hadn't even heard him making it in the kitchen.

"Dude...what was up Coach's ass tonight? He never goes that hard," he says, sighing as he shoves a handful of the salty snack into his mouth.

I groan at the reminder of tonight's practice and shrug it off, going on my phone.

"No clue and I don't care. I need a good brain rot sesh to forget the last three hours of my life."

My body warms as I find just the account I was looking for.

Viral videos and photos of Sienna dancing filter my phone screen as I select her most recent post from a few days ago. On this account, she only posts herself dancing, and it's how I've been able to sketch a few drawings over the time we've spent apart.

My fingers itch for a pencil as I watch her practice her dance from the recital last week in an empty studio. She's wearing all black with a black baseball cap, but I know it's her. She could have a paper bag over her head and I'd still know who she is.

The room is so quiet as I watch through Sienna's video that I think Blake might've fallen asleep mid-chew until he speaks lowly.

"Do you think Cleo's going to be at the game?" he asks quietly, effectively yanking my attention from my phone.

What did he just say?

"Considering Ryan is her brother…I'd say yes, but why do you care? Aren't you two doing a project or something?" I ask as I look my closest friend over.

I've seen Blake go off the deep end with women more times than I can count. From sleeping around to simply ghosting them after a night in his room, I've seen it all. If he thinks he's going to do the same thing to my best friend, he's out of his mind.

"Oh…uh…yeah." He coughs, clearing his throat as he runs a hand through his messy waves. "She and I have a project together…I was just wondering."

I don't like that…I can't look after my friends and stalk Sienna at the same time.

Something's gotta give, and it's not the ballerina.

EIGHT

Sienna

I GIVE UP.

Never in my near twenty-one years of existence have I ever given up on something, but *I* give up. My throat feels like sandpaper and my chest burns from overworking my heart.

Is this what death feels like? It fucking sucks if it is.

"Wait, Sienna, what are you doing? We need to run that move again!" ~~The psychopath~~ Daisy exclaims as I crawl across the dance floor towards my water bottle.

I don't know if it's a caffeine addiction or just her nature, but the girl is scary—and I thought *I* was scary when it came to dancing. We've been practicing nonstop for over *two hours,* and she has yet to take a water break.

Our dance isn't rigorous in terms of speed and agility, but it is *very* technical and demanding on the body. We've chosen to do a lyrical ballet duet. The work is supposed to simulate a black and white swan with each mirroring one another, but my dance partner is a nutcase who doesn't know what the meaning of a break is.

"I'm getting water before I die from heat exhaustion," I throw back at her, gulping half of my bottle down in mere seconds.

Daisy chuckles quietly at my response, taking a seat beside me, doing the same. We sit in silence for a few minutes with me trying to catch my breath and her...pondering. I guess.

Other than the few times we've talked in class, I know little to nothing about the red haired girl beside me. So, in honor of trying to make friends at this new school, I speak up.

"Are you going to the football game tonight? I hear it's going to be a good season opener," I say with a smile, lying through my teeth. I haven't heard a thing about this game other than the fact that my cousin is playing and so is his sexy best friend, Tatum.

What's up with my cousins having attractive friends? First Jace, then Tatum, and now Denver...they're all freaking beautiful.

"Oh no...I only date hockey players. Besides, football games are like a frat boy's wet dream, and frat guys aren't my type." Daisy shrugs, pulling two bottles of light pink tinted water out from her bag.

That's not weird at all...

I understand only dating one type of male, but only dating *hockey guys* seems a little odd.

My brows furrow slightly as I take Daisy in. She seems so calm and collected, and not at all like she danced for two hours straight. She must feel my gaze on her because she smiles at me, handing me one of the bottles of water.

"Here, drink this. It has electrolytes in it! It's how I stay so active during our practices."

Taking the bottle, I give her a small smile and throw it into my bag.

"Ready to get back to it?"

"She has to be doing hard drugs..." I mumble as I step into the apartment, my legs feeling like al dente noodles as I trudge inside.

Georgia, like the hyper sorcerous she is, materializes in front of me out of thin air.

"Who's on drugs? Did you take any?" she asks, her head tilted like a confused puppy as she pops a green grape into her mouth.

I'd think the scene of her standing in front of me smacking on grapes was comical had my body *not* been completely eviscerated just twenty minutes ago.

"No? Why would I—"

"Do you hear that?" Georgia cuts me off, holding her hand up.

Did this bitch just— *Wait.*

My ears perk up, the faint sound of sniffling and muffled sobs quietly sound out through the apartment. Eyeing one another carefully, Georgia and I make our way to the hall where our rooms are.

My heart drops as the cries grow louder.

"Is she sick? Did she get hurt?" My words are like vomit, tumbling out of my mouth uncontrollably as Georgia frowns at me, shaking her head.

She doesn't give me the time to think of a game plan for this situation. No, instead, Georgia Adams grabs the knob of Cleo's door, saunters into the room, and snatches the covers off of my cousin's back.

My heart cracks and falls out of my chest at the sight below me, my cousin—one of the strongest people I know—lies in a fetal position, hugging her knees to her chest as she sobs quietly.

"Cleo..." I breathe her name, my body moving on its own as I take a seat beside her on the bed with Georgia doing the same on her other side.

My brain feels as if it's on autopilot as I listen to what's been going on with her. I'd noticed she wasn't like her old self and has been distant, but I'd never suspected this.

Someone's been threatening and stalking her for *months* and she's just now speaking out about it.

I swear I'm going to kill everyone who ever dared to *think* badly about her, let alone threaten her. They've been texting her nonstop and it's sickening. If I had it my way, I'd go real life COD on their asses and blow everyone up.

Too much?

Sorry...

By the time we get to the game, everyone's spirits are up. Cleo's started to feel better, Denver's with us, and Georgia's had a margarita. I drank a little bit of those electrolytes that Daisy gave me earlier, and now my energy is through the roof.

We're sitting in center field, near the fifty-yard line, on the edge of our seats watching the boys get obliterated. Ryan was cocky in our cousins' group chat about how he and the guys would win, but it's not looking too good for them with this game.

The energy in the arena shifts just as Denver complains about the game being boring, and my spine straightens as a chill runs down it.

"Funny to see you here, Coach." Minty breath against my ears sends shivers across my body as Jace backs away from me.

"I didn't know they let crazy people on school campuses…" I roll my eyes as Jace looks me up and down, cataloging me in his brain.

My body thrums to life as I watch him analyze me carefully. My skin warms as his eyes caress the bare parts of it that my cropped shirt doesn't cover.

"Guess you can say I'm the exception." He shrugs, leaning back and spreading his legs wide.

My mouth salivates as he gets comfortable in his seat, his eyes never leaving my own.

"More like the rule…"

We stare at each other in complete silence, and I don't realize my friends are going back and forth with his friends until Jace interjects and Georgia groans.

She'd said before we left that she wanted a drama free night to watch "her man" in action. Her man being Ryan, though I don't think he knows that.

"Oh, fuck me sideways, why are you here? *Don't you have some girl to paint or something?*" Georgia asks loudly before whispering as her eyes flicker to the left, catching on Delilah and Derek—whom I hadn't realized were here—before falling back on Jace.

Why is Derek here? And what girl? Was the girl from the first day of classes really his girl—

Jace rolls his eyes. "Did Halloween come early, or have my nightmares come true, *peach?*"

I grimace as Georgia scowls—she's mildly allergic to peaches.

The two of them go at it, but I tune them out as my stomach gurgles and my head spins. Has Georgia known all along about Jace's girlfriend? And if she did, why hadn't she told me?

By halftime, my mouth feels cottony and my stomach is queasy. I don't know what I ate, but it obviously disagrees with my body.

My skin is hot, and I don't know if it's because it's too many bodies around me or because I'm coming down with something. The feeling of my curls being moved to the side and a cooling, wet sensation being rubbed against the nape of my neck brings me mild relief. I groan as a cool feeling flows through my skin.

"You feeling alright?" Jace's gruff voice is soft as he rubs circles against my neck, the cool sensation slowly fading to his fingertips.

Is he rubbing me down? At a football game, no less?

"No, stop touching me..." I bite, my body craving to get closer to him even though my brain refuses.

Continuing down that road with Jace would only lead to two things: failure and regrets. Two very, *very* disappointing things that I don't see for my future self any time soon.

As the game progresses, my skin grows clammier, and by the time the game is done, I'm hot all over.

What the hell is happening to me?

"You coming to the bar tonight?" Blake asks Derek, who's been awfully quiet all night as he declines, gesturing to his sleeping daughter.

I can feel eyes watching my every move as I wipe a bead of sweat from my forehead.

"What about you guys? Sienna, you coming?" Cleo asks, turning to face me, and it's then that I realize I'd been zoning out.

"Huh...?"

"She's not, she's going home and getting some rest." Jace cuts in for me, and I don't know if I want to thank him for saying what my mouth wouldn't or scold him for speaking for me.

"What?! No, it's the first game of the season!" Georgia groans, butting into the conversation.

"I don't know, G. I don't feel too good," I mumble, holding a hand to my aching stomach as Georgia's frown deepens.

"Fine...Hey, DILF, can you take her home? We live in the RiverView complex, but I drove here." My eyes widen as Georgia calls out to Derek, my *nemesis*.

Nemesis may be a strong word, but he's up there on my list right next to my former mentor at NYU and toe socks.

I look at each and every person around me before my eyes land on *his*. If a person could hold a storm in their eyes, then Jace's holds a wildfire. His eyes are brimming with heat and anger as his jaw clenches. I watch him as he folds his arms across his chest and my stomach churns. I don't know if it's from sickness or because of attraction, but I want him to say something...anything.

I want *him* to take me home, not this asshole.

Just when he's about to open his mouth, Derek cuts in.

"Of course, I'll take her home."

My heart falls. I don't know what I had expected—Jace isn't my knight in shining armor. Why would he give up his Saturday night at a bar just to take me home?

The car ride with Derek is silent and uncomfortable with him and I sitting in silence while Delilah sleeps.

It isn't until we get close enough to my apartment that he makes the first move and initiates a conversation.

"How long have you known Jace?" he asks. His eyes are on the road, but I can feel him looking at me through his peripheral vision. My head snaps to my left and I stare at him.

"What? It's not every day that my closest friend stares at me like I've committed treason...you two hookup or something?"

"God, you're unbearable," I groan quietly.

The first time he's spoken to me since the recital and he's asking if Jace and I have had sex? Typical ogre male mentality...

"You can just drop me off here," I offer as we get to the street light five minutes away from the apartment. Derek cracks a hearty laugh.

"I'm not letting you out the car at a random light—Shit, Deli's hair." He curses under his breath after quickly turning to look at the sleeping toddler in the back seat, snuggled into her stuffed lion.

I smile at the sight of Delilah's adorable sleeping form before my eyes widen, taking in the sight of her hair. When he'd put her in her car seat back at the stadium, it'd been in two long ponytails.

Now, her hair resembles a bird's nest, messy and tangled. When we pull up to my apartment, I waste zero time, hoping out of the car and gently pulling Delilah to be able to access her head while letting her sleep.

My nannies would always put two braids in my hair as a kid, and since that's the only style that I know how to do on another person, I do it to Delilah's hair in no time.

Derek watches silently as I finish the last braid before deciding to open his big fat mouth, spoiling my mood.

"Thanks, but she's not your kid."

My spine stiffens at his words, but I don't falter. I've had enough of his attitude, and though I want to repay his coldness with an attitude, I choose kindness.

"Oh, shut the hell up and take the help."

That was kind enough. My phone pings as I gather my things and I check it quickly.

Aric

Can't wait for tomorrow!!!

Fucking hell...

"Fuck, I'm sorry. I shouldn't have said that," Derek apologizes softly, reaching out for my arm as I snatch it away, backing up from him.

What's up with people trying to touch me these days?

My annoyance flares to an all-time high as I think over how shitty this week has been.

I need a shower and seven freshly baked chocolate chip cookies, STAT.

Turning to Derek, I exhale a deep breath. "Have a nice night, Derek."

NINE

Sienna

"S̲o̲ l̲i̲k̲e̲ I̲ w̲a̲s̲...s̲a̲y̲i̲n̲g̲..."

I cringe as Aric takes another large slurp of the spaghetti he'd ordered, watching as some of the soupy tomato juice splatters on the table and his chin.

If you'd had told the Sienna of four months ago that she'd be sitting in a cramped Italian restaurant watching a man sloppily slurp up pasta and talk about the magic of Van Gogh's brush strokes, I'd think you must've hit your head and entered a weird alternate planet in our multiverse.

Aric takes a huge gulp from his glass of water, his fingers leaving a red residue behind on the cup. My nose scrunches as the condensation on the cup causes the residual pasta juice to melt onto the table in a hopeless display of pitifulness.

I should've listened to my gut.

When Aric asked me out, I was skeptical—and for good reason. No man in this universe has had the accomplishment of *not* giving me *the ick*. You know what I mean when I say that—that feeling of complete and utter disgust from something no matter how big or small, it makes you cringe viscerally.

Art History and I have always been mortal enemies considering information refuses to settle in my brain for long periods of time. I can never remember a person whom I've just met name or when something occurs, which is why I hate the subject.

The same subject I've been forced to listen to for the past forty-five minutes.

"So as I was saying, little pig—get it, because you have pink hair?—Maybe you can snog something bigger a little later..." Aric winks.

Oh hell no...

Before I can stop myself, my chair screeches as it slides against the cheap hardwood floors of Mike's Italiano.

Are all men like this?

I wasted two hours of my Sunday getting primmed and pressed by Cleo and Georgia for this date, only to sit here and have this asshole make sexual innuendos, ride Van Gogh's dick for twenty minutes, and then proceed to relate my hair color to a fucking pig?!

Taking a nice long sip of the untouched glass of the cabernet that Aric had ordered, I grimace.

I fucking hate wine.

"Woah, baby girl...you ready to get out of here or something?" Aric questions me, biting his bottom lip. It takes everything in me not to let the two bites of the gnocchi I'd eaten come back up.

Aric had been a cool guy—until he shoved two glasses of cabernet down his thick throat and proceeded to make innuendos and talk dead artists for the better half of this "date".

"I'm getting out of here. I hope you have a nice date with yourself, Aric." I roll my eyes, snatching the mini gold purse I'd taken from Cleo's closet before leaving.

My legs are moving faster than my brain, and soon enough, I find myself standing in front of a random closed storefront wearing a designer lavender Asteri cocktail dress, stranded.

"Fuck me..." I curse quietly, searching the empty roads for any sign of life.

Good going, Si Si. Your prissy ass couldn't just sit there and take it? Look at you now, stuck in a city you're not used to at night, carless and hungry.

My heart drops and my shoulders slump as the little angry bitch on my shoulder reminds me of my faults. I just wanted to branch out, put myself out there, and try the whole dating thing. But why is it so difficult? What happened to romance? Holding doors, walking your date to their doorstep? It's almost like in order to date, I need to be willing to give up my body on the first date for things to work out...but why?

Maybe it's for the best that this whole dating thing was a bust...maybe I'm not cut out for it.

My phone buzzes in my pocket as a cool gust of early September air breezes past. My skin pebbles with goosebumps as I open up my phone to find messages from my uncle, Clef.

Uncle CJ

> Hey Sola girl, how's everything with school? You settling in alright? Your cousin said you're going on a date tonight. I can't believe my girls are growing up.

> Hit me back when your date's over, Sola girl. I love you!

Heat prickles my skin as my heart warms. Uncle Clef has always been like a father figure to me, considering his older brother, my dad, was never truly around. He's a busy guy, touring the world and DJing...it's normal.

Without missing a beat, I respond to my uncle.

Me

> Can you come get me? I'm in front of the creepy ceramic doll store by Mike's Italiano.

In less than ten minutes, I find myself sitting in the passenger seat of my uncle's Escalade, wondering where I went wrong.

Is my taste in men that horrible, or are all the good guys taken? Is this what normal dating is like? As I sit, stewing in silence, watching the dark college town scenery pass by, my skin prickles with awareness.

"Say it..." I sigh, chewing on my bottom lip.

The sigh Uncle Clef lets out is deep. "What's going on with my Sola girl?"

I grin at the use of my childhood nickname, Sola girl. It's a play on my middle name, Sola. My parents spent a summer in Spain and met an independent artist named Sola Lopez. She gave them a place to stay after my father was mobbed while my mother was pregnant with me...long story. Anyways, my uncle started calling me 'Sola girl' because I couldn't pronounce the L in my name and would say "Soa" instead.

"I don't know, Uncle CJ...I just want to be different. I'm tired of trying to live up to these perfect standards that I've created for myself...It's like I know that no one expects perfection from me, but *I* do. I want to be the best, I want everything to be correct and okay...and I just...I don't know." I shrug, looking briefly at my uncle then back to the window as Uncle Clef pulls into the parking lot of my complex.

He hums, processing my words before nodding. "Sienna...I'll tell you what I tell your cousins and the team," he says, putting the car in park before facing me. "It is okay to seek perfection, but it is also okay to fail. It's okay to start over and try new things, and it is more than okay to not have a plan. Your accomplishments do not dictate your worth or who you are on the inside, Sola girl." Uncle Clef frowns, patting my shoulder before sighing.

"I know that you believe that by being the best at everything then you'll feel validated, but it's okay to just sit back and breathe. You're twenty, you have your whole life ahead of you. Don't waste time stressing about whether everything is perfect or not. The only thing that matters is if you're being your authentic self, Sienna. You are a star, and I'm so sorry my brother doesn't tell you this more often, but just know that I see you and I love you."

As the weight of my uncle's words settle in my soul, I feel a mixture of things. Sad for one, that my mask of indifference has fallen and that he sees how much I crave my parents validation, but happy because I'm not alone.

I see you and I love you.

My uncle has always been one of my favorite authority figures. He took me in countless summers and traveled to be there for me whenever he could.

Just as I'm about to thank him, he stops me in my tracks and speaks.

"And stop going on dates with bums. There should be no reason that I'm picking you up on a *Sunday* of all days because you had an asshole for a date."

"Die, motherfucker...die!" I hiss at the monitor as I smash my finger against my mouse, aiming and killing my opponents. A flash bang flies across my screen, blinding me momentarily.

"Fucking bitch..." I mutter, reloading my gun before proceeding to take out the rest of my competition.

This is the calmest I've felt in weeks. Hell, maybe even months. Uncle Clef's advice was amazing, but in order for me to *truly* breathe, I need to annihilate something...or someone.

My grin is bright and wide as my kill cam pops up, displaying my last kill of the night as I take a bite of one of the fresh baked chocolate chip cookies Georgia made for me this morning.

"I needed this..." I sigh, spinning around in my seat to look at Oscar.

He's running around the cage slower than normal, taking his time instead of being the weirdly overactive ferret that he is.

Hmm...I wonder if he needs a break, too.

I'm about to walk over and check on the poor albino ferret when simultaneous dings from my phone, laptop, and watch alert me of a new text.

Checking the time first, my eyes widen. *Who* in their right mind is texting me at 3:00 a.m.?! Matter of fact...why am *I* up at 3:00 a.m.?!

It isn't until I read the text for a second time that my eyes almost fall completely out of their sockets.

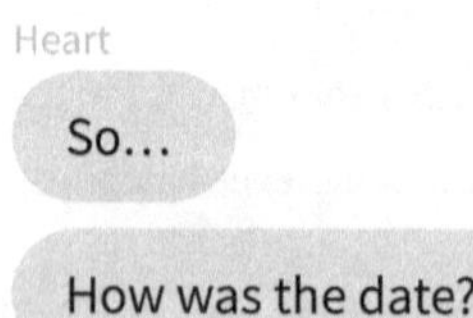

Before I can reconcile with the fact that Hades himself is texting me about a date that he should in fact have zero knowledge of, my phone rings.

It fucking rings!

What kind of sick psychopath calls their ex-lover—if you can call me that—at 3:00 a.m. to talk about boys?!

I shriek as my phone clatters against my floor, jumping back from the sparkly case on the ground.

Just breathe, Sienna.

Think about what this could look like.

If I don't answer, he'd get the wrong impression and think that I was with Aric...

But if I do answer, I look like a lonely sap who doesn't sleep and can't keep a date going—which I kind of am...but that's besides the point.

Making up my mind, I decide that texting Jace back instead of calling would be the smarter option.

Me

I didn't peg you for a stalker, Eros.

But then again, you rearranged my entire schedule so what would I know?

How'd you know about the date?

Heart

Answer the call

I'm craving to see the kind of guy who doesn't give a fuck that you're texting another man right now

Me

No.

Heart

So he's a poly guy...

Didn't peg my little angel to be into polyamory, but if that's what you like, just know we're cutting it out of our relationship

I scoff as I reread his message for the third time, and before I get the chance to respond, those three little dots pop up again, alerting me of Jace's next onslaught of messages.

I watch as the message bubble appears for a minute before disappearing and the phone vibrates. The image of myself being reflected on the screen appears as he video calls me.

Is he some kind of psycho? Even *if* I was with another man right now, I wouldn't answer his call.

So then why is your heart racing, Sienna?

Shut up, Christine...Yes, I named the evil part of my consciousness.

Dashing around the room, I throw on a hoodie and tug on my lavender bonnet, securely wrapping my hair up before answering the phone.

Don't look at me like that...

Jace won't stop until I answer the phone, so I might as well give in before he makes my phone die from constant ringing.

In seconds, the screen displays a shirtless Jace peering up at his camera with an annoyed expression. His dark blond brows are furrowed together as he squints at the screen.

"Wha—"

"Who's hoodie is that?" he cuts me off, his voice tight as he observes my surroundings, I scoff at his interruption, but it doesn't stop him from continuing his pestering.

"I'm busy." I respond through gritted teeth.

Yeah...busy playing video games and erasing that horrible date from my mind, but he doesn't need to know that.

"You're obviously not busy enough to talk to me...She's taken by the way, big guy. And if you so much as *think* about touching her, I'll—"

"You'll what?" I tease, poking the bear. My heart skips as I replay his words, but they're futile. He's only doing this because he's an asshole.

No other reason at all.

"I'll kick his goddamn door down, angel," he yawns, his entire body shaking with the force of it.

"Sleepy?"

"No...I was waiting for you," he replies nonchalantly before turning over in his bed.

Waiting for me?

I don't like the feeling that my heart has from hearing those words. The feeling is soft and warm and completely unreliable.

"Goodnight, angel," Jace yawns again, smiling sleepily after a few minutes of silence.

"Goodnight, psycho..."

TEN

Jace

I'M STARTING TO THINK the scientists were right...Sleep is an essential part of daily life and heartbreak can kill, especially if it's dealt to you by a pink-haired dance teacher who could care less about you or your feelings.

My minds been running off images of what could and did happen between Sienna and that fugly green sweater wearing jackass. I mean come on...my girl couldn't have at least picked someone with a sprinkle of style?

Last night, I purposefully fell asleep on the phone with her. You want to know what I woke up to instead of a purple bonnet and her soft snores?

I woke up to Blake fucking Wilder and Alec goddamn Tu staring down at me with devious smiles on their faces, dressed in their workout clothes for today's morning skate. My phone, the same one that I was almost certain Sienna fell asleep on, was dead when I checked it.

But to top everything off, when I checked my call log with Sienna, it said that our call time was only ten minutes. She hung up on me as soon as I shut my eyes!

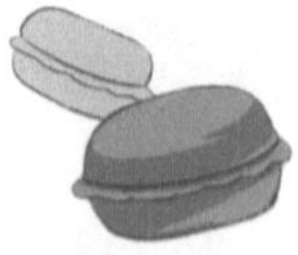

"Run that play again for Heart! Heart, get your head out of your fucking ass!" Coach shouts from center ice. His words are like icing on the cake to how shitty

I feel. I can't eat, can't sleep—granted, it's been less than forty-eight hours since I found out that Sienna was going on a date with a dude who dresses like Oscar The Grouch—but still.

By the time practice is over and I've sat through my Graphic Design course, I'm antsy and ready to get the hell off of this campus. But first, I need to eat. I hadn't eaten anything before practice this morning, and only had half a granola bar and a bottle of water in the middle of class today.

Stopping at Cafe Iteri, the new tiny industrial style cafe that was opened over the summer, I make my way up to the to-go line. This place has seen me every single week since its opening, whether for breakfast or dinner.

I order my food quickly, getting a Jambon Beurre—which is basically a fancy way of saying ham and cheese on fancy bread. I park myself at one of the tables near the large floor to ceiling windows before opening my laptop to start on some homework.

One of the waitresses, Kaila, brings my sandwich and water to the table, and I immediately dig in. The smoky flavors of the ham mixed with brie makes my mouth water. Fuck...nothing can ruin this—

"Oh my God, who let you in here?"

And just like that, it's ruined. Georgia sneers as she looks down at me, placing her food on the table right in front of me. My eyebrows furrow as my childhood best friend rolls her eyes, taking a piece of the chocolate chip cookie I'd been saving for later, popping it into her mouth.

My mouth drops as she smiles at me, the sandwich I'd eaten settling into my stomach like lead. Who the hell let *her* in here? Does this place have no ethical standards?

"So," she says, popping a French fry into her mouth.

"So?" I challenge.

"Why are you being so weird lately? What cat crawled up your ass?" she asks. Her word choice is harsh, but her delivery is sincere.

I'll bite.

"More like what girl..." I mumble, taking another bite of my sandwich, but the blonde hears it. She always does. Georgia has the hearing of a bat.

She takes slow bites of her fish and chips, contemplating my words. Nearly five minutes go by before she responds, I almost assume that she hadn't heard me.

"A girl?" she asks, her voice guiltily soft.

I tilt my head at her, eyeing the way she fidgets in the seat. She knows something...

We finish up our food in silence with me observing Georgia for her tells and her completely ignoring me.

We walk out of Cafe Iteri, and I'm thinking we're about to go our separate ways when Georgia speaks up.

"You know...I do miss our friendship a bit," she says softly. Pausing in my steps, I turn to take a good look at my oldest friend.

"It's just, we used to be best friends and yeah, we argue like siblings all the time...I just wish our friendship was back to how it was before I walked in on you two that night." Georgia frowns, her eyes falling to the ground as I stop to ponder her words.

I never truly thought about how that night with Sienna affected Georgia and I's friendship until now. Before New Years Eve, the three of us—Georgia, Ryan, and I—went into SFU closer than ever. We hung out on weekends and attended each other's events. Hell, Georgia went to a hockey game *alone* for me because both my parents were sick with the flu and couldn't make the hour long drive down here.

After Sienna virtually ghosted me, I now realize that I did the same exact thing to everyone else. I stopped texting Georgia back and kind of resented her for interrupting us that night.

Looking at my friend now, seeing the hurt in her eyes, my heart breaks.

I didn't mean to leave her behind, and we've just grown to be assholes to one another.

"It wasn't your fault," I say with a shrug, patting her shoulder. "You couldn't have known what we would do...We didn't even know we'd kiss one another...I should've talked to you about it instead of being a dick."

"Yeah, you were a dick." She chuckles, side hugging me as we walk.

It feels nice to have my best friend back, but I know it won't last long. Georgia and I are like fire and ice. Always arguing and fighting.

This moment feels too soft for us...all this sappy nonsense.

"You know our moms want us to get together?" I ask, smirking as her green eyes bulge out of her head.

"Eugh!" she gags. "You're not my type, I wouldn't touch a krampus like you with a ten foot pole."

"*Krampus*—" I'm about to start up an argument with the asshole when someone bumps my shoulder while walking, talking loudly on the phone.

"Yeah, bruh. That Sienna bitch wouldn't put out and then had the nerve to walk out, leaving me with the bill."

Now...growing up my mom would always say, *"Let sleeping dogs lie."*

Well, that stupid bitch is about to be lying his ass on the ground, because I'm 99.9% sure he's talking about *my* girl.

Georgia looks up at me, her eyes blazing with fury, but I could care less about how she feels right now. My issue is with him.

"Yo, watch your mouth." My voice is eerily calm as the jackass turns on his heels, his face scrunched up as he tells the person on the other line to hold on.

The style-less fraud tilts his head as if my words offend him.

"What?" he asks, squaring his chest. I want to laugh as he stands to his full height, because even though he's tall, I'm still taller.

"Did I stutter?" I ask with a humorless laugh. "I said watch your mouth."

The idiot has the nerve to laugh in my face as he takes a step closer to me.

Coach, I swear I have no control over my body if this motherfucker says—"And why the fuck do you care? It's not like the bitch would give it up for you—"

In an instant, my fist connects with his jaw, sending him flying to the ground like the little bitch he is. I clench my jaw at the burning sensation in my knuckles as the idiot tries to stand back up. I kick him down again, my mind blank as I pound into his face.

"Jace Eros Heart, you better stop this shit right now!" Georgia's voice filters into my numb brain as she tries pulling me off of him.

I send one last satisfying punch, leaving him on the ground, still alive and looking exactly like how he acts.

Idiotic and ugly.

Georgia, who'd just moments ago was eager to get me off the guy, runs up and kicks him in the balls.

"That's for being an asshole to my best friend, you dick!" she shouts, grabbing my sleeve as she runs off towards the parking lots near the cafe, leaving The Grouch where he lays.

When we get inside of my car, we sit in complete silence, thinking about our actions.

"Oh my...I was an accomplice to your crazy ass." Georgia breathes, her green eyes wide and crazed as she turns to look at me.

"No one told you to kick him! I was doing fine on my own." I sigh, resting my head on the seat.

At this, Georgia scoffs.

I need to call Blake, he'd know what to do.

Pulling out my phone, I hit the third number on my emergency contact list and sigh, running a hand through my hair. As soon as Blake answers, all of my actions flash before my eyes.

"I fucked up!" I shout into the mic as Georgia whispers something beside me. My ear tingles as I hear Cleo's name.

"Did you call fucking Cleo?!" I yell, twisting in my seat to glare at the girl.

"Yes! Because you're a fucking bleach blond sociopath who won't leave me the hell alone! You—"

Bleach blonde?! Won't leave *her* alone? Did she forget that she harassed me and interrupted *my* lunch? Or that she was the crazy person who kicked a man—albeit he was an asshole—while he was down?!

"*I'm* a sociopath?! Have you looked in the mirror, peach? I'm pretty sure your name is plastered beside the definition in the dictionary!" I shout, feeling my blood pressure raise just from the sight of her.

"You're such a fucking cunt, asshole!" she shoots back, her voice sharp.

"Takes one to know one, dick!" I say, sticking my tongue out at her as she scoffs, but Blake's chuckle causes me to go still as it echoes through *both* Georgia and I's phone.

He didn't...

"You fuckers are together without me?!" I screech just as the line goes silent. *Assholes.*

The air is frigid between Georgia and I as we sit in silence, thinking about our actions.

"I know why I kicked that fucker, but why did you punch him?!" she asks, spinning in her seat, her eyes accusatory.

My heart thumps out of my chest as I look at her, hoping my mask of indifference is still in place as I reply, "I don't answer to you."

Georgia rolls her eyes, scoffing at me. "Yeah, well...you're going to have to do a fuck ton of explaining if Sienna finds out you beat up her date."

I hadn't thought about that...Sienna could hate me for what I did. I'd hate myself for making her feel that way, but I'd do it again in a heartbeat if anyone decided they'd open their mouth to speak against her.

It's silent for a moment between us. Georgia's beady eyes stare into my soul before she gasps softly.

"You don't...You're not over Si Si, are you?"

My eyes widen as my neck snaps to face her. "Keep this between us. *All* of it. Cleo doesn't—"

"I promised you two years ago that I wouldn't tell Cleo about what I saw, and I'm not going to now. But you've got to figure this shit out. You can't just go around banging on your chest whenever someone talks bad about her." Georgia frowns, her eyes holding something close to pity as she looks at me.

Who says I can't protect her? I don't see anything wrong with teaching these guys out here how to respect women. Specifically, *my* woman.

"How am I a sociopath?" I ask, trying to change the subject, but Georgia only sighs.

"Oh…I don't know, you've only like the same girl your whole life and refuse to be a human around her…I don't know how you're a sociopath, Jace." She cocks her head to the side, rolling her eyes at me.

Memories of Sienna and I throughout the summers of our childhood play before my eyes as Georgia's words register. Every summer since I turned eight, I waited for the day Clef Jones would bring his niece home for the summer. Sienna was like the moon, quiet and shy, but always there when we first met. She'd pay attention to everything and everyone, but never spoke too loud or out of turn.

It wasn't until she and I were alone one day sitting in my backyard, eating chocolate chip cookies, that she opened up to me about not having friends. I vowed that day to always be by her side, and she did the same for me.

Sienna was the only person I could be my true, authentic self around for years. I didn't have to be the funny and outgoing friend when I was with her, I could just be Jace.

ELEVEN

Sienna

"No! You're doing it wrong, Sienna. Run it again." Daisy's stern voice is like hot coals to my ears as she speaks sharply at me yet again.

Heaving a deep sigh, I count backwards from ten to calm down. Since we've gotten started with our practice two hours ago, Daisy has been unbearable and irritable. We've gone over the routine countless times without a break, which isn't a problem at all. The problem is how bitchy she's been.

She acted like this entire dance was her idea and that she was running this show. I want to be annoyed and yell, maybe she's had a bad day, but fuck! I've had a bad *two weeks*!

I've had to deal with Jace popping back up in my life, adjusting to a new school, moving, Derek Perez, Aric turning out to be a douchebag, and I have yet to talk to my parents since the semester started.

We're all going through things that no one else knows about, but that doesn't give her the right to be a bitch.

"You know what, maybe we should take a break and get a breather—"

"No! We don't need breaks, what we need is for you to get your shit together," she cuts me off, her eyes narrowing on me.

I look around the room, trying to find who she's speaking to. Was it me? Certainly she wasn't—My phone's ringtone blares in the silent room. I chuckle as it saves Daisy from my new found wrath. I don't know what crawled up her ass and died, but I hope she relieves herself soon.

Daisy opens her mouth to reprimand me, but I silence her by holding up my pointer finger to go check who's calling.

My eyes narrow on the screen as I purse my lips.

It's just my luck that today's the day Eloisa Jones—my mother—decides she wants to speak with me.

"Hell—"

"Si Si, darling!" She greets. Her voice is in its usual high pitched tone as she interrupts my greeting.

"How's Ibiza, Mom? Is Dad there?" I ask, cursing myself quietly for the hopefulness in my tone as my mother clears her throat.

"No time to chat, honey, I was just calling to let you know that your father and I won't be able to visit as we planned this month. He's so busy with DJing and you know how it is…" she trails off, her light tone never wavering as I gulp.

They were supposed to visit for a weekend since they missed their last sched-uled visit in June…it's September, and I haven't seen my parents since February.

My bottom lip quivers as I pull it between my teeth. "I understand, Mom. Work comes—"

"You get it, I'll talk to you later. Ta, ta, darling," she interrupts, her breathy tone like nails on a chalkboard.

"Bye! I love—" The line disconnects.

I gulp, sucking on my bottom lip as I try to compose myself and slide the mask I've grown to know so well back on, but it's so hard.

Why me? Why can't my parents just *want* to see me? I try my hardest in school to get accolades that they'd be proud of. I was the top ballerina in my program at NYU, and I'm a damn good dance teacher, but it's never enough for them to just come and visit me. I haven't seen them in months, and the one time my mom calls this week is to tell me that her and dad won't make it to Maryland at the end of the month.

"Well if you're just going to stand there, I guess we're done," Daisy tuts from the corner of the room.

I sigh, rolling my neck as I snatch up my things just as my phone rings yet again.

Daisy raises a brow at me as if daring me to answer the call. Ignoring her, I slide the screen to answer Dupri.

"I need you at the studio immediately, we need to discuss your next steps." Dupri's voice is breathless and echoey as she speaks, presumably from my old studio.

"I'm on my way."

"Due to unforeseen circumstances, I must relieve you of this position."

I'd never thought that I would ever hear those words, but they blare in my ears loud as can be as I stumble my way through the studio.

Although Dupri didn't *fire* me, she did inform me that I was not to teach the Minis anymore, stating that my sole focus is to remain on my *new* student. I'd been given the opportunity to speak with the girls before officially handing everything over to Guillana, a new coach at the studio.

As I'm dragging myself to the Minis' studio, a man walks right into me. He apologizes briefly, but cuts himself off as he and I look at one another.

Just my fucking luck.

Derek stands in front of me, scowling as he looks down at me.

I look at him, waiting for him to do what my kids' parents usually do and ask questions, but he remains silent, staring me down.

"The proper thing to do would be to apologize," he sighs.

I reel back.

Did he just—

"Excuse you?"

"I mean, you bumped into me, and if I remembered correctly, you cursed me out... so." He shrugs.

"You've got a lot of freaking nerve. You don't show up for your kid then when you do, you're late. Not to mention, you've only picked her up from here *once* since I've started working here, and when I call you out, you have the nerve to say that *I* need to apologize?" I scoff, tilting my head at his audacity.

I mean, who does he think he is?

Derek looks down his nose at me. "You bumped into me."

"Yeah, well so fucking what? You're the only parent in this building who hasn't asked about their kid, so you know what? I don't give a damn." I roll my eyes, turning on my heels as blood rushes through my ears

"Fucking asshole, *que te folle un pez espada*[1]," I mutter as I stomp away from the pompous asshole.

Could this day get any worse? It feels like the world is suffocating me and everything is going the exact opposite of how I planned for it to go.

It doesn't take long for me to apologize to the girls for having to transfer rooms and handing over the reins to Guillana, who's already been working with them for some time now.

By the time I get to my apartment, my head is pounding from an oncoming headache, my feet hurt, and I'm pretty sure I didn't reach my daily water intake goal for the day.

I need a shower. I need to wash this day away.

Stumbling into the house, I say to myself, "I need a drink and some serious girl talk," as I plop down on the couch beside Cleo, laying on her lap and pulling her hand into my hair.

"Long day?" She asks, massaging circles into my scalp.

"That guy will be the death of me!" I shout, sitting up. I don't know if it's Jace, my dad, or Derek that I'm speaking about, but they're all going to send me to an early grave.

"Spill, girl!"

I jump slightly as the guy that Cleo has a crush on quips in a mock Valley girl accent.

I tell them everything from how Derek is the bane of my existence, how my Dad is absent, and allude a little to Jace being the psycho that he is. I don't say his

---

1. Que te folle un pez espada – fuck a swordfish (screw you) (Spanish)

name for fear of what Cleo would think if she knew that I've been dealing with Jace for the past two weeks, but she and the guy—Jake, I think—listen carefully.

"Do you maybe think you're projecting your feelings about Auntie and Uncle onto him?" Cleo asks, making my brain hurt as I groan.

"I don't know, honestly. But it feels shitty knowing that another little girl is out there being treated how I was." I sigh, hanging my head as Jake tells me to be there for her.

I don't know if it's me or just Delilah that I need to be there for, but I take the advice, happily.

I know just what to do to be there for her.

"You're so right! Thanks, Jake!" I squeal as ideas flow to my brain, skipping to my room.

I go straight to my bathroom and prepare for my shower, turning the water to its highest temperature. Stepping into the shower and in the comfort of my own bathroom, I allow myself to break.

I have to be strong in front of Cleo and her guy friend. She's already going through something way deeper than I'd ever know, and I barely know Jake.

In my everything shower, I'm allowed to be the sad, broken hearted girl that I am on the inside. I'm allowed to be mopey about my parents and feel for Delilah. I'm allowed to let my mind drift to Jace and wonder about him.

Soon after washing my body, the sadness that I'd had pent up boils into anger, and I find myself sitting in front of my PC, locked in yet another gruesome game.

I'm in my seventh round of playing COD when I feel a presence brush up beside me. The warm aroma of vanilla and leather invades my senses, and I know it's him before I see him. Moving my headset off of my ear, I ask, "What?" as I continue gaming.

"We need to talk." Jace's voice is gruff as he speaks, his voice closer than I'd expected as his breath dusts the shell of my uncovered ear, making my body tingle.

"What could we possibly have to talk—"

In an instant, a white sheet of paper is placed over my fingers as I'm typing away. I pause in my haste, eyeing it momentarily then back at my screen, but something in my mind tells me to look at the paper again. When I do, my anger boils over.

My heart stutters as the neat scribble of my hand writing comes into my focus. My eyes stay there, stuck on the scrawl of *my list.*

In an instant, I open my mouth to yell at him for not only invading my privacy, but also for keeping my list for all this time.

Jace intervenes by softly grabbing my chin, pulling my focus back to him and successfully shutting me up as his lip quirks slightly.

The bastard thinks this is funny...

"Before you go all 'Assassin's Creed' on me, can you please just listen to me?" he asks, lowering his head. His eyes track momentarily down to my lips before reconnecting with my eyes...

What the hell was that look?

"What?" I bite out as my heart races.

He takes a step closer, our breaths mingling with one another.

"Use me."

I gulp, looking up at him as his green eyes lock on mine, filled with determination and something else that I can't quite place.

"What?" I ask again, exiting my game in total, staring up at the man in clear bewilderment.

Has he hit his head or something?

"Use. Me," he repeats, shoulders back.

I sigh. "Jace, look...I don't have time for—"

He steps in closer, slamming a hand down on my desk as he sighs dramatically.

"Goddamnit, Sienna, just listen to me!" he cries out, and although he isn't yelling, I seal my lips shut. Jace has never, and I mean *never*, gotten serious with me before.

"I can see it, you want to break out of your shell...You went on that date to do it, right? But then you wouldn't have sex with him," he says matter-of-factly, taking me aback.

How would he know that?

"I know what you need, so let me give it to you? I feel like shit for going through your list, but I want you to use me. I mean...you can trust me and I trust you. I've experienced all of these things before, and I'd rather you do it with someone you feel safe with rather than a stranger." Jace takes his bottom lip between his teeth as he looks down at me sheepishly, red tinging his cheeks.

I'm speechless as I stare up at him.

He wants me to use him to finish my list? How did he even get the list in the first place?

Sensing my loss of words, Jace smirks knowingly.

"Marvel Rivals is the better game, by the way." He grins, leaning down, placing a heart fluttering kiss to my forehead before leaving me with my thoughts and video games.

TWELVE

Sienna

WHEN YOUR CHILDHOOD CRUSH—WHO'S also your first kiss, mind you—asks you to *use* him, what do you do? Because me? I've been up for the past two days thinking about it.

I groan as I scroll through the endless threads of Reddit users, all discussing their childhood crush, and I sigh as I come up empty...again.

On the one hand, I want to laugh in Jace's face for playing such a prank on me. But on the other, I want to give in. I want to do as he asked and use him, but what does that make me? An asshole? A bitch? Crazy?

I feel overwhelmed...I need to write. Ever since I was a kid, writing has always helped me to feel better. I would write letters, knowing I'd never send them, and vent all of my frustrations.

"Fuck..." I mutter, my nose burning after my phone falls from my hands, smacking it.

"Don't you have practice or something today?" Georgia asks as she walks into the living room.

I quirk a brow at her clothing choice of an off the runway Asteri couture three piece cropped pantsuit. I'd only been aware of what it was because the blonde wouldn't stop talking about how she'd gotten her hands on it.

Georgia sees my obvious perusal and grins brightly, doing a small spin for me.

"Like what you see? I had to find a good strapless bra for this top or else my tits would be on display for Fashion Forecasting." She grins, hoisting up her breasts before heading to the front door. I watch as Georgia pauses in her tracks, looking back at me before she sighs, slouching a bit.

"Is something going on with you? I feel like we haven't had a chance to talk to one another lately, and you know I'm always there for you, Si Si," she pouts, her plump lips frowning. I stalk towards her, grabbing my dance bag.

"I'm fine, G. Now, let's go…Wouldn't want to keep your admirers waiting," I say jokingly as we exit the apartment.

Cleo left earlier this morning for one of her courses, and since I purposefully made my schedule to where I didn't have courses on Friday, I'm free today except for work and practice with Daisy.

Daisy's been acting so odd lately, dodging eye contact with me and making snooty remarks when my back's turned. I just hope she doesn't turn into one of the girls from my old university and becomes a raging bitch. It'd suck to lose a new friend after just meeting them.

When I get to the small studio on campus that Daisy and I rented out for our session, we immediately jump into work. Today, she's a bit hostile towards me, eyeing me as if I'd kicked her cat, and it confuses me.

Did I do something to her? What could possibly be her issue with me?

Just as I'm about to question her, my phone dings over the Bluetooth speaker we're using.

"It's fine, we can ignore it…" I say, waving off the message as Daisy frowns, but just as we get back into the swing of things, more messages come in.

Daisy scoffs, her head rolling back as she looks up at the ceiling as if to ask God for the strength to deal with me. I cock my head to the side, watching her agitation grow.

"Can you be any more unprofessional? Go answer your phone!" She shoos me, flicking her wrist dismissively.

My imagination is overactive as my brain transports me into a combat video game. I imagine I'm a sharpshooter and Daisy's my target and I'm aiming to kill. Just as my finger rest on the trigger I—

Ping! Ping!

Oh for the love of…

Snatching up my phone, my heart stutters as I reread the two messages from the one person I'd least expected to text me.

Heart

Did you make your decision?

It's been two days

Me

Busy

Heart

Well get unbusy, we have a lesson today.

I reel back at his audacity. I don't have to do anything. What could we possibly have a lesson—Oh! He means for work...I forgot that he's my student...right. My heart triples in rhythm from the thought of being in a closed space with Jace ~~grinding~~ dancing with one another.

Get your head out of the gutter, girl...

Jace doesn't give me the opportunity to text him back. My phone vibrates as he shoots me another message, this one sending my heart rocketing in my chest as I read it.

Heart

Outside.

Don't make me wait, angel.

I look up to find Daisy already staring down at me, her expression pinched as she folds her arms under her chest.

"I'm sorry—" I try, guilt riddling my tone as I gather my things on the other side of the room, but she isn't hearing any of it.

"Save it. When you're ready to work, call me," she grits, turning away from me to the large mirrored wall in front of us.

Not wasting any time, I make my way to the parking lot, pausing at the sight before me. Jace leans cooly against the hood of his dark green Aston Martin SUV, his tanned, veiny forearms on full display from his sleeves being rolled up.

I tilt my head at him, and though he's wearing sunshades, I just know he's smug as all outdoors.

"Didn't your mom put you in ballroom dance as a kid? Why do you need lessons?" I quip, siding up to him as he smirks at me.

"My teacher's hot. Besides, we're not here to dance today. We have to do an item on your list," he says. Without giving me any time to process his words, he's pulling my dance bag from my shoulder, transferring it to his.

I stand in my spot, gawking at him as his smirk morphs into a grin. Jace leans in close to my face and my stomach flips as he grips my chin, closing my mouth.

"You'll catch flies, beautiful. Now go sit your pretty ass in the car, we're late."

Still in shock, I slowly make my way over to the door, but Jace beats me to it, opening the passenger door for me.

"Ladies first."

Ladies first? Did the demon that possessed this boy for the past three weeks die or something? My mind races as I sit firmly in the heated leather seat. Not only did I walk out on practice, but I'm sitting in a psychopath's car...

"How did you even know I was here? Stalking much?" I shoot at him, my head snapping to face the smug bastard as he chuckles.

"You call it stalking, I call it being aware of your surroundings..." The asshole shrugs as he pulls out of the parking lot. Low R&B plays on the radio, and it takes me a moment to realize that it's an unreleased song from my cousin, Zola.

I furrow my brows at the sound of the song, Jace must sense my confusion, but instead of acknowledging it, he turns it up.

How did I end up here...

I was supposed to go to dance practice with Daisy, check on the Minis at the studio, and then get a head start on my History of Modern Art coursework considering it's my hardest class right now. Instead, I'm sitting in the passenger seat of my childhood crush's car, on the way to God knows where.

I side-eye Jace as he taps along on the steering wheel to the beat of the music that plays.

"We need to talk," I say, turning off the radio, twisting in my seat to fully face him as he smirks slowly.

"Is this where you apologize for ditching me on the top of a skyscraper after tonguing me down and ignoring me for two years before professing your undying love for me? *Or* is this just a casual talk between besties?" he asks, briefly looking over at me. His quick gaze is playful, but I can hear the seriousness and hurt in his words.

I hurt him.

Suddenly, my mouth is dry and my chest hurts. A part of me wants to tell him to pull over and give each other the clarity we deserve. But I know that time has passed us. So instead, I push back my feelings and wet my dry mouth.

"Sorry, *bestie,* but no." I try feeling a bit at ease as Jace chuckles quietly. "We need some ground rules between us before we do anything on that list."

"Shoot."

My brows raise. *Is it that easy?*

It's *never* that easy with a Heart man. I of all people should know.

"*This* between us, stays like that. Between us. No one else knows. Hell, the girls don't even know that I'm doing this shit—the list, I mean—Cleo almost passed out when she saw my *hair.* I can't send her to an early grave if she finds out I'm sneaking around with her *best friend.*" I pull at my fingers, trying to calm my nerves as guilt racks my body.

I know that Cleo and Georgia would never judge me. They'd both be there for me no matter what, but how do I tell my best friend and closest family member that I fell for *her* best friend when we were eight and nine?

If Jace wants to interject, he doesn't. For the rest of our fifteen minute drive to who knows where, he's silent. I don't think I've ever seen a silent Jace Heart before, so the phenomena leaves me with an uneasy feeling as he pulls into the parking lot of an apartment building about five minutes away from my place.

"Listen, Sienna. I want to make you comfortable, so I'll agree to your terms. but you owe me, I'm not someone you can just hide...I mean look at me." He scoffs jokingly, but I know that he's serious as he gestures to himself.

My eyes betray me as they track Jace's movements, slowly trailing from his collarbone to his crotch.

He sure isn't someone I can hide...

My eyes trail up from his crotch to his mouth, my own mouth salivating as I stare at his plump lips before landing back on his eyes.

The air around me grows electric with tension as Jace's face grows closer, pulling me in. I want to kiss him, to get to know him again, but I can't. So, instead of acting on that instinct, I turn my head and look out of the front windshield, cursing myself.

Jace chuckles quietly, getting out of the car. He turns to me in the passenger seat, completely brushing off the interaction.

"Don't touch that door," he commands as my palm lies flat against the door handle.

Raising a brow, I watch as he jogs around the car to my side, opening the door with a smug grin. Chills rack my spine as Jace leans down, his lips brushing the shell of my ear.

"Atta girl, tonight you're mine." he whispers. A flutter of butterflies swarm in my belly as I try to hold a tight leash on my composure, but my body tingles from where he'd just lingered.

When we enter the unknown apartment, my voice catches in my throat as I take it in. I stand in stunned silence, looking around the modernized loft with a glass balcony.

Had I known this place existed, I would've moved here instead of my current place.

This apartment is like all my wildest dreams in one, with a bed the size of Texas in the loft area and a couch equally as big on the lower level. Pillows and soft throw blankets decorate the couch, but what catches my attention the most is the large flatscreen TV with the opening credits to one of my favorite movies in the world, *The Lovers*, on display.

My eyes brighten as I take in my surroundings.

"Do you like—" Jace starts, but my eyes immediately shift to the large vase of light pink Stargazer Lilies displayed intricately in a vase on the marbled kitchen island.

"Are those lilies?!" My shocked gasp is loud as I run over to the flowers.

My eyes brighten and the buds of my fingers tingle as I gently trace over the lines of the flowers.

Jace chuckles softly, making his way over to the kitchen. He quietly goes through the cabinets, pulling out instant popcorn and a large white box. I watch as he moves silently and efficiently through the place as if he owns it, and it isn't until he takes off his jacket, throwing it on one of the island's chairs that I voice my concerns.

"Uh...Who's place is this? I thought you lived with the rest of the team."

An amused grin falls onto his tanned face as he places the white box in front of me. "Keeping tabs on me?"

"More like being aware of enemy territory," I retort, squinting mockingly at him as he smiles.

"I bought this place at the beginning of the year when I thought I'd move out of the house. Love the guys, but Blake snores when he loses games and Alec is a loud dude in bed, which is odd considering he's the quietest out of all of us." He sighs, running a hand through his mop of blond waves. Opening up the box, he steals a cookie, making my mouth water.

He got cookies from SweetTooth.

Fuck, I love their cookies.

"So why—"

"Did I bring you here?" he cuts me off, raising a brow from across the island.

Instead of responding, I nod and take a cookie of my own, watching him carefully as I chew.

Jace doesn't seem to mind, though. Instead, he holds my eye contact, unwavering. He licks his bottom lip and my eye tracks the movement as his eyes glitter.

"Because I know you," he says simply, as if that was the answer to all of my questions and more before stalking into the living room, plopping down on the massive couch.

I reluctantly follow, taking the box of cookies along before settling on a cushion a few feet away.

Jace raises a brow at the action, but remains silent as he moves in closer to me, spreading his legs out to get comfortable.

My mind is like a warzone as I fight the urge to let my shoulders drop and melt into him, but something in me can't. I want to be able to lay here and watch a movie with him, but I don't know how. And yes, I know that sounds stupid, but can you blame me?

I've never done any of *this* before.

Jace doesn't seem to mind, though. Instead, he rests an arm over my shoulder and pulls me into him.

"You can trust me, Sienna. I won't do anything you're not comfortable with, I promise," he says softly, holding out his pinky.

The breath in my throat catches at the reminder of all of the promises we've made with one another over the years, and without hesitation, I lock pinkies with him, my head turning towards him.

This close, I can see his every imperfection, but let's be honest...Nothing about Jace is imperfect. He has these tiny freckles that decorate his golden skin like constellations, and those *eyes*. If I'd been standing, my knees would've grown weak from staring into them.

Jace takes his bottom lip into his mouth. His hooded gaze lowers to my lips, tracking my movements before settling on my eyes once again, dark and hungrily.

"Jace..." my voice trails off as I lean in close. We're so close that I breathe in his minty air.

"Angel—"

The sound of crashing on the screen jolts us apart. My heart rackets against my chest as my eyes snap to the screen to see Lolark, the female main character, screaming in pain as an arrow protrudes from her back.

Blinking my surprise away, I focus back on the screen, inches away from Jace. Just five seconds ago, I almost kissed him. And had the TV not interrupted us, I would've.

THIRTEEN

Jace

I was this close to having Sienna Sola Jones in my arms until my movie date idea came back to bite me in my ass. I had it all planned out. I wanted to just bring her here to show her a safe place, watch the movie, and talk more. I had zero expectations of doing anything sexual, but now that I know that she feels the same way for me, I don't know what to do with myself.

My eyes remain locked on the pink haired woman beside me who scooted a few feet away from me on the couch after the near kiss. From where I'm sitting, I have the perfect view of her as she laughs and watches the movie.

My fingers itch to sketch her, to draw and paint her, to keep her suspended in time for my eyes only.

Sienna giggles at something the vamp guy says on the screen, and my muscles ache to be right under her skin. My ears yearn to be closer to her, to hear her giggle and laugh for all eternity.

I don't know how or when, but by the second movie, we're sitting shoulder to shoulder again. Slowly, I move my arm to rest around the top of hers, grinning to myself as she settles into my side, cuddling into me.

"Did you see that?" she asks, looking up at me with large doe eyes, a small smile on her face. "Her being depressed for months because her man left is so real—"

My body moves on its own, pressing my lips to hers. The kiss is soft and quick, yet electric and fulfilling. Pulling away, I bite my lip, guilt racking me as I watch the stunned, silent girl.

Sienna blinks once, then twice too fast as she looks at me with wide eyes.

"What was that...for?" she asks breathlessly, still leaning on me as I rest my forehead on hers. I close my eyes, wanting to keep this moment locked in my brain.

"I just had to make sure you were real...Why did you leave?"

Sienna looks up at me, her gaze wide and searching as her hand travels to my cheek. "I was scared. Not just because of the fact that our friendship would change, but I didn't want to lose you too. We've been close all our lives, and then I kissed you and it changed everything. I left because it's the only thing that I know how to do...My parents always leave me, and I fucked up by doing it to you that night..."

Her face is a storm cloud of misery, as if she's reliving the moment everything between us changed on her birthday.

"Just so you know, I'll always catch you when you run."

Her lips part slowly, quirking slightly before she's pulling my face back to hers, sealing our fates together in a searing hot kiss.

The kiss is deep and aching as we battle for dominance of one another's mouth. My stomach clenches and my dick hardens as Sienna moans in my mouth.

Dear God.

She's fast with her movements, keeping our lips pressed together, hot and heavy, as she moves to straddle me. And as if we've done this dance before, my hands grip her waist, pulling her flush against me as she grinds into me.

My pulse screams from her movements, and before I know it, she's pulling away.

I can't open my eyes. My mind full of shock as I pull myself together, trying and failing to comprehend what just happened.

"What's your excuse?" I croak, my voice hoarse as I quirk a brow at her. Sienna smiles down at me, fully sitting on my lap as she chuckles lightly, hiding her face in my neck.

"God, this is embarrassing..." she mumbles, her voice vibrating against my neck as I chuckle, pulling her back and removing her hands from her face.

"Don't hide from me." The softness of my voice is unrecognizable to my own ears as Sienna perks up, uncovering her face.

She is stunning...

I haven't had a healthy relationship since she left that night. In a way, I think that her leaving caused me to not be able to fully give myself to other women. Yeah, I'd have sex with them, but Sienna is the only woman who has ever known my mind. She can read and see everything that goes on in my head without me letting her.

I haven't been dumped since then, either. I do the dumping. But with her here in my lap, I realize that I'd let her run away again, however this time, I'd chase her. I'd catch her and I won't ever let her go.

The incident broke me, but now I'm ready for us.

Sienna looks at me, and I mean *truly* looks at me. Her hazel gaze is unwavering and soft, holding the world beneath the depths of her irises. When she leans in closer to me, I don't hesitate to mimic her, but just as our lips are close to brushing against one another, a phone rings. Sienna jumps from my lap like she's been scalded, and I curse whichever one of the fates put *this* into our timeline.

"Fuck..." I quietly curse, eyeing my phone then back to the quiet girl on the couch, now cuddling herself.

"I'll be back." I frown, taking the call into the kitchen as my mom's name displays across the screen. I love my mom, don't get me wrong, but she just interrupted the most important moment of my life.

"Honey, hi!" My mom's voice is surprised as I answer the phone with slight rustling and whispering in the background.

"What's up, Mom? I'm kind of in the middle of something—"

She cuts me off, her voice cheerful as she says, "Oh! This won't take too long, sweetheart," before clearing her throat.

Immediately, my hackles raise.

"Oh for the love of—"

"Angelina and I were just speaking about you and her daughter, Kacey! I remember the two of you having something last year and—"

The last thread of my sanity snaps as I sigh, pinching the bridge of my nose.

I was cockblocked for this?

"Mom, you realize that I'm barely twenty, right? Besides, I'm kind of busy right now..." I try, but dear old Anna Heart isn't hearing any of that.

"Nonsense, sweetheart. Your father and I were your age when we got married!" she exclaims, her light southern accent peeking out as I groan. My nostrils flare with annoyance as I turn back to face the living room where Sienna sits, watching the movie.

She's quieter than before, but is now lounging closer to the spot that I'd sat in before getting up. My mom drones on about the importance of marriage and *blah blah blah,* but my mind drowns her out as I watch the pink haired girl before me laugh.

It's a soft, quiet laugh, with her covering her mouth briefly. Sienna must sense my gaze on her, as her laughter dies down while she turns to face me. Her eyes narrow on me as she tilts her head, as if to silently ask if I'm okay. Nodding, I mouth the word *Mom,* pointing to my phone just as my mother hangs up.

Heaving a small sigh, I round back towards the couch, plopping down right beside Sienna as she turns to fully face me. Her eyes searching my face for answers, but she doesn't say anything, and neither do I.

"So... you actually want to pet a monkey?" I ask, looking between her and the TV.

Sienna raises an amused brow at me, tilting her head. I groan as she looks at me. Those eyes of hers just do something to me. The scent of her vanilla and chai perfume sticks to my clothes, warming my skin with her fragrance.

I can never get enough of her.

"Huh?" she asks, but I don't elaborate. Instead, I hop up from my seat on the couch and head back into the kitchen and rummage through the drawers. When I find what I'm looking for, a huge smile plasters itself across my face before I take a seat by her.

"This here is your list, sweetheart. We're going to finish everything by—"

"December 31st...my birthday," she finishes for me sheepishly. My throat catches realizing the date.

"Right." I cough. "The 31st...Anyways...uhm...have a heart wrenching break up experience?" I muse, twisting to face her as she shrugs.

"I mean, why not? Everyone's got to have their heart broken at least once, am I right?"

I chuckle lightly as she scoots in closer to me, reading the list over my shoulder. We're so close that I can feel her heart beating against my arm. Chewing my bottom lip to distract myself from her, my eyes linger on one interesting choice.

"Try shibari? What the hell is that?"

Sienna's eyes widen, mouth dropping slightly as I fully face her. Our noses are just shy of touching with our faces being so close. She bites the inside of her cheek, tampering down her humor.

"I was supposed to erase that from the list—"

"Oh, so it's something kinky, isn't it? I know how you book girls get." I jokingly wink as she groans, punching my shoulder lightly.

"You're not funny."

Ignoring her, I move onto another part of the list. My eyes widen, heart dropping as I silently skim it once again. I don't know why I hadn't thought of this before when I first read the letter, but now my mind won't stop racing.

"Sienna, are you a virgin?"

I don't mean for my words to come out so bluntly, but they do. Sienna's silence is nerve-wracking as she quietly moves away from me.

I'll take that as a yes.

"You're twenty, babe. I don't expect you to be the next coming of Aphrodite or something...Come here." I reach for her, but she doesn't move. Instead, Sienna remains silently seated in the corner, watching me carefully.

Good going, asshole. You made her uncomfortable.

I stare at her, trying to communicate with my eyes since I clearly have the mental capacity of a four-year-old that doesn't know how to keep their mouth shut, but like my other attempts, she doesn't talk back.

Time to resort to my last option.

With a loud sigh, I get up from my spot and make my way to her at the end of the couch. Sienna yelps as I tug her legs from under her, straightening them out and opening them slightly.

"What the hell are–*Get up!*" she screeches as I lay my large body in the space between her legs, my back to her stomach.

"Nope, we have a list to go over. Besides, I see here that you want to kiss three people in one night. I'll let you know right now, angel, that isn't happening." I frown, mentally erasing that line altogether.

Sienna struggles to free herself from under the weight of my body on her torso before she gives up, her hands finding their way into my hair. I groan as she begins playing with the longer strands of my hair, reminding me that I need a haircut.

"What about it? Who says I can't kiss three consenting adults if I want to?" she challenges, tugging my hair slightly. Suppressing another groan—*God, this woman is going to be the death of me*—I grin, tilting my head up to face her.

"I say. If you want three different people, I'll buy two wigs."

Sienna laughs quietly, her body vibrating from doing so as I turn back to the list.

"Since we're keeping this a secret," she starts, shifting under me, her hands still massaging, "we need to come up with a code."

"Like special agents?" I annoyingly add, and I just know she's rolling her little eyes at me.

Sienna pops the top of my head. "No, you idiot...We just need something to say that the two of us will understand. Like, I have a minx to catch...something like that." She shrugs under me as my face scrunches.

"A minx? Like the weasel or the sex symbol?"

Sienna sighs dramatically. "You're infuriating..."

"Let's just say it's a work thing," I suggest, skimming the list.

"Technically I *am* working..."

Furrowing my brows, I turn to eye her before looking at the TV, the third movie in *The Lovers Saga* now playing on the screen.

"Let's be real…You're not working, I haven't learned a single move since being here at the school. Think of this as paid fun."

"Sounds like prostitution…" she says skeptically, halting all movement in my hair as I smirk.

"Good, we start tomorrow."

Fourteen

Sienna

I ONLY TRUST JACE as far as I can throw him, and let me make one thing clear: I can barely lift fifty pounds without feeling like I'll throw my back out at twenty. However, I also know that Jace wouldn't kill me, because if he tries, he'll have to answer to my uncle and cousins.

And we all know how that would end...

Anyways...

Jace wouldn't kill me, so that's why I'm excited for today.

He's the only person who I'm willing to complete my list with, and him being eager for me to "use" him is always a plus—but not in that sense...you know, because we're just friends.

Friends that have kissed...a few times.

"Si Si! How does this look?!" Georgia's voice breaks through my thoughts as she bursts into my room.

I watch with one eye open from my bed as she twirls around in a green, satin dress, tailored to look like the perfect spring gown.

Rising with my elbows propped behind me, I eye the blonde. "It's sixty-five degrees outside...Where are you going?" I chuckle lightly as she pouts at me.

"A spring wedding...duh!" she says in an obvious tone, as if I understand what she means. When Georgia senses my obliviousness, she plops down on the bed beside me.

"It's the start of a piece I'm creating for an internship! As we all know, I'm destined to be Eden Marlowe's protégé." She grins, sassily flipping her hair over her shoulder. I smile as she leans in closer to my face, her green eyes dazzling with excitement.

"What better way to show her that I'll be the next best thing than to create my own pieces? I'm thinking I wear this to a wedding in Tuscany!" she exclaims, her happiness evident as she jumps up from the bed, twirling. The dress flows prettily as she spins effortlessly, her hair blowing in the wind.

I admire my friend; her beauty, her charisma. Georgia Adams is like the sun, always happy and semi-peaceful.

She stumbles a little, dizziness overtaking her. Giggles fall from my lips as she grabs my hands to twirl with her, and I do. We laugh and spin, and everything in life is perfect. We're just girls, living life together for the very first time.

"Are you two having a dance party without me?!" Cleo's voice startles the two of us. Georgia and I pull away from one another like toddlers who'd just been caught doing something they shouldn't be.

The three of us stare at each other, Georgia and I breathing heavily as a slow smile breaks across Cleo's face, and soon enough, the three of us are in a blissful state. We dance and laugh and allow our inner children to heal with one another, and it's beautiful.

"Wait, wait, wait! You want to get married in Tuscany?" Cleo asks Georgia, putting a hold on our dance party as she turns down the music she'd begun playing.

Georgia gathers her breath, a shy grin spreading across her face as she shakes her head. "Nah, we all know I'm more of a Vegas chapel with an Elvis preacher kinda girl." She jokes, wrapping an arm around the two of us.

"Puh-lease...you wouldn't be caught dead in one of those," I say, rolling my eyes as she pokes my cheek.

"You're right! Someone give me a tall, dark, handsome man with more money than the US Treasury and a wedding on the Amalfi Coast, then I can die a happy woman." The blonde chuckles as Cleo and I grin.

We spend so much time talking and laughing with one another that I lose track of time. I almost completely forget about Jace until my phone dings with a new message.

Heart

Be ready in fifteen, I'm on the way

My eyes widen as my bottom lip finds itself tucked under my teeth. *Fuck.* I was supposed to be getting ready…I don't regret spending time with my friends, but I do regret not finding a cute outfit while doing so.

"So yeah, I'll just order some sushi from that one place in the quad and we should be good to go for a movie night?" Cleo's voice rings through my ears like warning bells being set off. My heart drops.

Georgia must sense my worriedness as we make brief eye contact, because she immediately saves the day. Pulling Cleo into her side, she walks the two of them out.

"I think Si Si has plans tonight, but we can watch…" Her voice trails off as they leave, and I let out a deep sigh.

"Thank God…"

It doesn't take long for me to get ready, seeing as I took a shower when I got home from the gym earlier today. Styling my curls is easier than ever, I add a little curling gel to ensure they don't frizz. I throw on a lavender two-piece short set and a jean jacket. In less than five minutes, I'm dressed and ready for whatever Jace has planned. This time, when my phone dings, I don't check it. I know it's him.

Jace stands outside his car, leaning against the hood of it. The perfect picture of sin. Today, he reminds me of a model for a coastal magazine. His fluffy, blond hair is free and messy in the way that men always perfectly achieve. He's dressed in jeans and a vintage, navy blue crewneck. My mouth waters from the sight of him and the small chain on his neck.

My goodness.

He smiles at me, and I swear something in my chest shifts. My palms dampen as I chew my bottom lip while approaching him.

Why am I so nervous all of a sudden? He's a guy…one who I grew up with. One who I've kissed more than once…so why do I feel like a giddy school girl? "So, what are we—Oh!" My brows shoot to my hairline as he pulls a bouquet of orange Stargazer Lilies from behind his back, a cheeky grin on his face as he holds them out to me.

"M'lady," he says, bowing his head slightly.

Th-Thump! Th-Thump!

Shut up, heart...Now is not the time.

"Wh-What are these for?" I cringe internally as my own question rings through my ears.

They're flowers, Sienna...What do you think they're for?

Jace doesn't mind, though. He simply chuckles at me, placing the flowers in my clammy hands.

"You like lilies, right?"

Hesitantly, I nod. My eyes trail over the intricate flowers, my fingers dusting the velvety petals.

"*That's* what they're for...Now get in, we have a list to complete."

FIFTEEN

Jace

I GUESS IT'S SAFE to say that the music gene that ran in the Jones family for the past sixty-five years, died with Sienna Jones.

Standing inside of Mulligan's, a coffee shop-bar duo, wincing as Sienna tries her own rendition of her grandmother's hit song, *Twilight*, was not how I expected tonight to go.

As Sienna hits her second high note of the night and the patrons of the bar wince, I clap, cheering for the tone-deaf woman.

"Woo! That's my girl!" I shout, pumping a fist in the air while my brain battles with the urge to explode from her horrible singing.

I'm pretty sure a run-over hyena could produce better vocals than her, but I digress.

On the small wooden stage, standing under a lone spotlight, is a girl who is allowing herself to be free. I won't stand in the way of Sienna's happiness. Not now, not ever.

She giggles as her voice cracks and shakes her hips off beat to the melody she'd concocted on her own fruition.

My brows raise, amusement littering my body as she somehow nails one note before failing every single one afterwards.

It's an art, truly.

But when Sienna bows, happy with herself, smiling brightly...I can't help but to do the same.

If she has no fans, then I am dead because in a fraction of a heartbeat, I'm standing. My smile is bright and proud of her as I clap for the pink-haired singing "aficionado."

Sienna bounces off of the stage, her hazel eyes greener as excitement takes over her. She's giddy by the time she reaches me, taking a sip of her Shirley Temple.

"How…Was that?" she asks between sips of her straw as she looks up at me, her eyes round and expectant.

My mom always instilled in me that honesty is the best policy, but how do I honestly tell her that she sounded like a mother cow giving birth to an antelope? Impossibly horrendous…

"You were great, angel! The crowd was amazed!" I exclaim, my voice raising an octave. Sienna's eye twitches slightly as if she'd heard my lie clear, but her smile doesn't waver. Instead, she grabs my hand and holds it up as if to guide me.

"Woah—"

"We have to sing a duet!" She grins playfully.

Mulligan's is on the other side of Summerfield, closer to another school, Nolince University. It's a smaller university with a population of around twenty thousand students to SFU's eighty thousand students. Their Men's Hockey and Women's Basketball teams are impressive, but not as good as ours.

I brought Sienna here because I know that this is NU territory, and most SFU students stick to our side of town. She must've sensed that when we first entered the place because she immediately lowered her inhibitions and let herself be.

When we get to the stage, Sienna is a ball of energy, bouncing as she looks for the next song for us to sing. Meanwhile, I'm silently dying inside.

She was supposed to be the only one "performing" tonight, yet I'm finding myself on stage, standing next to her like a dumbass.

Sienna doesn't care, though. Instead she smiles at the small crowd and waves as the beginning chords of *Start of Something New* from the movie *High School Musical* begins to play.

I groan inwardly immediately.

The girls used to force me to watch *High School Musical* every summer before high school.

Sienna nudges me, an annoyingly pleased grin on her face as I grab the mic.

Sighing, I roll my shoulders back, taking in my environment. I mean if I'm going to do this, I'm going to give it my all. We sing and dance around each other, shimmying back and forth and twirling one another as the music plays.

Sienna's smile is brighter than the sun as she giggles while I spin her in my arms. For someone who's been a trained dancer her entire life, Sienna's moves are wild and carefree as we move around each other.

We're getting into the last chord of the song, my body thrumming with excitement as we attempt to hit a note together. A tugging on my shirt pauses my singing as Sienna ducks behind me.

"Why are we stopping?" I ask, twisting slightly to see her nervous face. Sienna looks as if she'd seen a ghost.

"There's people here...from school." She frowns, pushing me completely in front of her. I squint at her, not understanding the problem until it dawns on me.

"Don't let them dim what we have going on. C'mon, angel." I pull her back to the front of me, nodding my head, and together we finish the song.

I don't waste any time, hoisting her into my arms fireman style, carrying her away. Sienna's body shakes in my grasp, sending a chill down my spine.

Maybe I pushed her too far, I think as we approach my car, but it's then that I realize she's laughing...*not* crying.

"That was so freaking fun! You should've seen that old guy in the front dancing to our song." She cackles as I place her in the car.

Our song.

I like the sound of that.

I stare at her, watching her as she speaks animatedly about the past hour and a half we spent inside Mulligan's. Even though I was there with her, Sienna spares no detail in her tale. She talks about how she'd gotten nervous seeing a guy from her Dance course with some girl, but then slowly stopped caring about them in total and it was like music to my ears.

As Sienna's eyes grow wide and excited the longer she talks, the more I realize just how much I've missed *this* girl.

This is the same girl who used to run me around downtown and had me dress up for whatever "showcase" she wanted to put on in the theater room of her uncle's house. *This is the same girl* who begged her parents to let her come to Maryland one winter to see my first ever Junior Hockey game, and stayed until I walked out of the locker room just to congratulate me.

This is the same girl who I've dreamt about for *years*, painting and sketching her from memory because of how much I missed seeing her face.

This is the same girl who kissed me on her eighteenth birthday, and then left me in that spot, heartbroken.

This is the same girl who I had a crush on at eight-years-old, became obsessed with at twelve, and now at nineteen have no idea what I'm doing with.

Seeing her now, I realize that that girl that I used to know is still inside her. She just needs to be taken out of her shell.

Sienna senses my inner turmoil; she always can. She grabs my hand and all breath comes back into my lungs, stilling me in my spot. My eyes flicker to the clock on my car's dashboard.

"We're going to be late..." My voice comes out like an avalanche of words as Sienna tilts her head to the side.

"For what? I thought that this was—"

"I'm going to take you somewhere special."

sixteen

Sienna

"Kiss me," he says, his voice just above a whisper. A shiver runs down my spine as his strong hands pull me against his muscular chest, holding me in place.

Jace's golden hair and sage eyes glimmer in the sun as he leans in closer, hungrily searching me. My body is liquid in his embrace, aching for the moment our lips touch. The second our tongues dance with one another's and our bodies become one.

There's a hint of mischief in the depths of his irises. He's having fun with me, and I know it.

"Why should I, Heart?" I tease, my eyes flickering to his plump lips then back to his eyes in a second.

He chuckles softly, the feel of his breath is cool against my skin.

I want to taste him, devour his mouth and savor it.

If I were an artist, this moment with him in this field would be set and hung up in galleries all over the world.

"Sienna...This is the skin of a killer..."

Wait...What?

Jace's eyes morph from the familiar light green that I know all too well to a light golden, cat-like color.

"Jace?"

"Bella—"

The world around us crumbles as my body shakes, pulling me from the reality where Jace Heart was a vampire and I, a human, standing in a green field, on the verge of taking one another. Instead, my view is replaced by sparkling green eyes, moonlight, and the dashboard of a car.

Fucking hell...

"Where...are we?" I ask with a yawn as I stretch my crooked neck.

Jace leans back from my face, grinning like the Cheshire cat, gesturing to the view before me, and that's when it comes back to me.

A gasp leaves my mouth immediately as I take in the wooded area and the multitude of vehicles around us, all facing a giant screen with the words *Twilight: Breaking Dawn Part One* plastered on the screen.

"We're watching *Twilight*?" I ask, my voice scratchy as Jace rolls his eyes as if to say *duh...what does it look like?*

"Eh...Only the last two, I know you put on the list that you wanted to watch the entire saga, but I also know that you only like watching the last two movies the most." He shrugs as if what he's saying is the most normal thing in the world, but it only heightens my shock.

I stare at the blond, my jaw dropped as he smiles softly at me, his brow furrowing for a second before softening.

How does he know that I only like those two movies? I mean I love the series, but those two movies are the best in the franchise.

Argue with your mom, not me. I said what I said.

My shock must not affect Jace, because instead of saying anything to acknowledge it, he simply pulls out a bucket of popcorn—from out of nowhere, by the way—and passes it to me with a packet of fruit snacks.

He has my movie theater combo, too?

Without thinking, I dump the fruit snacks into the popcorn bucket and shake the contents, mixing them. Throughout the entire process, Jace says nothing. Instead, he settles in his seat, attention set on the screen before us.

I stare holes into the side of his head, trying to gauge him.

What's his angle? Is this some ploy to get me alone in the woods?

"Yes, Sienna?" Jace's amused tone is mocking as he remains focused on the screen.

"What is this?" I ask, gesturing around the car, now noting the lavender blanket thrown haphazardly across my lap.

Cute.

"What does it look like, angel?" he questions curiously, a small amused grin tugging at his lips. We're closer than before, his eyes are smoldering orbs of the earth as they peer into my own, as if cataloging me into his memory.

"Well...*Hades*," I say, clearing my throat mockingly as I lean forward just a mere inch from his face. If he moved any further, we'd be kissing right now. "It looks like you're trying to seduce me in the middle of the woods while watching a vampire movie."

Jace's brows raise as he cackles in my face, unfiltered and breathless. "Hades? Is that what you call me, angel?" He chuckles.

"Oh, I call you many things." I roll my eyes but my words only bring his annoyingly cocky persona back.

"As long as 'yours' is in that little dictionary of yours, I'm cool with that...besides..." His eyes lower as he looks at me, taking me in. "You'd know when I'd try to seduce you."

The humor that'd once been laced in his tone dissipates as he gets closer into my space. My skin warms with his body heat, the center console of the car being the only thing to separate us.

My body buzzes to be closer to him, to touch and taste him. That dream from earlier flashes across my mind, and before I know it, I'm cupping his face, pulling his lips to mine.

The kiss is slow and languid, unlike our previous ones. His mouth moves with mine, and God, it feels like I've died and gone to Heaven. Jace's hand cups my jaw, his fingers digging into my skin, holding me in place. I'm beaming with energy as he dominates my mouth, tasting and claiming me as his own. My body thrums with energy, heat bellowing in my belly as his teeth pull lightly on my bottom lip.

I moan softly in his mouth and he smiles at the sound before pressing our lips together in one last kiss, a promise of more to come, not a finale.

When we pull away, it takes everything in me to catch my breath as Jace's eyes bore into my own. He sighs subtly, his mouth slightly ajar. The look on his face is something that I haven't seen before, I can't tell if it's desire or longing...or both, as he licks the remnants of my raspberry flavored lip gloss off of his lips.

My voice is raspy and breathless as I try to speak, but Jace beats me to it. His soft focus, still locked in on me.

"I—"

"That's three times, angel." He smirks, voice gruff, his eyes remaining fixated on my mouth as I gulp. "I'll grant you a wish next time." The bastard winks.

He fucking winked!

Also...is the asshole keeping track of our kisses?!

My mind is still trying to process the kiss, but I can't possibly think about anything else as my lips tingle with the sensation of him pressed against them.

Have we really kissed three times? Are we moving too fast? I've never done this whole *secretly obsessed with my childhood crush who is now practically begging me to use him to fulfill my birthday wish* kinda thing, and there's fucking zero other people on Reddit who have.

Without a word, Jace softly grasps my chin, turning it to focus on the large screen ahead. He doesn't say anything as he pulls the blanket over my lap, handing me the bucket of popcorn again, and leaving his hand planted firmly on my thigh.

And that's how we remain for the next forty-five minutes, a heated, almost *sexual* energy thrums between us as we sit in silence. His hand that'd been once over the blanket found itself under it, gripping and running circles over my bare thigh absentmindedly. I don't even think he's realized that the action has had me silently anticipating something more this entire time, something that blurs the lines of this newly established *agreement*.

The feeling of his thumb circling my thigh has me wishing it were other places, circling my core and begging for more.

"You want to cum?"

My ears ring as my eyes bulge out of my head. "I'm sorry–WHAT?!"

Jace furrows his brows at me, tilting his head, "I said do you want some? You've been grabbing air for the past two minutes…" He chuckles as I freak the fuck out internally.

Why…What—Who?!

What is he doing to my brain?

I blink. Once. Twice. Four times too fast before his words process in my head.

"Yeah…that's—Yep! Can you get water too please?" My voice shakes as Jace smirks, a singular brow raising.

"Thirsty?"

You don't know the half of it…

He doesn't wait for a response from me and instead slides out of the vehicle, heading to the concessions stand nearby. I watch as he walks away, and as soon as he's too far to turn around, I pull out my phone.

Me

Code purple

Her response is immediate, as if she were waiting for me to text her.

Gee Adams

Bitch I know you didn't dye your hair PURPLE omg…

You're going to get chemical damage with all of these new colors

This girl…

Rolling my eyes, I text Georgia again. This time with details.

Me

I just kissed him…again

Gee Adams

Wait where are you?

You're with him right now???

WAIt

KISS???

HUH

STOp

I—

Ok let me get this straight

The devil boy (who you weirdly are okay with being in presence) kissed and kidnapped you??

What's he doing right now?

Maybe texting Georgia wasn't a good idea...She tends to... *¿Como se dice? Overreact.* Sighing, I close my phone, leaving Georgia on read, and search the lot for Jace.

It takes two minutes to find him, but when my eyes land on the oh so familiar blond—*who tongued me down not even five minutes ago*—my heart plummets to my ass.

A girl, short and pear-shaped in physique, stands before him.

Do NOT jump to conclusions, Si Si.

She could be a friend...

I can't see her face, but I just know that she's pretty based on what she's wearing. I'm no woman hater, not in the slightest. Her outfit is stunning, with a small purple dress that compliments her deep brown skin and chestnut hair perfectly.

My head tilts as I watch them. Jace smiles down at the woman, listening intently as she talks. Are they close? How does he—

The temperature in the car plummets. My mouth feels cottony, my saliva is hard to swallow, and I feel as if I'll pass out. The image in front of me is *odd*.

I've never imagined something like this in my wildest dreams, and maybe I'm a masochist or just a confused girl, because I sit there, *watching*.

I watch as the brown skinned girl reaches up, cupping his face and pulling him in for a searing kiss. I watch as Jace grips her shoulders, and I take a deep breath as she deepens it, sticking her tongue in his mouth.

I can't take it. I can't watch anymore. My body moves before my brain can process and the large screen where *Twilight* plays is back in my line of sight.

In school, we learn that when the body is in danger, it chooses between two phases of defense. Fight or Flight.

This survival mechanism is an imperative response to danger and uncontrollable. What we don't learn about, however, is the Freeze response.

I am frozen in my seat, unmoving, unblinking. I want to move. I want to get out of this car, storm up to him and yell, because what the fuck just happened? We *just* kissed, just touched and shared an intimate moment, and not even an hour later, he's kissing someone just ten feet away from me.

My breathing grows shallow. *It's so cold*. I can see my breath as I let out shaky exhales.

Is he just using me?

Wouldn't that be funny…He'd asked me to use him—fucking begged me—and now he's kissing another girl?

Am I losing my mind? We're not together, but fuck…do I yell? Do I run? What should I do?

When the door opens, my stomach roils as pink strawberries and cotton candy assaults my nostrils. I flinch as Jace taps my shoulder, holding the popcorn out for me with a sweet smile on his slappable face.

Momma ain't raise no bitch—*granted, she didn't raise me at all*. You get the fucking memo.

My eye twitches as I watch him, my fingers itching to grab the door knob as he gulps. Is he going to acknowledge what happened? Reassure me?

I should be quiet. It's not my place and we're friends.

"So...what did I miss?" he asks.

I blink at him, my eye twitches a-*freaking*-gain.

Fix your face, Sienna. Don't let him see you sweat.

He moves again, shifting uncomfortably and something in me *snaps*.

Fuck that.

"Oh you missed a lot, considering your tongue was down that bitch's *throat*." My smile is filled with venom as he looks at me. The rapid rise and fall of my chest would be concerning had I not been on the verge of cursing the spawn of Hades out.

Jace flinches, "That's not what happ–"

"So you didn't *just* kiss her? Right, I'm delusional and Eren fucking Marlowe is standing right there. I think my eyes work perfectly fine, thank you. I know what I saw, *matter of fact*, I'm done. For someone pleading for me to *use them*, you sure are using the fuck out of me...Right now." My voice shakes as I face the front of the car, cursing my human body for letting its emotions take over.

In the corner of my eye, I can see Jace recoil, but I don't care. And clearly neither does he.

seventeen

Jace

—6 minutes ago

I SQUINT AS KARLIYA speaks, straining both my eyes and ears to hear what she's trying to say. The loud speaker blaring *Twilight* is no help for the soft spoken girl.

I'd been smiling originally, trying to be nice and placate the previous hookup, but it's already been three minutes and Sienna's popcorn is going to get cold the longer I stay out here.

Sienna.

My pulse quickens at the mere thought of her. My body is still vibrating with the aftermath of that kiss we'd just shared. Do you think she'd want to do it again? I mean, she kissed me first and I'm freaking amazing at it, so I'd like to think that she would.

I just don't want to push her too fast. Unlike other girls who I've been with—Karliya included—they were easier to get with and then dump. As bad as it sounds, it's the truth. I've had my fair share of women, and they'd wanted the same thing that I did.

To fuck without strings attached.

With Sienna, it's different, though. We're a mess of red strings tangled together by the Fates. She's my past, present, and future (hopefully).

I don't notice the signs as I lean in to hear Karliya better. She's in my Communications course, and so I'd *thought* that's what she wanted to talk about...I was wrong.

So...so very wrong.

Karliya pulls my face down to her level and kisses the hell out of me. It's sloppy and the pungent taste of grape soda and chocolate peanut butter fills my mouth. It takes everything in me to not gag.

My hands grip her shoulders trying to gently push her away, but when she drills her tongue into my mouth, I can't help but to put a little strength behind my second push.

"Wha—"

"What the fuck?!" I gag, spitting the taste of her out of my mouth onto the concrete beside us.

Fuck. I hope Sienna didn't see this shit. She already doesn't trust me enough, as is.

"You do know that sexual assault is fucking illegal, right? What the fuck—" I can't help the second gag. I think I'm going to be sick.

Fuck that.

I *know* that I'm going to be sick. I groan as my stomach roils. The scent of her wretched perfume sticks to me like a skunk's spray.

"I thought we had—"

"Shut the fuck up. Oh my God..." I spit again, frowning as the taste of Sienna completely disappears from my mouth. "You're lucky I don't report you to someone."

I can't even look at Karliya as I snatch up Sienna's snacks, taking them back to the car. The air is cold when I get back in, and I just know she'd seen everything when she gives me *the look* as I try to hand her the popcorn. You know the look that moms give when you're in deep shit? Yeah...*that* look.

She's mad.

"So...what did I miss?"

She blinks at me and her eye twitches. I don't think I've ever seen her this mad. I watch her, from the rapid rise and fall of her chest to her tapping on the door's armrest.

She rips me a new asshole so fresh that I think I've just been reborn. Never in my nineteen going on twenty years of life have I ever had a woman talk to me like that.

I blink, stunned and impressed as Sienna curses me from sunup to sundown, shredding my ego in a mere second, and *I love it.*

Her breathing is rapid as she finishes, trying and failing to focus her attention ahead, but I know she wants to do more, *say* more.

Had I been a smart man, I would've known not to touch her when she's like this. Instead of being smart, I reach out for her, softly tugging her chin back to face me.

"Angel, I think your eyes work perfectly; however, I also think that you should've watched a little longer—"

She swats my hand away, and I chuckle softly as I continue.

"What she did was not consensual. She forced herself onto me. I didn't kiss back, I would never do that to you. But while we're here, let's have a talk about trust and what this is that we have between us." I eye her, noting her hidden resolve as her brows dip with concern.

"Oh, fuck you—"

"Would you?" I raise a brow as steam billows from her ears.

Oh, she's *angry.* It's kinda hot...Should I poke the beast? I study her quickly and scratch that thought. She'd personally see to my castration if I did.

I like my dick. Me and JJ have quite a time together.

"That's not important right now, *this* is," I say, gesturing between us. Sienna frowns, side-eyeing me.

"What?" she huffs, eyeing me down as I smile, tempting her.

My next words are measured. "We need to fix your list. Firstly, this *thing* between us can't go anywhere if you don't trust me."

She shifts in her seat, folding her arms under her chest as she faces me. I smirk lightly as she sassily rolls her neck to look at me.

"I trust—"

"*Oh, bullshit!* Don't lie, Sienna. You trust me as far as you can throw me, and that's not much. We'll strengthen it in due time, but I need you to *try* to trust me."

She nods slowly, gnawing on her bottom lip. "So she kissed you...Who was she? Do you know her?"

This could go so many ways...If I tell her the truth, she could spazz out again. If I lie, I'm a hypocrite.

The truth will set you free...I guess.

"She was a hook up—"

"YOU HAD SEX WITH HER?!"

Well shit...

The truth might send me to an early fucking grave, my goodness. I'm going to be twelve feet under for good measure, dealing with this girl.

"Oh my gosh." She gags, putting a finger in her mouth like the childish woman she is. "Brush your teeth!" Sienna exclaims, twisting her face in disgust. I need to reel this conversation back to why I'd started it and quickly.

"Like I was saying, the list needs to be changed, and this thing between us will remain like that. You might think I'm a whore, but that side of me is only for you."

That shuts her up. Sienna's throat bobs as her eyes widen.

"I'll be anything you want me to be. You want me to beg, I'll do that. You want me to do your list, already on it. I'm *yours*. Everything that you want, Sienna, I'll give it to you, but let me make myself clear." I lean in, my voice lowering as my lips brush Sienna's earlobe, and she shudders for a whole new reason.

"No one else kisses these lips but me, and no one touches this pussy but me. Are we clear?"

Sienna gulps, her eyes raking my face. I want to kiss her so badly, take her in this car and let her stake her claim over me, for crying out loud, but I can't and I won't. She deserves so much more.

"What—"

Wrong answer.

"Are we clear?"

When Sienna doesn't say anything, my blood temperature rises. She should know exactly how I feel about her. The only girl who I have eyes for *is her*. There's no one else for me but Sienna Jones, and I'm going to make it my mission for her to know that, even if it's the death of me.

"And you know what?" I pause, waiting for her to respond and huff when she doesn't.

"Fuck the rules and fuck number three on your list, Sienna. I want you to be mine. No one else touches you but me. You have me, no doubt about that." My chest heaves from the speed at which my words tumble out of my mouth, but it's the truth. The only woman who I want and need is right in front of me, she always has been.

Sienna must get a bit of her confidence back after hearing what I said, because she clears her throat and lifts her chin defiantly. "You don't run this show, Eros...it was my list."

I tilt my head to the side, allowing the cocky smirk I'd been holding in to broadcast itself on full display. "And I'm orchestrating it, angel. You're mine, simple."

When I pull up to the girls' apartment the next day, I feel relieved and nervous all at once. What I'm about to do is derailing Sienna's schedule completely, and I don't know if she's ready for such a leap yet.

After I dropped her off last night, we talked more and made an agreement that although we're keeping what we are behind closed doors, what's going on between us will remain strictly monogamous.

She's a possessive woman, and I may or may not be a possessive man (I definitely am). It's the only way that this will work.

It's been fifteen minutes since I texted and told her that I'd be outside. Sienna had responded immediately that she was on her way down, but when I check my watch again, I chuckle.

For someone who's always on time, she's late today.

I'm reaching into my back pocket about to make a check-in call to her when a flash of pink rushes past me in a blur. I tilt my head as Sienna walks straight past me, her teeth gnawing on her bottom lip as she looks around.

Oh, she hasn't noticed me...my phone ringing in my pocket only gives truth to my hypothesis as I answer the Bluetooth.

"Good morning, angel."

"Where are you, psycho?" she deadpans, staring into the vast parking lot.

"On your left." I grin, knowing my smile is hidden as I wiggle my fingers at her in a mock wave, leaning against the vehicle behind me.

Sienna's gasp rings through both the speakers and my ears as she rushes over, her hands over her mouth.

"Jace," she breathes my name like fresh air, "who's bike is that?!"

"Get on, angel. We've got places to be."

EIGHTEEN

Sienna

WHOEVER IN THE WORLD decided to make biker boys seem like they were hot and that being a "backpack" is even hotter—has a special place in hell with their name on it.

My body feels like gravity is working against me and my knees shake as I press them tightly against Jace's thighs. My hands are wrapped so tightly around his waist that I may be cutting off my own circulation, and this man has the nerve to *laugh* as I bury myself deeper into his back.

"This isn't freaking funny!" I shout as laughter rings throughout the speakers of my helmet.

When Jace had told me he'd pick me up for practice, this isn't what I'd thought he meant, but I should've known considering *who* he is. Leave it to Jace freaking Heart to show up outside of my place leaning against a dark green Ducati.

My body thrums with anxious energy as Jace speeds up, the sound of the bike's exhaust growing louder, my eyes burning from squeezing them so tightly.

I don't wanna die.

I don't wanna die.

I don't want to fucking die!

When I left my apartment twenty minutes ago, becoming an organ donor wasn't on my list for today!

"You're going to kill me! I just know it. I know it. I know it!" I repeat, breathing heavily as I squeeze him tighter.

Jace chuckles softly as the bike slows down. He squeezes my hands that are clenched around his waist before landing a gloved palm on my clothed thigh, rubbing gentle circles on it.

"You're fine, angel...I would never let anything happen to you," he coos, making my stomach flutter as he squeezes my thigh reassuringly.

I'm shaking as I look at the side of his helmeted head.

"Really?"

"Of course, now hold tight."

You don't have to tell me—

My back slowly lowers to the ground and I swear that I can see the angels above grimacing as the front wheel of the bike *lifts* off of the ground.

"AHHHH OH MY FUCK—" My shout is cut off by the maniacal laughter of the asshole who holds my life in his hands. I hold on for dear life as he zooms, faster and further down the near empty street, whisking me away as I tuck my head into his back.

"Fuck. I hate you so much! I'm going to shoot your little cupid looking ass in the back, I swear it! Fuck. Fuck. *Fuck*!" I scream and mean every single word as we come to a stop.

My body remains glued to Jace's, not falling for the same old trick again as he sniffs a laugh.

"Although I love having you holding on to me, baby. I think you're going to want to see this," he says smoothly, patting my hands as he puts the bike in neutral, taking out the key.

My eyes are glued shut as my mind slowly picks itself up from the highway and travels back to its host. When my brain finally catches up to my body, I open one eye. The tension in my body rackets higher as I take in my surroundings.

Trees taller than skyscrapers and a graveled road that goes on for miles surrounds me. We're in a parking lot with only about three or four more cars surrounding us. Jace turn to face me with his helmet off, staring down at me expectantly.

So, this is where it ends...

I wonder what my tombstone would say...*Here lies a girl with pink hair and a fat ass*. Or maybe *death by psychotic blond dude*.

Sucks...

"If you're going to try to kill me now, just know I will fight back. I have bear mace in my pocket," I say, slowly pulling off the dark helmet he'd given me.

At this, Jace raises a brow, crooking his neck to face me with an amused grin.

"Bear mace?" he asks.

So what if I'm lying! He doesn't have to know that... Straightening my back, I raise my head with a confident nod.

"Bear mace! So you better not try anything funny, psycho... I'm watching you." I narrow my eyes as I wiggle a finger at him. Jace feigns his fright, jumping back with an exaggeratedly scared face and his hands up in mock surrender. I roll my eyes at him and take in my surroundings as he helps me off of the bike, his calloused hands wrapping protectively around my waist after he gets the bike settled.

The skin around my waist thrums with the heat of his touch, warming my cheeks as I look around the greenery.

"So what're we doing here? I was joking yesterday when I mentioned you trying to seduce me in the woods...that seems painful, with all the sticks and bugs." I shudder at the thought of my knees even touching the floor of a wooded area.

I'd rather sit and listen to Georgia drone on about Eden Marlowe's "excellence" before touching twigs and spiders in the middle of the woods.

Jace chuckles, his voice airy as he asks, "Isn't it obvious?"

I scrunch my nose as something pungent and farmy—if that's a word—assaults my nostrils.

"It smells like cow ass..." I grumble, tilting my head to look at the smiling man.

"It'll smell like a lot more than that when we get inside."

Jace doesn't give me the time to process his words before he's grabbing a hold of my hand, leading me in the opposite direction of where we parked, and it's then that I realize where we are.

A large archway in the shape of an opened mouth monkey is tall and inviting in front of us with the words *Lottie Exotic!* splayed on a sign under the mouth's opening. I furrow my brows as Jace walks us straight through and eye everything as we pass by a stand with different exotic animals on the top of bubble dispensers.

"A zoo? What are we—" I whisper more-so to myself, but Jace hears it all.

"Together, but we're not talking about that right now. Right now, we're getting number 10 crossed off that pretty little list of yours."

Number 10? Did he memorize the order of the list? No—that's silly...He wouldn't, right? Wait, fuck that—

Together?!

Did he just say we're together? Like as in man with woman who kiss and talk and date...together?!

Gaping at him like a fish out of water, I allow my body to be dragged and pulled by him. Jace tugs me all over until we reach a point where we get wristbands to enter the actual zoo. He gives me a green one and tugs a purple one onto his wrist before continuing with his pulling, and I allow it.

My mind is still grappling with what he'd just said that I don't realize we're standing right in front of a pride of peacocks. A rainbow of feathers and long necked birds stalk past us, completely indifferent towards the two idiot humans standing just a few feet away.

Peacocks have the most divine feathers and features. As a kid, I always thought that the female of the species was the flashier animal with blue and green tones, only to find out it was the male.

"Wow." I hear from the side of me, feeling Jace's body heat. Lifting my head to look at him, I gulp as our eyes clash with one another's.

My breath lodges in my throat, keeping me preserved in this moment as his hand squeezes my waist in a possessive yet gentle grip.

"Careful, Heart...Your feathers are showing." I smirk up at him, making the worst "bird" joke known to man, his lip quirks.

"Good, gotta let those ganders know whose hen you are. That little small one over there was about to try to make you their mate."

I roll my eyes, fighting my laugh off as the small wide-eyed peacock at the back of the group locks eyes with me.

Minutes later, I find myself standing outside of the monkey enclosure with Jace and one of the primate keepers, Janice. Janice is a taller woman with arms the size of tanks. She grins, looking down at me with the warmest brown eyes as Jace drones on and on about me wanting to pet a monkey.

"It's been her dream to pet one, you can just see it in her little hazel eyes—the excitement," he gushes as Janice *awws* audibly, her hand clutching her heart.

I roll my eyes, shaking my head with a smile as Jace turns to inspect the enclosure for "threats", also known as the 300 pound gorilla named Bessie, who shares the enclosure with the other primates.

"You are a lucky girl, I wish my boyfriend would drone on about my interests like yours…" Janice sighs, patting my shoulder lovingly.

Boyfriend? My body warms at the thought. Do we seem like a couple? Can other people see this?

"Who—"

"Babe, look at this one! He's small and doesn't look like he'd rip your finger off!"

I cringe at the loud man in the near empty petting zoo. It's now apparent to me why my parents never indulged in a "bring your kid to work" day. After spending more time with Jace, I *completely* understand.

Jace points at a tiny black and white Capuchin, and the monkey stares back at him with a glimmer of mischief in his large brown eyes. I think that this may be the cutest freaking animal that I've ever seen—don't tell Oscar.

The tiny Capuchin monkey is held in another large enclosure a few paces away from the biggest one in the center of the room with a bunch more smaller primates.

"Oh! That's Maurice, he's a sweet little guy. If you want to pet him, you can as long as you wash your hands before and after!"

Jace grins deviously.

"My girlfriend is obsessed with these guys, Thank you!" his tone doesn't waver as his focus remains locked on Janice. My eyes snap to him, head tilting in confusion as the infuriatingly handsome man grins.

Girlfriend?

"Of course! The cleaning station is just around that corner." Janice grins, pointing away, but I'm not paying her any mind as Jace wraps a protective arm around my waist, guiding me to the station.

"Girlfriend?"

He rolls his eyes at me, ever the sassy man he is. "Would you rather me say 'girl who's using me to complete her fantasies'?"

Pursing my lips, I remain quiet and wash my hands.

"Monkeys are very agile creatures. Maurice here is probably our calmest primate with him still being a toddler, but please remember that he is still a wild animal. Be gentle, and do not force contact with him. He will come to—Oh!"

I'm taken aback, my body stiffening before softening slightly as tiny, nimble fingers squeeze my nose. Large brown eyes peer up at me as Maurice adjusts himself in my hands. He'd been in Janice's care as she spoke until deciding to jump into my arms.

His small body reminds me of a baby as I cradle him carefully, holding him just as Janice tried to show.

Oh my goodness, he's so stinkin' cute!

Maurice nuzzles his face into the crook of my neck like a baby, and I swoon as the tiny monkey tugs on my ear.

As I hold Maurice, I can feel Jace's protective gaze on me, watching and recording the moment I spend with the small wild animal.

Janice tells us about the origins of the zoo, explaining how these animals are only in captivity for a small period of time here before being released to a better environment. Many of the animals here were born into captivity or on the verge of death due to animal poachers.

My heart breaks as Janice tells us about Maurice's origin story. His mom was born in the wild, but was so badly injured trying to escape from poachers that when she arrived in the states to the exotic zoo's rehab facility, she died shortly after giving birth to him.

He'd likely stay in the zoo's care for the rest of his life.

I hate humans. We always find a good thing and destroy it. The world is dying because of us, and instead of caring about our ecosystem, we're more interested in putting highways in the Amazon Rainforest.

I pet Maurice with a bit more care before our time is up and we have to leave for the next exhibit.

My mood bar is in hell by the time we exit the primate exhibit, but Jace is thrumming with energy.

"You were so cute with that little guy!" he exclaims, flicking through pictures on his phone, flashing a photo of me looking down at Maurice.

I try to smile, but it isn't as bright as before. Those poor animals deserve to be in their homes, not in a shelter.

"Let's check out one last place before leaving, I promise this will bring your mood up." Jace grins, grabbing a hold of my hand sending sparks of electricity up my arm as I follow behind.

His happiness and excitement warms my mood a bit, and soon enough I find myself grinning as I realize which exhibit we're waiting to enter.

The kangaroos.

Now, I don't know if this is because I had a strange obsession with Australian animals as a child or because I'm a grown adult who knows what flight or fight is, but the idea of being in a semi-enclosed space near kangaroos sends my hackles rising.

When we were kids, I would drone on about my fascinations and obsessions with Jace. Sharks, kangaroos, and monkeys were always a topic of discussion between us, and it looks like he'd remembered.

We're about to enter the exhibit when a small fur ball skitters past us, running across our feet. Jace lets out the shrillest, most ear-splitting shriek that I've ever heard from a man.

My jaw drops as my eyes register the small black cat that ran past, its eyes and paws too big for its body.

"Don't—" he tries to stop me, but my eyes are already filled with mirthful tears as I fail to conceal my humor.

"Oh my gosh!" I cackle, doubling over in laughter. Did this man just scream over a kitten?! I add in a knee slap for some extra *umph*.

"Ha! Ha! Ha! Laugh all you want, angel. When that little demon spawn tries to claw your eyes out, I don't want to hear anything," he pouts, causing me to laugh harder at his expense.

In all my years of knowing him, never have I ever thought that he'd be afraid of *cats*, of all things.

"So wait...let me get this straight: you're scared of cats, of all things, but a *kangaroo* is nothing?!" I ask in between laughs, still reeling from his pitiful scream. Jace purses his lips, sick of my antics as he ushers me into the exhibit.

"I'm not scared of kangaroos or cats...it was just a fluke," he mutters unconvincingly, guiding me to where one of the zoo's workers stands inside of the exhibit.

The woman is tall with deep brown skin. Her hair is in a beautiful array of blonde and brown French braids that are pulled into a bun with a few strands out.

I admire her hair, marking it in my brain for a possible style to try as she smiles at us, inviting us into the exhibit.

"Hi, guys! My name's Shayla. Did you two want to feed our joey here? He's Nox, sweet little thing, might I add. His brother and sister are over there sleeping." Shayla beams as she pets Nox's shoulder.

Jace doesn't hesitate to pull me towards the animal, smiling from ear to ear. I grimace, already knowing how this will play out before it starts as Shayla leads us inside the enclosure with Nox and his siblings.

The entire process is going smoothly with Nox letting me feed and pet him—or so I think. About two minutes into feeding Nox, his mother, Reina, wakes up, and *surprise surprise*...Jace Heart decides that he wants to feed her.

My back is turned to Jace and Reina, with Shayla mediating between the two of us. I'm just about to feed Nox another small carrot when my body is jerked back into a strong chest.

Jace wraps both of his arms around me protectively, squeezing tightly.

Is he trying to hug—

"I made her mad," he whispers calmly in my ear. My blood chills, eyes snapping up to the buff momma-roo in front of me, eyeing down the idiot using me as protection.

"She's docile..."

"Babe, have you not seen *Kangaroo Jack*?! These motherfuckers are psycho. Nope!" he exclaims, grabbing me up like a kid before dragging us out of the enclosure, completely ignoring Shayla's protest.

The walk back to the bike is silent with Jace stewing and me trying not to laugh at the idiot.

"Don't—"

The laugh that falls out of my body is immediate and loud as I double over, clutching my stomach. Jace rolls his eyes, handing the purple helmet from earlier back to me, shutting me up instantly.

"What was that?" He smirks, watching as I look down at the heavy chunk of metal in my hands.

"Shut up..."

My phone vibrates in my pocket as he's about to make another annoying retort, so I ignore him and pull it out to check the message.

Daisy

> Where are you?

> Did you forget about our practice??

My heart drops, my eyes falling to the time. It's 12:30...we were supposed to meet at 12:15. Shit. It's a Friday, so I know I don't have classes today, but I *did* have a dance practice with Daisy.

Daisy

> Are you with that guy?

> Your boyfriend?

Boyfriend is a strong word...I'd say an acquaintance who is male that I have kissed and hung out with.

Leaving Daisy on read, I look up at Jace who's already staring at me expectantly. It's then that I finally take him in.

The sun is at its peak, and though we're in a forested area, it shines through the trees. Jace's hair is a mixture of sunlight, gold, and brown sugar cookies. Sweet and light. Jace is like a golden boy, like Herc—

No!

"Want something sweet?" he asks, his words like music to my ears as I grin, trying to shake off my thoughts.

"Have you met me?"

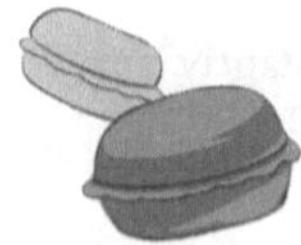

Jace may know me a little too well.

Our drive back to our side of town is seamless, with me cowering into his back and him singing early 2000s pop music over our Bluetooth connection.

When we get to Sweet Tooth, I'm surprised to find it empty with Saree standing behind the counter writing down an order on the phone. When she sees us, her eyes brighten as she waves before gesturing that she'll be with us in a minute.

Jace and I take that as a sign to look for what we want and make a bit of small talk until his phone rings, likely a call from his mom. He excuses himself in an instant, heading outside to talk.

"Hey, baby doll! What can I get for—" Saree's warm greeting is interrupted by *another* phone ringing.

The two of us pause, looking around for the culprit until I feel it. My phone's vibrating. *That's odd.* When I pull out my phone from my pocket, my brows raise and I answer it quickly, hoping she doesn't hang up before we're connected.

"Hello?! Mom, can you hear me?!" My words are hurried as I shove the phone to my ear. Saree's eyes widen. She knows a bit of my history with my parents. I watch as Saree starts to fill up plates with snacks for Jace and I as my mother's voice drones in.

"Sienna, darling. Is your hair still pink? It was so luscious and curly—" Her luxurious, posh voice is like glass shattering as my shoulders deflate.

Seriously? This...*again?*

When I'd dyed my hair, she'd had a fit over my "perfect curls" being ruined. *I* think that was just an analogy for her pristine image and daughter, being anything less than perfect.

But I digress.

"Is that what you wanted to talk—"

"No, darling. Your father has a surprise!" she exclaims into the phone.

I wait, chewing on my bottom lip for the ball to drop as Jace comes back into the bakery, frowning slightly.

"Your father and I are coming home for the holidays, Sienna!"

My eyes widen, jaw going slack as her words process. They're coming home...*for me?* They're coming home for my birthday!

I mean my birthday is a holiday, right?

"Are you ser—"

"Anyways, darling. Ta ta! Your father and I have a show tonight."

And with that, she hangs up. No *goodbye*, no *I love you*. Nothing, just her news.

Jace furrows his brows, raising his arms, unsure of if we're about to celebrate or if he's going to spend the night keeping me from having a breakdown.

"My parents are coming home for my birthday!"

NINETEEN

Sienna

AFTER JACE DROPPED ME off mid-day yesterday, the reality of what I'd done over the course of the day sunk in.

It's only been a few weeks we've started tackling things off of my list, but I already feel different. I feel safe, like I can be myself with him. I don't know what that says about him or what we have going on, but I don't want to fuck it up.

What I'm *not* happy about is the amount of work that I've allowed to pile up.

Not schoolwork or anything like that, I get most of my homework done after classes end.

I'm behind on practicing for the Winter Showcase. Granted, I only missed *one* practice, but I did leave another one early. Thoughts of failure and a horrible future plagues my mind as I get ready for today.

It's Saturday, and I have nothing planned for the day.

Cleo's home with that guy, Jake, studying for some project, and I'm pretty sure Georgia is on the other side of town, scouring different fabric shops for an internship she's looking into for next summer.

That just leaves Oscar and I, alone with my studies. Midterms are coming up soon, so I should probably get in all the studying that I can right now before I become too stressed to retain any knowledge.

I'd never really studied as a kid, school just came easier to me. But now that I'm in college, I need all the time that I can get to study.

Heaving a deep sigh, I take a sip of the peach kombucha that I'd left in the fridge and frown.

Maybe I could call Daisy over and we figure out some more choreo? I think just as the doorbell rings.

"Did Georgia forget her key again?" I say aloud, crossing the living room to the front door and when I check the peephole, my heart drops.

Jace stands on the other side of the door, smiling cheekily, holding his phone up to the small hole.

"Open up, gorgeous." His words bring life to my body, sending chills down my spine, leaving my mouth watering.

Oh my goodness, girl. Tighten up!

Schooling my expression, I open the door, stepping aside quickly before closing it behind me, thankful that I'd worn slippers to the living room.

Jace's eyes trail my body, slowly drinking me in from my legs to my hips, chest and lips.

I shift, skin burning. I'm not wearing the most inappropriate sleepwear, but I'm wearing a pair of tiny shorts and a loose Twisted Viper's band tee without a bra.

My nipples harden from his obvious perusal of my body as Jace clears his throat. His eyes that were on my lips flicker to my chest as I fold my arms before connecting with my eyes.

"What are you doing here?" I question him, yelling in a whispered tone as Jace huffs as if to say *do I really need a reason to be here?* He holds his phone out to me, as if that answers my questions.

Swatting it away, I frown. "Listen, I really need to study...I can't play mind games with you right now," I say lying through my teeth. I want nothing more than to play mind games with him. At least that way I won't be bored out of my mind.

"Oh trust me, babe, you want to play this one. Plus, it's Saturday night and midterms are in two weeks...This is the only time you'll get before you're studying your cute little life away." He smirks, dangling his phone teasingly as if to tempt me.

Frowning, I unfold my arms, tilting my head up and giving him direct eye contact. "You've got five minutes to explain."

"There's a party, and we're going. So go get your cute little ass ready."

My tongue pokes in my cheek as I think over his words. A party could be what I need to let loose a little bit more, and we can also scratch some things off of the list by going.

Jace must sense my skepticism because he frowns slightly, holding up his pinky to me. "You won't know anyone there but me, angel. I'll protect you, I promise."

"Fine but, wait in your car. Cleo and her guy friend are here doing a project together..." Conceding, I lock pinkies with the man. My skin heats at his touch as he gives me a devilish grin.

My heartbeat rackets against my chest as Jace's green eyes remain locked on mine as he leans down, sealing our promise with a kiss to our knuckles.

It takes me about forty-five minutes to fully psych myself up and get ready. I'm listening to Zola's new song, applying the last bit of my lip gloss when my door flies open. Freezing, I eye the blonde standing in my doorway.

Georgia gasps quietly, shutting the door quickly behind herself as she stalks into my room.

"Oh. My—" She widens her eyes, taking me in as I cut her off.

"Don't—"

She waves me off. "Oh I won't...You look fucking *hot!*" she squeals quietly, jumping up and down.

My cheeks heat from her praise as I eye myself in the mirror once again. My pink curls are slowly growing out and lightening to a light pastel pink with dark brown, grown out roots. Tonight, I'm wearing my hair out in a curly middle part with a bit tugged behind my ear on the right side. I picked a cute, sparkly, purple mini dress for the party that I've never worn, and paired it with a pair of silver, strappy heels. My makeup is light and airy with minimal contour and blush, leaving attention on my luscious lashes and lip combo.

I look damn good if I do say so myself. Grinning at my reflection, I do a small spin for Georgia. She pretends to be paparazzi, snapping pictures of me as we laugh before the mood takes a small turn with her sighing.

"Look...I won't tell her and I'll always have your back, but you need to tell her soon...The two of you have been going out a lot lately, and Cleo's not dumb. She may be a bit oblivious because of Captain Hockey Dick out there but, I'm not."

Her words hit me like a truck, and I know that she's right. Cleo isn't dumb, just distracted...and that's only going to last but so long. I need to tell her about my arrangement, but when?

She and I have never kept anything from each other...

"We'll talk about it later, babe. As of right now, I'm going to help you sneak out..."

And Georgia does just that, whispering and rushing me out of the apartment like we're in a spy movie, moving stealthily and carefully.

By the time I'm outside, I'm running to the familiar green Aston Martin in the lot. The car's owner stands outside, leaning against the hood of the car, eyes wide.

"You look—"

"I missed you so much!" I squeal, hugging the car's hood. After riding as a backpack on a Ducati for the better part of the day before Jace had to go to hockey practice yesterday, let's just say that I'm never wishing to be a backpack again.

"Wow, Sienna! I missed you, too, here's some sugar!" the asshole mocks sarcastically, kissing the air.

I flip him the bird, scrunching my face. "Ha-ha...very funny."

Jace blows an air kiss to me, humoring himself as he opens the door for me. His crisp, clean scent is intoxicating as he leans across me after I get in the car. My breath hitches and the air around us grows thick with tension as he buckles my seatbelt.

Our eyes lock. I drown in his mossy orbs and my breathing slows. Jace has the type of face that artists dream about. It's masculine beauty in its rawest form, and being this close to him, I can see everything from his long, dark lashes to the small splattering of light brown freckles decorating his nose and cheeks.

My eyes track as his lip quirks, smirking slightly.

"I could've done it myself," I say, trying and failing to add some bite to my tone. Instead, my words are breathless and lacking in punch as he breaks out in a full blown grin.

Dear God...

"Sure you could've, but I wanted to," he says simply before getting in the car himself, pulling us out of my complex's parking lot.

Jace's hand rests on my thigh, his thumb swirling small circles on my naked flesh as I get comfortable in the seat. Soft R&B plays on the aux, lulling me into a comfortable bliss.

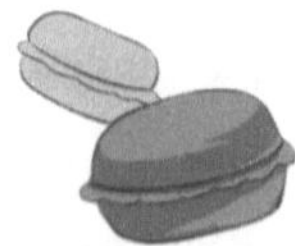

"ARE YOU READY TO GET FUCKED UP?!"

My body is jolted out of its quick slumber as Jace yells along to whatever fucking EDM artist he likes. He pumps his fist, chewing his bottom lip in a weird *bro* move as he pulls up outside of a packed neighborhood block.

It takes a minute for my eyes to adjust to my surroundings, but when they do, I smile.

There's nothing but drunk college kids, dudes in togas, and red and white streamers everywhere.

"Are we?" I furrow my brows looking over at Jace, jumping slightly when I realized he'd already been looking my way.

"At the Nolince U Omega chapter about to get fucked up? Yes. Let's go, hot stuff."

Jace holds my hand, guiding me through the packed Nolince U frat house. I grip his hand a little tighter as he leads me through to an empty space in the house's living room, coughing a bit as someone blows blue raspberry flavored smoke my way. Jace squeezes my hand, smiling as he pulls me into him by my waist.

"What number on the list are we doing?" I ask, shouting over the loud music blaring in the house.

"Six and eight, but don't worry, gorgeous, I'm on angel protection all night." He grins, wrapping an arm around my shoulder as he walks us to the kitchen. I watch, standing next to him as he makes us some drinks.

Jace's arms are on full display tonight, and my mouth waters at the sight of his thick veins popping up from his skin. He senses my obvious perusal of him and grins, holding out a cup to me. "Cheers. To getting blacked out."

"To getting blacked out." I nod.

We move back to the living room, finding a small space in the corner and take shot after shot—or I do, at least. Jace sticks to a singular shot of tequila, but I've had about six or seven.

Rap music plays on the house's speakers, and everyone in the party seems to be enjoying themselves even as the songs change to a more sensual vibe. My pulse quickens as Jace wraps his arms around my waist, perching on the dip above my ass.

He smiles down at me, our faces close as we grind against one another, getting lost in each other's bodies. I'm warm from all the shots I've taken, and I'm nowhere near done. Even though the house is crowded with people, it feels like we're alone as we dance against one another.

I don't know when, or how our positions changed, but my back is to Jace's hard chest now. The music is fast yet *just* the vibe needed for me to grind against him. My pussy clenches around nothing as Jace hardens behind me. If you were wondering—the answer is yes. It's huge. My breathing quickens as he grips my hips, grinding into me in tandem with my dancing.

His hands roam freely against my body, sending goosebumps and chills all over me. As I grind deeper against him, I throw an arm over his shoulder, pulling him closer.

Jace chuckles softly, almost inaudibly as he holds me against him, his hands on my stomach. My smile is lazy as he cups my chin, tilting my head up to his, melting his lips against mine.

I gasp as he kisses me, but he doesn't hold back. Taking it as an opening, he inches his tongue inside. Like muscle memory, I kiss back, my mouth moving against his as if to say *welcome home, we missed you.* It's sloppy, and sexy, and everything I could've ever pictured a kiss in this environment would be.

In a room where I don't know anyone, grinding against one another, we make out. I twist to fully face and give him my all. When his large hand grasps my ass possessively, I smile into the kiss.

Here, at this party, I can be free with a guy who I like way too much for my own good.

Jace may think that I don't trust him, and in a way, I don't. I don't trust him not to leave me when he's scared like I did to him two years ago. I don't trust him to not leave me alone after he's done with me like my parents had, and I know that this isn't something that I should put on him. I'm trying my hardest not to. But here, at this party, I can trust and be free with him because no one knows us.

They don't know our past or our present.

I'm scared of the fact that I may just still be in love with this man from my past. I'm scared that Cleo will find out and then want nothing to do with me because of this thing between him and I. I can't lose her, but I want nothing more than to lose myself in him.

To be with him.

And that fact alone scares me the most.

It's been two years since we've tangled ourselves deeply in one another's web, and over a decade of me pining after the blond boy from around the corner.

I want Jace Heart, but what would that mean for my sanity?

Jace kisses me again, softly this time before resting his head against my own. He clears his throat. "I want you more than anything, but I much rather you when you're sober."

Wait no! Don't stop the sexy kissing time...

Did I say that in my head or out loud?

Jace's answering chuckle has my eyes widening, Oh my goodness...I said it out loud.

"You're saying everything out loud, Sienna." He grins, kissing my forehead tenderly. "Now let's go do what we originally came here to do."

He doesn't have to tell me twice, I didn't watch YouTube videos on how to do a keg stand for nothing. After an extensive bit of research, I'm pretty sure that a keg will hate to see me coming.

I'm going to be the keg stand queen.

Jace looks me up and down, eyes assessing before he digs in his pocket, pulling out a crumbled lump of grey material.

"What's this?" I ask, crooking my neck at the glob as he smiles.

"Shorts...if you think I'm letting you do a keg stand in a dress, you're mistaken." He chuckles, handing them to me.

I roll my eyes as I take them, putting them on right then and there. I feel like Captain freaking Underpants, standing in front of him with a large pair of grey basketball shorts over my cute sparkly dress, but I digress.

Jace leads me through the house confidently, as if he's been here before, and guides me straight to the backyard where a group of people stand around, talking and drinking. The backyard is smaller than I would've thought, but it may just be because there's people crowding the space with two beer pong tables.

Jace grimaces as we stand in front of our mission, looking ever the skeptical man as I beam at it, smiling from ear to ear.

"Are you ready?"

Rolling my eyes, I put my hands on my hips.

"Baby, I was *born* ready."

TWENTY

Jace

Sienna Jones was not in fact "born ready", after her fourth attempt at doing the keg herself, successfully shooting beer up her nose. I pull her away from the keg, trying to mask my laughter.

The frustrated pink haired girl pouts as she's successfully taken away from the large barrel.

"Wait! The videos said that I need to do it like this!" she exclaims, her pout deepening as I roll my lips in trying hard not to laugh in her face—and failing.

"Babe it's a keg, not open heart surgery." I laugh as she glares at me.

Sienna huffs, her small body turning in an instant to face the monster of a keg next to us.

"I don't need your stupid help, anyways! I am a powerful queen..." she says, slurring her words as she positions herself in a perfect handstand once again, doing the exact same thing that resulted in her getting a shot of beer up her nostrils.

Chuckling quietly, knowing that laughing will only hurt her feelings more, I take a step back.

Sienna's handstand is flawless thanks to her years of gymnastics as a kid. I grimace, thinking of the summer she convinced Ryan and I to do it with her.

I can still remember the leotard wedgies we had...*Eugh.*

She's positioned in a perfectly straight handstand, but the longer she stays like that, the more she shakes on the keg.

This is not how you do a keg stand...not in the slightest.

Crouching to where her face is, I smirk up at her as she groans, "Need help?"

"Fuck...off," she replies shakily, getting more beer in her nose this time around, her legs begin to teeter in the air and I'm on my feet in an instant, holding them steady and pulling them to an angle so she doesn't drown herself.

In seconds, a crowd forms, cheering her on as she does the keg stand like a champ, chugging it. By the time she's done, there's people cheering for her and someone has gotten her a paper towel.

"Girl, you did that!" some random girl shouts as I escort her back into the house, parking her in the kitchen.

"More drinks *puh-lease*!" she shouts from next to me, I flinch as I hoist her up onto the kitchen island by her waist. I know my way around the Omega house after spending a considerable amount of time here, gaming with some of the guys who live here.

"Stay here," I command the girl, and she grins up at me, a flame sparking beneath her hazel eyes as she salutes me.

"Yes, sir." She nods sassily, making my cheeks warm as I leave her on the island to find some more napkins and liquor for her.

I promised myself, and her, that I would be sober. And after only taking a single shot almost an hour ago, I'm sober as hell. My only job tonight is to make sure my girl has fun and is taken care of.

A loud drill song plays as I'm looking through the different liquor bottles for something that won't mix badly with the liquor already in her system when a familiar giggle rings through my ears.

It's Sienna's.

What could she possibly be laughing—

A tall, brown-skinned guy stands in front of Sienna, towering over her. Her and I aren't officially together. No matter how much I "manifest" it, we haven't made anything official.

So why does my heart feel like it's about to be ripped out at the sight of another guy *talking* to her? Anger courses through my veins as the dickhead caresses her face gently, and I'm not thinking as I make my way over, her drink in hand.

"My boyfriend is not gonna *yike* that..." she slurs, loud enough for me to hear, warming my heart and heightening my anger as the asshole responds, "I don't see him around," shrugging carelessly.

Don't do it.

Don't do it...

Don't hit him.

He places a hand on her bare thigh, and Sienna flinches, trying to slip away, but he grips her tighter.

In less than a second, he's on the ground and my knuckles burn from sucker punching the asshole. The burn of the punch sends a smile to my face. It was well deserved, but did you *hear* what she said?

Sienna just called me her *boyfriend!* I need to get that printed and hung up somewhere.

On this day, Sienna Sola Jones, publicly announced to a stupid ass guy at a party that Jace Eros Heart is the love of her life.

Maybe I can get that printed at CVS or something...

Sienna's eyes are bright and wide as I slide the last shot of the night to her. I watch as she quickly downs it and holds her arms up for me. In an instant, my hands are on her waist, picking her up off the counter and placing her heel clad feet back on the ground.

"That was a good one, Jacey...Take me home?" she asks lazily, slurring a bit as she pats my cheek softly.

Chuckling lightly at her, I hold her hand, kissing the palm. "With pleasure."

Sienna steps over the guy on the ground, who's still clutching his face as I follow behind her.

This girl is making me insane...in less than a month, I've punched two guys on her behalf and feel zero remorse about it. For Sienna, I'd walk through the pits of Hell just to see her smile. Punching an asshole at a party is nothing.

By the time we're safely in the car and on the way to my apartment, I realize Sienna is asleep, her head at a weird angle where her neck looks like it'd been snapped as she lets out soft snores.

When I get to a red light, I immediately turn on her seat warmer to combat the short dress she'd been wearing in fifty degree weather. It'd been warmer when we left, but the chilly fall night is now upon us. Leaning over, I try to position her differently to prevent her neck from hurting as she shifts.

Our noses are practically touching, my skin heating around my cheeks and neck as she blows out a mint and alcohol flavored breath.

She looks so peaceful when she sleeps. Her nose twitches just a bit, and soon enough she's changing her position, cuddling her knees in the seat.

Careful to not wake her, I chuckle softly and begin driving when the light changes.

It takes little to no time for me to get Sienna out of the car without waking her, considering she's a pretty heavy sleeper. I carry her bridal style from the car to the top floor where the loft is located, making sure not to bump her against anything. Sienna only shifts once in my arms, her breathing changing as she adjusts herself before she's out like a light once again.

Carefully, I take off her shoes and place them down on the rack next to the door that she always ignores. Sienna may be the biggest perfectionist in the world, but she *never* puts her shoes on the rack. I like to keep everything neat. No mess, no bugs.

I may be an artist and a hockey player, but the thought of messiness makes my skin crawl.

As I carry Sienna up the stairs of the loft, I grimace as I realize what she has on. She'd taken off the gym shorts when when we got to the car, leaving only the sparkly dress on. There's no way in this world she'd be comfortable sleeping in this dress, but there's also no way in hell that I'd take off her clothes while she's asleep and drunk.

This isn't that kind of party.

I cringe as I lay her down on the bed in her outside clothes. *She's going to be so uncomfortable.* I plant a soft kiss on Sienna's forehead before going into the bathroom. Picking up the supplies I'd bought yesterday after practice, I make my way back out to the bedroom with a large purple bonnet, makeup remover, a wash cloth, and face wash.

I'm careful as I lift Sienna's head, cradling it in my lap. When we were kids, her and Cleo taught me how to braid their hair as a way to get me to stop bothering them all the time. Her hair is soft as I gather it in my hands, separating it into two sections to braid, mindful to not comb out her curls with my fingers.

It takes almost ten minutes to braid two plaits in her hair without waking her, but I do it successfully and put the purple bonnet I'd bought yesterday on her head to protect her hair as she sleeps.

She looks like an adorable, sparkly mushroom with her matching light purple dress. Softly, I kiss her temple and then get to work on her face, gently taking off her makeup and wiping her face down with a wet washcloth with cleanser on it.

By the time I'm done pampering her for bed, twenty minutes have passed. It doesn't take any time for me to shower and throw on an SFU hoodie and sweats. I'm careful as I slide in the bed beside her and sigh as I make myself comfortable. Sienna breathes heavily, deep in sleep. A singular curl pokes out of her bonnet, framing her sleeping face and my chest tightens.

She's a work of art, whether awake or asleep, Sienna's beauty is captivating, my fingers itch to draw. They itch to hold a pencil and capture this woman in all of her essence. Setting her in this moment on a blank page.

Sienna has been my muse all of my life. I've filled pages and pages of sketchbooks with her face and silhouette, but never have I been able to capture her asleep. In this state, she's comfortable and trusting. It's an honor for someone to feel safe enough to sleep around you, and she is out *like a light*.

Carefully, I crawl out of the bed and stalk towards the trunk at the foot of it where I keep all of my sketchbooks and supplies. When I turn back around to the bed, Sienna has shifted. Her body, once cuddled into itself, is now splayed across the bed and she's gripping the cover tightly in one hand.

I smile at the image of her under the paintings I'd created in honor of her hanging on the wall.

I don't think she noticed the angel wings above my bed or the ballerina silhouette when she'd first come over, but they're there.

Sliding back into my spot next to her, I flip to a new page in my book and begin sketching.

TWENTY-ONE

Sienna

I BLINK HARD AS sunlight beams down on my face, temporarily blinding me.

Sunlight?

Groaning, I roll out my neck and stretch letting out a loud sigh as my muscles loosen and I roll around my bed, the smell of vanilla and leather engulfing me.

Wait...

Vanilla and leather?

I come to an abrupt stop in my rolling and open my eyes. A scream ripples from my throat at my unfamiliar surroundings before another scream drowns it out.

Jace comes running up the stairs into the loft, shirtless with grey sweatpants hanging loosely off his waist, wearing a hockey helmet and defensively holding a hockey stick.

"Why are we screaming?!" he yells before pausing, taking me in from the way I clutch the blanket to my frightened expression. When his eyes linger on my hand a little longer, brow furrowing, I realize one crucial thing.

I'm *naked*.

The scream that rips from my throat is instant, "Why am I naked?!"

"You're naked?!" he asks, pulling off the helmet. "Can I see?"

Scoffing, I hike the cover up higher. "*Why* am I naked Jace?!"

He sighs, putting the helmet and stick down, "I don't know! You had on that cute little dress when I put you to bed... Look at this by the way." He grins, jogging over to the bed, uncaring of me being in my underwear as he plops down beside me, shoving his phone in my face.

I gape in horror at the screen.

Jace's lockscreen is an image of me, obviously from last night, knocked out with my mouth ajar and spread across the bed wildly. A purple bonnet covers my hair and my makeup is off except for a smudging of mascara near my eyes. I cringe, noting the small amount of drool near my mouth and look away from the phone.

He put me to sleep?

That doesn't explain how I...Oh!

Images of me getting up from the bed and stripping down to my underwear before crawling back in next to him flashes in my mind as my cheeks warm.

So maybe I stripped out of my clothes while we were asleep...Big whoop...

Jace sighs, pursing his lips as he stalks away from me around the room before tossing something at my head. I grimace as I peel the blue SFU hoodie away from my face. "If this is your way of getting me in your clothes, you could've asked nicely."

"Trust me, I want nothing more than for you to be naked in my bed...but I also have breakfast on the stove right now, so..."

At the mention of food, my stomach growls and my sense of smells heighten. The smell of something sweet and savory makes my stomach growl even louder. In an instant, the hoodie Jace had thrown at me is over my head and I'm following him down the stairs to the kitchen. The hoodie is warm against my skin and huge, with its material stopping just above my thigh.

Sitting on the kitchen island, facing Jace while he cooks, I admire him. His back muscles flex as he whisks something in a bowl, humming a tune that I can't place.

The air in the loft this morning is peaceful and calming, a complete contrast to the man before me.

"Now, I'll be so honest with you right now...This might taste like shit." He chuckles, still facing the stove as he pours a liquid into a pan, the pan sizzling lowly.

"Derek usually cooks and meal preps for us at the house, and since I live there more than here, I never have to cook," he says, smiling as he turns to face me, a hint of powder on his nose and hands.

I scrunch my nose.

Derek?

Derek *Perez?*

He must sense my confusion, because without thought, he elaborates.

"He's the guy who took you home after the football game."

I scowl immediately. I don't *hate* Derek, but I don't like him, either. He's never given me a reason to like him, especially with him not being active in Delilah's life.

Jace continues speaking, clearly unaware of my thoughts as he turns back to the stove. "He's one of the kindest people I know. Without Derek, a lot of us on the team would be lost. He helped Blake last year with his issues and always gave me a shoulder to yap on. His daughter's like my niece now, too. You taught her dance class...Delilah Perez."

I can hear the fondness and smile in his tone even though he's not facing me.

"I would've thought that you'd be interested in him since he's someone you'd go for."

At this, my nose crinkles, disgust flaring in my gut.

"Annoying and an asshole?"

"Nah, kind and nurturing. Your personalities are very similar, and I think you'd probably be friends. Derek's been raising Deli solo since he was seventeen, and has been raising us hockey heads for three years now. If anything ever happens to me, I want you to know that you can trust him to be a good friend."

I allow his words to resonate with me for a minute. Did I have it all wrong about the douchebag? Or is Jace only saying this because they're friends? I *know* what I saw *and* heard, but what if I was wrong to immediately assume Derek is a bad parent?

Jace twists around, a bright smile decorating his handsome face as he holds out a fork with a fluffy, fried dough on it to my face.

"Taste," he says, eyes dancing with intrigue as he holds the food to my mouth.

My eyes remain locked with his as I lean forward. I've never been fed by a man before, and as my lips coat the fork, Jace's eyes darken. I decide to play with my meal, slowly pulling the dough away with my teeth. I watch as he gulps, watching me intently.

As the flavors of the dough begin to settle in my mouth, my chewing falters. Rather than being the sweet pancake that I *thought* it would be, it's salty. I grimace as I swallow the piece of food.

"So?"

"Stick to painting." I grin, curling my lips to not burst out in laughter as Jace's smile drops and he flicks my forehead.

After deciding that we'd be better off ordering breakfast, Jace places an order for delivery from Doug's Diner. We sit in the living room eating our breakfast and watching movies.

My leg rests casually across Jace's lap as I eat my chocolate chip pancakes and scroll aimlessly on my phone. The silence between us is comfortable, almost like we both know that as soon as we talk, our comfortability will be broken, but that doesn't stop the blabbermouth beside me from speaking.

"We need a game plan," he tells me without preamble, sliding in closer to me so now my thighs are over his lap as I shove another pancake into my mouth, nodding for him to continue.

"Your list—I mean, today, we're doing nothing. But if we want to get everything on that list done, we need a schedule, especially with the hockey season starting back up next month."

The thought of winter sports quickly approaching leads my mind back to the Winter Showcase. I haven't seen or heard from Daisy all weekend, but I know that I can't afford to miss any more practices.

"I thought we had a plan? You and I meet weekly to get the list done, I don't work at the studio until we finish?" My words come out more like a question as I lean to put my plate down on the coffee table. I'm about to move my legs from their spot on Jace's lap, but his tightening grip on my thigh halts me in my tracks.

"We do, but what about my hockey games?" his voice is a bit softer as he asks this, a small pout to his lips as his gaze remains locked on the forgotten movie playing on the TV.

So that's what this is about...He wants me to be there for him. A small smile dusts my lips as I lean forward, grabbing his chin and tilting his gaze to me.

"I'll be there for you, Jace. I promise."

His eyes roam over my face, softening as his shoulders slacken a bit. All of my feelings over the past ten years crash over me like a tidal wave as he looks at me like *that*. I gulp as he licks his lips, leaning forward to rest his forehead on mine, our breaths syncing up with one another like we were *made* for each other.

"That's all I wanted to hear, angel..." His words are soft, tugging at my heartstrings. I allow myself to fall down the rabbit hole of them, closing my eyes as he places a gentle kiss to my forehead, his warmth remaining stamped against my skin.

Jace Heart, what are you doing to me?

"Now! Let's talk about Fall Fest."

That snaps me out of my softened mood. He immediately gives me a run-down of the three day fall centered event here on campus. Since we're keeping whatever *this* is between us a secret, we have to be extra careful with how we go about doing the event. There's no need for us to get caught with our pants down if we can help it.

After deciding on a meet up spot, a few activities to do, and my list, we start a new TV series together about a hidden queen in a school for assassins.

We're just about to start the third episode when both of our phones go off simultaneously, his ringing with a call, and mine a text.

Cleo

Where you at girl?

I'm thinking we make bows and donuts tonight

Oooh or we could watch the new F1 docuseries

Eren looked so hot in the teaser omgggg!!!!!!!!!!!

Guilt immediately trickles down my spine as I respond to my cousin, lying through my teeth as Jace gets up to answer his call—most likely from his mom.

Me

At practice, can't tonight </3

I watch as Jace goes, still shirtless because apparently wearing shirts is illegal in the Heart household. My eyes track his movements as thoughts of his entire body plagues my mind. His hands are probably my favorite feature—besides his face, of course. They're muscular—if that makes sense—with thick veins and long, slender fingers. Those are the hands of someone skilled whether with a hockey stick, paint brush, or in the bedroom.

When Jace returns back to the couch, he looks dazed, his sketchbook and pencils in hand, and I already know that the conversation wasn't one that he wanted to have.

"Tough talk—" My phone dings again. Thinking it's from Cleo, I immediately open it only to frown when I realize it's not.

Daisy

We have shit to do

Monday night, no games, and no dicks.

TWENTY-TWO

Jace

"Cupid…Where do babies come from?" I'm blinded by a mess of dark brown curls, a neon pink face, and large innocent brown eyes as Delilah stares into the depths of my soul—you know the *exact* look that I'm talking about, too. If you're around kids, that is.

I don't get paid enough for this.

"Buttholes? I don't know, kid." I chuckle weakly as she huffs, folding her tiny arms over herself. I mask my smile as Delilah's light yellow princess crown tilts on her head when she plops down next to me on the couch.

Tonight, I'm on little sunshine—also known as mayhem in a child's body—duty. Hanging with Delilah always brings me a sense of warmth…and confusion. Because even though she's only four-years-old, she's more progressed than most kids her age and asks the craziest things.

"When will you get a girlfriend? I think Uncle Lake has one…" Delilah whispers to me as if we're sharing the greatest secret known to man.

Reeling back, I cock my neck at the nosey four-year-old, gently plucking her forehead. Sighing, I pull her into my lap.

"When you can successfully count to fifty." I chuckle, tickling her. But as she giggles and laughs at me, my mind wanders elsewhere.

Sienna.

Her smile, the way she lights up a room without even noticing.

Everything about her is beautiful.

I know that I claim and say that she's mine, but I wonder if she actually believes that. How can I *show* her that she is?

As Delilah calms down and my thoughts continue to spiral, my hand itches to paint. I've got to get whatever this is out of my system before I start to overthink my every life's decisions.

Derek's in the kitchen, presumably making salmon alfredo—his usual. Groaning, I run a hand through my hair. I'm tired of salmon fucking alfredo, give me a burger or something, I beg.

Thinking about my situation with Sienna is making me crazy. I don't even understand why we're keeping this a secret—I mean *I do*, but I don't at the same time. Cleo tends to overreact...a lot, but would it truly be the worst thing in the world if Sienna and I dated?

After taking off my cow print face mask and washing Delilah's face off, I find myself sketching while the toddler watches cartoons.

My hands move on their own volition, sketching and drawing to their heart's content, and I don't even realize what I'm drawing until my phone rings. The sound snatches me back to reality and my heart stutters.

Sienna stares back at me on the page. Her smiling, dancing, everything. The page is filled with sketches of her in every state, whether it's happiness or sadness. Her beauty is something that philosophers preach about and study to grasp. She's ethereal and unreal. The face that artists dream about—I know I do.

Another loud ring of my phone has Delilah cutting a sharp glare my way and me answering it blindly as I smile at her.

"Why haven't you been answering my calls, dude? I called you ten times this week." My brother Jackson's voice is agitated as the line comes through.

I sigh, messing up my hair as I run a hand through it.

"There's this thing called *do not disturb*, Jackie. I think the name is pretty self-explanatory," I whisper as I double check that Delilah is okay before heading to the foyer to continue this conversation.

My older brother Jackson is the kind of guy you don't want to piss off, but has no qualms about annoying the rest of society. I have no idea how my sister-in-law, Corinne, puts up with his annoying ass. Everyone likes to think that the youngest siblings are the annoying ones, but no one pays attention to the irritation that is known as the oldest child.

Jackson huffs on his side of the line, clearly unamused with me. "Mom told me that you're not being serious about this whole marriage thing, munch—"

I roll my eyes at the use of his childhood nickname for me, 'munch', short for munchkin. Fucking stupid, if you ask me. Heaving a sigh from the deepest crevice of my stomach, I roll my head up to the sky.

"I'll tell you the same thing that I told Mommy dearest...I'm *nineteen*! As in one nine—nineteen. I'll get married off the day that Asa decides to date anyone other than his computer and the company's stocks. Until then, get off my back."

Jackson doesn't respond immediately, allowing me to stew in my anger for a second too long before he lets out a sigh.

"This family will be the death of me...Just know Mom is on *all* of our asses to get you to start dating. Don't shoot the messenger, munch." He chuckles heartily as I groan.

My mother is up to something, I know it. There's a gnawing feeling at the back of my head whenever she calls me. Whatever my mom has planned, I hope she knows that I have something even better already in store...If I can understand how Sienna truly feels for me, that is.

By the time Jackson and I finish our conversation, I realize that Blake's home, talking with Derek in the kitchen after being out late. Charlie, Braxton, and Alec all get to the house a little later and we all eat dinner together before shifting to the living room to play some games.

Charlie, Braxton, and Derek—all assholes who don't live in this house—have the time of their lives playing a game against some other user while Alec plays with Deli. I'm sketching in my notebook yet again when a body plops down next to me, a beer outstretched for me.

Blake raises a brow as I eye him and the silent offering of beer. He'd had a bottle of water with him for himself. Taking the beer, I place it on the table in front of me as he gets comfortable next to me.

"You're drawing?"

I look up from my work momentarily to eye him. "That's usually what people do when they have a sketchbook open," I say jokingly as he purses his lips, smacking me upside my head.

"Well duh, asshole. I mean you're *actually* drawing and not just doodling. Is it a girl?" he asks, his nosiness getting the best of him as he tries to look over my shoulder at the unfinished work. Clutching the sketchbook to my chest, I glare at him.

Why does everything have to be linked back to dating or a girl—I mean Sienna *is* the reason that I picked my pencil back up—but still. A guy can't just sketch the woman he's been in love with his whole life without everything being about her?

"Pshh... no," I scoff unconvincingly as he smirks, his eyes widening.

Oh please, no...

"It's a girl!" the asshole shouts, jumping up off the couch, snagging the attention of the guys and Delilah.

"Congratulations?" Charlie chirps, receiving a laugh from Braxton as Delilah claps and Derek furrows his brow. These reactions don't deter Blake's excitement in the least. Instead, he starts dancing as if he won the lottery.

"You *like* someone!" he cheers. "I know who, too!"

My heart proceeds to plummet to the lowest pit of Hell. Sienna and I have been nothing but secretive this entire time. I haven't even been *around* her with Blake present besides at the football game.

"I don't think you do—"

"Oh, I do! I mean it's kinda weird for you to be blond and like blondes, but–"

Oh for the love of God.

I'm going to need a forklift to pick up my jaw from the ground. I don't even need Blake to finish his sentence. Matter of fact, I don't want to hear the rest. The guys start hooting and hollering, all now aware of our conversation as I flip them off, grabbing my art supplies with me.

"Don't be such a P-U-S-S-Y, bro!" Braxton jeers, and I make sure to emphasize my lifted pinky finger as I leave the room, the sound of my friends laughter mocking me the entire walk to my bedroom.

When I enter my room and flicker on the lights, my eyes snag on Sienna's list on the desk and then on the old Halloween mask from last year hanging up on my wall. A small thought expands in the back of my mind as I look at the items, and I know just what I'll use them for.

TWENTY-THREE

Sienna

"AND THIS, CLASS, IS what I'd like to call one of the most engaging works of art in all of history, the *Mona Lisa*. The *Mona Lisa*..." My History of Modern Art professor drones on about the *Mona Lisa*'s significance, giving us all the details in the world about one of da Vinci's most esteemed works.

I try to focus and listen to everything he says, but it all goes in one ear and out the other. Class proceeds like this for two more hours, with him talking and me trying to remember what he's saying to me.

I don't really know enough people in this course to ask anyone for help, and my stupid pride won't even let the thought of asking for help linger in my brain.

"Can anyone name the artist behind this painting right here?" he asks, holding up a familiar painting. I squint my eyes to focus on the work ahead, raising my hand with all of the confidence in the world as I'm called on.

The painting depicts a man lying dead in a bathtub. From the few times my nanny Elaine would take me to Paris, she'd always gush about this painting whenever we'd go to the Louvre, even though the real one's not there.

"John Singleton-Copley?"

My professor purses his lips, running a hand through his greying hair, and there goes my confidence.

"No, you're about twelve years too early and in the wrong art style. The correct answer is Jacques-Louis David. Everyone, your homework will be due Sunday at 11:59..."

I cringe, ducking into myself as he continues on with his lecture. My grade in this class isn't horrible, but a C isn't great either, for crying out loud.

Don't you know anything, Sienna? How do you expect to ace a class when you can't remember an innocent detail like that?

I tug my bottom lip between my teeth, caving into myself as class continues on. Once Professor Hewin dismisses us, I'm one of the first people out of the door.

The air is a lot crispier than it has been these past few weeks, making me thankful that I wore a hoodie and leggings today instead of my usual wear. Parking myself by the large oak tree in the quad, I sigh as my butt hits its root.

That was so embarrassing...

Sighing, I fold my arms over my knees and rest my head on top of them. I know that honest mistakes happen and that I don't have to be the best at everything, but a part of me believes that I do. I need to be the best. I have to have my shit together. I have to be the greatest because at the end of the day, I'm the only person in my corner.

I'm rooting for *myself.*

Getting things wrong, not being perfect—it's like letting myself down.

I made my list to be able to free myself and let loose, but even with that, I feel like I'm doing myself a disservice if it's not perfect.

My body shakes as I try to compose myself, counting down from ten.

I'm *okay.*

I'm okay.

I'm okay.

Everything's fine.

Chills run up my spine as something brushes against my fingertips, and just as I'm about to freak out, my eyes land on a large pair of black and gold orbs. I blink, adjusting my focus on the orange and white cat staring into my soul.

"Hi...What're you doing here?" I coo, petting behind the cat's ear. When it purrs and leans into my touch, I grin.

His fur is dirty with little pebbles sticking out of it like he rolled in the rubble outside.

Hmm...I like the sound of that.

"I'm going to name you Rubble..." I smile, petting the top of the cat's head gently.

"You're a cute little guy but...Are you a little guy?" I ask the cat, chuckling lightly as it meows. I've never thought about owning a cat, but the cat distribution system just dropped one into my hands, so how can I refuse this one?

Rubble purrs as I hit a soft spot behind their ear, and they nuzzle their fur into my skin.

"I knew an angel came crashing down in front of me, I just didn't know she was this beautiful." Jace's all too familiar voice is loud, breaking Rubble and I's silent meeting as the cat flees away.

I groan, watching them leave, hoping to see them again before I look up at the man sidling up to me.

"You scared Rubble away," I tut, dragging my knees back up to my chest with a pout.

"Rubble?" Jace's amused tone has me scowling at him as I fiddle with the hem of my pants.

"Is there something that you wanted? Or did you just want to bother me?" I ask, my tone harsher than I'd intended.

Shit.

I wish that I didn't know Jace or watch him so intently, because then I wouldn't see it—the small flinch and wavering of his smile.

Jace chuckles unamused as he shakes his head. "Nope. I'll leave you to your cat business."

"Jace, no. I—"

He doesn't give me the time to apologize for my harshness, and instead leaves me to stew in my silent pity party.

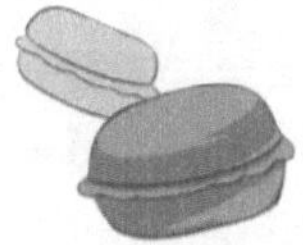

"Let's take a...break..." I say in between breaths, dragging my limbs over to my dance bag as Daisy nods, in the same state as me.

Sweat glistens on our foreheads, our chests heaving as we take seats against the mirrored wall of the dance studio next to our bags.

Daisy hands me a spare bottle of the pink liquid electrolytes that she always has, and I down it in one go, throwing my head back with a deep breath. My actions of the day still loom over my head even now, three hours later, at dance practice.

Daisy takes a careful sip of her drink, unlike me, and pauses the music on our Bluetooth.

"So..." she says, taking out her loose bun, running a hand through her waves.

"So?" I muse, my gaze locked on the missing panel in the ceiling. *Has that always been gone? Why have I only just now noticed that?* I take a sip of the flavored drink.

"Is that guy your boyfriend or is the other guy?"

I choke. My neck snaps to Daisy, eyebrows furrowed and mouth ajar.

What man? And who is this other guy she's talking about? Aric?

"Who–"

"The blond," she says with a shrug, cutting me off. My skin heats from the mention of Jace before instantly chilling as I remember how I treated him earlier. My mind looms over the thought of Jace and I being together, but then I recall the rest of Daisy's sentence.

Or the other guy?

"Wait...What other guy?" I ask as she takes a swig of her drink, shrugging.

"No one..."

That's not odd at all.

I eye her suspiciously once more and decide to ignore her probing. We've got a dance to complete and not enough time to do so. With our project for Winter Showcase being a dance, we have to create a portfolio and essay on how we came up with the choreography, the theme, and what artist inspired us. So far, we've completed about 40% of the written work, but with midterms peeking around the corner, we need to get in all the work that we can.

Daisy and I spend another hour working on our dance, but something feels off. I can feel her watching me, staring at me. And whenever I do something, she raises a brow at me before doing the same thing.

I don't know, maybe I'm tripping, but something is off.

All of today is.

When I get back home, it seems that everyone has had a shitty day, my cousin included. Cleo, my dearest friend and closest cousin, broke me as she cried and told Georgia, Denver, and I about what *really* happened at her old school.

She'd caught her ex-boyfriend, Marcelo, doing steroids and when she'd told him she'd speak up about it...He threatened her with revenge porn. That douchebag of an ex of hers is going to pay one of these days, and I'll be the one to make him pay.

Georgia, Denver, and I comfort her as best as we can. We listen to music to cheer her up, dance and drink a little until she finally decides to break and join us.

I want to feel happy that she's starting to let loose, but I can't. The mess that was my day still plagues the back of my mind, and all I want to do is release that energy. I feel like a bunch of nerves just bottled up, ready to explode at any moment—on anyone.

When the doorbell rings while Georgia and Denver sing their horrid duet, I feel like my prayers have been answered as Jake—the guy who Cleo has a crush on, stands on the other side of the door.

The two of them look like little puppies in love, and the rest of us know our time here is up when he pulls out a box of LEGOs for the two of them. As soon as Cleo has successfully ditched us, I make my escape.

Georgia and Denver pay me no mind as I leave the apartment, the feeling of happiness slowly washing over me. I immediately feel bad as I sit in my car and stare up at the apartment. From here, I can see Georgia and Denver laughing and drinking on the balcony—obviously in a good mood. I'd be the worst friend in the world if I went back up there in the mood that I'm in right now and brought them down.

Chewing on my lip, I note the time.

6:12 p.m.

Everyone at the studio should be gone since we closed early today...I could always go there. I mean, I have keys to the studio and no one else is going to just show up out of the blue.

Making a hasty decision, I put the car in drive and head to the one place that I can let out all of my negative emotions.

TWENTY-FOUR

Sienna

JUST AS I SUSPECTED, the lot for the studio is empty when I arrive. I waste no time, running to the trunk of my car and retrieving the one item that helps me when I want to relieve some stress through dance.

My dance heels.

I grin as I run my fingers over the leather and mesh material of the shoe, practically running into the studio. Something tugs me to Studio F, and soon enough, I'm getting myself set up in the room that I'd first saw Jace in again.

The air is a lot crisper and cleaner in the studio. It'd obviously been thoroughly cleaned and mopped, and I wouldn't be surprised if Jace, himself, cleaned it. He's a bit of a neat freak.

Hooking up my phone to the Bluetooth speaker in the room, I turn it on *do not disturb* and lace up my heels, allowing myself to be consumed by the sultry music.

No one else knows that I do heels dancing when I'm overwhelmed or that I play video games when I'm irritated, but it's what makes me feel free.

I stretch as I allow the music to consume me. The soft melody of the R&B song is all that I need to let go. I lose myself in my dancing, in the freedom of my movement. Though the dance is a little on the risqué side, I don't care as I freestyle.

I spin and flip and grind without a thought in the world, and as the song changes to one that I'm all too familiar with, I grin as I fully give myself to the music.

My body moves on its own accord, thrusting and touching itself seductively as I dance. I don't care who I am, who my parents are, or how shitty my situation could be as I dance.

In this room, I'm just Sienna.

A girl and her dance floor.

As I bend over slowly, my hands trailing down my thighs, a flicker of movement in the doorway catches my attention and halts me in my tracks.

Jace leans against the doorway, his eyes hooded as he watches me, his arms folded across his chest.

My heart stutters, chest heaving as I slowly rise. The skin on my naked arms pebble with goosebumps as Jace's eyes rake up and down my body. I'd only worn a sports bra and leggings to my practice with Daisy earlier, and haven't changed since.

"Oh don't let me stop you, angel. The show was just about to get good." Jace smirks, straightening up as I do the same, mimicking his actions.

"Show's over," I mumble, turning away from him to look back at myself in the mirror. Through the mirror, I watch as he strides towards me, his walk precise and absolute as he comes up behind me. Jace grabs my arm lightly and turns me to face him. My breathing quickens as I look up at the man, my panties dampening as he looks down at me. His gaze darkening as he clenches his jaw.

"Do you not know how to use a phone, Jones?"

I'm taken aback by his question as he laughs humorlessly. "I was worried sick about you. You had an attitude earlier and I left you with it—that was my fault. But then when Georgia called me, asking if you were staying with me tonight since you left without telling anyone—I freaked the fuck out."

My pulse quickens as his voice lowers. I can feel the rapid beating of his heart against my chest as he steps closer, his large hands settling at the small of my back as he leans down.

"Well, you found me." I breathe my words like a forbidden secret as I bite my bottom lip. His eyes track the movement like a lion on the hunt for its prey.

We hold each other in the palm of one another's hands, tempting the other to make the first move.

To do something.

Anything.

My eyes trail to his mouth slowly. He sees the opportunity, takes it, and runs.

Jace's lips crash against mine so feverishly and harshly, that I hold my breath as one of his large hands circles to the nape of my neck, the other snaking completely around my waist, melting me into him.

I'm his to take as he devours my mouth. Touching. Tasting. Biting. I moan in his mouth as he deepens the kiss. His hand on the small of my back travels further south and grips my ass. I sigh against him, my stomach fluttering from the action as he groans.

Fuck. This was not how I thought tonight would end, but I'm not complaining as Jace backs me into the mirrored wall behind us.

His hands roam everywhere, slowly and tauntingly as if he has all the time in the world. And when he reaches the bare skin just under my sports bra, he pauses.

Green eyes search my hazel ones, as if asking for permission. When I nod, he goes to touch me before pausing once again, "Are you sure?"

"I want you to touch me, Jace. Make me feel good."

His eyes darken to that of a forest green as he takes me in his mouth again, kissing my lips with the hunger of a man starved. Jace savors me deeply, his palm kneading my breast, and when I moan, he grins.

The little psycho is having a field day with me, and I want him to go further, to touch me everywhere right here, right now.

"Fuck, sweetheart, you're so beautiful," he curses, looking me over in the mirror and then back down at my physical self in front of him. He bites his lip, a hint of a smirk playing at his lips. "How flexible are you?"

"Don't play with me." I chuckle breathlessly as he kisses me again, lifting my left leg over his hip. I take it upon myself to jump, and soon enough, he's holding the swell of my ass against the mirror, kissing me breathlessly.

Jace's lips travel from mine, sucking and pressing deep licks and kisses to my neck. I moan loudly as the combination of him playing with my hardened nipples against my bra and him sucking the spot under my right ear combine.

His hand grips my ass tightly and my breath hitches. Jace pauses, leaning back to gauge me.

"Do you want to st—"

I blink hard. *NO! Absolutely not.*

"Don't stop. I'm not saying fuck my brains out...Not yet at least but—"

"Sienna, I'm not taking you in a dance studio—" He looks at me with pure bewilderment, still holding me as if I weigh nothing as I cut him off.

"But I *do* want you to touch me."

We share a look and say so much to one another without any words. The next kiss that Jace steals from my lips is soft. He sets my legs down on the ground gently, although it's hard due to them being wobbly.

Is he about to stop? I think before I'm smoothly corrected as his hand snakes up between my chest and my neck, gripping it firmly like the perfect necklace.

"You gonna stop playing around or are you too pussy to do what you want?" I ask, my eyes dazzling as I grin up at the man, holding my neck like a vice. Jace leans in close to me, our noses bumping.

"I like to play with my food before I feast, angel."

My breath catches as his other hand slowly travels to my pants, leaving goosebumps in their wake before they enter my underwear.

I've never been touched like this by anyone other than myself before. I don't know how to react or what to say, but when his darkened gaze rests upon mine, I relax as he circles my clit.

"Jace..." I breathe out as a single finger enters me, pumping in and out slowly.

"What were you saying earlier, hmm?" He smirks, his lips ghosting over my own teasingly as my breath quickens.

"That's a lot of talk for someone not...eating me out." I breathe deeply as he groans.

"It's hot when you talk like that." He kisses me, his thumb circling my clit as he pumps a second finger into me, causing me to clench around his fingers.

My pulse quickens, breathing racketing as he pumps faster.

In and out.

In and *out.*

My head rolls back against the mirror as he squeezes my neck, coaxing me. I want to hold out, show him that he can't unravel me that quickly, but when he leans back away from me, a teasing smirk on his face and the words, "Come for me," fall from his lips, I want to do just that.

However, my brain isn't as foggy as he thinks. So instead of following his "directions" like a *good girl*, I grin.

"Make me."

Jace wastes no time kissing me breathlessly before dropping to his knees. He tugs my pants and panties down with one swift motion, leaving my lower half bare to him.

"Beautiful," he whispers, his hands gripping my ass as he kisses the flesh over my pussy. My head lulls as goosebumps fleck my skin.

Jace's thumb circles my clit as he blows a small amount of air on it, teasing me. I moan from the sensation and the sight of him on his knees, watching my reactions as he pleasures me.

When his mouth circles me, replacing his fingers, I'm his. Jace takes his time licking and lapping me up, eating me out like I'm truly the one feast he's been waiting his whole life for. And when he inserts two fingers inside of me instead of one, I come undone.

My breathing escalates to an all-time high, my hands looping through the thick strands of his hair as I grind against his mouth, coming on his tongue. The hand gripping my ass to keep me centered squeezes as I finish in his mouth.

Jace chuckles lightly as he stands to his full height. "Taste yourself on my tongue," he commands, and without a thought in the world, I do.

I kiss him, lapping up my sweet juices mixed with his own minty taste, and almost come again from the pure eroticism of it all.

I'm sated and growing tired as Jace helps to redress me, taking my underwear and placing them in his pocket as he helps me into my leggings.

I'm silent, a small dopey smile wanting to break out after what we'd done.

Jace is smug as he walks me out of the studio, carrying my things out with us silently.

The chilly September air is brisk as it hits my bare arms when we reach my car.

"So what was all that shit you were talking, Jones?" he teases, gently placing my stuff in the car as I roll my eyes, failing to mask my smile.

"Whatever, Heart."

Jace leans against my car, the embodiment of sex as he tugs me into him by the waist. The gesture is intimate and domestic as he kisses the top of my forehead.

I'm about to tell him off for *not* kissing my lips when he grips the bottom of my chin, lifting it to meet his eyes.

"Tomorrow, wear your running shoes."

TWENTY-FIVE

Jace

"THE D TO P ratio in our group is—" Braxton's whispering is cut off by a cheerful apology as Cleo comes scrambling up to us, her face apologetic.

"Sorry we're so late. G couldn't find her keys and then I couldn't find mine, and Si Si–" At the mention of Sienna's nickname, my eyes lock on her immediately. I lick my lips as Sienna struts up to us with Ryan, Denver, and the blonde demon she likes to keep around.

My mouth waters at the sight of Sienna Jones in all her angelic glory. Her pink hair is the first thing that I notice, it's the most unique color of pink I've ever seen in a person's hair. Sienna stands bright and shining like the star that she is as Georgia throws a lazy arm around her shoulder.

Clad in an oversized cropped SFU hoodie—that looks a little *too* familiar—a mini skirt and sneakers, my eyes track her up and down slowly, remaining on her legs for a moment too long.

God, I love her legs.

I drink her in as she smiles, beaming at something Georgia says. The memory of those same lips being pressed against mine last night sends a shudder of pleasure down my spine.

Sienna Jones, what are you doing to me?

My body is pulled to her like a magnet, propelling my soul towards hers. I don't notice my own movements until she shakes her head subtly, telling me no.

It stings a bit, the rejection, but I understand where she's coming from. Her friends are here, and she still wants to keep this a secret. But I'd be lying if I said her rejection didn't fuck me up a little bit.

I want to be able to hold her hand around Fall Fest, show her the cute little stands with the stuffed animals she likes, and be able to take pictures of her while we're here.

Instead, we have to keep our relationship—if you can call it that—a secret.

It burns something deep in my chest as she slips a mask of happiness and indifference over her face while she talks to Georgia, when all I want to do is march over there, pull her into my arms, and be with her.

Somehow or another, Cleo and Blake slip away from our group—the excuse of working on their project being used as they run off, holding hands into the sunset, leaving the rest of us mortals to our own vices.

It doesn't slip my silent notice that Cleo's step-brother, Ryan, does the same with Blake's adopted cousin, Denver. As soon as Cleo and Blake were gone, the duo slipped away as well, Ryan tugging the girl off to who knows where.

I'm in the back of the group, letting Charlie talk my ear off, but all of my focus is on the small head of pink hair in front of me.

I watch silently as Sienna trails behind the rest of our group, in her own world. Derek and Delilah had met up with us sometime around us hitting a photo booth stall and Braxton wanting fried Oreos. Deli takes it upon herself to give Sienna some sort of company when she notices her previous dance teacher. My brow raises as Delilah reaches out for Sienna to carry her, even though she's in her father's arms. I almost lose my shit completely when Derek hands over Delilah with a reluctant smile dusting his features.

Sienna grins at the four-year-old, hoisting her up on her hip.

Never in my life have I *ever* seen Delilah reach for anyone other than her dad, and *never* has Derek *ever* willingly handed his daughter to someone else.

When did those two become friends?

I knew I shouldn't have told her she could trust him. Now he's going to steal my girl before I get the chance to fully make her mine.

"You've got a cute kid," Georgia coos as she talks to Derek, her full attention on the toddler in her friend's arms as Derek's ears redden. He scratches the back of his neck, tugging on the loose curls on his nape as he smiles at her.

My eyes narrow on the action as Charlie pats my chest. Dragging my gaze away from them, I raise a brow at him.

"We're about to go see what the girls at Gamma Gamma Nu are up to, you coming?" he asks, his usual loud voice making me cringe as I quickly eye Sienna before turning back to him, shaking my head.

Charlie furrows his brows at me, but doesn't push as he, Brax, and Alec dap me up, leaving the rest of us.

Sienna eyes me warily as Delilah talks her ear off about the new dance she's learning at school, but I don't do anything to stop her questioning gaze. Instead, I pull out my phone and open up our text thread, ready to get started on the next item on her list.

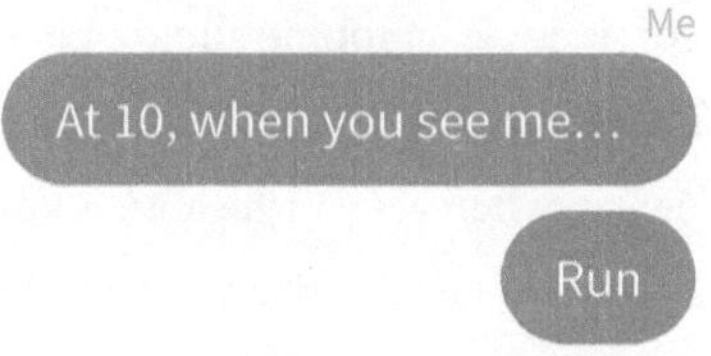

Sienna's brow raises as she watches me, still giving small chatter to Delilah to keep her satisfied. When her phone vibrates, she purses her lips and raises her brows when she sees the message, a hint of mischief playing on her features.

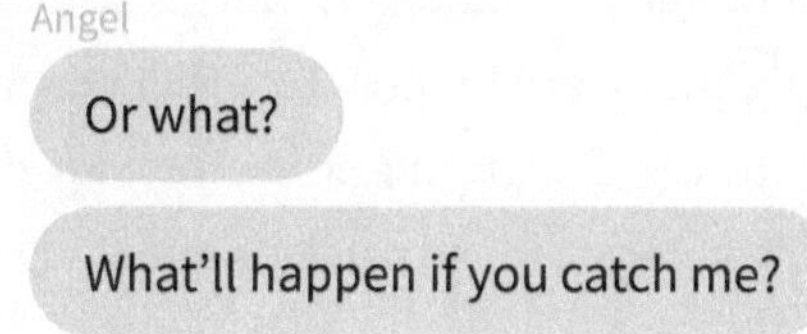

My words get lodged in my throat at her suggestive message. I'm going to have a field day with this one.

"Oh! Can we go there, Daddy?" Delilah's little voice snatches me from my phone as my eyes track to where she's pointing, widening slightly at the ride that she wants to go on.

Derek gulps at the sight of the ride that his kid wants to get on, and just as he's about to deny her request, Georgia snatches his hand. His eyes widen as she squeals, "It's the best freaking thing here!"

My brow raises as I see it, the change. *Something* in Derek's gaze snaps as he comes to terms with the ride and all of the girls' growing excitement. He *hates* heights, but the daredevil next to him and his daughter *love*s them.

Sienna's eyes gleam with excitement as she nods, agreeing with Georgia's sentiment.

"G's right! We have to get on that!" she says, turning to me with a smile brighter than Sirius.

Sienna looks up at me expectantly as Delilah jumps from her arms and runs to Georgia's side, grabbing ahold of her hand.

"You coming?" she asks, and my heart stutters for a beat.

"Sienna, wherever you go, always know that I'll follow," I say lowly, stepping closer to her as her eyes darken. She takes a step back when our breathing syncs with one another's, and turns on her heels to follow after our friends towards the ride.

I'm not a bitch, but I believe that carnival rides are some of the most dangerous things to ever be invented—Sienna Jones does not agree with this sentiment. After riding the spinning death thing known as The Scrambler, she drags me to every single high stakes ride known to man. Georgia and Sienna are like partners in torturous crime as they lead the poor single dad and daughter duo along with myself to every single ride at Fall Fest.

The only reason I'm doing these death traps is because of her.

Sienna, who'd been quiet and reclusive earlier, is like a butterfly springing from her cocoon as she talks animatedly with Georgia and Delilah, the girls all coming to some sort of kahoots with one another.

We begin to slow down a bit after the last ride has been done and soon begin to make our way to the annual lantern lighting at Fall Fest. Small lanterns with the SFU crest emblazoned on them begin to light the sky as I slip away from the group, and movement catches my eye.

Derek slowly makes his way towards Sienna. I watch carefully as I stalk towards the trees next to the fairground, eyeing them as Sienna and him laugh.

Georgia had taken Delilah to the bathroom, leaving the two of them alone together.

I check my watch and clench my jaw at the time.

9:56 p.m.

I still have time to kill before our next part of the list is started. Standing in my hiding place, my eyes lock on the pink haired girl immediately.

I check the watch again and smile.

9:59 p.m.

No better time than the present. Pulling out my phone, Sienna's name is pinned in the top of my messages. I click on it.

Let the games begin.

I smile triumphantly behind my mask as Sienna looks up from her phone, her face drained of all color as she looks around the packed lantern festival. Georgia's confused face is the icing on the cake as she mouths something I can't comprehend, but I don't need to because soon enough, Sienna sees me.

I've never done anything remotely *close* to what Sienna had on that list of hers, but I *did* read a few dark romance books similar to our current situation. If Sienna is predictable like the women in her books she'll take off in...

3...

2...

1...

I almost laugh aloud as she takes off in the opposite direction of me, Delilah pointing after her as I slowly stride towards her, avoiding the massive crowd of people.

Let's be real, if I chased Sienna with a mask on, someone would call the cops on my ass and then Daddy dearest would have to get involved.

So, instead of wearing my Halloween mask from last year throughout Fall Fest, I stick with a hoodie until we're alone. My smile is menacing as Sienna runs from me to a crowded part of the park, her footsteps heavy as she looks back at me while running.

Her eyes are a mix of emotions, but the one that prevails? Lust. Her hazel eyes are clouded with it as she bites her bottom lip, a sliver of fear laced beneath them.

The little minx is getting off on this...

My phone buzzes, pausing my following momentarily as I pull it out to make sure it's no one important.

Charlie

> Just saw coach's niece running from something

> Want me to make sure she's okay?

Sighing, I massage my temples, wishing Charlie wasn't as attentive as I type out a response.

When I look back up to make sure that I do in fact have Sienna, my heart drops when I realize she's nowhere to be found. I gulp as I come to a standstill in the middle of the grounds where all the funhouses are.

There's a large building with the words *Chili's Hot Fun!* on the roof with an clown as the mascot in the very middle, the mirror maze, I'm guessing. Scrunching my nose, I eye the two other buildings, one being a house of slides.

She isn't going in there...

When my eyes fall on the third and final building, I smile at the sign, *Cupid's Love Maze.*

Fitting.

There's people everywhere as I push inside the maze to chase after Sienna. Couples and friends line the maze, and I almost think that I won't be able to find her in this frenzy until a blur of pink flashes in my peripheral, heading into the employee only section.

What are you up to, angel?

I follow her carefully, sure to be discreet enough that no one will see us as I follow her into a part of the maze that's closed off. It takes nothing for me to slide the mask on as I slip in behind her. The room is lit with red and pink lighting, with mirrors all around and a heart shaped, red velvet bed in the center on a spinning showcase.

Sienna stands in the very center of the room, her back to me as I stand behind her, but I can feel her eyes on me through the mirror, watching my every move.

The lights in the room flicker nonstop between pink and red, emanating a strobe light effect as I slowly approach my girl. Loud laughs and cheers echo in the distance just feet away, but in here, it's only us.

Sienna's breathing is heavy, her deep inhales and exhales hardening me as I wrap my hands around her waist. She sighs as I pull her curly ponytail from her shoulder, the plastic lips of the mask tickling the skin of her neck, causing her to gasp.

"I'm gonna need you to be very, *very* quiet. Think you can do that for me, angel?"

Sienna's sharp intake of breath is all the push I need to move my hand up her hoodie, gripping one of her breasts as she melts into me.

"Take...Take it off," she gasps as I tilt her head for more access to her neck.

"Hm?" I hum, my fingers pinching her nipples as she groans.

"Take off the mask," she shivers, "I want to see your face when you take me."

I gulp at the implication of her words, she couldn't possibly... Did she say *'take'* her? Taking the mask off, I drop it near the foot of the bed, her words dancing around my mind and spurring me on as I kiss the length of her neck.

Sienna's breath is shaky, her mouth forming an 'o' shape as my fingers trail under her skirt, finding the hem of her lace underwear. I watch her in the mirrors as she bucks against the finger that I insert inside her, grinding against it. My thumb finds her clit, pushing down on it as I pump in another finger.

"Fuck Jace..." She sighs, her head rolling back against my chest as lick down her neck, blowing it with cool air, my fingers working her with ease.

"Kiss me?" she asks softly, and she doesn't have to ask twice. In an instant, my lips are locked with hers, my other hand decorating her neck like a necklace as I pump my fingers in and out of her.

I'd give this girl the world and so much more. She just needs to say the words, and it's hers.

Sienna's teeth tug at my bottom lip, making a popping noise as we part. I grin down as she gives me a pleasure-filled smile, her eyes clouded with lust as I kiss and suck on her neck.

"Jace, baby...I'm ready," she breathes out quietly as voices on the outside remind her that we're not alone. The lights in the 'room' flicker as my heart rate rackets higher.

"Huh?" is all I can say to her, and I feel like a fucking asshole for being tongue tied at a time like this of all times. My fingers fall from Sienna's warmth, her wetness coating them as she twists in my grip, a blaze of fire in her eyes as she faces me head on.

Sienna's gaze darkens, her eyes hooding over as she licks her lips and *fuck*, I might just come from the *sight* of her.

"I *said* I'm ready. I didn't let you chase me around just to finger me," Her tongue skates around her top row of teeth, stealing my attention as she smirks. "I want you to *fuck* me."

"So bend over."

My blood thrums loudly in my ears as Sienna does as she's told without question, bending over the bed and baring her ass to me. I send a quick thank you to the Fates as all the blood in my body shoots to my dick at the sight of her, ready for me.

In no time, I'm pulling a condom from inside my wallet and slipping it on. Knowing that Sienna is a virgin has me wishing that I could give her more foreplay and ease her into this, but seeing as I've known the impatient woman my entire life, I know that she's not going to wait for this any longer.

"If anything and I mean *anything* makes you uncomfortable, say the word and we stop this," I command, my voice stern as she smiles against the sheet.

"Yes, *sir*," she says mockingly. A smile cracks on my face at her sassiness. She's going to pay for that one.

Aligning myself with her opening, I let out a deep breath, slowly exhaling as I inch myself in. Sienna groans from the intrusion, my girth stretching her to a limit she's never felt before. I squeeze my eyes shut. Her tightness makes me see stars as I slowly pull away and inch myself in again. She moans and flinches, and I halt my movement.

"That's too much, you're not supposed to shove it all in at once!" she whispers, lifting her upper half up a bit to look back at me as I smirk.

"That was only the tip, angel." I smirk as her eyes widen.

She gulps, turning back around as the lights flicker to red, and I ease myself in again. Her hand shoots behind herself, gripping my forearm, pausing me.

"Just stick it in! You edging it in—" she gasps, moaning into the bed as I push my full length into her, her body shaking as I groan.

"What was that?" I taunt, leaning down to her ear as she sighs.

"Shut up and fuck me, psycho," she responds breathlessly as I chuckle, kissing her shoulder softly.

"Yes, ma'am." I push all the way in, chuckling softly as she screams into the sheets. Her hands shoot out to grip them as I adjust myself inside her, pumping slowly.

Sienna clenches around me so tight, my eyes shut in response as I groan. I push deeper into her, pumping slowly in and out. Sienna cries out, her arch deepening as she pushes up on her tiptoes, allowing me more access to her.

"Fuck…" I mumble, gripping her hips as I dive in deeper, pumping slow and hard. Sienna's moans are muffled by the bed, and I don't like it one bit.

I want the whole world to know whose dick she's taking. I lift her body up, my pace unrelenting as my hand settles in its rightful spot on her neck. I tilt her head back, encompassing her lips with my own as I fuck her faster.

"Oh! Ja—" she screams and I halt my movements, slowing my pace as she leans a little, looking me in my eyes.

"You gotta be quiet or I'm going to have to use my hands to keep you quiet," I tell her, holding her gaze as she smirks daringly.

"Do it then."

Fuck.

I don't know what comes over me. I don't know if it's the weirdly freaky room, the idea of being caught, the woman in my presence, or all of the above, but I'm changing positions in an instant. I pull out, picking Sienna up and dropping her down on my dick, drilling up into her.

When she tries to moan aloud, I seal my lips against her, kissing and swallowing her cries of pleasure. Our bodies are in sync as I coax us both to an orgasm, seeing stars as I drill into her.

Sienna clenches around me hard, her own climax building and exploding out as she cries loudly into my mouth, her covered breasts moving hard against my chest as I come to the brink of my own climax, happy to have given her an orgasm twice today.

My pace quickens as I burrow into her, my body tingling and balls tightening as I come, finishing inside of her with a loud, throaty groan.

"Angel."

Our breathing is rapid as we both come down from our highs, the clarity of what we just did settling in my stomach like a swarm of butterflies. Sienna's gaze searches mine as if for any signs that I'd do something to jeopardize this thing that we have going between us, and I'd rather be shot in the heart than hurt this woman.

Putting all of my feelings and emotions in a kiss, I hold Sienna close as I slowly pull out of her, discarding the used condom. She watches with a shy smile as I buckle my pants, and I can't help but to laugh at the unseriousness of this all as we help each other look presentable.

"That was…"

"Amazing." She blushes, hiding her face as I hug her.

We sneak out of the 'room', avoiding the crowd of people entering the maze. My arm is wrapped around her shoulders as we walk through the back of the building. I'm about to kiss her forehead again, feeling more affectionate than ever as she comes to a halt, intaking sharply.

"I...I have to go." She frowns, worry creasing her brow as she looks up from her phone at me.

"What?" I ask, taken aback as a line forms between her brows.

"It's Cleo...I-I'm sorry."

And with that, she leaves.

Again.

Sienna

My feet drag over the gravel of the fairgrounds parking lot as I walk behind my friends, my mind on the man that I *just* left.

Fuck, I should've stayed. I *wanted* to stay. To be with him, to let him take care of me. Instead, I'm semi listening to my cousin cry about kissing a guy who everyone *knows* she likes while my heart is somewhere else.

I'm silent on the ride back home, my mind replaying the moments prior. The chase, Jace wearing a Halloween mask, and then secretly taking my virginity in a public place.

After everything I've done today, I'm in dire need of some rest. I yawn as we file out of the car, heading up to the apartment. The girls are all chatting away, but my head is elsewhere as I walk beside Cleo.

I *really* fucked up this time. Leaving after a kiss is one thing, but running away after having *sex*? I'm fucking doomed.

A gentle tug on my hoodie sleeves brings my focus back to the present as Cleo furrows her brows at me, frowning a bit.

"What's up with—Is that a *hickey*?!" she screeches, eyes wide as she points at my neck, drawing attention our way as Denver and Georgia gasp.

I mimic her expression as my jaw drops and I clutch my neck. Georgia and Denver halt in their steps, both gasping as they eye me.

"Oh my gosh! It's from that hot dad isn't it?!" Cleo exclaims, her hands flying to her mouth animatedly.

Hot dad?!

My jaw drops as nervous laughter bubbles from my throat. She couldn't be *further* from the truth. Georgia eyes me over Cleo's head, her face scrutinizing as I laugh off my cousin.

"Hot dad? Did you bump your head on the Mind Eraser, CJ? It's a bruise." I chuckle as she tilts her head, confused by my deflection. My stomach sinks as Georgia sighs, pursing her lips, clearly unimpressed with my avoidance.

When we get into our apartment, we each take our rightful spots on the couch and loveseat. Denver and Cleo talk animatedly about what happened at Fall Fest while Georgia plays a fashion game on her phone.

I need to text Jace, see if our relation—situationship, whatever this is—is still salvageable. I mean, if I were him, I'd be pissed. The woman who ditched him on a rooftop two years ago ditched him again after getting her way with him.

What is the female equivalent to a fuckboy? If there is one, I'm pretty sure my name is mixed in the definition.

I can feel eyes on me as I chew on my bottom lip, my fingers itching to get in contact with Jace.

Fuck it.

Jumping from my spot on the loveseat, I practically run to the front door of our apartment, snatching up my keys as I do so. I *need* to talk to him, to get him to understand just how sorry I am for leaving him.

Cleo's up in an instant, her worried brown eyes searching my face, but I don't give her any signs of how I'm feeling. The only person who needs to be taken care of right now is a blond asshole that I'm pretty sure may be the spawn of Hades.

"What's going on, Si Si? Why do you look like someone just threatened Oscar?" She chuckles warily as I crack a watery smile, my heart stuttering as I lie to my best friend.

"Nothing, I-I just need some air."

I don't give Cleo the chance to respond as I leave the apartment, racing to my car in the parking lot. The sight of my light purple AMG GT 63 comes into view, but I stumble in my tracks at the car parked next to it.

A dark green Aston Martin SUV.

Jace's car.

He leans casually against the hood, watching me, the picture of utter perfection. I don't know what to do with myself, my hands squeezing and pulling at my fingers as I try to psych myself up to approach coolly.

But all of my carefully crafted nonchalance bursts as I catch his eye, and I fucking *run* to him, crushing him in a bear hug.

Jace is taken aback from the force of the hug, stumbling slightly as he wraps his arms around my waist, squeezing.

"I'm so sorry. I should've given you more, or at least *tried* to stay with you a little longer. Instead, I just ran and—"

"It's okay," he says softly, gripping me a little tighter as I sigh.

Jace is the kind of guy who puts everyone's emotions and well-being above himself. He always has been, hence him doing the list with me. He's selfless and attentive, albeit a little crazy when he wants to be. He means well, and that's all that matters.

I know that my actions hurt him, that he won't tell me they did in order to spare my feelings, and I feel like shit a little bit more because of that fact.

"We should probably get in the car, wouldn't want anyone to see, right?" he says quietly, and a pang of guilt hits my heart as I chew my bottom lip.

"Right."

In the car, neither of us speak. Jace sits staring out the car's windshield blankly and I sit next to him, watching him.

The silence between us is deafening and something I've never experienced with the man to the left of me.

I don't like it.

"Do you want to come up? We can all hang out and talk like old times," I try, preparing myself for him to reject me but Jace just sends a sweet smile my way, nodding.

He's like a kid in a candy store as I lead him up to the apartment, talking and joking like normal. My body releases its tension as Jace cracks jokes about the guys and fills me in on what's been happening at practice lately.

When we approach the hall for my apartment, his hand gripping my wrist has me pausing in my steps. When I turn to face him, I gasp as he pulls me by the waist and kisses me.

"That's not fair, I wasn't ready" I say, a small smile peeking through as he chuckles.

"Life isn't fair, Sienna."

I narrow my eyes at him, turning to face him in front of the apartment door as he raises a brow at me. I point a finger at his chest.

"Be on your best behavior here, no longing gazes and no flirting," I say, a hint of humor lacing my tone as he nods like a soldier, saluting me.

"Yes, ma'am. There will be zero funny business."

Nodding my head, I smile.

"Goo—"

The asshole kisses my cheek, green eyes dazzling.

"Starting now."

Everyone goes silent as we shuffle into the apartment, Jace striding in like he owns the place as I sigh, throwing on a fake annoyed tone.

"Look what the cat dragged in." I roll my eyes as he chuckles behind me.

"Time to party, motherfuckers!" he jeers, raising his hands in the air like the king of the jungle as Cleo races up to hug him.

Dragging my feet to the couch, I plop down next to Georgia as she eyes me curiously.

"What happened to fresh air?" she quips quietly as I cut my eyes to her.

"He was already outside." I shrug, licking my lips as Jace takes the loveseat.

I track his movements as he settles himself in the chair and my skin buzzes with a newfound energy as he spreads his legs widely, deepening himself in the cushion. Jace catches my obvious perusal of him and winks, smiling softly as Cleo offers him a donut from her stash.

He takes the donut carefully, eating it slowly, and my mouth waters at the sight of him.

What the hell is going on with me? And why do I find the sight of him eating a *donut* to be the most attractive thing in the world?

Maybe it's because of the hole?

Get a grip, Sienna...Oh my goodness.

"We should watch last night's race!" Denver claps excitedly, turning the TV to yesterday's Formula One race as Jace groans, the sound going straight to my...nether regions. Memories of him groaning my name not even two hours ago plague my mind as I eye him from my peripheral, my mouth watering when something dawns on me.

In the few times that Jace and I have done anything remotely sexual, he'd been the one giving pleasure—not receiving. The thought of making Jace feel just as much pleasure that he'd given me makes my pulse race.

I've read countless romance books and the one thing that these books have taught me is the art of giving a good blowjob.

Or at least I hope that they have...

I mean how hard can it be to suck dick? (No pun intended.)

All I have to do is give him those eyes—*fuck me* eyes for those that don't know—pull out his dick, and suck. *Without using teeth*. Seems pretty easy enough.

Now, I just need to find a way to get him to my room...I eye him momentarily as he talks with Denver and see my moment as she brings up being too short to do some things.

"Speaking of short, Jace, I need your help with getting some boxes in my closet. I've been trying to get them down, but uh..." I trail off as he crooks a brow at me as if to say *really, is that how you're going to try to get me out of my pants?* and yes, that's *exactly* how I'm going to do it.

Jace's face is unreadable as he stands, wiping his hands on his thighs. "What would you do without me, *shortcake*?" he teases, throwing a playful arm around my shoulder as I roll my eyes, swatting him away.

"Oh fuck off, I'm just using you for your height."

Laughter trails behind me as I dramatically sashay to my room, Jace in tow. He says something that I can't hear and Cleo's loud cackle is the only thing that can be heard as I enter my bedroom and immediately freak the fuck out.

"Oh my God. Oh my God. Oh my God..."

What the hell do I do now? I had the right idea, hell yeah I did, but now I don't know what the fuck to do! Do I say something cute? Maybe make him laugh...or just immediately jump his bones.

Do people even say "jump his bones" anymore?

Fucking hell.

My heart drops, my throat feeling cottony as Jace enters the room. His hair is cute and rumpled from the hoodie he's wearing, and that makes this all even worse as he softly shuts the door. When our eyes lock, my shoulders stiffen and Jace tilts his head like a confused puppy.

You got this! It's just a...penis?

Letting out a deep breath, I roll my shoulders back and push him back—thinking the action would be sexy like how I've seen in porn. Instead, Jace hits the door with a loud thud and his eyes widen animatedly.

"Are y'all okay?" Georgia's voice is loud and distant, drilling anxiety into my bones as I look up at the confused man in my room.

"We're fine!" I shout back, putting a finger over my lips, signaling for Jace to be calm as I wrap my arms around his neck. In an instant, his hands find my waist and I melt into his touch.

Now's the time...you got this girl!

I psych myself up and do the only thing that I *semi* know how to do.

I drop to my knees right in front of him. Jace's jaw drops like my knees as he gapes at me like a fish out of water.

"Wha...What are you doing?" he asks, gasping as I tug on the waist of his pants.

"What does it look like? I'm apologizing!" I whisper, gesturing for him to be quiet by putting my finger to my lips.

How does this go again? I just shimmy the pants down, right? Since this isn't the Omegaverse books that I typically read, he shouldn't be the size of Jupiter when I free him. Right? Fuck, I should've studied before doing this...What if he thinks I'm inexperienced—I mean, I am but...*Fuck.*

When I tug on his jeans, his hand clasps around my wrist, halting my movements. My breathing stutters as I look up. Jace's face is a torrent of emotions as he looks down at me, jaw still dropped, and that's when I see it...*Fear*.

This is a disaster.

"*No!* No no no...Get up!" he says, not giving me the chance to do it myself as he hoists me to my feet.

"Huh...I just thought—"

Jace cups my face, cutting me off.

"No...Don't *ever* feel the need to pleasure someone as an *apology*, Sienna. If someone ever makes you give them head as an apology, tell me and I'll kill them myself." He sighs, pulling me into him and my heart shatters.

Does he not want me? I just thought that would be something he would want...

"But at Fall Fest—"

Jace shakes his head.

"I was *not* going to let you give me a blow job at that place. The floor was more like a dirt road than concrete..." He chuckles softly, the vibrations of his laugh dancing on the top of my head as my shoulders slump.

"So, no head?" I ask, chuckling a bit as he pulls away to look at my face. The look in his eyes is sweet and playful before he kisses my forehead.

"No." He laughs, squeezing me a little tighter. When we pull away from one another, it feels like time has stopped. His eyes, the perfect swirl of light and dark green are full of light, no disappointment or pity—just light. The look he gives me is airy and sweet. Tension builds between us as neither of us backs down from our unintentional staring contest.

I break it, slapping a hand to his chest. "Don't look at me like that, psycho. I'm starting to worry that you're falling for me."

My words are playful, but I can't help the pit of longing that builds in my stomach as he grabs a hold of my wrist before intertwining our fingers.

"No need to worry," he says cooly, but his eyes speak another language. Breathing deeply, I untangle myself from him and lift my head.

I've got to get a grip because even though he's saying he isn't falling for me. I can't guarantee that I haven't already fell for him.

"I think you should stay in Cleo's room tonight—if you stay over that is...Wouldn't want to let our little secret out, y'know." I gulp, my eyes looking anywhere but his as he clears his throat, the sound awkward.

"Right...wouldn't want to fuck up our *arrangement*."

I flinch as Jace walks out of the room, leaving me with a confused and muddied heart.

I just fucked up...*again*.

TWENTY-SEVEN

Jace

"Of course I'll kiss you...Wow, Eren—"

For the love of...

"Cleo!"

The sound of a kiss fills the air of the silent bedroom as Cleo kisses her stuffed bear, Mr. Pickles.

"Cleo!" I whisper again, hissing as she sighs dreamily.

This girl...

"Cleo," I say her name in full volume but surprise, surprise...She remains fast asleep.

In all honesty, I'd think that her ability to sleep so heavily at night should earn her an award. However, my best friend sleeping next to me and having *sex dreams* about her celebrity crush while her cousin—the woman who I actually want to sleep beside—is in the other room, makes me a little less enthusiastic towards her.

Cleo shifts, her leg slinging over my hip, causing me to groan. She's the wildest fucking sleeper out of all the girls. With a sigh, I twist to lay on my back, knowing that I won't be asleep anytime soon.

Time to plan, Jacey...

How can I get Sienna to stop hiding whatever *this* is between us? It's only been a month, but fuck if I don't feel like my skin is crawling every time the guys mention hanging out with other girls or when I see another guy talking to her on campus. Sighing, I rub a hand over my face.

This would be so much easier if Cleo weren't her cousin...

Maybe I could take her out? Get rid of all of our problems.

Turning my head slowly to my right, I sigh. I can't kill my best friend, even if she's fucking drooling on my shoulder.

I'm going insane here just thinking about the fact that we're hiding this. I just want to love her out loud, not hide ourselves from the world because of other people's opinions of us. I want to be able to laugh with my friends and hold her in my lap whilst doing so, hearing her laugh the loudest in my ear as we all talk. I want to be able to hold her hand freely on campus and to be able to sleep in her room instead of this *beast's* bed for crying out loud.

I just want *her*.

And she's all I can think about as I drift off to sleep.

My brain pounds against my skull, and I cringe as my nose burns. Something just punched the shit out of me. Groaning, my hand shoots to my nose as a body moves next to me, pulling a brick off of my face.

"What the fuck, CJ?" I sigh, popping one eye open before she shoves a screen into my face.

It's only nine o'clock on a Sunday.

Why the fuck is she up before eleven on a *Sunday*?

"What the fuck is this?! Read it!" she exclaims as she shoves the phone in my face harder. My head pounds with the beginning of a headache as I open both eyes.

My mind is still on Sienna and how fucked our current situation is that anger boils in my chest as I read Cleo's phone, my jaw clenching.

Blake

Wat ER oui?

Fucking great...

"Let's go," I say, my voice stern as the pink loving girl next to me widens her eyes.

The confused, wide eyed look that Cleo gives me reminds me so much of her cousin that I have to look away because the longer I look, the more I want to go to her.

Cleo can't know about Sienna and I, and I'll be damned if I tell her when Sienna told me not to.

Happy wife, happy life, am I right?

Looking at Cleo, I frown thinking about what I've gotten myself into. Why the hell am I dealing with drama on a Sunday morning?

I'm annoyed as Cleo and I make our way to her car. I take her to get breakfast first because knowing her, she'd just complain about being hungry the entire ride over, and I don't want to hear it. Not right now, at least.

Right now, my mind is still focused on how I can get Sienna to let loose. She's an only child and has never done a lot of the things that I was able to do as a kid since her parents were never home.

What she craves right now is rebellion, and I'm the best man for her to lead through one.

When I pull up to my house, dropping off Cleo with a full stomach and her cow pajamas, I tell her that I have some things to handle and stay in the car. Cleo's a big girl who can handle herself so I'm not too worried about her as she marches up the steps of my porch and knocks shyly on the front door.

Now back to business.

Pulling out my phone, I find an image of Sienna's list and smile.

Hello, number 19...Let's see how well our girl is with needles.

I make a few calls and soon enough, the lovely Sienna Jones has an appointment at Ink and Tales this afternoon. Grinning like I won the lottery, I recline in the driver's seat and begin sketching a small piece, letting my fingers have a mind of their own.

Around five minutes later, the sketch is finished and my stomach is growling. Since it's Sunday, Derek should be cooking breakfast.

I could really go for an omelet right about now...

My foot is just about to make contact with the plush green grass of our lawn when the front door flies open and Cleo runs through it, *running* past me and to her car.

What the hell—

"Cleo! Wait, no—" a loud voice belts, but it's too late. Cleo drives away so fast, you'd think she was fleeing from a crime.

Deep breaths, Jace.

The sight of Blake standing on our lawn in his favorite cartoon boxers with the guys standing behind him, watching, has my blood boiling.

One job. The idiot had one job, and he fucked with my best friend's heart. I knew the asshole was going to fuck up eventually, but now I'm hangry and seeing as I was woken up because of this, I want to kill him.

"You're in deep shit," I say, pointing at the idiot as I jump into my other car, a sleek blue Maserati Granturismo. I shake my head as I think about Blake and Cleo, still not believing that Cleo really woke me up for this shit.

Driving the Maserati out of our driveway, I make my way down to the loft. I have two cars and a bike, but I never usually drive the Maserati because it's my favorite and I don't want anyone to ruin it out on the road. My mom and dad got me Lola, my Aston Martin, for my birthday, but this baby right here is all mine.

Running a few errands, I grab all the things that I need to make today's date the best one yet.

Sienna may like to call the things we do on her list "activities" or whatever she calls them, but to me, they're everything.

By the time I've arrived back at the girls' place, I've changed and gotten her and I breakfast. Knocking on the girls' apartment door, my veins thrum with excitement as I wait for Sienna. I'm smiling from ear to ear just at the thought of seeing her, but when the door opens, my smile crumbles to ash.

"You." I sigh, rolling my head back as Georgia rolls her eyes.

"They just let anybody in here these days..." She purses her lips, stepping to the side to let me in. "Now what're you—"

I don't give Georgia the time to finish her sentence as I make my way to the sleeping pink haired girl's bedroom, already knowing Cleo isn't home after checking her location.

Sienna is laid halfway across her bed in a cute little purple and white flower pajama set, snoring softly, when I enter her room. Chuckling quietly, I take a seat on the side of the bed that she's not occupying and snap a picture of her sleeping, but just as I'm about to put the phone away, a hand shoots out to grab it.

My heart falls out of my ass as I jump off the bed, looking at the now very *awake* woman. Sienna's eyes are unfocused as she groans, stretching and yawning.

Her voice is groggy and riddled with sleep as she rubs her eyes and asks, "What happpened?"

Instead of responding like a normal person would, I kiss her cheek and pick her up bridal style. Her eyes bulge out of her head as I walk her out of her apartment and down to the Granturismo.

She doesn't say anything as she looks around her new environment, taking it in as I put the car in reverse and take us to the loft.

On the way there, I hum whatever's playing on my Bluetooth and she remains quiet the entire trip. Sienna allows me to carry her back up to the loft, without a word. I think she may have fallen back asleep but when she looks up at me, I know that she hasn't. Entering the loft, I make a beeline to the kitchen and place her on the island.

Sienna hisses as her butt makes contact with the cold surface, and I kiss her lips quickly, stunning her before leaving to get our breakfast from the car.

She has no clue what we're doing today, which is great because if she knew what I had up my sleeves...She'd probably kill me.

When I get back up to the loft, Sienna has brushed her teeth and is lounging on the couch on her phone. Her face lights up like a kid in a candy store when I place our breakfast in front of her.

"You really know the way to a woman's heart," she mumbles over a mouthful of chocolate chip pancakes as I take a bite of my own blueberry ones.

We sit in a content silence, scarfing down our sugary breakfasts until Sienna clears her throat, her sharp gaze calculating as she eyes me.

"You didn't just drag me out of bed, feed me chocolate chip pancakes, and sat here quietly eating for nothing, Heart. Spit it out," she says, setting her food down and resting back in the seat.

I grin as I mimic her actions, setting aside my own food. She's going to have a heart attack when she sees what I have planned for her. Sienna might've thought that being a backpack on my bike was crazy, but this might just be insane.

"Finish your food, angel. There's so much that I have planned." I grin maniacally, twisting the stubble on my upper lip like a mad scientist with a curly mustache.

Sienna rolls her eyes at me. "That wasn't vague or creepy at all."

It takes her about forty minutes to finish her food, take a quick shower, and throw on some of my clothes. By the time she's done getting ready, we're cutting it close for our appointment time. Sienna comes skipping down to the lower level of the loft, a smile on her clean face as she stops in front of me. My clothes drown her, my white and orange SFU hoodie hangs around her thighs and my large basketball shorts make her look like she has chicken legs.

When we finally make it to the car with about ten minutes to spare before we're late, Sienna turns to me in her seat. "So...what's on the agenda for today?"

A lot...

Instead of answering her, I tilt my head, looking up at her with a daring smirk. "Do you trust me?"

She smiles sweetly, but I can see through her feisty mask as she gets closer to my face, her cool minty breath dancing against my skin.

"As far as I can throw you."

Sienna and I's ride to Ink and Tales is filled with laughter, singing, and her asking questions about where we're going. She reminds me so much of her younger self, and I love it. She's still the girl with the overactive imagination and too many questions to count that I remember.

When we arrive at the tattoo shop, Sienna's brows furrow, creating a deep V between them as her eyes track between the shop and my own green ones.

"Why are we here? Are you getting my name tattooed? I mean I'd be flattered, but–"

"No, you little pyscho...we're here to get number 19 crossed off of that list of yours." I chuckle, holding an arm out to usher her into the studio as she frowns.

"My name would've been hotter—especially on your forehead." She shrugs as I snicker behind her and her large pink curls.

This girl...

"Do you know what you want to g—"

"Tramp stamp," she says immediately, cutting me off as she turns to look up at me. Her hazel eyes are big and bright with amusement as I smile down at her.

The thought of Sienna having a tattoo above the swell of her ass does something to me. I shift in my spot in front of her as she keeps our eyes locked together before hers slowly roam down my body.

"Does that idea excite you, Jace?" she coos seductively, a hand on my chest. I cough, trying to reel myself in, but fucking hell this girl is mesmerizing.

"Yeah—"

"Can I help y'all with anything?" A deep, gruff voice pulls my attention from Sienna. A tall woman with tattoos for days, pink and purple split-dyed hair, and black lipstick stands before us, an amused smirk dazzling her face.

Sienna looks up at me as if I have all the answers to our problems, and I gulp, still thinking about our interaction as she grins at the woman.

"Jacey here is getting a tattoo."

TWENTY-EIGHT

Sienna

THE LOOK THAT JACE Eros Heart sends my way can be described as three things.

1. Confused as hell

2. Mortified as fuck

3. Acceptance

Somewhere in the mix of his confusion and mortification, Jace agreed to get a tattoo. I know that he has a few on his legs and one on his rib cage, but I didn't think he'd actually agree to get a tattoo today. Hell, *I* didn't agree to get one. Which brings me to my next issue.

The sound of a buzzing asshole in the shape of a tattoo needle sends blood rushing to my ears as Bertha, the woman who *so graciously* checked us in for our reservation that I had *no idea* about, tests out her equipment.

Jace's only two stipulations for getting a tattoo of his own was that I'd gotten one, too—that's fine, it's on my list anyways. But the other was that I get something that *he* designed without seeing it beforehand.

"Do you trust me?"

"As far as I can throw you."

I groan at the memory of his words from earlier, wishing I'd paid attention to the way he'd been so giddy and excited about what we're going to do today.

The first red flag should've been the chocolate chip pancakes! He was buttering me up, I just know it.

"Ready, doll? This shouldn't hurt at all." Bertha's thick voice is full of lightness as her cold, gloved fingers prep the area just above my right ankle to be assaulted by a tattoo gun.

"As ready as I'll ever—*Ouch*, that hurts, Bertha! Are you trying to chisel into my bone?" I wince, looking down at the smiling woman as she adjusts her seat.

"Hon', I only pressed down a smidge on your ankle...there's no ink on you."

Oh...

So *maybe* getting tattoos and riding on the back of motorcycles aren't for me. *Big whoop.* I can always– OH MY!

The feeling of a rapid drilling in my ankle sends me spiraling. My eyes bulge out of their sockets as I peer down at the pure mutilation occurring towards my beautifully soft and empty skin.

*Scratch what I said earlier...*Getting tattoos and riding on the back of motorcycles are DEFINITELY *not* for me.

By the time Bertha is done nailing into my skin, I want a batch of chocolate chip cookies—all to myself, obviously—and a nice long everything shower.

As agreed with Jace, I'm not allowed to see either of our tattoos until we make it back to the loft. When Jace joins me back in the lobby, his entire neck and cheeks are red, but his bicep is covered by a plastic wrap. Mortification and confusion run through my bones as I eye him suspiciously.

"What did you do..."

"Let me see! Let me see! Let me see!"

"Jeez, girl, I'm starting to think you want to see more than the tattoo." Jace chuckles as I yank on his arm, clearly amused by my antics as we enter the loft.

I groan as I tug on him again and to my displeasure, he doesn't react to the tugging. Instead, he tilts his head at me as if to say *are you done?* and *no*, I'm not done.

"Let me see it! Why were your neck and cheeks red? What did you do? Is it a dick? Did you get a dick on your neck? How would I explain that to anyone—Oh my goodness, your *mom*! How would I tell her that her son got a *phallus* on his neck instead of only in his pants!?" My exclamations are drowned out by the loud cackling laugh of the man beside me.

Jace kisses my forehead, his body vibrating with humor as I frown, folding my arms over my chest.

"Come here," he says stalking towards the couches in the living room, his voice a mixture between a command and soft plea.

I comply, following behind him with narrowed eyes as he takes a seat on the couch.

He looks between the seat next to him and me, his fingers twiddling with one another nervously as he bites his lip. Is he...is Jace Heart nervous?

Anxiety flares in my gut as I take a cautious seat next to him, his usual comforting scent of vanilla and leather leave a feeling of dread in my stomach as I turn to stare at the man beside me. Without speaking, Jace softly grasps my ankle where the tattoo he'd designed is covered. I lean forward, expecting the worst as he draws out the reveal of the tattoo, taking his sweet precious time to rip off the (literal) Band-Aid.

"Oh for Pete's sake!" I cry out, reaching out to rip the dang thing off only to be popped quickly by his cold fingers.

Did I just get popped by a grown man?

I stare at him, my jaw dropped as he ignores me.

"You were going to ruin the surprise," he chides, slowly pulling back the wrap once again.

I'm sorry but...Did this man just *pop* me?

I mean...truly popped. Like a four-year-old getting popped by their nanny in the mouth for saying *"shut the fuck up"* in Turkish after hearing it on a soap opera, *popped*.

That may or may not have happened to me...Moving on.

My brain is still reeling from the fact that Jace popped me like a bad ass kid that I don't notice his silence or the cold air hitting my skin.

"This is beautiful..." he murmurs, examining my ankle closely, catching my attention.

I lean forward, the eagerness and excitement from earlier now back in full throttle as I take in the small, dainty tattoo he'd insisted be put on my skin.

My breath catches in my throat as I take in the intricate swirls of black ink embedded in my skin permanently. He'd drawn a small and intricate key, the bow of the key a detailed swirl of lines curving into a heart. The key reminds me of something I've seen before with its vintage and old-timey art style.

I'm transfixed by the tattoo, so much so that when I look from it, I'm startled slightly to find Jace already looking at me.

His eyes are a wild range of emotions, drawing me in.

"Do you like it?" he asks softly, his thumb caressing the skin under my leg as I nod.

I love it.

Jace grins, holding his arm out expectantly.

"Rip it off of me," he quips, and I have to blink a few times to understand that he means the tattoo wrap and *not* his clothes.

Slowly and with the ease of a ballerina on stage, I undo the wrapping and my body reacts before I can at the sight before me. A stopwatch, old and vintage in the exact same art style as the key, sits at tilt with its chain drifting away. I tilt my head, leaning in closer, taking in the complex detailing and shading of the stopwatch, down the little heart in the center of it.

"A key...and a stopwatch," I whisper aloud, trying to paint the full picture, but I can't. Curiosity rings through my mind as my eyes flicker from the key on my ankle to the stopwatch on his inner bicep.

And then it hits me.

"Everything's got a moral, if only you could find it."

Alice in Wonderland. His favorite tale, one of curiosity and growth. A thought transports me back to my nine-year-old self, the day that started it all between us.

The day that I met Jace Heart.

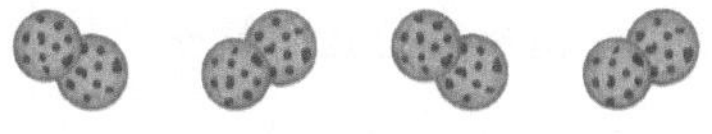

Twelve years ago

I huff dramatically crossing my arms over my chest. This isn't fair! I should be able to go with Mommy and Daddy on their work tour. Why do I have to stay with Uncle Clef all summer?

"Now I know you're not pouting, Sola girl," Uncle Clef admonishes, his expression playful as I frown, shaking my head furiously. The long and thick twists in my hair swing, hitting my face with the large, round, purple and white balls that Nanny Roshelle put in my hair before I was brought here.

"No...I'm not pouting," I say sighing as he pats my head lovingly before grabbing my bags from the trunk of his car.

"Good, now run inside. Your cousin and her friends should be inside with Ryan."

At the mention of my cousin Cleo and her new brother Ryan, my ears perk up. I haven't seen Cleo since last year when Uncle Clef said that I could sleep over at his house for a playdate.

I march up the front porch of my uncle's house, still upset because my mommy and daddy left without me.

I mean, I just don't get it. It's summertime and I don't have any school or dance classes...Why can't I go with Mommy and Daddy?

My shoulders slump as my eyes fall to my feet. Rounding up the stairs to Cleo's bedroom, I stop when a voice calls out to me, "Everything's got a moral, if only you could find it."

I stop in my tracks at the unfamiliar sound and turn to find a boy. I've never seen him before. I would've remembered if I had because I have great memory. I know I do, my dance teacher says it all the time. So that's how I know that this boy in particular, is not someone I've met before.

He has hair the color of gold, vibrant like the sun, and rosy red cheeks like they were painted with a cherry, but what catches my attention are his eyes. Light green and vibrant all the same, his eyes are interesting. They remind me of a fairy meadow, light and dazzling.

"Who—" I try to say, but the eager golden skinned boy cuts me off.

"You're sad, why are you sad? I heard you talk about your mommy, are you okay?" he asks, taking a step closer to me on the stairs.

I tilt my head as he grins at me. The grin is bright and I giggle as I notice the two missing front teeth in his mouth, but then his words come back to me.

Defensively, I turn away from the boy.

"I'm not sad. I don't get sad, that's not how big girls handle their problems," I huff, folding my arms over my chest.

The boy's grin widens as he rolls his eyes like we're joking with one another, I raise an eyebrow at him.

Who is this kid, anyways?

"Well obviously, silly, why would parents name you 'Sad'? That's an odd name..."

"They didn't." I furrow my brows, leaning closer to him as he raises his brows.

"So then what do I call you, Sad?" he asks as if he were genuinely confused, tilting his head like the puppies I'd seen on TV.

"Sienna, you can call me Sienna."

The boy's grin returns as he holds an abrupt hand out for me to shake. "And I'm Jace."

Loud laughter and the thundering sound of footsteps catches my ear as Jace's eyes brighten. "Cleo, Georgia, and Ryan are upstairs. Would you like to play with us, Sad Sienna?"

"I am not sad," I grumble, seriously becoming annoyed by this smiling, golden boy.

"No, but you don't seem happy, either. I'll tell them we'll watch a movie and then all your sadness will be gone, what'd you think?"

A movie? Together? It's been so long since anyone has wanted to watch a movie with me. I think the last time may have been last year when I spent the weekend with Cleo.

"Sure." I shrug, trying to play it off cool, but inside I'm ecstatic!

Someone wants to watch a movie with me! Does that mean that we're friends now?

"Good. We'll watch Alice in Wonderland."

When the memory subsides and my eyes land back on Jace, his eyes tell a mixture of stories and emotions beneath their irises.

The key that Alice used to open the door to Wonderland and the White Rabbit's stopwatch. Jace tattooed the first ever memory we shared with one another on our skin.

Emotion builds in my throat as I go to speak, but he beats me to it.

"What do you think?" he questions softly, eyes glimmering as I draw in a breath.

"That you may just be a little bit of a sweet guy." I chuckle jokingly. He dramatically clutches his chest as if he'd been wearing pearls.

"A little?"

I roll my eyes at him, twisting my body to fully face him. In the time since we started this whole list together, Jace has proven time and time again that he is a caring person who just wants the best for me.

"You're an amazing guy, Jace...Don't ever forget that."

Twenty-Nine

Sienna

"Shit, I don't understand…Explain it one more time." I sigh for the fortieth time, running a hand over my face as Jace gives me a warm, patient smile.

He places a soft hand on my knee and squeezes gently before diving back into his spiel on columns and their different art styles. And just like before, I can't process a single thing he's saying.

We've been going at this for hours now. Him tutoring me for my History of Modern Art course with me looking like a confused puppy in front of him.

Around hour two, I ordered Chinese takeout. Now, an hour later, zero information has been soaked into my brain and all of my shrimp fried rice is gone.

"Babe, are you listening?"

No, not at all, I want to say. But instead of being truthful, I nod.

Jace dramatically and playfully rolls his eyes like a toddler before adjusting our position to where his legs are open and my back is to his chest on the ground. I relax under his touch, something that I've grown accustomed to over the past few months as he holds up my flashcards before my eyes.

"I'm going to fail…and then I'll be a miserable loser who has no food, house, or money for chocolate chip cookies. Then, I'll grow old and grey and no man will look at me." I frown as Jace chuckles from behind me, the vibrations of his laugh warming my body.

"I'll still be here." He chuckles, but that only ups my antics. I sigh loudly.

"This is a disaster!" I yell, throwing my head back against his chest.

"Sienna... A "C" in a college course is not a bad thing," Jace soothes, his voice soft and gentle against my ear.

My body caves in on itself, slouching as I process his words. "But it's not perfect..."

I hate to be that person, but my grades are my everything. I didn't have too many friends growing up, and school was the only constant in my life.

My parents were never around, and I barely got to see my uncle and cousins.

If I don't have good grades, then who am I?

"Listen, we'll get through this...I'll stay up all night to help you. Always," Jace says, massaging my shoulders, causing me to roll my neck from the deep touch.

"Promise?" I ask, my voice lazy and soft as he kisses my shoulder gently.

"I promise."

We sit for two more hours, studying and working on both of our class work. Jace helps me through everything, and for the first time since I've started this course, I truly understand it.

"You're really smart, y'know?" I say, watching him as he works out some of his work for his Communications course.

I hadn't even known that he was a double major until tonight.

He's minoring in Business Management and majoring in Fine Arts. It's a hard task when not doing any extracurriculars, but Jace is also a hockey player for a D1 team and the owner of a small business and art gallery.

The man's work ethic is impeccable.

"Gee thanks..." He chuckles as I playfully roll my eyes, leaning my head on his shoulder.

"I don't mean it like that, I just mean that I admire you. You're really smart and you work hard," I say with a shrug, but my heart racing in my chest tells a completely different story.

"I admire you too, Sienna, more than you'd ever know."

Sienna

"And now class, I'd like everyone to think deeper. What does Impressionism mean to you?" Professor Hewin's monotone voice travels across the lecture hall.

My head lulls as I try to think back to our course on Impressionism, only for my thoughts to stray back to Jace. Last week after getting tattoos and *almost* trying shibari—which ended in us realizing rope play is *not* for us—he'd helped me study for midterms. And for the first time since I started this course, I learned something.

I don't know if it's because a hot guy was teaching me or because Jace is just *that* good at explaining things, but I learned so much more in our hours of studying than I have in the nearly two months that I've been in this course.

Sighing, I bite the end of my pen as my mind wanders back to Jace. He's been busier lately with the start of the hockey season quickly approaching, and I want nothing more than to see him play the sport that he loves. The last time I'd seen him play was four years ago, and he—

My phone's buzzing halts my thoughts. With a small frown, I pull it out only to chuckle at who the sender is.

Heart

Juliette, where art thou?

Speak of the devil...

Me

Up your ass.

What's up?

Heart

Kinky

I like it

Anyways…come outside. I'm in lot B

When I reread his texts for the third time, his words still don't comprehend in my mind.

What does he mean, "come outside"? Like outside of my class, *outside?*

Me

What's in it for me?

Heart

Wow.

Is my beautiful face not enough?

Me

Nope.

Heart

Move your cute little ass, Sienna

Time is ticking and we're late

My mind wars with the decision. Do I stay in this boring class? Or do I go? I haven't seen Jace all week, but I also know that I *need* to pass this class more than anything. Then again…I could also learn way more from Jace. He *did* help me retain information better. Buuuuuutt then again, I have perfect attendance—I can't just leave…or can I?

Girl, you're in college. You can leave whenever, the devil on my shoulder chimes in.

Fuck it.

Making my decision, I gather my things.

Oh my gosh, am I doing this? Like *truly* doing this? My mind races, palms sweating as I approach the lecture hall exit.

Why does it feel like I'm about to fuck up my life catastrophically? I can see it now…The dean of Summerfield University plastering my name everywhere after I walk out of my lecture into "no man's land" with Jace Heart…

Am I overthinking this? *Maybe*. But you would be, too! I've never skipped a class before. Could I get suspended for skipping? Can you get suspended in college?

"Don't do that—Ouch!" Jace yelps, holding his shoulder as I clutch my frightened heart.

"Why would you sneak up on me?!" I shriek as he scoffs, clearly offended by me *softly* punching his arm.

"You were standing two steps away!"

Touché…

Jace doesn't give me the time to respond to his retort, and instead grabs my hand and pulls me closer to him. The exposed skin on my waist tingles as his large hands slide firmly against it, he softly squeezes me, smiling boyishly. My cheeks heat and goosebumps litter my skin from the look.

He kisses me soft and quickly, startling me momentarily before he pulls away. "We're going to have so much fun…Get in!"

That's how I find myself standing in front of Wishland, the 304 acre theme park an hour and a half away from my History of Modern Art lecture hall.

I've never actually been to a *real* amusement park before, only carnivals and fairs. My parents were always busy on the road and I've never wanted to go to one alone, but I don't think that Jace knows this.

Instead, the guy is standing next to me like a kid in a candy store, grinning from ear to ear at the park's entrance. Without a word, I allow him to drag me through the park's metal detectors and into the world of Wishland. Iconic

Wishland characters like Princess North and Princess Lyra decorate posters at the very front of the park, but what steals my breath away is the iconic Wishland "Luna Blue" star at the very middle of the park.

"What do you want to do first? I'm thinking we try Gemini Jumpstart and then—"

"Can we get Staries? I've never had them before..." I trail off, my eyes locked on the girl just a few feet away from us, giggling with her friends, dawning the esteemed Wishland stars on her head.

"Whatever you want, angel... Always."

After getting my Staries and forcing Jace to get his own in a different color, the two of us set off for the Zodiac's Quad section of the theme park.

Since Wishland is a theme park based off of the solar system. Everything in the park and company is named after different constellations, including the characters.

When we get to Gemini Jumpstart, I halt in my steps at the sight of the ride. It's a massive roller coaster with purple and pink coloring. The ride is full of loops and turns with two carts running at the same time to seem as if they are twins. My jaw drops when the ride goes upside down and fire—Yes, *FIRE*—shoots into the air just a few feet away from the carts.

"What the hell..." I breathe, but Jace clearly doesn't hear the hesitation in my voice because instead of stopping to think about getting on the ride, he drags me towards it.

What happened to the guy who was scared of rides at Fall Fest? Where did this stranger who doesn't care about life come from?

"Come on, babe. I want to get a good seat at the front!" he exclaims, marching us to the rides line.

When we get settled in the line and my heart returns back to my chest, I turn to him.

"What happened to the boy who was scared of carnival rides not even a month ago?"

Jace scoffs, a hint of a chuckle in his tone as he looks down at me, wrapping an arm around my shoulder. I settle into his touch, grinning as he rolls his eyes dramatically.

"If you think that I'm about to *willingly* ride something that can be put up and taken down in less than twenty-four hours, you're *severely* mistaken, angel." He shrugs as the line moves forward.

I frown. "What's so good about real roller coasters, anyways? They're just rides..."

Jace's eyes nearly bug out of his head as he looks at me, shock and amusement dancing in his irises.

"Have you never ridden a real roller coaster before? Your parents are celebrities..." he says, completely baffled as I shrug.

"They also were *never* home for me to hang out with them, besides I've ridden rides before...Just not a rollercoaster at real amusement park since I've never been to one..." I trail off, my eyes darting to the carts in front of me instead of the man beside me.

Jace does a double take, looking down at me with a whole new perspective as we move closer to the front of the line, just a few feet away from the ride.

"You've never been to Wishland before? WishWorld? Wishtis? None of the Wish brand theme parks? They're the biggest company in the world...I could've sworn you went with us as kids." He gapes, chuckling in his confusion.

"No."

"Well then, today's your lucky day, angel. We're going to make your wish come true."

And that he does.

Jace and I ride every ride under the sun, starting at Zodiac's Quad and ending at Dipper lane where the main food halls and stationary games are. Somewhere along the way, Jace won me a giant Luna Blue plushie, warming my childhood heart. I grin down at the large blue and white smiling star as we step forward in line to order at The Carina Cafe.

"What can I do for you today?" the worker behind the counter asks as we take a step forward in line. Taking in the worker's attire, I smile at her miniature pirate hat and corseted dress, completely on brand for the constellation Carina.

"Can I get a deluxe funnel cake and lemon—" Jace steps in closer to me, his arms tightening around my waist as he shakes his head.

"Wait babe...What are you doing?"

"Huh? What do you mean?" I ask, titling my head to look at him as his brows furrow.

"You can't eat that..."

I can't eat that? Who does he think he is to tell me what I can or *cannot* eat? I am a grown woman and can make my own damn decis—

"It's littered with strawberries *and* strawberry preserves," he says, looking pointedly at the menu where it clearly states the food and its ingredients.

Oh...

"Are you trying to send yourself to an early grave or what, woman?" he asks jokingly, squeezing my hip before turning to the worker. "She'll have a regular funnel cake with all the bells and whistles of a deluxe, minus the strawberry—she's allergic."

I look at Jace with a newfound interest as he continues ordering for us and pays. No one, not even my family, is that thoughtful of my allergy, especially since it's so rare.

Hell, *Cleo* eats strawberry donuts all the time.

But Jace? He remembered my allergy and made sure that I didn't consume any part of it, even though I would have been the one to order without fully checking the menu.

"I love you Sienna, but shit, don't scare me like that. You almost killed yourself." He laughs as we place our food on the table.

Did he just...?

We both pause in our tracks and I jump up from my spot, hovering over the table to stare at him. Jace Heart just told me that he loves me, in the middle of The Carina Cafe at *Wishland*.

Jace's cheeks are redder than a tomato, his eyes wide like a deer caught in the headlights as he gapes at me, processing his own words.

What do I say? Do I say it back? Did he mean it as a friend way or something *more?*

Jace Heart loves me.

Jace Heart loves *me?*

Jace Heart loves me.

Jace fucking Heart *loves* me!

Oh my...My jaw drops as he schools his expression and shoots finger guns my way, slowly sliding back away from me.

"Wait—"

He doesn't hear me because he's turning on his heels and *running* back up to the register. I mean full on track star running to the register...

He just told me he loves me and then ran away like a school girl!

When Jace gets back to the table, two cups of water in hand, he makes a point to look everywhere but at me. It's kind of cute the way that he avoids eye contact nervously, but it's also confusing. Did he really just say that he loves me and ran away?

"Uh...Jace?" I poke, and when he doesn't respond, I keep trying. "Want to go on one last ride?"

Instead of responding, he nods, leaving us in complete and utter silence. Awkwardness builds between us, turning a day full of happiness and exhilaration into one of tension.

When we finish eating, I begin to lead Jace to the two towers located just behind the Wishland star. When we step in the path of Ursa Major, the largest drop tower in the state of Maryland, and Ursa Minor, the second, Jace halts in his steps.

"Is this *really* the last ride that you want to get on today? A drop tower?" he asks skeptically as I grin.

"Yep!"

The queue for the line is short and quick with only four other people in line, making it our quickest wait time of the day. And in no time, we're being strapped to the constellation themed ride.

Jace squeezes my hand, holding me tightly the entire way up, still completely silent as we climb to the top. My skin dances with nerves and the anticipation of the peak, scared shitless of the drop.

When I turn my head, I realize that I can't see Jace, but I know that he's there beside me. He always is.

"Hey, Jace?" I call out, more like shouting, as we climb up the ride, reaching the top in just mere seconds.

Now's the time, Sienna...don't dick out, I tell myself, my heart thrumming hard against my chest.

"Yeah?!" he calls back, his hand squeezing mine.

My heart skips a beat as we pause momentarily at the peak of the ride, the entire theme park surrounding us in glittering lights as sunset begins to fall.

A feeling of peace and happiness washes through me as I smile and say, "I love you, too!"

And then, we drop.

THIRTY-ONE

Jace

THIrTY-TWO

Jace

TODAY'S A GOOD FUCKING day. Sienna Sola Jones loves me, the sky is an array of pink and orange as the sun sets, I spent the whole day with the woman that I've loved my entire life—Did I mention that Sienna loves me?

Great fucking day indeed.

When we finish up at Wishland, Sienna and I walk back to my car hand in hand, grinning like mad men.

This is *our* place—Wishland. Me saying I love her may have been accidental in timing, but I meant every single word, and I'll continue to scream it from the rooftops.

I love Sienna Jones, and Sienna Jones loves me.

I should get that tattooed on me.

Maybe I'm turning into Derek with all of these spontaneous tattoos, but who cares because Sienna Jones loves me!

"Your first game is coming up, right?" Sienna asks as we get settled in the car. The thought of our first game brightens my mood even more as the team that I've been a part of for the past three years, flashes at the back of my mind.

"Yep, are you coming?" I question as we pull on to the road, heading for the highway.

Sienna's quiet for a second after my question. Does she not want to come to my game? Am I moving too fast? Before I can voice my concerns and outright ask her if she's okay, she responds.

"Do you want me to go?" she sheepishly asks, tugging with the hem of her shirt, bringing a smile to my face.

I reach across the arm rest and squeeze her thigh softly. "Of course, I want you to be there."

Sienna brightens at this and turns to me, even though I'm driving. "Then yeah, I'll always be there for you."

"Promise?"

"Promise." She nods, a note of finality in her words causing me to smile as she locks her pinky with the one that I have settled against her thigh.

Looks like that's become our thing, too. We have *things!* Can you believe that? I mean, I can...I manifested this relationship every day for years, but now that it's forming, I'm happier than ever.

When I drop Sienna back off at her apartment, we sit in the car for a little longer than anyone would deem normal. Sienna is an angel incarnated as the lights of her building and the streetlights brighten her features in the car. She smiles at me, her smile brighter than the night sky.

My heart skips a beat at the sight of her. Her hazel eyes are a light brown, reminding me of warm toffee. I want to kiss her and set this moment in time between us. I mean we said we *love* each other not even eight hours ago.

My eyes must translate what I'm thinking because without a word, Sienna leans into me and kisses me softly. The kiss reminds me of a walk in the park, warm and full of happiness. I pull her in deeper, kissing her with intent, she groans softly before pulling away.

This girl is everything.

"I'll see you later?" she asks, eyeing me up and down with a small smile as I kiss her one last time.

"I'll see you later, angel."

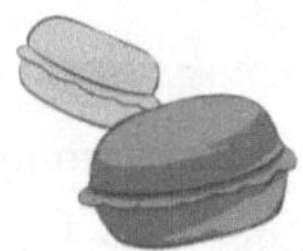

"So yeah, J...I just don't think that we're going to the game. I mean it's still awkward with Blake and I and the other girls don't even like hockey that much. I think Denver–" I zone out as I reread Cleo's text about not coming to tonight's game.

I could understand why she wouldn't go considering she had Blake chasing her in his underwear like a lunatic just a week ago, but why wouldn't Sienna be there? I mean she has no reason to not be in attendance.

She and I just swore on it that she'd be there for me.

Fuck. I *cannot* go into this game angry. Maybe she and the girls are still going to be here and Cleo's the only one not coming...Yeah, that sounds right!

Sienna's still coming...

Then why hasn't she texted you back yet? My phone burns with my unopened text to Sienna.

I'm fucking pissed.

She *promised* me.

She also ran away after kissing and having sex with you, so...

Now is not the time to go back and forth with my conscience over this, especially when the game is an hour underway and I'm in the locker room with the culprit of this whole thing right beside me.

I should kill him.

"Leave her the fuck alone, Wilder," I mutter as Blake sends Cleo yet another text about how he fucked up.

Him fucking up with Cleo is fucking with *my* relationship!

"Don't tell me what to do," he snaps.

And that's how my best friend and I end up on opposite sides of the locker room, our chests heaving with Braxton, Derek, and Charlie between us.

Blake and I haven't fought one another since freshman year when I pissed him off with my strict housekeeping rules in our dorm. And yet, fighting him made me feel so much better about everything.

I don't know what that says about me, but hey...At least I'm honest.

Blake and I hash things out, apologizing to one another before stepping into the rink's tunnel, the two of us putting our minds back on what's really important today.

The game.

We're about to hit the ice, the entire team standing in the tunnel waiting for the announcer to introduce us as the home team when Blake nudges my shoulder. Since I'd been the one to technically start our little tiff in the locker room, I'd lost my anger towards him shortly after it fused.

"You okay?" he asks, his blue eyes deep with concern as I shrug.

"We've got a game to win," I say instead of giving him my real answer which is, *why are girls so confusing?*

Two days ago, Sienna and I were screaming to the rooftops that we love each other, and now, she's not answering my texts and her cousin is claiming that they won't come to tonight's game.

Before I can start to overthink this even more, the lights in the arena dawn their familiar orange and blue hue.

It's showtime.

Blake is the first out on the ice with me, ripping right behind him. The chill of the rink has nothing on the anger coursing through my body.

Is Sienna really not here?

Fuck, she has to be here. I mean she wouldn't break a promise like that...I don't even know why this is suddenly so serious to me, but the thought of her not being here does something to my heart.

The game goes by so quickly that I don't even realize that it's over until Blake scores the winning goal, and there's still no sign of Sienna.

I search high and low throughout the crowd, and yet I don't see her. When we took our intermissions and talked over plays with Coach, I hadn't been able to check my phone to see if she responded to my texts.

The guys are all celebrating tonight's win, some patting Blake on the shoulder and others discussing whatever party they're going to tonight, but my mind is set on one thing, and I can smell it now.

My fingers itch to paint, to let out this emotion that I'm feeling and just be back to my old self. I don't even think that I'm angry about Sienna not being here to support me, but I am disappointed.

You don't break a promise to someone you love.

I wonder if that's how she felt when she was a kid and her parents didn't show up for her recitals.

Was she disappointed? I know that she was sad, but was that feeling as deep as the one that I feel right now?

Blake is a chipper fucking camper, happy and talking like he wasn't sulking in the corner earlier as we walk out of the locker room with Derek ahead of us.

My brow furrows as he stops in front of something before walking the opposite away, revealing *my* girl.

Sienna stands next to Georgia, wearing a black beanie and one of our special white and blue hockey sweaters. A smile breaks on my face at the sight of her wearing our jersey, only for it to fall as she turns to the side, looking up at Georgia.

What. The. Fuck.

The number 52 sprawled on her shoulder sends my blood pressure to an all new high and the vein in my neck pulsing.

Last time I checked, the number I wear on my back weekly is 26...*Derek* is 52.

My jaw clenches as I sidle up to Blake, agreeing and nodding at whatever he has to say, but my eyes are locked on *her*.

"Give your keys to Sienna," Blake tells Cleo, and my brow furrows as I look between the three of them.

Sienna tilts her head at me, as if she's confused on why I'm staring *her* down, but I remain silent, seething as Cleo and Blake skip off to wherever.

Out of respect for my girl, I wait for the two of them to walk away before I sidle up to her, plucking the keys out of her hands and tossing them to Georgia.

"Excuse—"

"You're excused," I dismiss her, turning my attention to the wide eyed girl in front of me. Sienna gapes at me in shock as I take her hand in mine, silently leading her away from her friends.

"Where are we going?" she blubbers, completely off guard as I lead her out to my car.

"Babe, wait! Jace, are you okay?" Sienna digs her heels into the asphalt, making me stop to look at her, and when I do, my heart skips a beat.

"Take that off."

She blinks at me twice before furrowing her neatly arched brows. "What?"

"Take. It. Off," I say, stepping closer with each step.

Sienna's breath hitches as we stand toe to toe with each other, her looking up at me in pure bewilderment.

"Have you lost your mind? Jace, what are you on right now?"

"Nothing. Get in the car," I say with a sigh as she tilts her head to the side, giving me that annoyed look that she does.

"No, I—"

"Get in the car, Sienna." My command has her eyes widening, but she does as she's told and gets in, albeit a little hesitant.

The ride to where I'm taking her is short, only a ten minute drive away from the rink.

Sienna is quiet, watching me with sharp eyes as I walk around to her side of the car.

"What are we—"

I don't give her the time to finish her sentence as I toss her over my shoulder and unlock the door to the art studio. I give her ass a smack, grinning as she gasps.

When I find the room that I'm looking for, I place Sienna down on the white tarp in the room. I leave to get my supplies before coming back to find her still in the same position as I left her, wearing *his* jersey.

Sienna raises an expectant brow at me, folding her arms over her chest. "Well?"

"You've got two seconds to take the jersey off or I'll do it for you. I need to paint, and right now, I'm staring at my canvas."

A hint of a smirk tugs at her lips before she licks them. "So take it off me then."

Our eyes lock, holding one another in a dance that I never want to be through with. I look her up and down slowly, drinking her in.

"Well," she tilts her head, "what are you waiting for?"

Taking a step closer to her, I cup her face with both of my hands and tilt her eyes to lock on mine. Her eyes are what tempt me the most; they call out to me as if to say *do it*. And I do.

I take her lips between my own, tasting and sucking her soul into my own with a deep, devouring kiss. Sienna grins, her hands gripping the back of my shirt, pulling me into her.

I want this girl more than anyone will ever know, but first, I need to get this itch scratched. Without wasting time, I pull away from her and pull the jersey off her in one swift movement. She blinks back at me in shock, but it's fleeting as she brings me back down by the nape of my neck to seal our fates together yet again.

I'm hesitant as I pull back from her, unsure of if I should continue with my original plan or keep whatever *this* is going, but when I pull back and look into her eyes, I know what must be done.

"Take those off and stand right here, I need to see you under the light," I command, stepping away from her to the giant canisters of gold and lavender edible paint.

When I'd first bought these, I honestly had no idea what I'd use them for, but now that Sienna's here, I have quite the idea.

Sienna folds her arms over her chest, raising a brow at me as I approach her with both canisters and a paintbrush.

Dipping a clean brush into the canister of lavender paint, I make my first swipe at her thigh, only to pause at the sight of a roadblock.

"Why are these still on?" I ask, staring at the lavender lace panties hiding her from me as she scoffs.

"Why wouldn't they be on?" she taunts me.

She's right, I should've been more thorough with my words. Instead of responding, I yank them down and stuff them in my pocket for safe keeping.

I don't have to look at her to know that her jaw is on the floor as I swipe the paint deliciously up her thigh, stopping just a few inches from her center.

"All of this is mine. I told you this once, but it looks like you need a refresher, angel." I kiss her inner thigh before swiping the paint even higher and lighter, trailing over the spot where my lips had been.

Sienna shivers as the cold paint dawns her warm colored skin, sending goosebumps to her flesh as I continue to paint her entire body. When I get to her breast, I take my time, flicking and smearing the paint across her nipples. They look like little mounds of purple by the time that I'm done, and I want nothing more than to take them in my mouth and suck them clean. I'm about to make good on that thought until Sienna places a hand on my chest, stopping me in my tracks.

"You want me at your mercy? Fine. But we're going to be equals through it all. Take this off and those. I want to see all of you."

I smirk, standing to my full height and pulling her wet skin against my dry clothing.

"Such a needy little thing, aren't you?" I taunt, bite my lip as she looks up at me.

Sienna swipes her tongue across her teeth with a grin. "I know what I want..."

Covered in paint unashamed by anything at all, Sienna looks up at me like she could walk me like a dog...and she knows that she can.

"You want me?" I taunt, looking down my nose at her as she nods. "Show me. Get on your knees."

I've been hard from the moment I saw her, but the sight of Sienna on her knees causes something in both my chest and dick to stir as she looks up at me through her thick lashes.

"Pull it out," I direct, adjusting my hips for her to have better access.

Sienna's hands work fast as she quickly undoes my jeans and pulls down both my pants and underwear, freeing my dick in one swift movement.

My skin tingles where she holds me in her hands, pumping twice before wrapping her warm lips around me.

I gulp, tightening my core to stop myself from coming at the sight of her on her knees painted purple with my cock in her mouth.

Sienna sucks in and out twice, her head bobbing before her teeth grazes my tip, causing me to flinch.

Fuck, that hurts...Sienna's eyes widen momentarily and she moves to pull away.

I cup my hand under her chin and give her a reassuring smile, stopping her.

"Open your mouth a little wider, use more spit, and suck."

I throw my head back, groaning in complete ecstasy as she does exactly that, my hand on the back of her head guiding her as she takes me in her mouth, bobbing up and down.

"Atta girl, you suck my dick so well," I tease her as she deepens her throat, sticking her middle finger up.

Fuck, this girl is going to end me before we even get started.

Sienna pulls away from me, her mouth making a popping noise as she looks up at me, drool connecting her to my cock. Her eyes dance with fire as I lean down and kiss her sloppily, mixing our erotic flavors together.

Pulling her up to her feet, Sienna grins devilishly at me. "That was easy, now turn around. I can't be the only one who's messy."

Instantly, I rip my shirt off and turn around for her as a cold yet wet sensation travels across my entire back. Unlike me, Sienna used her hands to paint my body gold, and when I turn to face her, she's grinning like a mad man.

Her hands trail up and down my skin, leaving flames of desire in her wake as she rubs all over me, stopping at my neck.

"Come here," I say, not wasting any time before pulling her by the nape of her neck and connecting our lips, kissing her all the way to the ground. I lick Sienna's body, my fingers trailing up and down her thighs before landing at her center, finding her wet for me. But just as I'm about to sink a finger into her, she grabs my forearm.

"Stop playing and put it in," she huffs, angling her body to open her legs for me.

"Angel, if you want me to fuck you, you're going to have to beg."

Instead of answering me, Sienna rolls over on top of me, her eyes full of lust and defiance as she straddles me and aligns my dick with her entrance. "Well it's a good thing that *I* want to fuck *you*."

The groan that escapes me is out of this world as she sinks down onto me, taking my full length inside of her before bouncing up and down on my dick. I can see the universe behind my eyes as pressure builds in my stomach. I bite my lip hard as a distraction and lean forward, pulling one of her breasts into my mouth, licking and sucking her nipple as she moans. She throws her head back before pausing.

Sienna stiffens, her body stopping as she looks down at me, placing her hands on my chest.

"I...We never..." she breathes, her chest rising and falling as she looks down at me, worry clouding her gaze.

Reaching up, I gently cup her cheek. "We can stop right now if you're uncomfortable...Are you—"

"I'm on the pill. Are you okay with this?" she asks, biting her lip. The feeling of her clenching around me has my muscles tightening.

"I'm okay..." I grit out, my vision blurring as she begins to ride me. As soon as I feel her slow down, I take over, thrusting up into her. Fuck, I need to see her, feel her deeper.

Flipping us to where she's on her back, I let out a grunt. My pleasure grows at the sight of her ready, and I immediately plunge back into her, fucking her into the tarp as she moans aloud.

"Come on, baby. I know you can be louder than that...I want the whole neighborhood to know my name," I tease her, my thumb circling her clit as I pound her deeper and harder.

Sienna screams with pleasure as my thrusts quicken, mercilessly drilling into her as she clenches around me. "Fuck, Jace! I'm gonna—"

"I know, I love you so much," I groan, my hips pumping faster as she squeals under me, a moaning, writhing mess.

"Jace!" she yells, bucking up to meet my thrusts, a plea in her voice as our skin slaps against one another, creating a wet noise.

"Come for me, angel," I groan. She clenches so hard around me that my eyes roll to the back of my head. I clench my jaw, holding out for as long as possible as Sienna writhes against me. Her ecstasy washes over the both of us, and just as I feel that all too familiar tightening in my stomach, I pull out. She smiles dreamily at me as I stroke myself hard and urgently, spilling my arousal on her breasts.

The perfect pearl necklace.

Kissing her one last time, my tongue finding its way home in her mouth, I savor her. The feeling of our cold flesh pressed together and her mouth on mine has my brain short circuiting as we pull apart.

"Come on, let's go get you cleaned up."

THIRTY-THREE

Jace

ANOTHER LINE HERE WOULD make this pop...

My pencil glides across my sketchbook effortlessly, tracing and outlining a small piece that's always plagued my mind but has never been finished. Before Sienna and I reconnected, I hadn't picked up my sketchbook in almost seven months, but now that we have, I'm sketching more than I have in my almost twenty years of life.

"And another one here—" I'm about to add some more detailing when a girl pops into my line of view, pausing me momentarily in my craft.

She smiles at me and I reciprocate the action skeptically as she plants a seat next to me, pulling a sketchbook identical to my own out of her canvas bag. My nose scrunches as the pungent scent of her perfume intoxicates the air, reeking of an old cotton candy smell.

"Is this seat taken?" the blonde questions, turning to face me as I erase a minor mistake on my page.

Mumbling, "All yours..." my mind flashes with thoughts of Sienna and her upcoming birthday. She turns twenty-one on New Years Eve, and though her birthday is two months after mine, I'd rather plan her birthday first seeing as I have a good idea on what to do for my twentieth already.

"Wow! Your line work is gorgeous," the woman next to me gasps, leaning in to get a better look at *my* sketchbook. I tense as her breasts rub against my arm and her pervasive smell suffocates me.

"Oh...Thanks." I awkwardly rub the back of my neck, looking down at the unfinished dancer that I always sketch just as she turns to look up at me, her face mere inches from mine.

My nose itches.

I scrunch it, my eyes watering as I try to place where I know this girl from, but I can't.

"Oh! I'm so sorry...I'm so nosey." The woman giggles shyly, pulling back abruptly as I try to shake away my sneeze.

Rubbing my nose discreetly, I wave her off. "You're fine..."

"I'm Amber, by the way." She smiles hard, holding out her hand for me to shake before turning back to my sketchbook and previous thoughts.

My heart aches as my mind wanders back to how excited Sienna had been after her mom told her she'd be coming home for her birthday.

The hope in her eyes, the pure happiness that radiated off of her...I fucking hate her parents for putting that look on her face, because in the end, I don't trust them.

They weren't there at that recital all those years ago. They didn't see that angel lose her wings for the very first time or how hard I worked over the years to put them back in their rightful spot. They didn't see how dim the light in her eyes were at the beginning of every summer and winter fucking break.

I did.

For years, *I* was the one watching over her even when I had no idea what I was doing. *I* was the one who held her when she cried on the porch. *I* was the one always there for Sienna because at that age, I knew that when you love someone, you fight for them. And when you love someone, you show up for them.

They didn't, but I damn sure did.

Heaving a sigh, I shake off the little tiffs of anger settling in my bones as Amber leans in to say something only to be interrupted by our professor.

"Again everyone, there isn't any homework due for this week. I need you all to be rested and focused for the upcoming midterm."

Thank God.

This course has been a walk in the park so far with my professor assigning little to no work and only discussion boards. I'm gathering my things and walking out, thoughts of Sienna's birthday still raging through my head, as someone grabs a hold of my bicep.

"Do you think we'll have homework?" the girl from earlier asks.

Was she not paying—

My phone vibrates Sienna's custom alert. Giving the girl a tightlipped smile, I open our text thread.

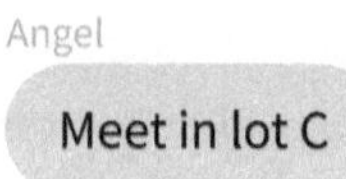

My brows dip as I read the text. Is she still trying to hide us? Lot C is the furthest lot from the Arts section of the quad where the majority of both of our classes are located.

Sending a thumbs up emoji, I look back down at Artemis—or whatever her name was...

She grins up at me cheerfully.

"Bye."

I don't give her time to respond back before I'm making my way to parking lot C and the woman desperate to hide me.

"Well color me gray and tie me to a tree stump, you look mighty fine, Mr. Cupid," Sienna coos in a horrible southern accent, tilting the cowboy hat on my head.

Catching her wrist, I smirk down at her. "Wear the hat, ride the cowboy, darlin'," I drawl, smiling as she rolls her eyes before playfully swatting at my chest.

Sienna walks over to a full body mirror a few paces from where I'm standing and turns, analyzing her butt in her reflection.

"Oh hush…Now what do you think we should wear? I'm thinking the denim set and glasses, what do you think?"

I feel relaxed as I watch her through the mirror, slipping my arm around her waist. "Whatever you like…"

Sienna doesn't give me the time to be dreamy, instead she abruptly turns in my arms and smiles up at me like a mad man.

"Good! You can wear the giant glasses!"

And that's how I found myself standing inside of a mall's photo studio, taking "awkward couples photos" with the crazy girl.

Granted, this item was on her list…I'd thought she wanted us to take nice professional pictures that weren't done inside of a mall.

Instead, we stand in a reverse dominant position, staring into a camera in our first outfit. I don't know what convinced my girl that we should wear stitched sweater vests, but she somehow managed to get me into one. Sienna's small frame is wrapped behind me like we're taking prom photos, with her holding my waist.

"I need more seriousness from you, blondie!" the photographer shouts, snapping away at us as Sienna giggles. My lips quirk at the smile only dying down fully when the photographer groans.

We've been at this for an hour.

"Show your poker face, *blondie,*" Sienna taunts, stepping in closer to my back side.

"I liked it better when you called me psycho…had a better ring to it, don't ya think?"

She chuckles behind me, unraveling her hands from around my waist to poke my cheek.

The photographer snaps a few more photos in this odd outfit before we change into the fully denim one with glasses from earlier at the store. This outfit reminds me of a bad jeans ad with awful stitching and actors.

Sienna's southern accent from before is back in full force as she orders me around, positioning me to her heart's desire. She pokes and prods at everything and even musses my hair, claiming it adds more "ummph" to the pictures, or whatever that means.

All I know is that I'm here and doing whatever this woman wants me to for however long she'll keep me around.

"I love you, Heart, but my goodness you're stiff." She frowns, yanking my arms back and forth as my heart swells. Hearing her say she loves me will never get old.

Grinning, I quip, "Not the only thing that's stiff," as she gags.

"Eugh! That was gross...I'm going to make a jar for all of your little douchebag comments," she tuts, running a hand over her slicked back hair.

After a few minutes of pushing and pulling me every which way, Sienna positions us to where her back is to my chest. She makes me hold my head over my fingertips, and I feel like I'm a toddler at a dance competition. The pose is awkward to say the least. As she mimics it under me, I place my chin on her head.

"Don't move...This is perfecto!" the photographer exclaims, snapping away as Sienna snorts.

"You think this is funny?" I peer down at the pink haired woman as she looks up at me.

The world stops as soon as Sienna's deep hazel eyes lock with mine. The way she looks at me triples my heart rate. The glow in her eyes, the soft yearn beneath her irises. Sienna Jones could be the only girl in the universe, a million light years away, and I'd still be able to identify her just from her eyes alone.

"And we're all set. Your pictures will be ready in two to four days. Please return back to pick them up." The photographer's voice pulls us back to reality, and my heart slows back to its normal rhythm as we check out.

Sienna and I walk out of the photo studio hand in hand, on a mission to explore the mall just as my stomach grumbles. I let go of her hand momentarily, rubbing my stomach how Delilah does when she's hungry.

"You hear that? Psycho needs food, angel...Feed me."

Sienna pretends to gag, sticking her finger in her mouth animatedly. "Gross! Don't ever do that again…"

"Oh you love it…" I taunt, going to grab her hand again and putting it back where it rightfully belongs, when she suddenly flinches away.

What the hell…Furrowing my brows, I go to reach for her again when she takes a step back, shaking her head. She stares wide eyed in the distance, and when my eyes land on the group of SFU cheerleaders, my blood boils.

"Why are you still so hell bent on hiding us?" I huff, standing in her line of view.

Sienna looks taken aback as she looks up at me, confusion souring her face. "What?"

Heaving a deep breath, I sigh. "You're hiding us. We can't be seen together on campus, I can't stand too close to you because of what other people will think. Hell—I can't even hold your hand at a mall, *thirty minutes away* from campus because some bobblehead cheerleaders might see you interact with me! You literally just told me that you love me not even an hour ago, but you're embarrassed to be seen with me." My chest heaves as Sienna draws back, her jaw slightly dropped.

"I'm not embarrassed! I just don't want anyone to see us," she counters, and her words hit me like a knife.

It hits its intended target and I stagger back, wounded.

"Wow…"

"No, Jace…What I meant was—" she tries to say, but I don't want to hear it.

"Sorry I'm not *perfect* enough for you, Sienna," I spit, unflinching as she blinks back rapidly before turning on my heel and leaving her there in the mall.

I'd known that Sienna didn't want us to be public—it was one of the first things she said to me regarding this little arrangement—but for her to say it so bluntly has my head pounding and blood thrumming with anger.

My parents love one another loudly. Dad will brag about my mom to everyone he meets, talking about his beloved wife so animatedly to anyone who'd listened and vice versa.

They'd passed that down to us, making it a mission for everyone in our family to be loved and celebrated for their accomplishments no matter how big or small they are.

I just don't want anyone to see us.

Her words from earlier ring like sirens in my head as I walk into the guys and I's house off campus. Blake and Braxton sit in the living room, playing video games when I walk in. The two of them groan and shout at the TV as I plop down on the couch with a sigh.

They eye one another briefly, playing for a few more minutes before pausing their next round.

Blake is the first to speak. "What happened?" he questions, furrowing his brow as Braxton smacks him upside his head.

"Obviously a girl happened..." Brax shakes his head, annoyed, before turning to me. "Why did you and the mystery girl fight?"

At his words, Blake smacks his chest, his eyes wide like he's trying to communicate with our friend, but Braxton ignores him.

"Dude, it's obvious they fought...look at his little puppy dog eyes..."

Blake groans, throwing his arms up.

"Yeah, but—"

I tune them out, putting my headphones in and turning the volume up as a sad song begins to play.

My mind immediately goes back to the mall, and even though I try to move past it, I can't.

It shouldn't have gone that far, *that* I know. Sienna was raised completely different from how I was. Her accomplishments, no matter how big or mediocre they were, went unnoticed. She didn't have people who were there for her or celebrated her just for being herself besides her uncle, cousins, and me. But that doesn't mean that my feelings aren't justified, as well.

This is so fucked...

I sigh, my mind roaring with images of her face before I left her standing there in the mall wearing a large pair of nerdy glasses.

I shouldn't have left her there alone. We could've talked it out...I should've just did the right thing and took her home instead of leaving. All her parents and everyone in her life ever did was leave, and I just did, too.

We fucking sucked tonight. We, as in the team. Tonight was an away game against Harborview, one of the worst teams in our conference and yet, we came close to tying. I don't know if it's because everyone is having girl problems lately or just have their heads up their asses, but there should be zero reason we were just a hair shy of losing to them.

I sigh as I sit next to Derek in the back of the bus in our usual away game spot and close my eyes. I like sitting next to Momma bear because he rarely talks after away games, especially if we sucked. And when he does talk after, it's always good conversation.

As the bus begins moving and the guys begin talking about whatever they got into while we were here, I feel eyes on me. Popping open an eye, I flinch from the close proximity of Derek and I.

"What happened with the demon spawn?" he asks, eyeing me suspiciously as I raise a brow.

Demon spawn? I only know one of those, and she doesn't respond to my texts.

"Georgia?" I frown as he rolls his eyes.

"No, dimwit. Sienna. Why was she upset and why did I have to take her home a few days ago?" Derek's questions have a bit of an edge to them as my brows squeeze together, catching the tail end of his words.

"You took her home?"

He sighs exasperatedly. "That's beside the point."

The fuck does he mean *beside the point*?

I reel back unamused. "No, I think this *is* a point, considering you took my girlfriend home."

Could I even call her that?

Derek's eyes widen, amusement flashing in them as he raises his brows. He looks around the bus cautiously, but everyone else is still in their own worlds. Lowering his voice, he leans in closer to me and I can just feel the anger radiating off of him. "Then why the fuck did you leave her in a mall stranded and on the verge of tears?"

Gulping, I shift my gaze from him to the window, chewing on my bottom lip.

It was never supposed to end like that...What had originally only been a question turned into an angered rant. She won't answer my calls, and I can hardly think without seeing that look of hurt on her face.

"Did she cry?" My voice is unrecognizable, hard and rough as I voice my concern.

Derek scoffs. "I don't know how she didn't, but that girl saved every single drop. She even helped me with Deli's hair and gave me some advice, so I'd like to think of her as a friend now. And since both of you are my friends...I'm going to ask again. Why did you leave her?"

Derek's never been the serious type, but right now, the look he gives me is the same one he gives to opposing teams on the ice: cold and deadly.

I rub both hands over my face, thinking deeply about my situation before turning to face him and telling him everything from start to finish.

I tell him about our childhood, from when we met to our first kiss on her birthday, to now. I tell him about how I was like Sienna's self-appointed protector and how we made it a mission to be there for one another. I even told him about the tattoos we got before finally rearing back to today. When I finish, Derek sighs as if he'd lived everything himself.

"Dude...go get your girl back. Life is too short to end something great because of miscommunication."

THIRTY-FOUR

Sienna

"Should we take it from the top?"

Sweat beads down my forehead, trickling to my brow. I'm heaving, my chest rising and falling like I'd just ran a marathon after practicing for the Winter Showcase with Daisy. She, on the other hand, looks like a freaking runway model.

I don't think I've ever seen this woman break a sweat in our months of practicing together.

She's silent for a moment, her eyes on me through the mirrored wall before she lets out a small chuckle, stalking towards her bag at the front of the room.

"Here babe, drink up..." She smiles, placing the all too familiar electrolyte flavored drink in front of me.

Nodding, I pick it up and down the entire thing as Daisy laughs.

"Did you sleep last night? You downed that like you're starving." She cackles as I flip her off.

"I slept horribly yesterday, but I got this! Let's run it from the top again and fix the eight count at the very end—I don't like the last turn that we added. It doesn't flow...Then after we should do a run through and be done. How does that sound?" I ask, after downing the entire bottle of electrolytes and turning to Daisy.

The smile she sends me is like a proud mother as she claps a hand on my shoulder, squeezing lightly. "It sounds like we're about to nail this showcase."

When Daisy and I finish our practice, I feel lighter than I have in a dance studio in months. My body is drenched with sweat, my heart is happy, and I've worked up an appetite. Daisy, who'd been a lot meaner in our last practices, is now the perfect friend, laughing and walking with me out of the studio.

"No girl, did you see that new video that MarjaDance posted last night? I've been running through it all day in my head." She laughs, opening the door for me as we exit out of the studio.

My eyes widen as I turn to her. I love MarjaDance. She's been my favorite dance influencer for the past five years, and I get a lot of inspiration from her.

"Of course, I did! She combined acro and ballet, I was tuned in!" I say pridefully as if I knew MarjaDance myself. Daisy's laughter slowly dies down, and when I no longer feel her presence beside me, I slow my steps.

"Hey, isn't that your boyfriend?"

I stutter in my steps, my eyes slowly tracking to where Daisy's light ones are, and low and behold, Jace Eros Heart stands at the entrance of the Arts building in all his glory. I tuck my bottom lip into my mouth as I eye him carefully.

Today, he's wearing his orange SFU hoodie and grey sweats—a typical outfit for a guy, but still hot and laid back.

He and I haven't spoken since he left me at the mall almost a week ago, and not because he hadn't tried—he did, but because I didn't *want* to talk to him.

I don't know how to face him...

I do feel like an asshole though, he sent flowers to the apartment and called me more times than I can count, but what kind of man leaves their girlfriend inside of a mall? We could've talked it out. If he'd just let me finish speaking, he would understand that I'm not embarrassed of him.

Far from it.

I'd just rather keep us a secret a little longer so I can figure out how to tell Cleo about us. It would kill me if I lost her over a guy. No matter how much I love him, I can't lose my best friend. To lose her would be to lose a piece of myself.

After the misunderstanding, Derek found me in the mall and offered to take me home since he'd saw everything go down. In the car, he let me vent to him and was a true friend to me, like Jace said he would be all those months ago.

Derek had even given me some advice afterwards, and I agreed to help him with Delilah's hair, seeing as he wrangled her curls into loose ponytails that always ended up a mess by the end of the day.

It felt nice to have a new friend.

Like a magnet, my legs propel me to Jace. We could be miles apart and I will forever be drawn to him. I need to talk to him and apologize. I was in the wrong for my words and I want nothing more than for him to understand what I meant. I never wanted to make him feel that way, especially after everything we've been through. I just—

My heart stops and my feet halt in their tracks, my brain sensing danger before my eyes ever lock on the blonde girl who pops up behind him.

I note the look of discomfort clouding his usually cheerful face and the way he subtly tries to back away from her.

The girl is persistent though, she continues to smile up at my boyfriend, tugging at his arm in a way that makes it seem to the unknowing eye that they're together.

The quickening of my pulse is like that of an F1 cart as the woman lifts on her tip toes.

It all happens so fast.

My legs propel me forward with a mind of their own, taking me to the pair and planting me right in front of Jace.

I'm fucking livid.

"You have five seconds to leave my boyfriend alone or I swear to all things great, you're going to learn how far I can shove my fist up your–."

A hand over my mouth stops my words. His warm scent of leather and vanilla engulfs me and my body relaxes under his touch. Jace chuckles nervously as the woman's eyes widen.

The girl takes a deep breath, mumbling as she turns on her heels running away like a cat with its tail tucked between its legs.

When Jace lets me go, it's like all the air between us thickens. He tilts his head at me, a knowing smirk on his face. Rolling my eyes, I sigh and smoothen my hair down.

"*So,* I'm your boyfriend." He teases, raising a dark blond brow at me as I roll my eyes.

"I guess you are."

Jace makes an amused sound, a small smile playing on his lips before he looks down at me.

"Listen..." We say in unison, the awkward tension from before building as the both of us laugh shyly.

"I shouldn't have left you, and I damn sure shouldn't have gotten mad at you at the mall. I understand why you are the way that you are and I–"

I cut him off, shaking my head. I can't let him go on... Not like that.

"No Jace, I'm the one that should be apologizing for what happened at the mall. It was wrong of me to flinch away from you when all you wanted was affection. I've never done this before and I got scared... but I never should've made you agree to hiding this... *us.* You mean the world to me and when I realized that I hurt you, I didn't know what to do with myself." I lay out my heart as Jace nods.

"So why didn't you answer my calls? I left you flowers daily..."

I couldn't stand to see that look of hurt on your face again... I knew that I'd hurt you again and I just couldn't, I think but don't have the courage to say aloud.

"Embarrassment. I was embarrassed that I didn't realize that I was hurting you sooner... I should've acted like an adult and talked it out with you instead of ignoring you then marking my territory like a jealous toddler..." I trail off when Jace laughs, the vibration of his laugh rattling me.

"It was hot, I'll give you that." He grins, nudging my shoulder.

Laughing, I nod as he pulls me closer into his chest.

"I'm sorry that I left, Sienna. I love you, okay? I love *you.* I would never do anything to put you in a situation like that ever again. I've been in love with you for my entire life and plan on loving you for eternity after that. I'm sorry." He says, the vibration of him gulping moves against the top of my head and I hug him in just a little tighter.

We needed this.

"Are we good?" Jace asks, his voice taking on a sobering note as I nod.

"Always."

Jace nods in agreement, "Promise?" he holds up his pinky to my line of view.

"Promise."

THIRTY-FIVE

Jace

"Are you in love with her? I'm not saying I'll back off, it's every man for himself—" Blake's words drone on as he rambles about Cleo, and I wonder how I ended up in this situation.

The more he talks, the longer my mind wanders back to Sienna. It's been a week since I'd seen her head of pink curls, smelled her chai vanilla perfume, or even heard her sassy ass voice.

She's been practicing for the Winter Showcase and taking up shifts at the dance studio. One of the teachers is sick, so she's been a stand-in. I've had practice with the team every single day this week also. Is this how my life will be if I go to the NHL? Will I ever see my wife and kids?

Sienna could be in a different country for all I know.

Blake continues to drone on about his date tonight with Cleo, asking me questions about her and being his true dramatic self. I do my best to placate him, but the only thing that my mind can focus on is *her*.

Sienna.

I need to see her.

Trying her phone again, hope builds in my chest only to die a quick death.

"Hey… You've reached my voicemail!—"

Just as I'm about to hang up, another call interrupts me. Thinking it's Sienna, I answer immediately, only for my shoulders to fall as my mom's voice flows through the speaker.

"Sweetheart, I've got such great news!" Mom cheers through the line, and I can just imagine her doing her happy dance as amusement laces her tone.

Walking out of Blake's empty bedroom, I go to my room and shut the door, kicking off my bedroom slippers.

My mom takes a deep breath, pausing for a dramatic effect before shouting, "Your brother has a girlfriend!"

"I think Corinne would be slightly offended if she heard you call her a 'girlfriend', Mom." I chuckle as I throw on a hoodie and plop down on my bed, sketchbook in hand.

Mom giggles before brushing me off. "No, silly! Asa has a girlfriend! She's pretty and tall, and that's all I know since someone—" she coughs exaggeratedly, "—is hiding her from us."

I can hear Asa in the background objecting to my mom's words before she laughs loudly.

"Anyways, honey, I'll talk to you later! I can't wait to see you on Thanksgiving, I have a big surprise for you. I love you!" she coos into the speaker as I grin.

"I love you, too, Mom."

The next day, Blake and Cleo's disgustingly happy and sex riddled faces find me at the house's front door while I'm on the phone with the local Summerfield florist.

Today's my birthday brunch that the girls and I usually do the Saturday before my birthday.

Cleo and Blake stand awkwardly in front of me, and had I not been on a strict schedule today, I'd stay to chat and rib them some more.

But I've got a girl to find.

Sienna has been M.I.A all morning, not answering calls or texts.

Leaving those weirdos on the stairs, I make my way to the flower shop, Lola's, just a few minutes from the house. Picking up some lilies and some chocolate chip cookies from The Sweet Tooth, I make my way over to the studio.

I refuse to go another day without seeing this woman.

My heart beats rapidly as I stand in front of the studios door, and just as I'm about to raise my hand to knock on the door , it swings open.

Sienna screams, jumping into my arms, and I catch her instantly. I grin as I inhale her warm scent, holding her as I set down the flowers and cookies.

"I missed you so much! These kids are going to be the death of me." She chuckles, kissing me quickly before grabbing the box of cookies and stealing one.

"Did you miss me or the cookies?" I ask jokingly as she speaks directly to the sweet treat.

"You." She grins, moaning lightly as she takes a bite.

We walk in a comfortable silence and settle inside Studio F. Sienna's dance class from today ended about five minutes before I got here, which is perfect.

I'm not sharing her with anyone today. She's all mine.

She leans her head on my shoulder, sighing contently as I hand her another cookie. As she turns to thank me for it, I instantly remember the gift I'd gotten for her.

It may be my birthday weekend, but spoiling my girl is an everyday thing.

"Close your eyes for me," I say, smiling softly as she scrunches her face.

"If you're about to try and get freaky in this studio, then you've lost your damn—"

I shove a cookie in her mouth. "That's enough from you. Close your eyes."

Reluctantly complying, Sienna closes her eyes. I turn her body to where her back is to me and pull the small back box from my pocket. I've been holding onto this for *weeks*.

Smiling to myself, I untangle the necklace and wrap it around her neck. The singular pearl lays against her skin perfectly with its silver chain shining brightly.

"Open."

When Sienna opens her eyes and turns to the mirror behind us, they widen a fraction.

"This is so..."

Biting my lip, I fidget with my fingers. "You like it?"

"Jace, I love it," she says before gently cupping my cheek and kissing me.

We spend about an hour in the studio, laughing with one another until her next lesson. It's bittersweet knowing that I have to leave her again, but the kisses she gives me makes up for it.

"I'm sorry I can't go to your party tomorrow, but I'll have a surprise for you! I can't have my boyfriend go without a gift on his birthday," she says, wrapping her arms around my neck as I sigh.

I've been looking forward to seeing Sienna on my birthday and the costume she decided to wear, but I understand that she has to work now.

I should just hire more people at the studio...I mean, I own it now.

That's not a bad thought—

"Look out for your gift, babe. I'm sure you'll fall in love with it when you see it."

Jace

I'M FEELING FUCKING GOOD; my veins thrum with energy and liquor. My skin buzzes and my stomach is warm as I dance around the top floor of Breeze, the newest addition to my parents ever flowing string of nightclubs.

Shots of colored liquor get passed around to all the people on the floor. About twenty minutes ago, I decided that if I were to be sad on my birthday, I was going to do so while being drunk as fuck.

I wish Sienna was here. I mean, I understand why she couldn't be, but my heart yearns for her to be here next to me.

"Bro, take another shot! Let's get you fucked up!" Braxton jeers, passing me a shot cup filled to the brim with purple liquid. My heart beats triple its normal speed as I look down at the single drink that I wanted passed around at tonight's party: The Angel.

It's a banana rum shooter, mixed with everything to create a miniature Caribbean storm—Sienna's favorite type of margarita.

Downing it in one go, I inhale deeply, cheering as I turn to Brax who pats my back a few times.

I cough from the impact and stumble my way back over to the table where all my friends and the team are seated. Blake and Cleo talk amongst themselves while Georgia and Denver laugh at something Alec says. I go up to Georgia, Alec, and Denver first.

Stumbling, I rest my elbow against Georgia's shoulder, smiling droopily at my three friends.

"Happy birthday, Jace! Are you happy to be twenty?" Denver asks, smiling at me as I grin.

"I'd be happier if I had a drink right about now!" I say, shouting over the loud music as Denver hands me her cup.

I don't think twice before downing it.

The guys make me play all types of drinking games, and I'll admit, they're fun as fuck. But my mind keeps wandering back to Sienna. I wonder if she's having fun with her students.

I know she was signed up for the Halloween party at the studio. It just sucks that Halloween is also my birthday.

Heaving a sigh, I pat Alec's shoulder and leave the table where the team is.

What does a guy have to do to get a solid drink around here? I'm getting fed up—

"Announcement for the birthday boy!" the DJ shouts into his mic, stopping me in my tracks as I look down at the floors under me. Breeze has four different levels shaped in a square pattern with a large dance floor on the bottom level. I can see everything in the building from where I'm standing.

"Jace Heart, an angel has arrived!" the DJ shouts, and all air in the room is sucked out. My body vibrates as I look everywhere, searching for her, but I can't see anything or anyone with pink hair that isn't so obviously a wig.

Without thought, my legs pull me away from my spot and to the elevators. I don't think as I let my legs propel me to the ground floor. People dance and grind around each other as strobe lights flare through the lower level. I'm pushed around as I squeeze through the crowd looking for a head of pink hair.

"Where is she—" The air in my body is expelled through a sharp intake of breath as I stop in my tracks.

On the bar, a girl in a red lace corset that forms a heart shape around her chest wearing a red lace garter with matching angel wings and horns dances freely to the seductive music playing in the club.

I almost look past her and the guy who's trying to get her attention, but something draws me in and that's when I notice it.

Her hair—it's black.

And that's *my* girl.

Sienna

I SEE IT, THE moment that Jace realizes it's me on the bar, dancing and living my video vixen dreams. He stumbles slightly, his head tilted adorably as he looks at me.

And I mean *truly* looks at me.

When he spots the guy who's been hackling me since I got here, a flip seems to switch in Jace's mind. In an instant his once drunken stature is sober as a doorknob, and he's hauling me over his shoulder, flipping off the guy on the bar.

"Bye-bye—" I yelp, cutting my sentence short as my ass stings from Jace's harsh smack.

"Ouch..."

He chuckles darkly, smacking my ass again before barging into a room at the back of the club.

The room is colder and the harsh LED lighting sobers me up as I take in the man in front of me.

His blond waves are longer, stopping a little closer to his ears. There's a dusting of light brown scruff decorating his face and he's shirtless, dressed like a sexy firefighter. His jaw clenches as he looks down at me, inhaling deeply.

For a moment, there's nothing but silence between us. He eyes me carefully as if he'd been craving to get a glimpse of me, and when his eyes land on my freshly dyed silk-press, they stay there.

I've never had black hair before, seeing as I've only worn my natural brown curls until I decided to dye my hair pink back in May.

Jace's eyes wander from my hair to my contact covered eyes before he takes a deep breath. And for a moment, I think he'll be calm...collected, even.

But the words *calm*, *collected*, and *Jace Heart* have never belonged in a sentence together.

In an instant, his mouth is attached to mine, his hand cupping my cheek as he takes me in his mouth, savoring our kiss.

My body comes to life as Jace runs his hand delicately from my jaw to my neck, giving it a light squeeze.

I wiggle against his front as his fingers trail from my neck, toying with the necklace he'd given me before cupping my breast, massaging me.

I groan, throwing my head back in pleasure as his kisses trail from my mouth down the column of my neck.

"Fuck..." I mumble, pulling him closer as he laps at my skin, sucking and biting my neck.

"Spread...your legs," he commands, his voice breathy against my neck as I roll my head back, opening up for him.

"Atta girl. I want you to ride my fingers. Take them in you like the bad girl I know you are." He smirks, eyeing me devilishly as I sigh.

The pressure of his thumb circling my clit as one finger pushes my panties to the side and enters my core has me seeing stars. Jace grins, his unused hand wrapping around my neck as he pulls our lips together in heated kiss.

The chaos of the nightclub outside dissipates as the heat between us mounts.

He adds another finger.

"Oh my—"

Another finger.

He pumps in and out so quickly, so enticingly, that before I know it, I'm coming undone.

Jace smirks lazily at me, pulling his finger out with a pop.

"Taste yourself," he says, putting his index finger in my mouth.

I suck his finger hungrily, lapping up my sweet juices and smile at him as he takes his finger out my mouth.

He throws his head back with a contented sigh.

"I'm going to take you home now, and then I'm going to eat my birthday cake. Understood?" he asks, tilting his head slightly as I sheepishly look away.

"Understood. Happy Birthday, baby."

THIRTY-EIGHT

Sienna

Daisy eyes me curiously for the third time as my phone buzzes again, signaling a new incoming text message.

"It's okay if you want to answer your texts, Sienna, I won't get mad." She chuckles softly, stalking towards her bag at the front of the studio.

Hastily, I make my way over to the phone and snatch it up, chuckling as I read the five separate texts from both Derek and Jace.

Heart

> Congratulations, angel

Heart

> Maybe if you're lucky…I'll show you how big my column is

The laugh that erupts from me is from the bottom of my core as Jace sends a string of smirking emojis my way.

This morning, we got our midterm test results back and I freaking passed! I got a 93% on my History of Modern Art midterm, which was way better than I thought I would do especially after the hell that this class has put me through.

With a bright smile on my face, I open my message thread with Derek and double over in laughter, clutching my belly.

It's a picture of Delilah with cake all over her face and her hair in two terrible buns…if that's what you can call the lopsided balls in her hair.

Derek

> I'd like to think that I did amazing

Derek

> SOS SHE LOOKS LIKE AN ANGRY GREMLIN

> HELP

Clutching my stomach, I hold the phone up, showing Daisy the screen. When she comes over smiling, her lips quirk when she eyes the phone.

"My friend is horrible! Look at my poor baby's hair!" I joke as Daisy laughs lightly, her eyes lingering on the phone as Derek texts again.

Derek

> I need you.

I shake my head, chuckling at his audacity.

Me

> You ruined her hair

Derek

> Shut up and come over. I need you to fix this

Sighing, I turn to Daisy, slightly noting the way she'd already been eyeing my phone. Daisy's lip quirks as she looks over the picture of Delilah, her hair in disarray with cake smeared on her face.

"She's adorable, is she yours?" she asks, her curious gaze washing over me as I snort.

"Nah...She's his daughter. Do you mind if I leave right now? We're nearing the end of our practice, and I'm pretty sure he'll leave her hair like that if I don't help out."

Daisy looks me over, her stare quizzical before agreeing, a large smile breaking out on her face. "Yeah...go save that little girl, I'll catch you later."

By the time I get to Derek's house, I can already tell that I'm going to need an energy drink and some pasta when I'm done with everything. Delilah is running around like a chicken with its head cut off, war crying, with cake *everywhere*.

She comes to a halt when she catches me standing in the foyer, nearly falling when our eyes lock.

"Where's your dad?"

Delilah tilts her head at me as if she has no clue what a "dad" even is. I raise a brow at her, trying to convey seriousness. The act must work because in an instant she buckles down.

"He's hiding..." she frowns, jutting out her bottom lip as I roll my own in to keep from laughing.

This man...

"Where?"

She doesn't answer me and instead points to the bathroom. Nodding, I don't head for her father. Instead, I lock the front door and pick her up, placing her on the marbled kitchen island. Cleaning the cake off Deli's face and getting her to settle down in the living room takes me less than five minutes, but also gives me time to look at Derek's apartment.

The apartment is industrial-styled with red brick accented walls and floor to ceiling windows. It's bigger and more luxurious than I would've expected for a single dad in college. There's all types of things showing that a child lives here from the toy box in the corner of the living room to the small kiddie chairs in the dining room.

However, the thing that makes me laugh a bit is the fact that this apartment is in the same building as Jace's loft. It's cute that they bought units in the same building.

Derek comes out of the bathroom, dark under eye bags making him appear older as his eyes widen, finding me in the living room.

"She said you were hiding..." I snicker as he sighs, running a hand through his hair.

"You would be too if a miniature Bigfoot was chasing you around...Want some tea?" he asks as he opens the cabinets in the kitchen, rummaging around while I take a seat behind Delilah. Her hair bow box and hair care products are already in the living room.

"Water's fine."

We move in tandem with me doing Delilah's hair and Derek handing me each product that I need while I instruct him on what to do with her mane of curls.

He listens intently to everything that I say, and fifteen minutes later, when I'm done with the two braided pigtails, he looks like a new man.

"So...How's everything with Jace? No more arguments that I have to save you from?"

I roll my eyes at him, my heart swarming with butterflies at the thought of my boyfriend.

"Everything's fine...He helped me pass my midterm and look, the photos from our photoshoot came back!"

When Derek spots our partnered picture, a smile breaks out on his face. He laughs lightly, catching Delilah's attention and soon enough, she's in his lap laughing dramatically how kids do.

I hate to admit it, but Derek is a good freaking dad and a good friend. He helped me without question and would do anything for his daughter. I know that I hated his guts originally, but he's pretty solid.

We're talking about my participation in the Winter Showcase when there's a knock on the door. The three of us are dressed in princess gowns, playing tea party with Delilah, all of us rocking Delilah's makeup. Derek raises a brow at me, looking as confused as I am.

"Did you order something?" I ask only for my question to be answered by a shout.

"Open up, dickhead! I know my girlfriend is in there!"

My boyfriend, ladies and gents...

Derek raises an amused brow at me, finding this hilarious as I sigh, following behind him to the front door with Deli in my arms.

When the door opens to reveal an angry Jace Heart, three things happen. Deli screams, "Uncle Cupid!" Jace gasps like he's in a telenovela, and then proceeds to grasp his heart like a woman scorned.

Biting back my laughter, I watch as realization dawns on him and smirk when Jace pouts, his emotions directed at Derek.

"Well, aren't you going to let me in, you big oaf? And why didn't you tell me you lived here too?"

My eyes widen as I look between the two while Derek lets Jace in, the latter immediately kisses my cheek as soon as he gets inside.

"Wait, let me get this straight...You two have been friends for *years* and neither of you knew the other lived in the same building?" I ask, looking between the two as Jace makes himself at home on the couch after taking off his shoes at the front door.

"Pretty much...Hey Momma bear, you feel like making chicken parm? I'm *starving*!"

Derek chuckles at his friend's antics, agreeing to make the dish as I settle beside Jace with Deli in between us. He turns, smiling warmly in his spot.

"Loving the whole undead princess vibe, angel."

Rolling my eyes, I reach behind Deli and smack him upside his head.

"Enough...Anyways, I think that it's time," I say, twiddling my fingers.

Jace's eyebrows crinkle quickly as he gives me his full, undivided attention. "Time for what? To get married and say F U to college or—"

I can't take him seriously...

Chuckling, I shake my head. "No...I mean that it's time for us to tell Cleo."

Delilah, who I hadn't known was listening, nods her head. "Yeah, bro. Tell her, dude."

Did she just...?

"Hey, Derek?" I call out, my voice filled with humor.

"Yeah?" he shouts back, pans clanging in the kitchen as Jace and I laugh.

"Please find a girlfriend," I chuckle, pinching Deli's cheeks, "Dels is starting to sound like a frat guy!"

THIRTY-NINE

Jace

THREE DAYS AGO, I was sitting in Derek's place eating up chicken parmesan with him, Sienna, and Delilah. Now, I'm rushing to get to my best friend.

"CJ's in trouble."

That was all Georgia said to me before I found myself, Braxton, Alec, Charlie, and Derek racing to the girls' apartment after free skating all afternoon.

The guys are as quiet as ever, no one daring to talk as we rush to the girls' place. My mind and heart aches to be there for Cleo, but another part of me *needs* to see Sienna. Knowing her, she blames herself for the things happening with Cleo, and though I don't know everything, I know that it's not her fault.

When Sienna opens the door, her expression is clouded. She looks like she's one second away from having a breakdown herself. I step to the side, allowing the rest of the guys into the apartment to head for Cleo. When the coast is clear, I pull Sienna out of the apartment and into the hall and engulf her in a bone crushing hug.

Her body shakes beneath my touch as if ready to cave in on itself, but I don't let her. So long as I'm here, she will forever stand strong.

"Sienna..."

"I should've been there for her. I shouldn't have lied to her about us or did anything to hurt her feelings after finding out about the tape. I should've went home immediately after practice today, I should've—"

Grasping her face with both hands, I look into her eyes and softly say, "What happened?"

"Everything."

Georgia opens the front door and we separate. She looks me over once before sighing and stepping out of the apartment. Without prompting, Georgia tells me everything from how Cleo and Marcelo—a grade A asshole from her old school—broke up, to the releasing of their shared sex tape today.

When Sienna detaches herself from me, leaving Georgia and I in the hall, I pause.

Georgia's eyes are as large as saucers, crystal lacing the brim of them. In an instant, she's stepping towards me and I can see the little girl trapped deep inside her begging to scream and cry for her friend. So, without words, I open up my arms and let her cry in them.

The sounds of the women around me breaking down in such a horrific way can be heard around the world. The heartbreak and anxiety of knowing that someone you love is hurting and not being able to help them is soul crushing.

What was supposed to be a calming day after practice turned into one of horror. Georgia and I silently pull apart from one another. I watch quietly as she pulls herself together and holds her head up high before reentering the apartment.

When it's my turn to hug Cleo, my heart breaks as she burrows into my chest.

I swore to protect these girls with my life a decade ago, but how am I supposed to protect Cleo from this? From her past?

When Cleo and I part, she remains on the floor next to the balcony no matter how much I beg for her to come to the couch. She wants to be there.

After getting all of the tears out of the way, we began brainstorming. It's been twenty minutes of us bouncing ideas off one another and yet nothing is sticking. Everything is either too outlandish or not enough.

"Look...I think the only true option is to track down the IP address. We may think it's Marcelo targeting her, but what if it's not? We can't just dive into water when we have no idea what's lying inside of it," Sienna says, running a hand through her dyed hair. She takes her time massaging her scalp, and I just wish it was me relieving her of this stress .

Georgia agrees with her and so does the rest of the guys, including Blake and Ryan who'd both showed up a while ago.

"Once we track down the IP address and user info, I think it'll be a piece of cake to sue whoever posted the tape," Sienna says as she grabs all the plates in the living room. I reach out to help her then think better of it when I take in our mixed company.

For once, I don't want to tell Cleo or anyone else about us, either. In the end, Braxton helps her in the kitchen while the rest of the guys head out to go pick up Deli from Derek's mom's house.

I stay where I'm seated as Braxton comes from the kitchen, brows raised as he takes in his empty surroundings. "Did he just leave me?"

"Yup." Georgia chuckles lightly, patting Braxton's shoulder as she passes him by.

I take this as my opportunity to move and slide into the kitchen where Sienna is.

"Talk to me, angel," I whisper next to her ear. She softens as she sighs.

"I wish I was there for her..." she trails off, turning to face me, her eyes downcast.

"You were—"

"No, in New York. I should've been there. I would've told her to leave his stupid-ass right where he was and threatened to feed him to Oscar if he so much as *looked* at her. She doesn't deserve this, she—"

I slip my hands around the nape of her neck, resting my forehead against hers.

"I wanted to tell her about us so bad, Jace, but how can I do that when she's hurting?"

There it is.

"Come on...I know what will make you feel a little better. Cleo's in her room with Blake, and it's time for me to take care of you. Let's go?" I don't wait for an answer before turning Sienna and walking her to her bedroom.

"What're we—"

"Get your gaming controller, I'm about to kick your ass in Mario Kart."

FORTY

Jace

MY MUSCLES STRAIN AS I finish my last set, pushing my body harder than ever in the gym. Our game against Brighton is approaching and some of the guys decided to workout at the on campus gym before practice. Since I'm co-captain, I'm automatically involved.

Blake has been stricter than ever lately, and I don't blame him. If Sienna was in Cleo's position, everyone would be dead.

I'm getting ready to leave for practice when I spot the girl who'd tried to kiss me a few weeks ago eyeing me in the corner of the gym.

"Why are you following me?"

The girl's cheeks redden as she looks between me and the window in front of her. "Someone paid me to."

Paid? Like prostitution paid? Like paid to stalk me, paid?

I blink at her trying to understand what she meant, but I can't. Why would someone pay her to stalk me?

"Yeah, it was some redhead...Listen, I'm sorry. I had no idea you had a girlfriend, I'll—"

Redhead? Who in the world...

Grabbing her wrist gently, my brows furrow. "What the hell do you mean someone *paid* you?"

The girl gulps, her eyes darting from me to the wall, "Listen...I didn't think it would be this serious. The girl who paid me didn't tell me her name, besides it's over...I won't try this ever again."

"See," I chuckle humorlessly, "that's not gonna cut it with me. Who paid you?"

"I-I don't know. It was just a hundred dollars, I'll give it to you right now."

Raising a hand, I silence her. "I don't want your fucking money. Leave me and my girlfriend out of whatever sick game you're playing. Just back off." I leave her there, her jaw agape, and turn on my heel back to the guys.

Who could possibly want to harm our relationship?

A few hours later, I find myself running through drills and playing with the rest of the team. Coach has been working our asses off all day, and for good reason.

We need to win.

Summerfield University births legends, especially on the men's hockey team.

Losing isn't an option.

About ten minutes ago, Coach left Blake and I in charge, telling us to finish running a new play we'd been working on. Our newer guys are strategic, but they lack connection with one another. Between Blake and the rest of the first line, we can communicate with one another effortlessly.

I don't know if it's a product of us working together for years or because of team bonding on campus, but our line is solid.

It's the other lines that need help.

I'm skating up to one of our freshmen, Mark, when I hear one of the twins on the team, Jonah, speaking about the coach's "other daughter".

I halt in my stride towards Mark and turn to face Blaise and Jonah.

"Yeah dude, Coach's daughter is fine as fuck, but have you seen the other one?" Jonah asks, making his hands outline an exaggerated curvy figure. I tilt my head at him.

Coach only has *one* daughter, and I've known her my entire life. Following their gaze to the stands, my blood crystalizes when I see Sienna speaking with her uncle in a hushed tone.

Her shoulders are slumped and hair is in a curly bun. She looks upset and when the coach pulls her in for a hug, I know that something's up.

"I mean look at her, have you seen her ass—"

"Shut the fuck up and get back to work," I snap at the two, rolling my eyes as they tuck their tails and skate back to their lines.

Sienna catches my eyes briefly before she nods her head at whatever Coach says, and my hackles rise. Something's wrong.

In a second, I'm off the ice. I waste zero time following her, yelling something about using the bathroom as I chase her.

When I find Sienna, I sigh in relief only to hold my breath as she looks up at me.

"They're not coming to Thanksgiving."

Moments like this make me thankful that there aren't any firearms in my vicinity. Sienna doesn't have to explain any further who "they" are. I already know. Frowning, I pull her into my arms, my heart breaking as she sniffles, relaxing in my embrace.

Her parents are the worst people in the world. I mean, who tells their kid that they'll see them for Thanksgiving and then cancels two weeks before?

"You can always come with me. Matter of fact, you're coming with me to Thanksgiving," I decide, not budging as Sienna tries to pry herself from me.

"No, I can't–"

"You can and you will, Sienna. Plus, my family loves you. What's the worst that can happen?" I ask, tilting my head down to her as she looks up at me, rolling her eyes with a smile.

"And do a little spin, show off my girl! Let me see you, baby!" I direct, recording Sienna on my mom's doorstep as she rolls her eyes.

Today's Thanksgiving, and even though Sienna was upset about not seeing her parents a few weeks ago, she's smiling from ear to ear now.

Humoring me, Sienna does a small spin, showing off the leather vest and all black outfit she's wearing, but the real show is her hair. I've been trying to convince her to go back to her pink hair, but she refuses.

So tonight, she's wearing a wig. I tried to understand what she meant by a lace frontal, but after watching a few videos on it, I'm still a bit lost.

Sienna grins as I pull her into a hug, opening the door and letting ourselves into the house.

On the day before Thanksgiving, my immediate family has a dinner that we like to call "Pre-Giving", where we all sit down together and eat before our extended family shows up.

I grin as we step into the foyer. Nothing has changed in my childhood home. The house is still warm as usual with photos of the entire family decorating the walls in chic picture frames.

"I'm home!" I yell, Sienna and I kicking off our shoes as Asa rounds the corner.

His smile is huge when he spots me, but when his eyes land on Sienna, they widen.

"Si Si?" he asks surprised, jaw slightly agape and brows furrowed as he hugs her.

Weird.

"Hey Ace," she greets, hugging him back and using his nickname.

The entire interaction is odd. Between my brothers, Asa is the chill one and almost never looks confused about anything.

He just goes with the flow.

Right now, he looks like he just tasted something sour as he stiffly walks Sienna and I to the living room.

"You need to get the two of you out of here right now," Asa whispers to me, and I don't have time to question him because that's when I see her.

My ex-girlfriend, Kacey.

Forty-one

Sienna

It happens all so fast.

Jace's mom gasps, shouting my name with a confused edge. The girl sitting next to her jumps up from her seat, eyes solely fixed on the man next to me. Jace gives me a concerned look before his eyes fall back on her. She pushes through us and pulls his body against hers, hugging him like her life depends on it.

I tilt my head, watching the hug, noting the way Jace's wide eyes flicker from the girl wrapped uncomfortably around him to me.

"Uh...who are you? And why are you attached to my boyfriend?"

The girl pulls away from Jace slowly, her eyes trailing up and down his sturdy body with hunger before drifting to my own.

"*I'm* his girlfriend. Who are you?" The girl tilts her head at me, causing me to reel back.

I chuckle, but it lacks all humor as I eye the woman who Jace desperately tries to pry himself from.

I scoff.

He's not cheating on me, that's for sure, but did he tell his mom about me? It's hypocritical of me to ask that when I haven't even told Cleo about us but...did he?

Obviously not if his mom invited another girl over...

I let out a deep exhale.

The air in the house is thick with tension. Everyone is sitting on the edge of their seats, looking around the room as if waiting for an imaginary ball to drop.

"Let's eat!" Asa claps, cutting some of the thickness in the air, and immediately everyone begins washing their hands and preparing to eat dinner.

"Sienna, I'm so happy you're back. I made sweet cornbread, you liked it as a kid, right?" Jace's mom, Anna, asks as I take a seat at the table after washing my hands.

"Yeah, I loved your cornbread as a kid." I grin, trying to brush off the awkward tension in the room.

Jace is seated next to me on my right with Asa to my left. His mom, the girl, and Jackson sit in front of us while his dad takes the head of the table.

The feeling of Jace's hand rubbing circles on my thigh soothes my fraying nerves as we eat.

"Oh my goodness, Anna, did you make these deviled eggs for me? You know how I much I love your deviled eggs!" the girl who's name I have yet to learn exclaims.

Anna gives her a tight-lipped grin as the girl giggles. I take another deep breath.

Stay calm, Sienna...

"Yes, honey. Your mom reminded me that you like them." Anna coughs awkwardly taking a bite of her food.

I eat a bite of the mashed potatoes on my plate and frown as I watch their interaction.

It's only been a few years since I've last been over here, but they seem well acquainted.

"Oh my gosh, wait, I remember this cornbread! Jacey baby, you remember when you fed it to me last year?" the woman says in a babylike voice, and I cringe.

What the fuck?

Jace stiffens, the movement on my thigh pausing as the girl's words silence the room.

Last year.

He brought her home for Thanksgiving last year...

"Oh...Uh..." he stammers.

"Oh really, *Jacey baby?*" I mock the girl, eyeing him.

He doesn't say anything though, his golden skin is dim of its naturally bright hue and he looks like he's just gotten caught doing something he shouldn't have.

Jace doesn't deny what she says, he just avoids eye contact with me.

Wow...

"Anna, thank you so much for having me, but I fear I've overstayed my welcome. I'll uh...I'll see myself out. Happy Holidays, everyone."

Jace's gaze flickers to my own, a torrent of emotions clouding them, but I don't stop walking.

I'm overstimulated to the max.

I wish he would've at least told her off or said something. *Anything.* Instead, he just sat there.

Without thinking, I march my way out of the house, leaving everything and everyone behind.

My mind is roaring with different thoughts of the two of them—Jace and that girl. When was the last time they've seen one another? Did they spend Christmas together—New Years?

Fuck.

I don't realize that Jace is following me out the door until I hear his footsteps hit the porch, thundering my own.

"Listen, I'm not mad or anything, and I want you to tell me all about the years we've been apart, but right now my mind is going at a pace that I can't help and I just need a break. I'm okay. I just need to breathe..."

When my words are out in the open, the world around us comes crashing down. Jace is closer to me, his hands finding their usual spot on my cheeks, guiding my eyes up to look at him, but I just can't.

"Is there anything that I can do?"

My chest heaves and everything feels too small, too close.

"No." I say, prying myself away from the man who I've loved my entire life and walking away.

FORTY-TWO

Sienna

LIFE ISN'T EASY. NO one ever said it was, but people have said that love is.

Those people lied.

If loving was easy, then why does my heart feel like I left it on Jace's lawn?

My hands shake as I walk, studying them.

I'd left my phone and coat at Jace's house, not caring at the time, but now as the crisp November air blows against my skin, I wish that I hadn't left so abruptly.

Headlights flash as a car drives past, but I ignore it. They're probably on their way to see their loved ones, something that I should be doing right now.

Instead, I'm walking through my boyfriend's neighborhood alone.

"Get in the car, Jones." My heart stutters, coming back to life at the sound of the person's voice. I'd know it anywhere.

It's my cousin, Zayden.

"No," I pout, quickening my steps as I walk to God knows where.

"Sienna, don't make me park this goddamn car and get your ass. I'm already sleepy as is and then I got some weird ass white boy calling me talking about come pick you up? And why are you walking around without a coat on?"

I snort at my cousin's words and turn to him. Zayden's smiling his perfectly white teeth my way with one arm on his steering wheel. His locs are pulled back with a headband and he's wearing his pajamas.

Was he asleep?

"He called?" I ask, getting in the car as he sighs.

"Did he? That motherfucker called me, Ry, *and* Uncle CJ. I don't even know how he got my number, Si Si." Zayden smacks his teeth as if truly perturbed by Jace as he pulls off.

"Yeah...He has a way of doing things." I sigh, resting my head back as Zayden drives.

He looks over at me momentarily, a small frown on his lips as he says, "Don't ever do that again, you hear me?"

I don't answer, already knowing where he's going with this.

"I know you hear me, Sola. Don't ever walk away from the person you love ever again, especially at night. And don't you dare leave *anywhere* without your phone and protection. Do you hear me?" he asks, turning to me as we come to a stop sign.

"I hear you, Zayden." I roll my eyes, smiling at his care for me as he begins driving again.

"Good, because that kid loves your stupid ass, and I can tell that you love him, too," he says, and then there's silence.

I watch quietly as we drive, ignoring the looks of my cousin as we exit the neighborhood.

"I'm sorry about them, by the way," he quietly adds, and it doesn't take a rocket scientist to know who he's speaking about.

My parents.

"Yeah, well, they could give a fuck about me, so."

"Si Si..."

I shake my head, cutting him off as my lip quivers. I bite on my cheek to stop the onslaught of tears. "No it's okay, they've neglected me for almost twenty-one years...What's one more holiday?"

When I think about it, I'm not mad at Jace. Did that girl trying to stake a claim over him piss me off? Hell yeah. Did him not telling his mom that I'll be at their Thanksgiving upset me? Of course. But all of this anger and overwhelming feelings aren't because of him.

They did this to me.

Zayden takes me back to his place in downtown D.C., about an hour and forty-five minutes from Summerfield and where Uncle Clef lives. I sigh as I step foot inside his penthouse, kicking off my shoes and heading to the guest bedroom that I normally stay in when Zayden lets me come over.

He hugs and kisses my forehead before heading to bed, claiming to need all of his energy before Turkey-Day tomorrow, and leaving me to my own vices.

Without thought, I head to the ensuite bathroom, don my clothes, and get in the shower.

I don't turn on the lights or music. Instead, I cry. I let it all out and for the first time in hours, I feel free.

Laughter follows me as I walk throughout Uncle Clef's house, smiling at the different family photos claiming the walls.

A small frown dusts my lips as I take in our childhood photos.

I sigh, never feeling more alone than I do now.

Maybe I shouldn't have left last night...

Making my way further into the house, I find myself standing outside of my uncle's study, and don't hesitate before letting myself in.

"I was wondering when my Sola girl was going to appear. What's been going on, Si Si?" Uncle Clef's warm voice greets me as soon as I enter the room. I sigh as I plop down on the brown leather couch next to him.

It'd become our thing to watch home movies together on Thanksgiving, reminiscing and laughing at both of our childhoods on film.

"I'm okay," I say with a shrug as he side eyes me, placing his photobook in his lap to look at me.

"Want to tell me the truth?"

"Nope," I say popping the 'p' as he laughs aloud.

"Fine, it was a boy. Which one? The guy who left you stranded or someone different?"

I chuckle, considering both Jace *and* Aric left me stranded before, but instead of answering, I play the home movie that he'd paused when I walked in the room.

"So it *is* a boy. Did you forget what I said about bums? I told you not to date them...Why didn't—"

Sighing, I cut him off, "He's not."

"Is he broke?"

I laugh. "He's richer than me and probably the prince of Wales combined."

Uncle Clef blows out a huff of air. "So he's a rich bum?"

I smile, loving my uncle. "You like this one."

Uncle Clef is silent for a moment, my words sinking in. It doesn't take a full five seconds before his neck is snapping my way and his jaw drops. "No!"

Cue the theatrics.

"The team is OFF limits! No, they are the worst of the worst. Besides Heart, I like Heart...he's a good—Oh for the love of God, it's Heart, isn't it?"

"It's Heart." I nod.

Uncle Clef smacks his teeth, shaking his head like the disappointed uncle his. When he looks up at the TV, a video of Jace and I dancing on the screen plays.

The way he looks at me, holds me. Even at ten-years-old, Jace's eyes have always been the same whenever he'd looked at me, and it warms my heart.

The video shifts and it's one I'd never seen before. The camera wobbles slightly as Uncle Clef's voice blares through the speaker.

"Come on, kid. Record her right!" *He coached even then.*

The boyish, childlike giggle has my spine stiffening as Jace's voice calls back, "I'm trying, I'm trying! She's moving so fast...God, she looks like an angel."

The last line is mumbled, but I hear it loud and clear as the video cuts.

The recital. The first ever recital that my uncle and everyone flew to California to see. He'd called me an angel, even then.

Jace had been my number one supporter that day, showing up with my first ever bouquet of flowers and a smile on his face. At the time, he had green braces, and they were the cutest things in the world to me.

I remember it like it was yesterday, when I'd looked around and couldn't find my parents in the crowd. I instead saw his mess of blond, wavy hair and knew that he was there for me.

That same day, he called me an angel and gave me flowers.

Stargazers.

They were bright and the most beautiful thing that I'd ever seen.

Jace Heart *saw* me, and dare I say he may have even *loved* me, all those years ago. Little did I know then, but I felt the exact same way.

Jace

THANKSGIVING WAS MY FAVORITE holiday until twelve hours ago. I can't even *think* of smelling food let alone being around it because I know that I'll throw up.

I kicked Kacey out as soon as Sienna walked away from me, I don't even know what possessed my mom to invite her, but I ended up telling her and everyone else in this family off as well.

Asa and Jackson could've told me, hell, they could've *warned* me that my ex-girlfriend would be sitting at our fucking dinner table when I got home.

Instead, I walked in the house blind, thinking I would surprise my mom with Sienna and everything would be fucking dandy.

The thought of Sienna being alone on Thanksgiving has my chest hurting.

The look on her face, those diamond-like tears brimming in her eyes…They were enough to make a grown man cry, and I did. Vulnerability and showing emotions is masculine, and I did both last night when I cried in the shower, thinking of Sienna and her parents.

Knocks sound on my bedroom door and I groan for the fifth time as Asa and Jackson try to get into the room.

"No!"

They don't care, instead they open the door and tumbling in like the large assholes they are.

"I don't want to talk to you cunt pockets. Get out or I'm telling Mom."

They have the nerve to *laugh* at me.

I squint my eyes, lifting my head from my pillow as Asa lays down next to me and Jackson pushes me over to be in the middle of them.

"Putting me in a brother-wich? What are y'all, five-years-old?"

They ignore me, instead making themselves comfortable before Jackson speaks.

"We're sorry. Mom didn't tell us her plan...She just said she had a surprise for you," Jackson says, turning to face me, but my eyes are trained solely on the light-up stars on the ceiling of my childhood bedroom.

"I knew. Whenever Mom says she has a surprise, I just assume it's a girl. Jacks is dumb," Asa quips, shrugging carefully as Jackson sighs.

"You're dumb," he retorts with a pout.

Asa twists to his side, "In my defense, dickhead, I thought you liked Cleo...Whole time, her cousin looks *exactly* like her. I mean Cleo's cute and you were always going to her house in the summer—"

"Ew! I thought he liked Georgia...But then again all they do is argue and they're both blondes..." Jacks adds.

Closing my eyes, I say, "Both you are fucking disgusting."

"So you went to the Jones' every day because of the cousin? I mean Sienna is gorgeous, had she been a little older I'd—"

I cut Asa a sharp look as he rolls his lips in.

"So, she's the one." He smiles as I huff, turning my head back to the ceiling.

"Get out of my room, I hate you both. Go play on the side of 210," I tut as my brothers cackle at my expense.

"The highway?"

"Did that little asshole just tell us to play on the highway, Jackson?" Asa asks, humor riddling his tone as Jackson chuckles.

"He did...He's whipped." Jacks smirks, patting my head as Asa copies him.

"Whipped!"

Footsteps alert us of another person's presence, and soon enough my mom's voice sounds throughout the room.

"Boys, leave your brother alone. He's sad and doesn't need to deal with your jokes right now," she reprimands them in her most motherly tone, and immediately all pets to my hair stops and both of the cowards walk out.

I turn on my side, watching as my mom walks around my room, eyeing the walls littered with paintings and sketches of the same person.

"Was she...Is Sienna the unknown girl—the dancer?"

My breath catches in my throat as I sit up, my shoulders deflating.

"She's the only girl I've ever drawn. Sienna has been my muse from the moment I first saw her, Mom."

My mom watches me, the crow's feet in the corner of her eyes softening as she takes a seat by me.

"I should've did more. I could've told you about her and made sure she was comfortable. Sienna has been freaking out because of her parents and I just made it worse by coming here without telling you she'd be with me. I...I should've went after her or at least called out Kacey's odd behavior last night in front of her. Instead, I did nothing." I sigh as my mom wraps an arm around my shoulder, pulling me into her.

A mother's comfort can heal all wounds, and that thought alone sends me spiraling because when I think back to Sienna, I realize that she's never had that form of comfort before.

"Tell me everything. How do we get my future daughter-in-law back here with us?"

My eyes search my mother's for any hint of playfulness, but there isn't any. She's as serious as can be, and that's how I find myself spilling my guts to my mom on Thanksgiving.

Her jaw clenches as she looks down at me, her face stone cold and impassive.

"So what the hell are you waiting for? Do you love her?" Mom asks, her tone mimicking the one that she uses in the boardroom, and it's then that I realize that this isn't my mother, it's Anna Heart.

"Of course."

"Then let's make a plan and I'll apologize to her myself for inviting Kacey. I just want you two to be happy. Now, get your girl and get the fuck up. You two need each other."

FORTY-FOUR

Sienna

Zayden sucks his teeth for what feels like the thirtieth time today as he looks at me. I roll my eyes at him, looking like someone's nosey ass grandma in the blinds, watching the front lawn like a creep.

"Man, Sienna, you got this boy standing on our lawn looking crazy." He smacks his teeth while shaking his head, but my stomach drops.

Jace is here?

Looking down at my watch, I note that it's only noon.

"Want me to get rid of him?" Ryan asks, standing next to Zayden. The two of them looking like Tweedle Dee and Tweedle Dum as they share a plate of sweet potato cake between them.

"No, you asshat...Jace would probably punch you if you tried and I don't want to have to explain to Pop Pop why some kid is beating his grandson's ass on Thanksgiving. I'll handle this."

The boys look between one another skeptically before nodding. I can hear Ryan saying, "That motherfucker could *try* to beat my ass," as I leave and I shake my head, chuckling.

When I get outside, I close the door behind me and sigh. I want nothing more than for this situation to be over with. I'm not mad him, I'm just upset at our current circumstances.

Jace tries speaking, but I don't let him, instead grabbing a hold of his wrist and leading him to the backyard away from prying eyes.

"Sienna, I need you."

"Keep talking, I like the sound of that," I try to joke, but the serious look in his eyes has me curling my lips in.

"Listen, I understand completely where everything went wrong yesterday. You were over stimulated from the jump, and I knew this. I didn't know that my mom would invite Kacey, and I truly didn't understand how to react while in there. I'm sorry I couldn't give you that reassurance then, but you have got to stop running. I will chase you forever, yes. But I'd rather it'd be us running from the problems together than you from me." He steps forward, his eyes reflecting emeralds as he uncrosses my arms, wrapping them around his neck. I don't fight him on it, either.

"I'm sorry for not expressing myself as clearly as I could. I just really needed space to breath. Will you tell me about those years apart? I think I'd like to know about them," I say, chewing my bottom lip as he softens.

Jace's eyes search mine, his demeanor open to me completely as I gnaw on my bottom lip. The instant my teeth connect with it, he tugs my lip out with his thumb.

"You are worth fighting for, Sienna."

"Promise?" I ask, stupidly holding up my pinky as he chuckles.

"I promise." He smiles, leaning forward and connecting our lips in a soft kiss.

FORTY-FIVE

Sienna

IT'S BEEN A WEEK since Thanksgiving, and everything between Jace and I has been perfect...Dare I say, too perfect? We've been in our own little bubble, thinking that we're safe in the world, but I have this nagging feeling in the back of my mind that shit is about to hit the fan.

Jace snuggles into my stomach, his face in my belly with his arms wrapped around my back as we sit on the couch, watching a movie.

It's early in the morning and SFU plays Brighton today. However, since the Winter Showcase is tomorrow, I have to spend the entirety of today practicing with Daisy to fix things up.

"Don't worry...We'll kick their asses, angel," he mumbles, sleepily drawing circles in my back as I play with his hair.

He's been super exhausted lately working on art pieces and practicing with the hockey team. It's been so hectic between us that we haven't even had time to keep knocking items off of my list.

"I don't know, Heart...Something just feels off." I frown, eyes trained on the screen as he pops his head up.

Jace studies me for a moment before a devilish smirk dances across his lips. "You know a good way to relieve stress and burn calories?"

"Yoga?" I tease, watching him as he jumps off the couch before he hauls me over his shoulder.

"Jace!"

He smacks my ass. "I'll be sure to bend you like a pretzel, angel."

That uneasy feeling doesn't dissipate after Jace and I have sex, it *heightens*. He had to leave shortly after we finished, which was fine seeing as I needed to head out, too. Only I'm not going to the studio first. No, first I'm heading to the pharmacy.

Sienna, you are just anxious about your recital…That's all. It has nothing to do with your late period.

I sound fucking dumb even in my own head.

A late period could mean a lot of things, and maybe I'm just a few days late since sex throws off your hormones, but this feeling of unease gnawing at my gut won't go away unless I do *something* about it.

Denver calls me on video chat as soon as I pull up to the pharmacy. She's smiling brightly wearing an SFU Men's Hockey jersey with a margarita glass raised in the air, but when she sees my face, her smile falters and she exits the room heading outside.

"What happened?" she questions almost instantly, closing the balcony door behind her as I put in my headphones.

"I'm getting a pregnancy test."

Denver's brows crease as she puts the phone closer to her face. "But you're a vir—Oh my God, get the test right now. How late are you?"

This is the part that I know she'll look at me funny.

"Two days…"

I know that she doesn't mean for it to happen, but she snorts quickly before masking her humor.

"If getting a pregnancy test will make you feel better, then get it. However, buying a test when you're not a full week late may not do anything because your period could always come tomorrow." Her lips deepen in a frown, as I mimic her facial expression.

"I'll tell you what...I'll sit on the phone with you while you take it, and if it's positive, we'll have a beautiful Sienna look-alike running around. If it's not, cheers to the freakin' weekend," She cheers, taking a sip from her margarita.

I laugh at my friend and continue through the store to the aisle where all of the tests are.

"Which one do I get?" I ask, whispering as she shrugs.

"I've never had a scare before, get the cheapest one with quick results..." Denver grimaces, downing the last of her drink as I scan the aisle of pink, white, and blue boxes.

If the Sienna of two years ago could see me now, she'd have an aneurysm.

Heaving a deep breath, I pick up three identical tests, them all guaranteeing an early result, and head to checkout.

"I don't know, girl, I highly doubt you're pregnant...I mean, do you use protection?" Denver's voice echoes loudly as I approach the register.

The cashier, an older woman with short, grey curls, purses her lips as I slide the three tests to her. My cheeks and neck feel warm as she eyes me from head to toe, her eyes lingering on my black coils for a little too long.

"$21.72," the woman blandly announces just as I tap my card awkwardly on the screen. "Good luck." I hear her words trailing after me as I race to the bathroom in the back of the pharmacy.

"What if it's positive, Den? I can't raise a baby...I've barely just started having sex—I haven't even used a vibrator yet! Oh my gosh...I don't even have my own place! Let alone a degree. What am I going to—"

My rant is cut off by Denver's soft sigh. She's been the more levelheaded friend out of the four of us, always seeing all sides of the coin before making a rash decision or freaking out.

"We'll worry about all of those things when the time comes. As of right now, you just need to worry about taking the test and whether or not it's positive," she answers, her voice resolute.

I gulp, looking at myself in the cracked mirror of the pharmacy bathroom and sigh.

It's okay. You got this, Sienna.

Denver and I wait for three agonizingly long minutes. My skin is hot to the touch as anxiety gnaws at my throat and ears.

Never in my life would I have thought that I would end up in this type of predicament. I mean surely if I am pregnant, then maybe it won't be so bad. I'll have Jace by my side and we'd have miniature geniuses on our—

"Time's up!" Denver's voice snaps me out of my stupor and immediately my shoulders slacken.

"Oh, thank heavens..."

Negative.

I'm not pregnant.

That's good, right? Me, not being pregnant right now. I mean I have my entire life to have a family. I wouldn't want to bring a kid into the world while I'm still learning it myself. I'm young. Besides, Jace and I aren't ready. We've barely been together for three months, but, why do I still feel like there's everything's about to go wrong?

FORTY-SIX

Jace

Wind billows around me, ice kicking up off the rink floor as I whizz around, tracking the puck back and forth between SFU and Brighton.

I'm on cloud freaking nine tonight. Everyone is in the stands, my friends all wearing the jerseys I'd given them, and we're up by two points on Brighton.

When I skate past the box where my friends are, my mood dampens for a minute when I remember that Sienna has to work on her dance for the Showcase tomorrow. I wish she could be here to see me kick some ass on the ice.

I skate harder and faster, my eye on the little black puck and that only. Eyeing my surroundings, my gaze locks on Blake's, and right when I shoot the puck to him, a motherfucker the size of Goliath checks me.

Now, I'm not a small guy by any means, but when a tall kid from Russia checks you, it's bound to leave a bruise, no matter how soft the hit is.

"Dude! What the fuck!?" I call out, my annoyance growing as I focus my eyes back on the puck.

I'm so close to it that I can see the high and low lights of the small disk.

We've worked so hard for tonight's game and all that training is damn sure going to pay off. Racing to the puck, I can almost taste the stellar shot I'm going to make when the air is knocked from my lungs and the room spins like shooting stars.

The world is a mix of colors. Orange, blue, dark purples, and then it's black as pain laces through my bones, sharp and unyielding. My arm hurts so bad I can barely breath. Everything around me is a cacophony of sped up heartbeats and hushed whispers.

Someone screams, loud and guttural, cutting through the silence. The sound alone is something that'll keep me up at night, only I don't realize that it's coming from me.

I'm making that horrid sound, and my arms feel like it's hanging on by a thread.

I roll my head back, my brain pounding against my skull has me wishing that I played something less dangerous like golf.

My right wrist is limp. The colors are a devastating painting of angry purple and red swirls. Had this been any other circumstance, I would say that this work of art is beautiful, but it's not.

It's painful.

"Does it hurt—"

"Fucking hell, Wilder! Do you see him? Of course it hurts." Braxton sighs exasperatedly, rubbing his gloved hand over his face.

My eyes track the movement before landing back on my ungloved hand and wrist before shifting a little bit away to the ice, my glove lying just a few feet away from the puck that I'd almost scored a goal with.

"CAN. YOU. HEAR—"

"I'm not fucking deaf, my wrist is fucked up," I snap at Charlie as he sighs, a guilty sheen in his eyes as they land on my wrist.

"Let's go...Give them some space," Blake directs the rest of the guys. I hadn't even noticed we were surrounded by players from both teams until our team's medics appeared on the ice.

"We saw everything, Heart...Ready?" Jonae, our newest medic asks, wrapping an arm around my waist as our other medic, Kai, does the same.

I don't answer them as they usher me off the ice and into their office where we have our physicals and evaluations. I watch in complete silence as the two of them lower the medical chair for me, a sheet of new dressing on it, before hopping on.

I need Sienna here with me. She'd make me laugh or at least tell me that everything will be fine and hockey's overrated.

I chuckle softly, thinking about the times she'd tried to convince me to switch to dance as a kid instead of doing hockey.

If Sienna were here, all of this pain festering in my most used limb wouldn't be here. I'd still be on the damn ice and she'd be watching me score.

It's only been a few hours, but God, I miss her.

Maybe she was right to be anxious a few hours ago. Had I listened to her, I wouldn't have a potentially broken wrist *and* pride right now.

Never in my life has something like this happened to me. I drink my milk, eat all the protein in the world, and eat sea moss daily to keep my immune system and bones healthy.

I've never broken a single bone in my body.

Fuck.

Resting my head back, I close my eyes as the throbbing pain in my wrist continues. Maybe if I just close my eyes and envision her, my wrist will be healed when I open them.

The room is eerily quiet, the only sound to be heard being the light footsteps of the medics as they gather supplies. My body lulls, the vibrations of pain coming in and out like waves just as I try to calm myself down.

"How's your—"

"You idiot! Did you not see that bastard coming up to you? I can't get a hold of anyone—Sienna, your mom, hell, I tried to call freaking Jackson!"

And there goes my calm...

I pop open an eye as Georgia storms into the room, smoke trailing behind her as her laser green eyes zero in on me. Rolling my own and closing them again, I sigh.

She's overreacting.

"Mom's probably working, and so is–"

"I *called* Sienna." The stress and emphasis on the word 'called' has both of my eyes opening, tilting my head. I note Georgia's body language. It's stiff and tight like a coiled screw. She stands with her shoulders damn near to the moon and her green eyes are wild.

My pulse skyrockets and I'm on my feet in an instant, the throbbing pain in my wrist dull as fear grasps me in its clutches. Sienna has been worried all day about something happening, and now she isn't answering her phone? That's the only thing she does. She's never more than five feet away from the device. Ever.

"Where is she? Is Sienna okay?" My heart races, sweat beading at my brow, but the pain in my wrist skyrockets when my feet fully hit the ground. My breathing rackets, clogging my throat. I feel like I'm drowning as my mind races with thoughts of Sienna and her whereabouts.

She's *never* not answered a call.

She's always on time, always answering when a friend needs her. She's always there.

Where is she right now?

Why isn't she here when *I* need her.

I groan, the pain shooting to my elbow as the feeling of hands pulling and grabbing me heightens my panic.

"Jace?" Georgia's voice echoes, the sound far away and close all at the same time as the pain intensifies.

"Where is Sienna?" I grumble before everything goes black.

FOrty-seven

Sienna

—1 hour before

"AND WE'LL TAKE IT from the top once again. Hit! One, two, three, four, five, AND six...seven, eight." Daisy claps back to back as I hit each move to her count.

After my freakout and five minutes of panic in the pharmacy bathroom, I went to practice. We finished our choreo for the Winter Showcase and our exams weeks ago, so now we're just perfecting everything.

My body is tired, I'm hungry, and I'm jealous that all of my friends get to watch the guys play Brighton tonight while I'm stuck here going over choreography for a grade.

When Daisy starts her individual run through, I count for her, marking each step.

Tension between the two of us completely dissipated after we'd found Jace being tormented by that girl in the quad a few weeks back. Now, we talk like we did when first met, calmly and like friends.

It's kinda odd since Daisy is nothing like my other friends, but I enjoy her presence. It's warm and nurturing in a way.

When she finishes her last turn, a triple pirouette, I applaud her. We've been going at this for hours.

"My kids would kill to know how to do a triple." I chuckle, my mind thinking back to the Minis group that I used to teach before my life was upended by a sneaky blond man.

Daisy gives me a confused look, her head tilting.

"No! I mean my kiddie dancers! I used to teach dance to toddlers. See, this is them!" I grin, jogging over to my phone, grabbing it and heading back over.

Daisy grins as she looks down at my phone with me, my lockscreen is an image of the girls and I after the recital in August. It'd been my first ever recital where I was the choreographer and not solely a dancer.

I've never felt so proud of those girls in my life. They came and performed their little hearts out.

"Aww! This little girl is so adorable!" Daisy coos, her pink stiletto shaped nail pointed at Delilah just as a text from Derek rolls in.

Derek

> About to hit the ice, the guys are pumped and after this you NEED to tell me who's been giving you those shitty Spanish lessons.

Derek

> I mean seriously, "que te folle un pez?" that's child's play

Rolling my eyes, I swipe his messages away.

Since becoming "friends" with Derek, the big bastard has texted me daily. He reminded me to eat healthy yesterday, and the day before he decided that I was going to be the person in charge of teaching him how to do Deli's mane of curls instead of YouTube University.

"Ignore him, he's been going on a serial texting spree lately," I say, laughing at my own joke as I turn to Daisy.

A muscle in her jaw tics a bit before she smiles brightly at me.

"I'm a little dehydrated...Want a drink?" she asks, stalking over to her bag just as my mouth dries.

Damn it, we have been working for hours. When was the last time I ate or drank water?

"Sure, I'll take anything you got!" I reply, turning on the music we'd been using for practice just as Daisy approaches with two bottles of pink liquid in hand.

Thanking her, I take the bottle she'd had for me, and gulp down its entire contents with a sigh.

I needed that.

Daisy watches me carefully, her eyes dancing with joy as I smile at her. She's been awfully cheerful this past week, hopefully it's a guy. I've been dying to go on a double date with someone lately.

"All good?" I ask looking back at her as I stretch my limbs once again, eyeing myself in the mirror.

In my reflection, I watch as Daisy nods, her lips pursing as she repeats my words, "All good."

Gulping, I'm about to go back into our routine, but freeze when I can't swallow my spit. I try again, struggling to swallow as an itching sensation travels through my body and I tense up. My tongue feels like it has fur on it, itching and scratching the roof of my mouth as my neck begins to burn.

"What's wrong?" Daisy's voice vibrates throughout the room, the sound everywhere and nowhere all at once.

"I-I don't know...I can't..." I swallow, but my tongue thickens and my face itches yet again.

"Call Jace...His numb...My phone," I wheeze, my lungs closing in on themselves as a fiery sensation travels all through my body.

What is happening to me?

Why can't I—

"Sienna? Are you—"

I don't hear her next words, or anything after that.

I don't see when Daisy calls for an ambulance, or when she walks away. I don't hear her packing up her stuff and leaving me on the floor as my body asphyxiates itself.

I don't hear the paramedics shouting at one another to get a dose of epinephrine ready for me. I don't hear their curses when they can't find my veins or even their sighs of relief when they finally stick.

I don't hear any of it.

I don't see any of it.

Instead, all I see and hear is *him*.

Jace's laugh when I fake an attitude after losing a round of Mario Kart that he'd clearly cheated at. His lazy smile in the morning when he wakes up and I'm already awake, staring and analyzing him. Because when Jace Heart is asleep, I'm at peace. I see Jace running after me as kids, chasing me through my uncle's backyard in the summer. I can hear the way he says my name when he's pissed off at something that involves me, but never at me. Jace is *never* mad at me. I can see him at his first hockey game, the one I begged my uncle to record since I wanted to be there for him but couldn't physically. I hear Jace's snarky retorts and sexual innuendos. I can picture our life together, him and I somewhere down south because we both hate city life. He'd be there for everything, for *me*, and I'd *always* be there for him.

Scientists believe that in the last minutes of life, your brain plays seven minutes of your happiest moments. You see the people and memories that meant the most to you, the ones that count.

You recount everything, the moments both big and small. Your brain sets the moments in a way that brings you peace even when death looms to claim your soul.

In my last seven minutes of life, all I could see was him.

Jace

I HATE HOSPITALS.

They reek of sick people, bleach, and death.

"Can we just go? I don't see why I need to be here! It's just sick dying people everywhere! I'm *fine*," I huff, wincing as my wrist makes contact with my other hand.

"You're not fucking fine, and your girlfriend isn't answering the goddamn phone. So help me God, if she's somehow found a way to end up in the ER too, you two will send me to an early grave!" Georgia laments, her eyes wild as she paces the room.

"One can wish..." I mumble, biting back my laugh when she stops in her tracks, eyeing me.

Georgia points at me, her eyes slicing me in half. "Don't make me break the other one."

Sighing, I lean back in the hospital bed and frown. We've been waiting in the ER for over ten minutes, and still haven't been helped. Our stall is open to all of the other patients in the emergency room, allowing everyone to see what's happening in my stall and for me to see what's going on out there.

"I can't believe they're taking so long...Literally everyone just ran out of here like there was an emergency or something." Georgia frowns, plopping down next to me on the stiff hospital bed.

"Wow! It's almost like we're in an emergency room, George." My dumbfounded voice must annoy her because instead of responding, she rolls her eyes and pulls out her phone.

"I need someone to get eyes on her STAT! Someone check her heart rate, she's dropping too fucking fast for her to be this young!" a doctor yells, barking orders at a few others as paramedics and other hospital staff roll in a gurney.

My eyes dart to Georgia then back to the moving transporter before they snag on something.

Lavender nails.

I don't know why this makes my heart drop, or why I'm on my feet in an instant, but I am. The world seems to stop as I stand, clutching my red and blue wrist as my eyes land on the person laying prone in the gurney.

Dark midnight colored hair, skin that used to be a deep brown color now ashened and marred with rashes, and lips that remind me of home, pass by me.

My heart stops.

No, actually...my heart is laying right in front of me, on a stretcher.

Georgia's cry is guttural and heart aching, but I can care less about consoling her because right now the only person who has ever been worth more than a miniscule of my time, is being rolled into the emergency room like a corpse.

My feet have a mind of their own, traveling quick and after her. I need to see her, be *with* her. What happened? She was just okay, not even eight hours ago.

I was just with her, and now this?

Had she come to my game and ditched practice, would she be here right now? Would the butterfly effect be so kind as to grant me her? Or would this still happen?

The Fates are never in agreement with one another after all, could this just be fate dealing us an awful hand?

Rage billows in my chest at the very thought of this being the last time I see her. The last time I do anything that involves her. I've waited over a decade for her, and I'll be damned if fate only gives us five months to get it right. To let me love her the way I've always dreamt. To hold her how she deserves at night.

I'll be damned and a dead man fucking walking before I let Sienna Jones leave me like this.

The muscles in my body work before I can stop them, dragging me to her as the string that connected our souls tugs me towards her.

I'm late...I'm too late. She's dying and I'm late.

I don't realize that I'm yelling, or hear myself scream for her. Everything around me moves around her, revolving around her.

I revolve around her.

I'd never compare Sienna to something as mediocre as the sun or the moon. No, she's so much bigger than that, so much fuller and beautiful. If you look too deeply at the sun you'd get blinded, if you focus on the moon, you'd see it's overrated.

Sienna is like Saturn for me. She's this big person in my life, unique and charming with her own traumas and baggage that build her up to be this exquisite person. To know Sienna Jones is to see her, and I do.

I see every single part of her.

My muscles are tight and fraught as someone holds me back, and it's then that I realize that I'm thrashing around like a wild animal with Georgia crying and screaming beside me.

"Let him go! That's his soulmate right there!" she shouts, her voice vengeful as she gestures wildly at the woman on the bed.

Soulmate.

Sienna's more than a soulmate to me. She's my entire existence, my soul. We don't share pieces of ourselves with one another, we *own* each other. She has my soul, and I hers.

"Sienna..." I call out, my voice scratchy as I twist from the guard's grip.

There's so many people around her, so many machines and sounds buzzing about.

"Sienna!" I say again, my voice louder as I full on thrash out of the man's grip.

"Hold him back!" someone shouts, but *fuck that.*

"Sienna, wake up!" I scream, my voice breaking, my soul aching as it feels the impact of her loss.

The room goes silent, or so that's how I think it is. No one talks, no one moves. We just stare at the unmoving woman on the bed. I choke on a sob, my body breaking down, heart shattering at the sight of her.

There's bruises on her body from where they'd stuck her, her skin...it's marred with red and purple welts. Tiny rashes decorate her arms and collar.

"Oh, baby..." I gasp, sucking in a deep breath as realization dawns on me.

"Strawberries—she's fucking allergic to them. Who gave her strawberries?!" I shout, my vision blurry as water falls from somewhere.

Rushing to her side, I look up at the sky and pray that God would show mercy on her. She has so much life to live, so much hope.

We hadn't even finished the list yet.

The list would never get finished, and she won't be able to graduate. It's all she's wanted.

"W...Wake up. Please, angel, just wake up. I need you. I need you so, *so* bad. Angel, don't do this to me, don't leave like this. I'd rather you run than this. Run away from me, but don't ever leave me," I sob, crying as I slide into the bed next to her, careful of my arm.

We had forever to go...It'd only been five months, but we still had forever to go. A lifetime with Sienna Jones is too short, I need eternity. I need forever. This moment with her cannot be our last.

My breath catches as my thoughts spiral, a life without her is a life I've never lived before.

"W...Why are you wet? Wh...Where are–" a scratchy voice, almost unrecognizable mumbles.

My heart starts to beat again as confused, golden eyes peer up at me.

"Sienna," I breathe her name, my prayers answered.

"Where am I? Why do I feel like—Jace? What happened? Why are we here? Are you okay?" Her voice rises as panic seizes her. I cup her face with my uninjured hand and press my forehead to hers.

"You do not ever get to do that to me again."

"Do what—" she tries, eyes searching mine for answers, but I don't give her any. Instead, I turn to the group of doctors in the room and Georgia.

"I want her moved to Johns Hopkins VIP suite. Airlift her—do whatever the fuck you need to do, but she needs to be there within the next thirty minutes. Georgia, call my mom and tell her what happened to Sienna. Call Coach, too, he'd want to know, and for the love of all things purple, someone get me a fucking cast."

FORTY-NINE

Sienna

"ARE YOU SURE YOU'RE okay?" I ask for the millionth time as Jace sighs, his chest rising and falling slowly as he tries to get some sleep.

"Angel, I was fine six minutes ago when you last asked," Jace says quietly, holding me tighter with his left arm.

I eye the lavender cast on his right wrist and frown.

I should've been there. Had I been there he would've gotten help quicker or maybe wouldn't have gotten hurt in the first place.

"Stop it."

Looking up at him, I furrow my brows and pout. "Stop what?"

"Stop pitying me and blaming yourself. That asshole was going to hit me regardless," he huffs, kissing my forehead.

I know he's right, but a piece of me just won't accept that.

"Well, are you hungry? I can call for some grilled cheese and maybe I can find a way to get cookies in here and—"

Jace's small laugh stops my rambling. "I am fine. Besides, you practically died. I should be the one asking if you're okay."

At the mention of my allergic reaction earlier, I sigh. I know it was something I had gotten from Daisy, but I highly doubt she gave me something that she knew I was allergic to. It could've just been an accident.

A nearly tragic one...

Jace shifts us in the bed to where I'm laying fully on his chest.

"This is the life..." he mumbles, kissing the top of my head as I relax into him.

I wish we could stay like this forever, cuddling and living quietly.

"Yeah...too bad I have the showcase tomorrow," I say, wrapping my arm around his waist as he makes a gruff noise.

"Nuh-uh."

"What do you mean?" I raise a brow at him as he pulls away from me, pulling out his phone.

Jace smirks down at the screen, typing away before responding smartly. "You heard me, you're staying here. You almost died not even three hours ago, and you think you're about to go prancing on stage tomorrow? We don't even know how you ended up having the reaction, and I'll be damned if I watch you almost die again."

My resolve softens as I look at him. "Do you think that I'm going to just crumble up and die if I hit the stage tomorrow? It was an allergic reaction! People have them all the time. *I'm okay*, Jace."

"You're okay now, but a few hours ago, I thought you were dead, Sienna. So, the answer is no. I already emailed your professor— you're not performing tomorrow, and that's the end of it."

When he looks up from his phone, his brow raised at me as if to say *test me*, my stomach does a flip. Jace had gotten rid of his shirt the moment we'd gotten settled in the hospital bed, his blonde waves tousled and mussed from him running his fingers through it, and he'd been wearing black rimmed blue light glasses.

I frown at him. Fine. If he wants to be that way, then so be it.

"No is still no, babe...Keep pouting, though," he says with a small laugh just as the door to the room opens.

"How's my favorite sick bitch and...you? I guess. How ya feeling, Si Si?" Georgia asks, rounding the corner to my side of the bed as Jace groans.

"Uh...Thank you for asking about me, seeing as I broke my wrist! Besides, why are you here?! We could've been naked!" he exclaims, folding his arms awkwardly over his chest.

"Gross, dude. This is a hospital." Dereks familiar voice calls out as he appears behind Georgia, entering the room still in athletic wear.

Snickering, I look between Derek and Georgia.

"How was the game?" I ask, steering the conversation from a blondie melt-down as Derek steps in.

"Kicked their asses, as usual. How's the asshole beside you?" he asks with short laugh as Jace flips him.

"Grumpy as usual."

The December air chills around Derek and I as we briskly walk towards the entrance of a cafe just a few minutes from campus.

One thing that I've learned about Derek since we've become reluctant friends is that the kid can eat. He's always snacking or sending me videos of new food places.

He'd even made a group chat with Georgia, Jace, and I where he only sends food recipes to try. The chat was originally made to remind everyone not to spill Jace and I's secret until we were ready, but it soon turned into Derek's personal recipe book.

"Look at this one, Heart Jr., I think this would be good, too!"

Ahh...that too. He's given me a nickname.

Rolling my eyes, I follow the big oaf around, checking my phone as he goes on and on about the pastries around us when I get a text.

Daisy

> I'm so so sorry about what happened at practice! I know we haven't been able to see one another be-cause I left last week to visit my grandma but can we please talk??? I'm sorry

Sighing, I swipe out of our texts. Yesterday, I did our showcase dance alone for our professor after Daisy hadn't respond to my texts for the past week. And after a few hours of grilling from Jace, Georgia, and Derek while I was in the hospital, we'd all come to the conclusion that my dance partner had given me a strawberry infused drink.

I know that she didn't mean to, you know...almost *kill* me, but I'd rather eat drywall than talk to her right now. Sure, she didn't mean to give me something that I'm deathly allergic to, but she also left me there after I collapsed.

The EMTs told us that I was alone when they found me, Daisy was nowhere in sight. Something is up with that girl, and I can't place a finger on what it is...

"So, do you have a plan for your birthday? Georgia told me it was on New Year's Eve," Derek questions as we sit down at a booth, three eclairs on his plate.

I tilt my head at him, smiling a bit. "You and G are getting closer."

He sighs dramatically. "That's because we're keeping you little nympho's secret. I need someone to talk about it with."

"Mhm...Right."

He and I eat the rest of our pastries—or more like I take one of his eclairs and he grumbles throughout our small lunch break.

Jace claimed he'd had a small surprise for me today, so when we finish up with lunch, I head over to his house with the guys. I've never truly been here, but he'd sent over the address claiming it was needed for "list purposes".

When I get to the house, the first thing that I notice is the empty driveway, save for Jace's car.

Odd.

My car door swings open and Hercules himself stands in the doorway in all his glory.

"Welcome home, angel." Jace grins broadly, holding out a hand for me. Narrowing my eyes at him, my hackles raise.

He's up to something.

"Hi? What's going on?" I muse, grabbing the held out hand.

"We're about to have the best sex of our lives—no one's home and I can finally show you my real room. Besides, we still have a few things on that list of yours to tick off."

His words process instantly. My eyes flicker to his for a brief moment, and before I know it, our lips are slamming against one another in broad daylight.

I've been waiting for this part of my list—rip off clothes like in the movies.

Jace hoists me up, my legs immediately wrapping around his waist as his hands cup my ass—our kiss unbreaking.

I sigh into the kiss as he walks me up the porch stairs of his house, and when he sets me down on my feet, my smile is bright and wild for him.

Jace doesn't hesitate to kiss me again, his tongue playing with my own as my fingers fumble to rip off his shirt.

We're kissing and pulling at one another's clothes, a feeling of pure euphoria washing over us as we tangle ourselves around one another. We're going at it like rabbits, grinding and tugging at each other, so deeply enthralled in our kiss that we don't pay attention to anything around us.

At this moment, I only see him and he only has eyes for me.

We grind, slamming against a wall. My mouth leaves his momentarily as he begins to tug on my shirt, and that's when it happens.

A low gasp stops us in our tracks. My eyes widen opening to find Jace looking down at me with a confused face just as someone screams.

"OH MY FUCKING GOD—"

Fuck...

This can't be happening.

Jace goes stark still, his mouth slightly agape as he winces.

"Sienna?!"

Shit.

FIFTY

Jace

THIS IS *NOT* HOW I expected tonight to go.

Sienna and I sit on the couch, my shirt in her hands as we bow our heads in shame while Cleo and Blake scold us like angry parents. The situation would be comical—had any of this been funny. Instead, it's kind of heart breaking.

Sienna hasn't spoken a word since Cleo screamed her name like she'd been attacked. She just sighed, accepted her fate, and sat on the couch. And like the good boyfriend I am—I sat next to her, equally as guilty.

"You two have been sleeping together? For *months?* I mean come on, Si Si—what happened to telling each other everything?!" Cleo's voice raises an octave as she peers down at Sienna.

I position my shoulder in front of her, shielding her as she flinches from the impact of Cleo's words.

"What you won't do is attack her. Sienna and I wanted to tell you about us—"

"*Us?!* There's an us...Oh my God, Blake—they're an *us* now!" Cleo's pitch raises. Blake winces, mouthing *sorry* my way as I shrug, already used to it.

Growing up with these girls, I've learned their every mannerism, and though Cleo is yelling like a lunatic, I know it's just her masking her hurt.

She's hurt that Sienna kept this from her, and Sienna is upset that her cousin is hurt—typical girl stuff.

Grabbing a hold of Sienna's hand, I squeeze it in an attempt to comfort her. Wrong choice.

Cleo's gasps is so loud I think the astronauts in freaking Mars can hear her as she stumbles back.

"This is why you were being so fucking weird! You weren't coming home you...you snuck out! I saw it myself and you've been gone for days at a time. Oh my gosh...I thought it was just dance practice and work that had you so busy—did you ever even have a job?" Cleo's brows crease, hurt lacing her tone as she looks Sienna square in the eye.

My girlfriend, to her credit, doesn't back down. Instead, she meets Cleo's glare, looks at me momentarily, and then rolls her eyes.

"I had a job—until he bought the studio."

"He bought the studio?! What're you, Richie Rich?" Cleo looks me over momentarily then puts her attention back on Sienna.

"Yeah...he was being a bit of a psycho then." Sienna frowns, clearly at unease with this conversation before rolling her shoulders back with a deep sigh. "I wanted to tell you, Cleo. We planned to do it, and then your tape leaked and I couldn't do that to you. You were...broken. I'd never seen you like that, and then to add more stress to you? I couldn't do it." Sienna frowns, her shoulders slumping, almost caving in on themselves as the weight of her words settles in the room.

Cleo's shoulders fall, her brows softening as she kneels in front of her cousin, taking her hands into her own.

"Oh Sienna...you could never hurt me—we're sisters." Cleo tears up, her words shaking as Sienna's head snaps up.

My own tears ducts open as I watch the two girls.

And then there's Blake...

"Wait—I thought your hair was pink..." he mumbles, clearly not reading the room. I smile at my friend, recalling Sienna's dramatics.

"She surprised me and dyed it." I chuckle, the memory of her dancing on the table at the forefront of my mind, unaware of the girls until I hear Cleo's voice again.

"You changed yourself because of *him*?! Have you lost your fucking mind?!" Cleo yells.

"Calm down a second...Let's take this outside and talk?" Sienna says her eyes wide, darting around the room as Cleo eyes her suspiciously.

The two nod simultaneously and head for the backyard.

Fuck. I hope they don't fight. I haven't broken up one of their fights since we were kids.

Blake plops down on couch beside me. "You know she called me Jake?"

Chuckling I turn to face my best friend and laugh in his face. "Who?"

"Your girlfriend. She's kinda cool, though, I like her for you." Blake shrugs, turning on the TV, settling into the couch.

"Me too. You and CJ are kinda cute, too," I admit, getting comfortable as Blake laughs.

"I know."

We're sitting in silence, watching the movie when Blake speaks up.

"So wait...Does this mean that we'll be in-laws, Jace?"

FIFTY-ONE

Sienna

CLEO AND I SIT in an awkward silence, eyeing one another carefully. It's been five minutes since we've gotten outside.

"So..." we say in unison, laughing nervously at one another.

"I'll go first if that's okay, Ceej," I say, placing a hand on her thigh and squeezing gently.

"Jace and I kissed two years ago," I admit. Her eyes widen like a cartoon characters, and I'd laugh if this whole thing was funny.

"What?! Who kissed who? Was I there? Does G know? Why didn't you guys date then? Wh—"

Laughing, I tilt my head at her.

Cleo mimes zipping her lips as sighs, her shoulders deflating.

"To answer your questions, I kissed him. I don't regret it, either, you were there, just not near us. Georgia does know, and we didn't date then because I was a coward," I admit, running a hand through my black curls as Cleo tilts her head at me.

"Sienna, you are not—"

Sighing, I cut her off.

"No, I was a coward. I ran away from someone I knew I loved because I was afraid that he'd leave me just like my parents. I was afraid that if I told you, that you'd want nothing to do with me, and Cleo, I just couldn't live like that...so I ran."

The cool December air bites at our skin, the two of us only having blankets to keep us warm out here. I fiddle with the necklace Jace had given me, shifting uncomfortably as Cleo eyes me.

"You hid him? Why did you think I'd be upset? I'd never be upset with you, Si Si. Especially over something like this..." Cleo frowns, taking hold of my fiddling hand.

Taking a deep breath, I turn to fully face Cleo and a piece of my heart warms.

"I shouldn't have hid him or did a number of the things that I did. I thought you may be upset since he's your best friend, but listening to myself now, I know that I had the wrong idea. I think that he and I have silently loved each other for years, and now that we're in the same place at the right time...I got scared and wanted to prevent myself from getting hurt."

Cleo pulls me into a hug, kissing the top of my head. "Never do that again. I love you and I will always accept you and who you love...Even if it is my crazy ass best friend."

Chuckling at her words, I hug her tightly.

"Now, what happened with that Aidan guy? I thought you were dating him and doing a project together," she questions pulling back slightly as I give her a confused look.

Who the hell is Aidan?

"Girl, do you mean Aric? My date from the beginning of the semester?" I ask snorting as Cleo's eyes widen.

"So let me get this straight: you're not dating your dance partner?"

Rolling my eyes jokingly, I shake my head. "She's a girl and not my type."

"Then who's Aidan?" Cleo furrows her brows as I laugh.

"I have no clue, but let's check on the guys...I'm sure they might know who you're talking about."

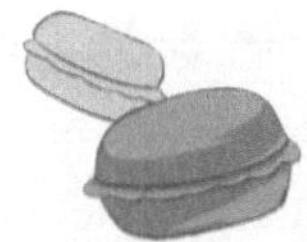

"Come on! Christmas with the in-laws isn't *so* bad, my parents love you!" Jace exclaims for the tenth time, walking back into the living room with a bowl of popcorn in his hands.

Sighing, I sit up from my spot on the couch and grab a hold of the buttery goods. "Jace can we please just watch the movie?" I ask for the second time.

Christmas is officially two weeks away, and the only thing on his mind is where we're going. My parents had told me that they'd be here for Christmas and my birthday, so I'm putting my faith in them and not making plans.

"But babe, my mom *loves* you, and Nonna wants to meet you! I can't say no to my Nonna—you've met her. She's *scary*!" he says with a shudder, and I laugh.

His nonna is an eighty-four-year-old badass who spends her days on yachts in the Amalfi coast with sangrias and her crochet needle—*Scary*.

"Heart."

"Jones." He raises a snarky brow at me as I gasp.

"Did you just—"

"I did, whatcha gonna do about it?" He smirks as I lean into him, kissing him silly. I'm about to deepen the kiss when my phone rings.

"Hold on..." I say, unlocking myself from him and jogging over to the device. My heart drops when the caller ID flashes my mother's contact.

This can't be good.

It's never good when she calls.

"Honey, I'm so sorry—" Are the first words my mom says to me in months. I don't need to hear the rest to know what's next. It's always the same with her: she'll call and have some stupid apology before hanging up on me. I don't get a word out before she does, and then the cycle repeats.

My dad doesn't have to call me because he sends his wife to do it. I don't think he and I have talked all year...

Sighing, I nod...I don't deserve this and I never did. I'm *their* kid, not the other way around. The night they decided to have unprotected sex and then keep me was the night they became parents.

I'm an innocent in this equation, the fucking constant variable to their experiment. I didn't ask to be born, or to be loved, and it shows.

"You know, Mom…I'm *really* getting tired of this shit. You call me once every blue moon to get my hopes up. You'll say, 'darling, we're coming home!' or 'Si Si, we're going to be there for you' and yet you have yet to see me *perform*, you have yet to physically show up for me and you…you could care less about me, Mom." My voice cracks as all of the unshed tears from my twenty years of life spill out.

"I have never—"

"*I'm* talking now," I cut her off. "I have worked endlessly for you to see me. I have broken myself daily to fit a mold of perfection, but you don't even care to *visit* me. The last time I saw you was a year ago! You don't care that I was bullied relentlessly, or that I couldn't look at myself for months because I wasn't perfect enough for you." I sniffle as Jace turns on the couch, a deep frown on his face as I continue to break.

"Mom, I am human. I am your *daughter*. You and Major are my parents, and yet I don't even *know* you. All of my life, I've had nannies and caregivers, but never a mother or a father. I set myself up to be perfect for you, and then you call to say that you can't see me on my birthday and Christmas? Do you know how much I've struggled just to be seen by you? I needed a mother and got the one person who never deserved children." My words hang in the air as my mother's sobs echo through the line.

"Oh, Sienna…I'm so sorry. I never meant for you to get hurt—"

"But you did. You did and that's fine, don't lie to me. I'm an adult now. I set the moments up perfectly. I made sure that I was there each and every single time you claimed you'd show up. I was the perfect daughter and you were the perfect, absentee mother—"

Something in my mother snaps. She riles herself up and then yells, "I gave you everything, Sienna! You were difficult—you would scream and cry and I—I *never* wanted to be a mom. I wanted *him,* but he wanted you!"

The silence between us is loud and my heart cracks just a bit more as her words saw at my heart.

"I wanted to be free, Sienna, and then I met you. I loathed you—I did. But then I fell in love with you, and it was too late. You were maybe five or six—you didn't need me, you had your nanny at the time. You would've been so much better off without me, and that's the truth. I was never meant to be a mom, but I *never* wanted to hurt you. I didn't know about the bullying or the standards you gave yourself. I didn't know."

I sniff deeply, inhaling her words and blowing them out. She's right. She was never meant to be a mom, and she didn't know.

"You're right, Eloisa, you didn't know. But you also never asked. You claim that you fell in love with me and that I didn't need you, but I was six...I needed a mother and you craved fame. You say Dad wanted me, but where is he? You may have thought he wanted me, but he's with you, right now. *Neither* of you deserved me," I say, and don't give her the chance to respond before hanging up.

I don't notice Jace standing next to me, or feel the small circles he traces on my arm, but when he pulls me into chest, I realize that this is where I belong. With him, I'm loved. With my friends and with the rest of my family, I'm cared for.

Sometimes the people you meet are more of a family to you than the people who birth you.

"I'm sorry, angel," he says, kissing my hair as I shrug.

"Don't be. Tell your mom and nonna I'd love to see them this Christmas."

FIFTY-TWO

Jace

"Babe."

Poke.

"Babe..."

Poke. Poke.

I squint, twisting in my spot on the bed, groaning I open one eye and immediately jolt awake at the sight in front of me. Sienna stands over the bed, hovering above me with an evil smile on her face.

Yawning, I stretch a bit. "What time is it?"

She plants herself in the small corner of the bed between my body and the edge. My arm immediately wraps around her waist and my cheek warms as she kisses it.

"4:00 AM..."

Four...

Four AM?!

Why do both Sienna and her cousin think that sleep is for the dead? What the hell is she doing up so early?

Before I can voice my question, she places a small envelope in front of my eyes and smiles triumphantly as I eye it.

"Merry Christmas." She beams at me, her eyes dazzling as I sit up, turning on the lamp beside us. My resolve softens at the sight of her, and I pull her in, kissing her softly.

"Merry Christmas, angel. What's this?" I ask noting the way she's buzzing with joy as she smiles nervously.

"I may have wrote you a few letters and lists as a kid, and I uh...I wanted to give them to you if we ever dated in the future. Don't read it now, but please read them before New Year's. Is this an okay gift? If you want something like a new paint brush set or cologne, I'll get it but I just thought that you'd—"

I cut her off with soft kiss to her lips. "This is all I could've ever wanted. Thank you."

"Really?" she asks, pulling away with a small shy smile as I nod.

"This is the best gift ever, now let's go back to bed...Wouldn't want you sleepy while you and Nonna play games tomorrow."

"Pour me up a shot, motherfuckers!" Nonna jeers, holding up her holiday shot glass as Asa and Jackson cheer, clapping and laughing hysterically in the corner of the room.

Sienna jumps from my lap where we're seated by the fireplace and Christmas tree. I watch her butt, clad in a purple holiday set to match the rest of my family, as she heads towards my nonna, grabbing the shot glass.

Nonna grins at Sienna, her hand clasping around my girlfriend and the glass. "Oh Sienna, honey. Get you one, too! Jacie tells me that your 21st is on New Year's Eve, we *have* to get you drunk!"

"Uh...No?" I scrunch up my face as Sienna laughs at my grandmother's request, running off to get another glass.

Nonna sighs. "Jacie, don't be such a wuss. Your girlfriend can have a little vodka with your nonna."

Asa snickers. "Nonna...I don't know what's worse. You saying wuss or insisting Si Si has a shot of *vodka* with you."

Nonna waves Asa off, rolling her eyes as Mom clears her throat.

"Doris…I think that's enough vodka…Poor Sienna is probably vodka'd out—" Mom tries to save Sienna, but my girlfriend clearly doesn't *want* to be saved. Because instead of bringing back just a shot…she brings the whole damn bottle.

Nonna's grin is large and manic when she sees Sienna, and I'm about to butt in and interrupt them when the doorbell goes off.

"Who's at the floor?" Sienna asks, stumbling as Jackson catches her, settling her in a chair next to Nonna.

That's enough vodka for her…

Running a hand over my face, I answer, "That, my love, should be a drop off. You've been looking all over the loft for your gifts, so I had to be a bit creative with hiding them."

Sienna has been looking for her Christmas gifts ever since she and her mom had that falling out two weeks ago. She's searched everywhere from her room, to my cars, and even the dance studio.

Hell, I think she tried to search Derek's place, too, before he told her off.

I kiss her forehead as she pouts and rolls her eyes at me before heading to the door where Derek and Delilah should be standing with the three gifts I'd planned for her.

What I don't expect to find is the whole damn student body for Summerfield University.

Cleo, Georgia, Denver, Delilah, Derek, Blake, and Ryan stand on my parents' front porch with a handful of presents. I gape at my friends, my eyes darting between every single one of them before landing on Deli.

"Chief Mischief…What're you doing here?" I question her, hoisting her up and holding her.

Delilah's giggles are sweet as she responds, "My daddy said that we're bringing Christmas to Ms. Si Si."

Nodding, I put her down and step aside to allow them all in. My eyes snag on Blake's pajama bottoms that eerily resemble the ones that I'm wearing.

"How did you—"

"Anna sent me the link!" Georgia squeals, thrusting a box into my chest. "That's for Si Si, don't open it."

"What—"

I'm about to throw a slew of questions her way when Ryan clasps a hand on my shoulder. "Merry Christmas, man."

Sighing, I throw an arm around his shoulder.

"Merry Christmas, Ry."

We hug for a moment, letting the Christmas spirit take over us just as my mom's shouts call out for us to join the rest of my family.

The guys and I all lounge around, watching as every single woman—Delilah included—sing their own horrible rendition of some musical about witches.

Sienna's singing voice is like nails on a chalkboard, and Cleo is no better, sounding like a dying mewl.

We each wince simultaneously as the girls continue with their songs, and when they finish, we're forced to clap.

"Again! Aga—" Delilah's cheers are cut off by her dad picking her up.

Derek smiles at his daughter, his finger unclogging his ear as he says, "How about we save some songs for next time, Dels?"

When we're all settled, the fire roasting fresh wood and the girls happily drinking whatever Nonna's whipped up, it's time for presents.

We'd opened presents this morning as a family, but since my friends so graciously decided to join us, we have a few more gifts plus Sienna's Christmas gifts to open.

Cleo and Blake go first, exchanging their gifts of matching necklaces and digital cameras. Originally, Blake was supposed to head to New York for the holidays, but he'd missed his flight back home two days ago and couldn't make it.

Cleo preens as Blake wraps her necklace around her neck, a shiny, diamond encrusted, cursive "B" hanging from the silver chain.

My family and I watch as each of my friends exchange their gifts, laughing when Sienna opens a cook book from Derek and when Georgia and Denver give each other the same thing—get out of jail free cards.

When all the chaos of my friends' gifts die down, my happiness grows as I look at Sienna.

She's going to flip when she sees what I got her.

I'm vibrating with nervous energy as I hold out one of my gifts to her, smiling as she eyes me skeptically.

"Why is the box so big?" she asks, eyes narrowing on me as Blake and Ryan snicker somewhere in the background.

"Sienna Jones, I love you so much..."

Now she's on edge, her face scrunching like she's preparing to wince. "You're not proposing, are you? I mean we just started dating and–"

Chuckling softly, I shake my head. "Not until we've both graduated—"

"I mean, I wouldn't be opposed if you did, but—"

Tilting my head, a soft smile grazes my face.

"Angel?" I ask, softly grasping her hands, my friends and family blurring into the background as she locks eyes with me.

God, I love this woman.

I've loved her my entire life, but this feeling grows in my chest at the sight of her... *This* is what love feels like.

"Hm?" Sienna hums softly, her eyes softening as a small smile breaks on her face.

"Would you just shut up and let me finish my question?" I ask jokingly, laughing as she pushes me off her with a teasing smile. "Like I was saying before *someone* got in her head... Will you make me the happiest man alive and be the mother of our new child?"

Sienna's jaw drops, her eyes large and bright as her hands shoot to her mouth. "What?"

The box rustles a bit more, and a small head pops up from the lid, impatient and annoyed.

Sienna gasps, her eyes widening, "Rubble?!"

"Surprise!" our friends shout. The air grows with excitement as Sienna squeals, taking Rubble out of the box. The cat's ears twitch as he purrs for her.

"You got me a cat?! This is *my* cat! How'd you find him?" Sienna exclaims, jumping up and down, hugging me with Rubble in hand.

"You like him?" I ask, hoping she says yes.

This cat has been the bane of my fucking existence. I'd originally planned on getting Sienna something completely different, but a few weeks ago, I'd been in the quad and this cat parked his ass next to me and wouldn't leave me alone.

My fear and dislike for the odd creatures lowered a bit when I realized Rubble wasn't too bad of an animal.

He's just *clingy.*

I can't eat, shit, or sleep without the monster being in the same room. I thought cats were supposed to be aloof, and that maybe this motherfucker is broken, but when I took him to the vet, they said he was normal.

It's been hard hiding him from Sienna considering she's crazy perceptive, but Derek's been watching him for me.

"So does this mean we're cat *and* ferret parents?" she asks, the smarmy cat looking up at me with a knowing smirk.

I'm sick of this cat. It's only been a few days that I've had him with me solely, but he's odd.

"Sadly, but I have one more gift," I announce, letting the room and Sienna settle as I pull out the small card at the very bottom of the box, handing it to Sienna.

"Jace..." she breathes my name, the sound like music to my ears.

"How do you feel about going to Vegas?"

Dear Jace,

    I wish I could've saw you today, but your mommy said you were sick and I don't want to get sick, too! When you get better, we're going to do everythingggg together. I miss you and I hope you *feel* better. I mean who else's butt am I going to kick in Mario Kart?

Okay, Bye for now.
Ten-year-old Sienna J

Sienna's List for the perfect husband

I'm Sienna, and if you're reading this, then you're my husband. I'm currently twelve and here's a few things that I'd like for my hubby to know:

1. You have to be SMART
(I want my husband to be the smartest most handsomest man in the world)

2. Buy me cookies DUH

3. Be kind
(You might not know this because I don't like talking about my feelings, but my mommy and daddy aren't the nicest. I want you to be nice to me...I know I can be mean but I'm trying!!!!)

4. Be funny
(My friend Jace is superrrrr funny, you have to make me laugh more than he does or this wont work LOL)

5. Last but not least PLEASE have green eyes.
(This can be discussed if you don't have them, but I think green eyes are sexy)
(DON'T TELL ANYONE I SAID THAT!!!! I DON'T WANT TO GET IN TROUBLE)

Anyways, hubby, if you saw this then I guess you fit the list. I love you teehee :)

Dear Jace,

    Today you and I held hands!!! I know we're just friends and that I shouldn't say this, but is it crazy to think that I may have a crush on you? It's a good thing you'll never see this. That would be awkward *LOL*. I had to leave today and I'm so sad I won't see you until Christmas. Mom and Dad are in town for a while and want to hang out. It's odd that they say "hang out" when I'm their daughter *LOL*.

Anyway, I hope you have a great school year.

Think of me and I'll think of you.

Okay, Bye for now.
Thirteen-year-old Sienna J

Dear Jace,

I can't fucking believe the nerve of my parents. I was supposed to come to Maryland this summer! The only reason I'm not is because they said they'd spend time with me. Now I'm stuck in the house alone. How am I going to have the most epic summer of my life when I have no one to be epic with? I know that you would've made this summer unforgettable. I miss you, Cleo, and the gang.

Think of me and I'll think of you.

P.S. I may stow away on a flight to Maryland (don't tell my parents)

Okay. Bye for now.
Sixteen-year-old Sienna J

Dear Jace,

I'm so sorry. I haven't written to you in months lol...The paper may be a little wet and I can't control that because I haven't stopped crying yet. I just need to get this all out and into the open so we can move forward. Jace, you mean the world to me and have since we were kids. I always thought that this was a stupid crush, but tonight I kissed and you kissed me back.

The kiss was beautiful and more than I could've ever dreamed of— considering it was my first one. I should've stayed right there with you, but I ran away like a fucking idiot. I'm so sorry. I miss you and it's only been twenty minutes since we last saw one another.

Maybe in another life, I'd actually stay and we'd have our moment. Maybe in another life we'd get the chance to make this thing between us real and seal our fates together on New Years like we tried to do today.

In another life, we'd party and have spontaneous trips to Vegas because we like the fast life. In another life, I wouldn't run from love and you'd love me the way that I've dreamt for the past decade.

I miss you. I'm sorry.

Think of me and I'll think of you always.

I promise.

Okay, see you later?
Eighteen-year-old Sienna J

FIFTY-THREE

Jace

"I'M GOING TO VEGAS, BITCHES!"

I watch in amused silence as my girlfriend proceeds to bend over the stairs of my private jet and shake her ass for the world to see.

Sienna cheers for herself, giggling and laughing as our friends cheer and record her behind me. I turn my head, eyeing the guys and smirking as they all find different spots in the sky to look at, the only one with a scrunched up face being her cousin.

I'd planned today so that everyone would arrive at the airstrip before Sienna, surprising her on the tarmac. Sienna jumps and cheers when my flight crew appears at the plane's door, a bottle of tequila and a furry, purple *21* crown in hand.

Like a princess, Sienna curtseys, allowing the crown to be placed on her head and taking the bottle with a loud cheer.

"She is going to be so fucked up..." Cleo mumbles amused by her cousin as Sienna dances her way inside the plane.

"Good, she's been asking about this trip every day since I brought it up."

We follow Sienna inside the plane, all of us laughing when she screams, running around the medium sized private jet.

I'd gotten a team of event planners to decorate both the jet and our hotel suite in Vegas before we arrived. Lavender feathers and clusters of balloons and glitter decorate the expanse of my jet. I'm shocked by the amount of purple that covers the green machine, down to the seats and carpet.

"This is the best birthday ever!" Sienna squeals, her eyes bright with excitement as she points to the large banner over the back of the plane with her name printed in glitter.

There's cut outs of her face in different expressions decorating each seat and two boxes of cookies from The Sweet Tooth on one of the tables.

"She's definitely not making it to tomorrow. Good luck, Heart," Ryan says, patting my back as he enters the plane and takes a seat next to Denver in the front.

Shaking my head, I laugh lowly, taking a seat next to Sienna, smiling when she turns to me.

"I'm serious, Jace, this is the best birthday ever." She frowns, but her eyes are full of light as she pecks my lips.

"Hm...I need a little bit more," I pout, sticking out my bottom lip as she rolls her eyes.

"Oh fuck you...I can't wait to see what Vegas has to offer for us." She sighs, leaning back in the seat, getting fully comfortable.

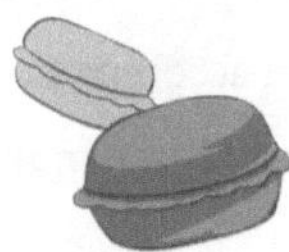

Strippers.

Vegas has strippers to offer. Male fucking strippers at that.

When Denver told me that she had the best birthday idea for Sienna, I thought she meant getting drunk and hitting up the club—not sitting front row at a Lovely Larry show.

I grimace as some asshole thrusts his leather clad junk in my face, rolling my eyes as the girls cheer for it.

"You're dead when we're done," Derek tells me, swatting away the male stripper dancing in front of him.

I also promised Derek strippers—just not male ones.

"Oh don't be such a sour bear," I tease, handing my friend a "Lucky One", the money that the club provides.

"I need a drink. Want one, blondie?"

"Nah I'm—"

Georgia cuts me off, her arms in the air as she dances with one of the strippers. "HELL YEAH!"

Blondie?

That's what he calls me!

Scrunching my face, I watch as Derek nods, walking away to get more drinks for him and Georgia, stunned at the pure fact that he'd just ignored me.

My gaze flickers back to the stage and my eyes nearly fall out of my head as I watch Sienna prance onto it.

"What the fuck?!" I shout, standing as hands push me back into my seat. Looking up, I make a horrified face at the smiling blonde.

"Unhand me!"

"No!" Georgia shakes her head at me and Ryan has the nerve to laugh.

"My girl would never—*Shit*," he curses seeing as his girl definitely would.

We all watch—except for Georgia—as all of our girlfriends are led onto the Lovely Larry stage, each of them accompanied by a man in nerdy clothes.

"This is my worst nightmare..." Blake mumbles as Cleo squeals when one of the strippers picks her up.

"Who's bright idea was this?!" I ask, watching in horror as Sienna laughs on the stage.

"Hers!" Georgia giggles, sipping on her drink as she points at my girlfriend.

In less than five minutes, a few things happen. The stripper instructs Sienna to rip off his shirt, my legs move on their own accord, and we end up on the curb of Lovely Larry's—banned for life.

"You couldn't have waited?! I wanted to see the rest!" Georgia groans, stomping her feet like a toddler as the girls agree.

I cut Sienna a sharp look. "What're you agreeing for?! He *groped* you!"

Sienna looks down at her feet. "He asked before he did it."

"And you said yes?!"

Cleo steps forward. "In her defense, she nodded and *then* shook her head."

"Not helping." I sigh, grabbing a hold of my loose cannon of a girlfriend's hand. I need to keep her right beside me. One minute she's dancing, then the next a Lovely Larry stripper is grinding on her.

Sienna pouts as I pull her close, her golden dress shining under the Vegas dome as we walk.

"We can't call it a night! We didn't even party or kiss! How can we call it a night when we haven't kissed?" she asks, puckering her lips at me.

Sighing, I lean down and peck her.

"She's right—we need shots!" Derek cheers, already past his limit of one beer as he and Georgia stumble together.

"WOO HOO! SHOTS! SHOTS! SHOTS!" Georgia cheers, dancing against Derek as he body rolls.

What the fuck is up with them?

"Are y'all down for another club?" I ask the guys, completely ignoring their drunken girlfriends.

Ryan and Blake look between one another before shrugging.

"Eh...Why not? What happens in Vegas, stays in Vegas." Blake shrugs, holding Cleo up as she joins in Derek and Georgia's dancing, creating an odd, three-way body roll.

Grimacing, I hold Sienna's hand tighter, so she doesn't join them and we over head to LUX, Asa's newest nightclub in Vegas.

LUX is filled to the brim with people, the four-story nightclub on the top of The Portsmith, one of the most luxurious hotel chains in the world, is all anyone can talk about.

The first two floors are huge with couches and small sections on the bottom floor and clear LED boxes for sections on the top two, overlooking the bottom. The lights in the club are set to purple tonight, and every single person in the venue is dancing their hearts out.

I laugh as the girls dance their way to the elevator and grin as I let us up to the rooftop club, exclusive to VIPs only. Up here, the party is lively and full of A-list celebrities, athletes, and young moguls. The true elite of our world.

"Oh my...He's here," Cleo gasps, frantically slapping at Denver's chest, her eyes trained on a man standing a few feet away, drink in hand.

Denver's eyes bug out, tracking the man's every movement as she stands ramrod straight. "No. Freakin'. Way."

My girlfriend being the nosey woman that she is, looks around everywhere, and when I gesture in the right direction, she gasps.

"Eren Marlowe?" Sienna's jaw drops as she stares the F1 driver down.

"He isn't all that." Blake rolls his eyes, trying to tug Cleo away, but she is immovable.

"How's my bow? Is it centered?"

"The fuck it is," Blake tuts, dragging her away as Sienna tugs on my hand.

"So many tattoos..." Denver drools as Ryan scoffs.

"I have tattoos."

I hold in my laugh as he pouts, grabbing hold of Denver's hand and pulling her away.

"Do you want to go talk to him?" I ask Sienna, already knowing she'll say no. She isn't into sports like that, the others are—

"Hell yeah! Do you think Alejandro Sanchez is here, too?"

How the hell does she know Sanchez? That's it...no more Cleo time for her. She's pulling my girl down the wrong path.

"On second thought, I think we should just get some drinks."

Derek and Georgia have already beat us to the chase, throwing back shot after shot at the bar. On the other side of the room, I watch with a content smile as Blake tries his hardest to not fanboy over Luka Espinosa—the leader of Twisted Vipers—while also trying not to let Cleo go after Eren Marlowe. Ryan on the other hand, has failed his mission, standing like a sad and kicked puppy as he listens to Denver drone on about something to the F1 racer.

Once Sienna and I get a few drinks, we settle in a spot near the balcony. She sips her piña colada, eyes on the stars as I drink my Manhattan behind her, my casted hand wrapped around her waist.

"This has been perfect, Jace. I mean it. Thank you for today and every day before it." She sighs, resting her honey blonde dyed hair against my chest.

I chuckle at the sight of it, grinning down at her. "Anything for you. Happy birthday, Sienna."

"Five!"

"Four!"

Sienna turns in my arms, her eyes bright.

"Three!"

She tilts her head up, smiling.

"Two!"

She gets on her tippy toes, arms thrown around my neck.

"One!"

She kisses me just as the New Year comes in.

FIFTY-FOUR

Sienna

I GROAN, MY HEAD pounding as Jace hands me a bottle of water on the terrace of our hotel room. He chuckles softly, his thumb wiping at the syrup on my bottom lip.

"I told you that drinking four margaritas would give you a migraine."

Pouting, I nod my head. "I know but they were sooo good." I sigh.

After the club last night, everyone sort of went their own separate ways. Derek, Georgia, Blake, and Cleo were nowhere to be found, and I'm pretty sure Denver and Ryan went back to Eren Marlowe's hotel room.

Sighing, I rest my head in my hands, looking out at the scenery before grimacing.

"It's too bright...Turn off the sun for just a second," I moan as Jace cackles like an asshole behind me.

"Turn off the sun? Angel, go lay down and I'll bring the food in."

I pout. Does he really think that *I'm* going to use my own legs to carry me to bed? Does he not see the condition that I'm in?

"I'll carry you to bed." He gives me an amused sigh as I throw my hands up, waiting to be carried only for the loud ringer of his phone to go off.

"Block them," I say, holding my hands over my ears.

Who the fuck uses their ringers these days? Is he eighty?

Jace sighs, holding his phone out for the both of us to see as our friend's face pops up on the screen.

"Dude, it's fucking 8:00 am, why are you—"

Before Jace can scold them, he's interrupted by a loud scream, "I fucked up!"

The air in my body is knocked loose as a four carat engagement ring stares back at us.

Holy shit...

"I don't know what happened last night, but this?!" They scream and my blood goes cold as the phone hangs up.

My mouth is on the floor as I look up at the robe and sunglasses wearing man beside me.

Jace's jaw drops, "How the fuck did they get married before us?! I've been in love with you for twelve years!"

THE END.

Epilogue

— two years later

"I SWEAR TO ALL things holy, Sienna Jones, if you cry and ruin this makeup, I will kick your ass on this fine Saturday morning," Georgia huffs, dabbing under my eyes for the second time today.

I let out a deep shaky laugh, my skin itching as I look around the room surrounded by the people I love and cherish. Clothed in lavender silk robes with their hair and makeup done, my girls look stunning.

I sigh, an overwhelming feeling heavy on my chest as I think about today's activities.

"Oh hush, G. It's not every day that our girl gets *married*." Cleo giggles, exaggerating the word "married" as she squeezes my shoulder.

"No, it's not every day that she gets married—but she does wear makeup daily. Crying off makeup that she paid for is just sinister. I honestly think the blond heathen doesn't deserve it," Georgia tuts, pursing her lips.

Her words make me laugh. You would think that after almost twenty years of friendship, the two of them would stop arguing like cats and dogs.

Sighing, I toss my head back.

"I *can't* calm down. I'm getting *married*, haven't seen my fiancé in over three days—which is crazy considering we're in the same fucking country. And I'm pretty sure I may spill wine on my first dress of the night because of how nervous I am."

The girls all pause, eyeing me through the vanity mirror I'm sitting in front of.

"Oh, Si Si, It's okay to be nervous. Marriage is a big deal, I would be more terrified if you weren't nervous about this," my cousin Zahria says, coming up to stand behind me.

"No, I don't think you understand, Zahr. If I don't see Jace Heart within the next ten seconds, I'm going to freak the fuck out," I say, my jaw clenching as my nails dig into the armrest of my chair.

I just need to hear his voice—smell him, even. I just need something. *Anything*.

As if the angels heard my plea, a knock sounds through the room.

"Knock. Knock. Knock. Mother of groom, here." Anna's sweet voice rings through the bridal suite, and I instantly feel a weight lifted off of my shoulders.

Throughout the wedding planning process, Anna has been a gift sent from above. She's helped book our wedding venue–Chateau de Versailles. She's brought on the best wedding planners in the industry and has even taken time out to book our dream honeymoon for us.

I couldn't wish for a better mother-in-law.

Anna's eyes are bright as she eyes me at the vanity, her smile warm as she heads towards me.

"Still nervous?"

I inhale sharply, "I—"

Shit! She wasn't supposed to know that I was nervous about today. What would she think? I'm supposed to be marrying her son—

"It's okay to be nervous, Sienna. I was nervous about marrying Julian, and I still get nervous whenever we renew our vows. Nerves and giddiness are a part of the wedding process, my dear," she says, gently placing a purple envelope on the vanity.

Our eyes lock, a look of love and trust dances in her irises as she gives me a small smile before pulling me into a hug.

"I am so proud of the woman that you have become, Sienna. I couldn't have asked for anyone better to be my daughter. Thank you for loving my boy, I love you." Anna's words hit me like a love filled freight train, but instead of bringing about more nerves and anxiety.

I feel a sense of comfort.

When she lets go of me, she sends me a small wink. Chuckling, I squeeze her hand.

When planning out this wedding, I made the brave decision of not inviting my parents. I only wanted to be surrounded by people who I know have love and care about me rather than those who brought about heartache.

After telling Anna about my parents, she was immediately on my side and has treated me like one of her own ever since.

I smile to myself, thinking back to the memory, only for my smile to falter as I realize that she's gathered up the girls and left the suite.

Odd.

My eyes land on the purple envelope on the vanity, and I tilt my head at the neat scrawl on the front of it.

To my wife.

My heart rackets against my chest as I eye the envelope and I waste zero time in opening it.

Did Jace write to me? When did he have the time? Did he write this today?

Thoughts swirl around my mind until my eyes drag on the first line.

Dear angel,

Merry Christmas. If you're reading this, then that means that I put a ring on that sexy ass finger of yours and declared you mine for all eternity. Today is Christmas, and you're drunk with my nonna and the girls...I can't say that I blame you considering Nonna's been feeding you vodka since 9:00 AM. I snuck off around you girls' fourth karaoke song, and have I ever told you that your karaoke voice is freaking terrible? Babe, I love you, but you purposely sing bad only during karaoke. Sorry—got a bit side tracked.

As I was saying, I snuck off and read every single letter that you gave me today. Who knew twelve-year-old you was so obsessed with me? I HAD TO SAY IT. YOU LOVEEEE ME.

Today is our wedding day (Yes, I know I'm writing this on Christmas, but sue me...I have a plan) and I already know that you're freaking out in typical Sienna Jones fashion. You've probably gotten cursed out by the she-devil for crying and have yet to put on your dress. You're probably worrying yourself about where I am and what I'm doing, but just know that I'm doing the exact same thing.

I've wanted to marry you from the moment I met you all those years ago. I've wanted nothing more than to change your last name and make you mine for a lifetime.

Sienna, thank you for always being your sassy, caring self. Thank you for loving me in your own way and helping me to see that I can love someone other than myself.

You are my light.

Marrying you has always been a dream, and today it is a reality.
I'll give this letter to my mom tonight to give to you on our special day. No matter how far away in the future our wedding day is, I want you to have this letter no matter what.

I love you, to Saturn and back.
Okay. Bye for now.
Your husband, Jace H.

Looking up at myself in the mirror, I smile. Through all of the pain and hardships that I've been through, there's always been a light at the end of the tunnel.

A few years ago, I wanted to change everything about myself. I hated how others perceived me and let their opinions effect everything about me. Looking in the mirror now, I'm proud of the woman I became.

Pushing back my shoulders and holding my head high, I nod.

"I got this."

When the girls reenter the room two minutes later, all hell breaks loose.

"I can't fucking believe you cried while we were gone! It was only two minutes!" Georgia screeches, her brows scrunched as she dabs away at my makeup.

Cleo and the twins fuss over my falling curls, the three of them a mess of hairspray and curling irons, but I'm just happy to be here.

The ceremony goes off without a hitch. There wasn't a dry eye in sight as Jace and I professed our love for one another. He'd gotten choked up a few times himself, stuttering and laughing like a nervous school boy.

When the ceremony is over, Jace looks at me as if I hung the moon. His light green eyes sparkle with love and joy as we walk hand in hand down the aisle, on the road to forever.

Stopping outside of the ceremony doors, we smile at each other. His eyes are soft as kisses me gently, his hand still in mine.

"We can always just sneak off now…" he whispers, his grin filled with mischief as I roll my eyes.

"Or we can go to the reception that we spent a million dollars on," I say cheekily as Jace cups my face, bringing my lips to his once again.

When he pulls back, his voice is husky as he replies, "We've got an hour…A lot can happen in an hour, angel."

"You gotta make it quick and my makeup must stay intact—"

A flashing of a camera followed by loud chatter interrupts my words as our photographers snap away at our intimate moment.

"We must get the shoot done before the reception starts, Mr. and Mrs. Heart, would you like to start in the gardens?" our head photographer, Chloe asks, lowering her camera.

"What do you say, Mrs. Heart? Where would you like to go?" Jace questions, his eyes rooted in a deep hunger as he whispers in my ear.

Chills racket my spine, but I stand my ground. We need to get these photos done now while the sun is up.

In that hour, Jace and I are posed in every way that you can imagine all over the Chateau's grounds. We take more pictures in an hour than we've had all year, and I just hope they all turn out amazing.

By the time our reception has started, the two of us have changed into our third outfits of the day, had our first dance, and have been blissfully separated from one another.

The last time I'd seen my husband, the sun was still up. Now the crisp, Parisian sky is littered with stars, fairy lights twinkle around the gardens grounds, and everyone has some semblance of liquor buzzing in their veins as they dance the night away.

I'm talking with Gizelle Banks, the PR manager of the Washington Eagles, the hockey team that Blake is signed to, when a hand grasps around my wrist, pulling me away.

Sending her a quick apology, I allow myself to be tugged away from the intruder, smiling from ear to ear as his cologne wafts through the air mixing with my perfume.

Jace doesn't say a word as he drags me throughout the palace before we land on a balcony overseeing the garden.

"If you wanted to get me all to yourself, you could've just told me that, Mr. Heart," I say, grinning as he tilts his head at me.

Jace wraps an arm around my waist, his other cupping my cheek as he leans in close. "Oh, but I did, Mrs. Heart. *You* didn't want to be whisked away. Besides, I've got a small surprise for you."

The first thunder and crack of a firework causes me to jump in his arms. My eyes wide as I look around the venue below. Half of the guest are peering up at us, some recording, others smiling, while the rest of the guests are facing the sky.

Bright fireworks go off in a series of purple and gold sparkles. My heart feels full of love and warmth as the display fills the sky.

"You didn't!" I gasp, turning to face the man of my dreams.

Jace only grins down at me, pulling me closer to his chest.

It'd been on my list of wedding requirements for us to have fireworks go off during the reception, but I'd been told that it may be out of our wheelhouse to have it happen.

Was I sad about it? Of course. What girl wouldn't want fireworks at her wedding? I was upset for about two weeks, moping around until Jace convinced me that he had something better up his sleeve.

Looking at the sky now, from this angle, I know that nothing could ever compare.

This wedding is everything younger me could've ever dreamt of. We had a harpist play our song as I walked down the aisle, ballerinas dancing around the reception, and photo booths all over to capture our wedding in real time.

Jace pulls me in for a searing kiss and I melt into him, welcoming him warmly. When he pulls away, resting his forehead atop mine, I grin.

He kisses my forehead once, the loud crackling of the fireworks the only thing to be heard as he turns me around to face the show and crowd, his arms wrapped around my waist.

We stand in a comfortable silence, but I know that it won't last long. My husband and the word *silence* do not belong in the same sentence as one another.

"I still can't believe we weren't the first in our friend group to get married," he says, an obvious pout in his words as I chuckle.

"No, but we were the first ones to meet and fall in love," I counter, twisting slightly to look up at him.

When Jace looks down at me, it's like the world stops as our eyes lock.

"Valid...Suck it, Blake, SiJace on top," he beams as my jaw drops.

"SiJace?" I ask, laughing as he winks at me.

"Our ship's name, baby. I've been working on it for years."

Giggling, I relax in his hold. Jace and I have had many ups and downs throughout the years, but they've all been worth it for this moment right here.

"I love you forever, Mr. Heart."

Jace kisses the top of my head. "I'll love you forevermore, Mrs. Heart."

Smiling to myself, I hold up my pinky. "Promise?"

His chuckle vibrates against my back as he locks pinkies with me.

"I promise."

Acknowledgements

Thank you so much for reading Set the Moment. This book means everything to me and couldn't have been made without countless tears, crash-outs, and laughter. I want to thank a few people for helping me stay sane during the crazy, long hours of writing and stress, hoping that others will love Sienna and Jace's story as much as I do. In Capture the Moment's acknowledgments, I said that it takes an army to write a book, and that is the "realest" thing I could've written.

First, I'd like to extend my gratitude to my family. My family has helped me tremendously through this writing process, from helping me get through some of my toughest battles as a "fresh adult" to simply asking about what I am writing and being there for me. I don't say this enough, but thank you so much for your everlasting support. You do not know what it means to me to have you support me through every wild endeavor I set my sights on. From wanting to be a "rockstar" at age five to writing romance novels at twenty-one, I thank you for your support.

To my boyfriend, thank you for always helping and inspiring new ideas for my books. Sienna—I love her to death—is a gamer and let's be very honest... I know jackshit about video games. If it's not The Sims or Mario Kart, I can't tell you anything about it. Thank you, love, for making sure that I take breaks from writing or whenever I feel stressed, it means the world to me.

As for the ones that are my OG "gworls", a.k.a Natalya and Shay, THANK YOU SO MUCH FOR KEEPING ME GOING. Without you two, Set the Moment would NOT be what it is today. You two have helped me more than you would ever know. You've kept my head on track, fought for Sienna and Jace when I didn't think there was much to fight for, and have helped me every step of the way with this book.

To my best friends, thank you for your everlasting support. My best friends, Kamryn and Erika, will not pick up a book even if it were the thing to save them from the world ending, but they never stopped supporting me. When I told them in high school that I wanted to write books, they didn't make fun of me. Instead, they downloaded Wattpad and read my books. They bought Capture the Moment when it came out and told everyone who'd listened, "My best friend wrote a book". I love you, idiots, forever.

My lovely girls, Briana, Essance, and Aryana, you will always hold a special place in this writer's heart. Bri, we've been friends for nearly a decade now, and you are truly one of the reasons that I will forever write romance. Your support has always been unconditional, and I love you for it. Essance, thank you for always wanting to help me, for being there when I have a crazy idea and saying, "Do it." You've pushed me to be who I am and not care two craps about it. Last but certainly not least, Ary, my girl, thank you for always supporting me and being the person to tell me "yes". You're like my partner in crime, always on my side, and rooting for my characters. Thank you, girls!

And lastly, to my amazing readers, thank you so much for all of your support! There truly would not be an STM without CTM. The support that you all have given me for Capture the Moment and now, Set the Moment, has truly made me want to keep going even when things were ROUGH. You all stuck by me, saw me, and supported me. Thank you so much. You are the best readers a girl could ask for.

XOXO,

Author Z

About the author

Ziye' (ZYE-yay) Taylor is an American author born and raised in the DC, Maryland, and Virginia area. She currently lives her live writing romance novels with her dog, KoKo while attending college.

When Ziye' was 11, she began to write her own short stories on the app, Wattpad and the began to publish them on the app at age 13. Ziye' has surpassed 300k reads on the app and has accumulated a small loyal fanbase of readers. She became an author because of her love of reading and whilst being on Wattpad, she noticed that there weren't a lot of books that represented herself. This prompted her to begin writing stories of her own. She wants to write books that everyone can relate to, no matter their shape, gender, or race. Her sources of inspiration are music and her environment. Often times, ideas come to her randomly and she jots them down in the notes app of her phone.

Ziye's favorite shows are The Vampire Diaries, New Girl, Teen Wolf, and The Originals. If she isn't watching these shows she can be found watching the movies White Chicks, Harry Potter, or The Princess Diaries 2. Her favorite music genres are Pop and R&B with SZA and Sabrina Carpenter being her current favorite artists.

For more information on Ziye's upcoming works please check out her website at https://authorziyetaylor.com